A New Shade of Paint

Emily Dana Botrous

Dedicated to:

Zahger, my husband.
For all the late nights I spent typing... I love you!

And to all my DAA girls.
You know who you are.
You were my inspiration.

Emily Dana Botrous is a wife and mom of four. When she isn't busy concocting inspiring plots and people, she enjoys playing with her kids, going to the beach, cooking, and long walks. And reading. Always reading. She lives in San Diego with her family. *A New Shade of Paint* is her first book. To learn more about Emily, visit her blog www.yourstrulyemily.com.

Chapter One

"Do you see him?"

Shannon scanned the faces waiting beside the small baggage claim. "No." Not like he could blend in.

"Isn't that yours?"

She turned to find Laura pointing at the purple bag moving toward them. Shannon reached for it, but she struggled to lift it. Just when she was about to teeter onto the conveyor belt, a hand reached over and hoisted the suitcase into the air.

"Shannon?"

She spun around to stare at the young man clutching her bag.

"I'm—I'm Andy. You remember me?"

Laura collided into her as she swung her duffel off the moving belt.

"Who's that?"

Shannon slowly turned to look at her sister, then back at Andy. She could see some of the ten-year-old she remembered. Same Roman nose and eyes like a cloudless sky. What used to be fiery orange hair was now a dark auburn disaster.

"This is Andy, our—" She couldn't make herself say it. "Kevin's son. You probably don't remember him much."

Andy's stance was hesitant as he shifted from one foot to the other, but he had a confident smile on his face.

"Well I sure remember you." He nodded his chin toward Laura. "You made me climb to the top of a tree once to get a bird's nest for you, and I got stuck up there, and you were just mad that I never got the stupid nest!"

Laura let out a little laugh, but Shannon didn't even smile.

"Is Kevin waiting in the car?"

"Dad?" Andy began to move toward the exit. "He's not here."

"What?" Her voice jumped an octave.

Andy gave her a strange look. "He had to work."

Shannon stopped, anger prickling at the back of her neck and shooting its way into her face.

"Wait a sec. You're telling me he couldn't take a couple hours off to meet us at the airport, when he's the one dragging us here in the first place?" Her voice rose again, and Laura tugged at her arm. Shannon took a deep breath and massaged her forehead. When had this headache shown up?

"Look, he wanted to be here." Shannon forced herself to listen as Andy spoke again. "But he had to work overtime. He'll be home by the time we get there."

Yeah, whatever. She let the words go unsaid and started walking again.

"I, um—" Andy paused and shook his head.

"Go ahead." Shannon nodded for him to continue as they crossed the airport road.

"I just—I wanted to say, you know, sorry about your mom." He glanced at her quickly, then at Laura. "It must be really tough."

Shannon took another deep breath. "Thank you."

Andy led the way inside the parking garage, pulling Laura's suitcase with one hand, Shannon's backpack slung over the opposite shoulder. The only sound echoing in the cement structure was the scraping of the suitcase wheels on the pavement until Andy asked, "Did you have a good flight?"

Shannon sighed, knowing he was trying. The least she could do was answer him. "It was fine. We're in Tennessee?"

"Yep. Tri-cities is the closest airport. Claywood's an hour from here." He stopped so suddenly Shannon almost ran into him. "Well, this is it, good ol' Jimmy."

"Jimmy?" Laura echoed, looking around.

"My car." He smiled broadly and slapped the trunk of the bright red two-door Mustang GT next to them.

"You named your car *Jimmy?*" Shannon smirked as she dumped Laura's duffel bag to the ground. "Very cute."

"Don't be jealous, now." Andy winked at Shannon as he popped the trunk, and she offered a weak smile. He reminded her of Todd. Painful.

Laura claimed the backseat before Shannon had a chance. She would much rather crawl into that small space than sit up front with Andy. Now she'd have to talk.

She checked the dashboard. Four o'clock. No wonder she was hungry. As they emerged from the parking garage into the October sunshine, she glanced at Andy.

"Can we stop to grab some food?" Anything to delay their reunion with Kevin.

"Well, Dad is planning on a big dinner for you guys tonight. Think you can make it until we get home?"

Home. The word hit Shannon like a misaimed baseball to the gut.

"I—I'll be fine."

Would she ever be fine again?

They drove in silence for almost ten minutes as Andy maneuvered through the rush-hour traffic. It was a big enough city, but nothing like Chicago.

Andy cleared his throat and began crooning off-key with the Oldies song playing quietly on the radio, and Shannon wondered if she should say something but didn't care enough to.

"So...do you like Italian? That's what Dad's making."

She nodded. "Sure."

"You don't sound too excited there."

"No really, Italian is great. It's just been a long day."

Andy leaned forward and snapped the radio off, and Shannon crossed her arms. He was a complete stranger to her. She may have known him for eight years once upon a time, but that seemed like a dream ago.

"Look." A small sigh caught in his throat. "I'm no good with words, but I'm gonna try, so just bear with me here." He sighed again. "Alright, I know—I know that you don't want to be here. And I know you just left behind—literally—everything you know. And on top of that I know I'm next to a perfect stranger to you, and—and so is Dad. And I get the feeling you aren't very happy with him. Dad...he's made a lot of mistakes in his life. A lot that he regrets. But—but right now he is trying..."Andy was frowning, like he was searching for the right words. "He is trying to do what's right for you guys. And, I know you probably think that would have been leaving you back in Illinois with whatever his name is—"

"Alan, his name is Alan." Shannon's voice was explosively tight as she stared out the window at the blur of passing trees. They zoomed past a sign that read "Welcome to Virginia."

"Sorry. Alan." He paused. "Look, I don't want to upset you. I'm just saying that Dad is trying to make up for not being around in the past—"

"That's impossible."

"Would you stop interrupting me? I know it's impossible, but he's doing his best. He wants to be the father to you guys that he never was, okay?"

Shannon chomped on her lip to keep in the offensive reply about to leap off her tongue. No sense making an enemy out of Andy in the first twenty minutes. Instead, she scratched her brain for memories of him growing up. He had, after all, spent every other week with them for the first eight years of her life.

One time he had joined her and Laura for a tea party—until the slightly older Todd showed up, and Andy was suddenly too cool for tea. She remembered when he had tried to "help" Mom make brownies. The details were hazy in her mind, but something about a kitchen covered in dripping chocolate. The recollection of Mom's laughter as she sent Andy to change out of his gooey clothes while she mopped up the would-be brownies brought a smile to Shannon's face.

"Hey, do you remember that time we went camping by Lake Michigan?" It was an abrupt break out of the silence, but Andy burst out laughing.

"Yeah, yeah, yeah! Ah, man, I'd forgotten about that. Wasn't that when the raccoons ran off with our food?"

Shannon laughed, too. First time all day. "I think so. I mean, I was pretty little, but that rings a bell."

Laura leaned over Shannon's shoulder. "I don't remember this. Was I there?"

"Oh, you were there," Andy replied. "I think you were like four or five, so you probably don't remember, but trust me, you were there. I had to rescue you from 'a bear,' also known as a tree stump. You wouldn't budge, just stood there screaming, staring at the stump like it was going to eat you."

Laura hooted with laughter. "I was such a little dork!"

"Nah, you were cute. Plus, it made me feel like a hero." The three of them laughed together. "Todd was the only one who behaved that trip. I think our parents decided taking four kids under age twelve on a camping trip was simply aiming too high."

Laura chuckled, but Shannon said softly, "It was our last family trip."

They lapsed back into silence for a few miles. Glorious autumn colors shimmered on the nearby mountains as the road led them higher through the terrain. It was more colorful than anything Shannon had seen back home.

"Tell us about Kevin's—other children." She winced at her awkward wording, but Andy smiled.

"Gabby is eight, but sometimes she thinks she's 13. She's pretty good most of the time. Daniel is four and totally adorable. They're great kids."

"What about you? You're, what, 19 now?"

"Yup. In my first year of community college, just taking some generals." He glanced in the rearview mirror. "How old are you, Laura?".

"Fifteen." She popped her head in between the two. "What's the high school like? Is it big?"

Shannon turned to Andy, ears wide open. This was important information. Transferring to a new school in the middle of her senior year was going to be no picnic. She might be 17 years old, but there were days—many days—she felt closer to 12.

"Well, it's bigger than you'd expect for a small town because the school district is spread out. Very rural. Lots of kids from surrounding areas. But everyone from Claywood knows each other."

"Cool! So it must be easy to make friends and stuff."

The two chattered while Shannon sank out of the conversation. She didn't want a new school. She didn't want to get to know anyone. She would rather blend in until she disappeared.

Again she turned her attention to the window, noting the desolate, mountainous area, beautiful in a different way than she was used to. Gone were the high risers, dense apartments and houses, and never-ending busyness of cars and people. She hadn't seen a car for miles on this back road. All that remained were rolling hills, rising mountains, and rocky cliffs, decorated by the fall foliage and fading greenery. Occasional houses seemed to have been dropped into the trees here and there. She stared wide-eyed at a deer, flicking its tail by the roadside.

"Well, this is Claywood."

Shannon leaned forward as they entered a small residential area.

"That's the high school." Andy pointed at a large brick structure on the right.

"Where's your community college?" Laura asked as they passed a dilapidated grocery store. George's Family Food Mart. Shannon raised an eyebrow. Looked like they'd be shopping in style.

"Oh, it's a twenty minute drive from here, in Clifton. Claywood's too small for a college."

Shannon listened in silence as Andy continued his tour. It was a small, old town that needed a facelift.

"Where do you live?" They seemed to be getting to the outskirts of town, which only took about two minutes. Andy looked at her, startled. It was the first time she had spoken in fifteen minutes at least.

"A couple miles outside town. Almost there."

A few more turns had them surrounded by woods on either side of the road. It felt like they were about to head up a mountain. When Shannon glanced back at her sister, Laura wrinkled her nose.

"Great. We're going to be pioneers on the frontier."

They had lived their whole life in the city suburbs. What a change this would be.

Andy was slowing down now, his directional blinking for the right. They turned by a grey mailbox that sported in black letters "Conrad 152." The narrow driveway led up a steep hill and around tight curves, all the while shrouded by dense forest. Then a burst of light flashed through the trees ahead, and a few seconds later they broke into a sunny clearing. The driveway ended in a wide circle, at the top of which sat an enormous grey house.

"Here we are!" Andy announced cheerfully, putting the car in park at the side of a detached three-car garage.

"Is Kevin—er, your dad, is he here yet?" Shannon tried to steady her breathing as they removed the suitcases from the trunk. Her pulse was hammering in her throat.

"Good question." Andy peered into a garage window. "Looks like it."

"How come you don't park in there?" Laura asked.

"It's full. This is my spot."

"Your dad has *three* cars?"

Andy shrugged helplessly. "Yes, he has three cars. And he's your dad too, by the way."

Shannon scowled at no one in particular. She had no plans of calling Kevin "Dad." Ever.

Laura was looking around with her jaw hanging open, amazement branded on her face. Shannon wanted to reach out and smack her, maybe knock some sense into the impressionable girl. All the riches in the world couldn't measure up to what a real father was. Or make up for what he wasn't.

They followed Andy up the side steps onto the L-shaped porch that graced the front of the house and came around to the side. Andy pushed open the maroon side door, calling out, "We're here!" Laura and Shannon filed in behind him, pausing beside a mudroom.

Two heads peaked around a corner before a young girl led the way, a small boy behind.

"Hey guys." Andy gave the girl a ruffle on the head and swept the boy up into his arms. "I want you to meet your big sisters, Shannon and Laura."

Shannon took a sharp breath. Big sisters?

"They're going to be living with us now, remember?"

The girl stepped forward with surprising poise. She held out her hand.

"Pleased to meet you."

Shannon accepted the hand and shook it, not knowing what else to do. How old had Andy said she was? Eight going on 13, something like that.

Andy set the boy down, who was shyly assessing them. "You can leave your stuff here for now. Let's find Dad."

Let's not, Shannon thought, but she bit it back and followed Andy into the kitchen. Kevin was standing at the stove, apron secured around his neck. He froze with a spatula in his hand.

"Ah, you made it. Good." They stood, Shannon and Laura staring at their father, he staring back at them. An awkward silence stretched between them, and Shannon shifted her eyes to examine the beautiful wooden cabinets complimented by frosted glass panes. Kevin's smooth-talking lawyer had been truthful about at least one thing—Kevin was clearly financially stable.

"Hey, so why don't we bring your stuff upstairs?" Andy came to the rescue, looking uncomfortable himself. Kevin exhaled, clearly relieved. He had acted so cocky in court the other day. Was he regretting things now? If so, Shannon would gladly go back to Chicago.

"Good idea. And then dinner will be ready in about fifteen minutes. That is, if you girls are hungry?" Uncertainty again. Shannon pulled her lips down into a frown. This hardly lined up with his previous behavior. He'd practically threatened Alan in the court room.

"Shannon?"

"What?"

"I asked if you're hungry."

"Oh. Yeah." She nodded, managing to avoid eye contact.

"Right. So let's get your stuff upstairs." Andy tugged Shannon's arm and hauled her toward the entryway. They grabbed their belongings and trucked them through the living room toward a wide, wooden staircase that curved upward in the far side of the room. Shannon's mouth parted at the sight of a grand piano to one side of the living room.

"Do you think I could use that sometime?"

Andy's face lifted in surprise. "You still play piano?"

"A little," she fudged.

"That's what it's here for. Gabby started taking lessons, but I'm sure she'll share. By the way, what'd you put in this thing?" Andy grunted as he hauled her suitcase up the stairs, his muscles straining.

Shannon didn't answer. She wasn't going to admit that there were only about five articles of clothing and one pair of shoes in the bag. Clothes could be gotten anywhere. Most of the space was filled with music and art supplies, pictures in frames, scrapbooks, journals, books, mementos, gifts. Memories. The ceramic clock her best friend Brittni had painted and given to her on her 11th birthday. The picture frame from Alan containing a photo of him and Mom on their last anniversary. These were treasures worth more than any clothing, no matter how dearly she would miss her favorite outfits.

"For now you two will have to share a room," Andy explained as they entered a large room. Two twin beds sat on opposite sides of the room, covered in bright pink comforters. Pink curtains fell away from the windows. Two dressers sat side by side, painted a pastel pink. Everywhere Shannon looked, she saw pink. Not her favorite color to begin with, but this was the very definition of overkill.

Andy smiled. "This is Gabby's old room, specially designed for sleepovers. She decided a few months ago that it was too 'childish' for her, so Dad remodeled a room for her. Sorry you have to sleep in Pink Paradise, but it's only for now. I'm moving out soon, so one of you can have my room. It's right here." He stepped across the hallway into another room. "Whoever keeps this one"—he pointed back to the room where Shannon and Laura still stood—"can redecorate in anyway—and any color—you'd like." He flashed his irresistible grin. "You guys doing okay? You look shell-shocked."

"Well, this house is huge. I'll get lost trying to find a bathroom." Shannon just wanted to go home.

Andy shook his head. "Nope, there's one right here." He flicked on a light in a small room between his bedroom and theirs. "We also have a basement with all sorts of fun. But I'll save that for later. Come on down for dinner when you're ready."

Shannon sank onto one of the fluorescent beds when he was gone, her energy depleted. Laura plopped herself down next to Shannon and leaned her head on her shoulder.

"I want to go home."

Shannon reached her arm around her sister. A second later she felt the shoulders shaking beneath her arm as Laura began to sob. Shannon wanted to join her. Then maybe she wouldn't hurt. But no tears would come. She had shed no tears when Mom died three weeks ago. No tears at the funeral. No tears on Wednesday when what remained of her life fell apart in court. And no tears when she'd said goodbye to her family this morning. No tears.

"Dinner's ready!" Andy's big voice called a few minutes later as Laura was touching up her makeup in the bathroom.

"Come on, Sis. Time to show our faces."

The food was decent, but that was the only good part of the meal. Kevin didn't speak the entire time, and by seven o'clock, Shannon was certain she hated him. Andy tried talking at first, but even he gave up since neither of the girls were responding. Daniel was the quietest four-year-old Shannon had ever seen, although she had to admit he was cute. Gabby was the only one who made much noise, prattling on the whole time about something at school. Shannon never did figure out what she was talking about before the torturous meal ended.

Kevin was putting the leftovers away when she took a deep breath and approached him.

"Do you mind if..." He hadn't looked up yet. "Kevin?"

His head snapped up, blue eyes wide. Shannon wondered if he expected her to call him "Dad." Slim chance of that. His face became rigidly expressionless as he waited for her to continue.

"I need to call Da—uh, Alan and let him know we got here safely."

"There is no need to do that." The Kevin she'd seen at the courtroom returned in a flash, his voice slicing the air like a sword. "If you hadn't arrived safely, Alan would have already been notified."

"But—"

"No." He raised his chin, beckoning for a challenge to his authority. "Don't you girls have some unpacking to do?"

"Not really. You didn't give us a chance to pack much." She didn't try to keep the accusation from her tone. If he wanted a fight, she'd be the first to comply.

"You had plenty of time to pack the things you most needed." His comeback was quick and controlled, but anger simmered in his eyes. "Remember, I could have taken you back with me the moment the judge gave me custody. But I gave you two extra days." He paused. "We're going shopping tomorrow, and you can get anything you need. Money is not an issue."

"Oh, I think we know that by now." Sarcasm edged Shannon's words as she turned around and exited the room in disgust before Kevin could make another sound.

She stalked onto the side porch and took a deep breath. A penetrating chill was spreading through the air as the sun sank below the trees. The woods made it appear darker than it probably was.

She'd had a cell phone until two months ago. With all of Mom's medical expenses, they couldn't keep up with the bill, so the company had shut her phone off. If only she still had it.

The screen door opened, and Shannon turned and found Andy.

"You need anything?"

"A phone?" she asked hopefully.

"Really? Sure." He pulled a sleek iPhone from his pocket. "Anything else?"

"Can you find Laura?"

A few seconds later Laura emerged onto the porch, and Shannon dialed the familiar number, saying in a hushed voice, "We better make this quick, before Kevin finds us."

Her step-dad answered on the second ring.

"Dad!" Her whole body relaxed at the sound of his voice.

"Shannon!"

The relief and love in his tone caused a lump in her throat so big she could barely breathe.

"I was so worried! I thought I'd hear from you sooner. Are you girls okay?"

"Yeah. Our flights were fine, and we're in Virginia now at—at Kevin's house."

"Good, good. Oh, I'm so glad you're safe. Is Laura around?"

Shannon hated to part with the comforting voice, but she handed the phone over to Laura, who chatted hungrily with Alan. Shannon was practically dancing, begging to have the phone back when Kevin's form filled the doorway.

"What are you doing? Whose phone is that?"

Laura's hand slowly fell, holding the cell phone, and Shannon could hear Alan's faraway voice calling, "Laura? Laura— Shannon, you there?"

Kevin reached over and grabbed the phone, ending the call with a beep. Laura made a small yelp of protest, but Kevin silenced her with one look.

Shannon felt something building in her, rising, boiling, about to bubble over. She yanked the phone out of Kevin's hand.

"Excuse me, we were in the middle of something, and it did not involve you."

Kevin's face went slack with shock before an angry flush spread across it.

"Actually, I think it had an awful lot to do with me, considering it was something I told you not to do."

Shannon took a quick step so that she stood inches away from Kevin. Her petite frame didn't even make it to his shoulders, but she didn't care.

"I know why you don't want us to talk to Dad—to Alan. Because you don't want to admit what a terrible father you've been, and that's what Alan reminds you of." She wagged her finger at him. "If you think keeping him from us will win us over to you, you're dead wrong. You don't know anything about love. Alan has loved us since the day he met us, and he's been everything that a father should, while you—you've been *nothing*." She spat the word out like it tasted bad. "You walked away. You left us and never came back. I don't know why you're oh-so-concerned about taking care of us now, when you've ignored us for the last nine years."

"Shannon—"

"You made us leave behind everything that we love and come to a new place—what, so you can bully us around? Does that give you a power trip? Is that what you want?" Her voice had reached a screech, but it dropped to a growl as she looked him straight in the eyes. "You're nothing but a jerk, and I hate you."

She heard the gasp that came from Laura, but she didn't care. She turned to walk away, but Kevin reached out and grabbed her arm.

"Stop right there, young lady. We are not finished. You can't attack me like that and just run off." His eyes were blazing, his face glowing so intensely that it clashed with his unruly red hair. "Sit down." Shannon stared in defiance until he reached out and forcefully pushed her onto a porch chair. She jerked her head up, but he pinned her down with the look on his face.

"Now you listen to me." His voice was tight, strained with anger. "I know I haven't been around the past few years, but that does not mean I didn't want to be a part of your life or that I was not concerned about you and Laura. When your mom and I split, I didn't want to fight over you two, so I let her have you both. I wanted to stay in your life, but it was complicated."

"Complicated? *Complicated*!" Shannon exploded. "You tell me what's complicated about the fact that you paid stupid child support every month for the past nine years but we never got a birthday card? A Christmas present? A phone call? *Not even one*?"

She didn't realize she was crying until Kevin's face blurred before her. He opened his mouth to reply, but she ignored the tears streaming down her face.

"After you abandoned us, Mom was crushed, but she loved us and took care of us. *You* walked away. As far as I'm concerned, you've never been a part of my life, and you never will!"

She fled into the house, stumbling on the stairs, not stopping until she collapsed onto the bright pink bed. Steady sheets of rain fell from her eyes, a waterfall plummeting onto the pillow. She sobbed until she couldn't breathe, holding her aching sides with her arms wrapped around her. Finally she slept, but even then she didn't escape the pain, dreaming the saddest dream she'd ever had. When she woke up still crying, she knew it wasn't a dream.

It was a memory.

Shannon glided back and forth on the wooden swing hanging from the monstrous oak tree in the backyard. The fading yellow rope burned her hands, but she didn't care. The feel of the wind through her hair kept her legs pumping, pumping, until she thought she would soar through the sky like one of the birds Mommy liked to feed. She let out a happy giggle, relishing the warm embrace of the summer sunshine. Above her in the tree house, Laura's high-pitched voice rang as she told her dolls to sit up straight for tea.

"Come play with me, Shanny!" Her little sister poked her head out the fort's door. "It's more fun with you." The pouting lip tugged at Shannon heart, and she dragged her feet in the dust, slowing the swing to a jerky stop.

A car pulled into the driveway.

"Daddy's home!" she shrieked, taking off at a run for the house. Behind her Laura scrambled down the sturdy ladder, yelling "Wait for me, Shanny. Wait!"

By the time they got to the backdoor, Daddy was inside, and Shannon kicked her shoes off as fast as she could. She didn't want to get scolded by Mommy again for bringing dirt in the house, but she couldn't wait to see Daddy! He'd been gone what felt like forever, and she missed him. Laura tore her shoes off, too, and they raced through the house, eagerly searching for signs of Daddy. Shannon spotted him standing in the living room and surged ahead.

In the doorway she came to a sliding halt, her socked feet slipping on the hardwood floor. Mommy sat on the sofa in front of Daddy, her hands covering her face. Her shoulders shook as loud sobs came from her mouth. Shannon felt confused. Why was Mommy crying? And why didn't Daddy turn around and look at them?

Laura slammed into her from behind with calls for Daddy erupting from her lips, but Shannon reached to shush her. Something was wrong. Another force bumped her, and she looked back to find Todd and Andy peering over the girls, eyes wide with curiosity.

"I'm sorry, Elise." Daddy's voice reached out to Shannon, sounding foreign to her. Empty. Cold. She stood transfixed, holding onto her little sister. "It's been a long time coming. You and I started off on the wrong foot, and I can't do it anymore."

Shannon cocked her head, trying to process the words of her beloved Daddy. What did he mean? He didn't want to be with Mommy?

Laura suddenly broke free from Shannon's grip and flung herself across the room, landing at Daddy's feet. "Daddy! I missed you!" She glanced at Mommy, who seemed to be shrinking into the couch as tears gushed from closed eyes. "Wha's a'matter? Why's Mommy cryin'?"

He looked down at Laura blindly, then glanced back at the sobbing form before him.

"I'll send someone for my things." He turned and strode away without a glance at the confused little girl who followed him to the doorway. Knocking into Shannon, he didn't look at her either or apologize. He grabbed Andy by the arm and kept walking.

"But Dad, where are we going?" The older boy tripped to keep up with his father, looking up at him with worry. Shannon's feet finally released from the floor, and she ran after the two, grabbing at Daddy's free hand. He jerked it away, and Shannon stopped, her fingers stinging.

"What's wrong, Daddy?" she whispered, tears forming in her eyes. He ignored her, just opened the door and walked out, pulling Andy with him. Todd and Laura trailed out the door behind them, looking bewildered, but Shannon stole back into the living room. She found Mommy crumpled in a heap on the floor.

Mommy didn't tuck Shannon into bed that night, or Laura, either. Shannon made sure Laura got in bed, and then she crept down the hall and stopped outside Mommy's closed door. There was only silence, so she began to slip away. But then she heard it: sobbing, choking, gasping, heaving, and bitter weeping. The sounds of Mommy's shattered heart. Not able to bear it a moment longer, Shannon fled back to her room, dove under the covers, buried her head in her pillow, and cried.

Daddy was gone.

Chapter Two

The first thing Shannon saw when she cracked open her eyes was pink. Everywhere. She closed her eyes, swollen and sore, as memories bombarded her, colliding with the hole in her chest that gasped for air. Mom was gone. Now she lived with Kevin. Life would never be the same again.

"That was a nice fireworks show last night."

She turned to look at her sister as she toweled her hair dry in the room twenty minutes later. A warm shower had soothed her face. Nothing done for the heart.

She raised her eyebrows in question.

"You and Kevin."

"Oh." Shannon let out a humorless laugh. "Yeah. I kinda' exploded."

"Kind of?" Laura shook her head. "I don't know where you get the guts to say the things you do. But you sure know how to say the truth in a way that hurts."

Shannon frowned. It wasn't exactly a compliment she wanted.

A quiet knock sounded on the bedroom door

"Breakfast time, girls." Kevin's firm voice contrasted with his soft knock. Shannon froze. She wasn't ready to see him. She wasn't sure she'd ever be.

"Okay, be right down," Laura called. When they got to the dining room, Andy, Gabby, and Daniel were already seated, and Kevin stood at the head of the table waiting. He smiled at them. Well, it was more of a grimace. Lips squeezed together and a nod of the head.

Shannon wasn't hungry, but the few bites of blueberry waffles and scrambled eggs she got down were tasty. She didn't want to say anything, but her mom had raised her right. "This is good."

"Thank you." Kevin nodded at her, looking satisfied.

She arched her eyebrows. "You made this?"

"Yes. Why so surprised? Alan didn't cook?"

It was the wrong thing to say. Shannon let her fork fall to her plate with a loud clatter. No one said a word as she stared at

Kevin, her cheek twitching with sudden anger. What was this man's deal? Why dig in a wound already wide open?

She swallowed several times and tried to stop her hands from shaking, not used to this much anger surging through her. Finally she took a deep breath and said into the tense silence, "Yes, he cooks very well." That may have been a stretch, but still… "I just didn't know a busy doctor such as yourself had time to practice culinary skills." There. She had been civil.

She heard Andy let out his breath.

"So who's ready for some shopping?" The enthusiasm in his voice sounded forced.

"I am." Laura perked up considerably. "Where are we going?"

Kevin looked over at her. "Wherever you girls need to go. We'll head to Bristol first, near the airport. There's some good shopping there."

"Sweet! Let's hurry up then. I still gotta shower."

Andy chuckled at Laura. "Well no need to rush *too* much. The mall opens later on Sunday, you know."

Sunday. Today was Sunday. Shannon sat up straight. "Wait, we're going shopping *this* morning?"

"I thought that was clear." Kevin stared at her. "Problem?"

She gazed back. "Mom and *Alan*"—she stressed his name— "always took us to church on Sunday." Another and larger stretch. But Kevin didn't need to know that. She shrugged casually. "But you don't strike me as the church-going type."

She heard Andy sigh but was surprised when Kevin countered with a dry "neither do you." Not knowing what to say in response to that gibe, she stuffed a piece of waffle in her mouth.

After breakfast, Laura steamed up the bathroom with a long shower while Shannon tried to do something with her hair. Blowing it around with Laura's blow drier brought out some of its natural bend. Her hair couldn't quite be called curly, but it wasn't naturally straight either. She usually left it in long waves past her shoulders. Laura's blond hair was as straight as a pencil, just like their mom's. Shannon wrinkled her nose as she realized that her hair was more like Kevin's. It had started out blond when she was a baby, but the older she got, the redder it got, until now she knew "strawberry blond," as she preferred to describe herself, was being generous. She hadn't minded until she saw Kevin. She didn't want to look like him. She didn't want to be connected to him in any way.

When she stepped out the door an hour later behind the others, she snuggled her jacket close.

"Wow, it's cold! This is the only coat I brought."

Kevin heard her from where he was fiddling around in the hatch of the van. Without looking at her, he said, "We'll get you a good coat today, and everything else you need."

Shannon ignored him, making herself busy by looking around at the other vehicles in the garage. In addition to the blue Kia minivan they were loading into was a forest green SUV and a white Chevy Silverado truck.

Andy buckled Daniel into his car seat, then backed himself out of the van. He threw a smile their way as he headed out of the garage.

"You guys have fun, ok?"

Panic welled up in Shannon, and she took a step after him. "Wait, you're coming, right?"

"No, I have to work." He paused, probably noting the terror on her face. "You'll be fine." He offered a reassuring smile, then disappeared into the yard.

Shannon closed her eyes and took a deep breath. How far away was Bristol? Like an hour? She'd never make it that long in the van with Kevin *without* Andy.

She went to the side of the van, but before she could get the door open, the window on the front passenger door rolled down.

"Saved the front for you, Shannon," Kevin called. "We better get going."

Shannon swallowed back a groan. Now she'd be in the front with Kevin for an hour. Perfect.

* * *

Kurt was crunching numbers at his dad's desk in the office of their woodworking shop when the bell above the main entrance jingled. "Be right with you!"

Footsteps approached.

"Hey, man."

Recognizing Andy's voice, he didn't look up.

"Hey." He kept pushing buttons on the large calculator. "I thought maybe you weren't coming today." He paused to look at his calculations.

"Sorry, we had a slow morning since my sisters got here."

Kurt swiveled around in the brown chair. "I totally forgot they were coming. How's that going?"

Andy drew in a big breath and blew it out, then glanced around for a place to sit.

"That good, huh?"

His friend grunted as he picked up a pile of papers that were on top of a bar stool and sat down. "It's pretty tense at home."

Kurt frowned. "Why? I guess I don't really remember why they're coming to live with you. Did you tell me?"

"I don't know. Their mom died three weeks ago."

"Oh man," Kurt moaned softly, stunned by the thought. "That's gotta be tough."

"Yeah. And my dad hasn't had much to do with them since they were little."

"Why?" Kurt fiddled with the receipt in his hand absently, wondering what it would be like to lose a parent.

Andy sighed again. "I really don't know. Their mom left custody to her husband in her will or whatever. But my dad took it to court because he wanted to have them. He flew out to Chicago last week for the emergency hearing, and the judge ordered him custody, of course, since he's the biological parent. Shannon—she's the oldest—is really upset. She's won't accept that my dad got custody."

"Hmmm. Sounds messy." Kurt made a face. "How old is she? Thirteen?"

"Where did you get that from?" Andy laughed. "She's seventeen."

"Oh. Why did I think they were younger?"

"No idea. Laura is fifteen. She seems to be handling it a little better. The problem is Shannon's way too much like my dad. She would hate me for saying this, but they have the same personality, and right now they are egging each other on."

"How so?" Kurt wished he could meet this little fireball.

"Well she is so—so—" Andy paused, searching for the word. Kurt waited patiently. His friend did this all the time. "Ah— antagonistic, that's it. She makes as many digging comments as possible. It's like she's trying to make my dad fight back. Which doesn't take much these days, with Carmen leaving. You shoulda' heard them last night." He described the blow-up on the porch, and Kurt was shaking his head by the end of the story.

"Man. If I get bored, I'll come over to your house! Seriously, though, you gotta give her time to heal. I mean, she probably hasn't even had a chance to grieve for her mom with all the legal stuff that happened right away. She'll come around."

"I guess." Andy nodded thoughtfully. "I feel bad, and I wish I could do more. But it's exhausting to be around them for long. That's why I decided to work today. I was thinking of going with them to Bristol, but I opted out after the breakfast conversation. Too many sparks flying."

Kurt started stacking up all the financial papers spread out on the desk. "What are they doing in Bristol?" He put the adding machine back where it belonged. He had decided to balance the books for his dad since his parents were out of town. His dad had taught him basic accounting a few years back, and now that Kurt was in the middle of an accounting class at the community college, he had a pretty good handle on the financial aspect of his dad's business. It would be his some day if he wanted it.

"Major shopping. The girls didn't bring much."

"Oh fun." Kurt stood up and scrunched his face. "Well we better get to work out in the shop. Oh, and I haven't forgotten about helping you with your project. How 'bout I come over tonight after dinner?" Andy was working on a new oak desk for his dad, trying to get it done for his birthday. The deadline was looming, and there was still a ways to go. Andy was handy with woodwork, but Kurt had more experience.

"That would be great." Andy rose and replaced the stack of papers on the stool. "This place is a mess!"

Kurt shook his head. "Tell me about it. No time to keep the office clean, you know?"

* * *

"Figure out where you're going first?" Kevin's voice made Shannon jump. She pretended to study the mall map when really her eyes were too blurry with tears to see.

"Nope."

He reached around her and tapped one of the colored blocks on the map. "This place has a great selection of winter gear. I'd start my coat search there."

She nodded. "I'll check it out."

"You going to be okay on your own? Where's Laura?"

Long gone with Kevin's credit card in hand. How she'd managed that one, Shannon was sure Kevin was still trying to figure out. She'd even convinced him to give Shannon one, too.

The ride had been tolerable. Kevin hadn't talked, so neither had Shannon. Once inside the mall, Laura disappeared, and Shannon had no idea where to start. She had never gone shopping without Mom before. The mall had been their thing. Laura always wanted to shop alone, but Shannon had stuck with Mom. She couldn't imagine doing this without her. How could Mom really be gone?

"Shannon?" She realized she hadn't responded to Kevin's questions, too caught up in her sorrow. A tear took the plunge from her bottom lid just as she turned to this man who was her dad.

"What's wrong?" he asked, eyeing her face.

She angled it away. "Nothing you'd understand."

He didn't try to cloak his sigh. "Okay. Do you want me to show you where Archie's is, the coat store?"

She wanted to say yes. She hated wandering around alone, not sure where she was going. "No, I've got it." No way would she look weak for him. "I'll see you later."

"Alright, Shannon." His quiet voice followed her as he watched her go.

Eventually she found the store, and Kevin was right, the coat selection was impressive. She settled for a cream colored pea-coat and a bright blue down hooded coat and picked out several sets of hats, gloves, and scarves that matched or contrasted nicely.

Too many hours later, she paid for her last purchase at the shoe store. Winter boots were in order, for sure. The only pair of shoes she had brought from Chicago, besides the Toms currently on her feet, was her running shoes. She couldn't live without those. In fact, she planned to go running tonight when they got back. She yearned for that satisfying burn in her legs and lungs.

She headed toward the fountain where Kevin had said to regroup at 4:30, bags bumping against her thighs. Buying an entire wardrobe in one shopping trip was quite a task, not to mention getting all the other necessities of life that hadn't fit in her suitcase. She had run into Kevin two hours ago, and he had taken her earlier purchases out to the van. She had no idea how much money she'd spent today. A lot.

Kevin, Gabby, and Daniel were sitting by the fountain when she arrived. "Sorry if I'm a couple minutes late," she panted. "This stuff is heavy."

"You're fine." Kevin glanced around. "We're still waiting on Laura."

"She's always late."

Ten minutes later Laura showed up with a teenage boy in tow.

"Hey guys, sorry I'm late," she announced, still 15 feet away.

They were all staring at the boy behind her, loaded down with shopping bags.

"This is Troy." Laura dumped the bags in her arms on the ground. It looked like she really had bought something at every store. "He was nice enough to help me carry my stuff."

Kevin stepped forward and rescued the scrawny kid from the mountain of bags.

"Thank you, Troy. I think we can handle things from here." He came short of saying get lost, but his tone said it for him. The boy nodded quickly, glanced at Laura, and then back at Kevin.

"Do you need something?" Kevin's nostrils were flaring. That boy would run if he knew what was good for him.

"Well um, I was wondering, uh, Laura, can I have your phone number?"

Laura's eyes bugged out, but before she could reply, Kevin answered for her.

"No, you cannot. You need to go."

The boy took off at a trot, throwing one more glance back at Laura.

"Laura, really?" Shannon asked immediately. "You're picking up guys at the mall?"

Laura's face was red. "He was desperate for attention, so he was willing to follow me around and carry my stuff." She rolled her eyes. "I never *dreamed* he'd ask for my number! How embarrassing. He was such a little nerd!"

"Well then you shouldn't have led him on like that." Kevin looked hard at Laura. "I don't ever want to see behavior like that from you again. Do you understand?"

Laura was redder than ever as she looked down and muttered, "Yes, sir."

"What is it with you and guys?" Shannon exploded, shaking her bags in the air. Laura wouldn't look at her. Somehow Laura had been able to carry on with life, including dating some bozo, while their mom had been dying. Shannon simply couldn't do it. One guy back in Chicago had wanted to date her, but that was right after her mom's diagnosis. He had kept asking, and finally she told him she didn't feel right going out with him when her mom was fighting for her life. He never spoke to her again, and a month later he was dating someone else. She was disgusted with boys in general and honestly hadn't given any guy much thought in about a year.

Kevin shook his head and picked up a load of bags, giving some to Gabby and even Daniel.

"Come on, let's go. Can you manage yours, Shannon?"

If she could manage two years of Mom's cancer, Mom dying, leaving Alan, Jaime and Todd, and living for the immediate future with the likes of Kevin, she could manage a few measly shopping bags. She could manage the whole mall inventory. Piece of cake.

Chapter Three

Kurt ate a quiet dinner in the kitchen. His parents were out of town for his uncle's funeral. He had volunteered to stay at home and keep things running. While he chewed, he made a mental list of what he needed to do tomorrow—besides going to classes and squeezing in three or four hours of homework.

His accounting class wasn't too hard , but business statistics was taking a lot of time, as was freshman comp, and those all met three times a week. Tuesdays and Thursdays he had American history, which was a breeze, and developmental psych, a lot of reading and memorization. Every Tuesday he also had a one-credit tennis class for fun. So far he was enjoying college, but it kept him much busier than high school had. He found it exhausting trying to keep up with homework and working about 30 hours a week for his dad. Tonight he desperately needed to work on statistics homework due tomorrow. But he'd promised Andy.

He shoved the last bit of sandwich into his mouth, wiped the crumbs off the table, and dumped the plate into the sink. Cleanup could wait.

He grabbed his favorite DeWalt circular saw from the woodworking shop and hopped into his Dodge Ram. He liked walking to Andy's, only fifteen minutes on the path they'd made through the woods. But it was two minutes driving, and every minute saved now was one less he'd have to stay up tonight. He'd stayed up too late the night before watching a movie when he should have been either sleeping or doing homework.

"Priorities, man," he mumbled to himself as he guided his truck down his steep driveway.

He parked in the circular drive in front of the Conrads' house, intending to go straight to Andy's woodworking nook in the back of the garage. Andy kept it curtained off with a drop cloth, and Kevin was so busy it didn't seem he had even thought to peek and see what Andy's latest project was. Andy was hoping to surprise his dad with the new desk.

He was walking to the garage when he heard music. The breeze was carrying it from the front of the house. Kurt cocked his head. Piano music. And much too advanced to be coming from Gabby's little fingers.

Curiosity overcame him, and he changed course, making a beeline for the front door. He slipped inside so quietly that the figure at the piano never looked up. Her hands kept gliding up and down the keys, creating the most beautiful, haunting melody he'd ever heard. Her whole body moved with her hands, as if she and the music were one.

He heard a sniff and realized the angel at the piano was crying. Glorious golden red ripples of hair flowed down her back, some spilling over her shoulders like a glowing waterfall.

She looked up and jolted at the sight of him. "Who are you?" she demanded, the song ending abruptly. Wide, blue eyes stared at him, and to Kurt they were an ocean, and he was immediately drowning. He shook his head, trying to clear the mud that had so quickly settled like sediment on the ocean floor.

"My name is Kurt. Please keep playing." He couldn't tear his eyes away from her beautiful, sad, ocean eyes.

But she didn't keep playing. Instead she got to her feet, wiping the tears off her face as a frown creased her soft features.

"Do you normally walk into people's front doors unannounced?" She edged toward the opening in the room where she could make an escape.

"No," he responded, pulling himself together. "I usually let myself in the side door."

Shock sprang to her lovely face.

"Kurt, is that you?" Andy popped into the room. "Thought I heard you. Why'd you come in the front?"

"Well, see, I heard—I heard the music, and I was curious. I wanted to see who was playing. It was... really nice..." He trailed off, focusing on the beautiful girl who was still looking at him through suspicious eyes from her stance beside the piano.

"Allow me to make proper introductions." Andy stepped in to smooth the way, his specialty.

"Shannon, this is my friend Kurt. You'll see him around here a lot."

So this was Shannon. Kurt had assumed as much by now. She was still watching him, but her expression was less annoyed than at first.

"And Kurt, this is my sister Shannon. As you have already heard, she is a talented musician." Andy narrowed his eyes at Shannon, and Kurt gathered that she hadn't been exactly forthright about her musical abilities. Blushing under Andy's scrutiny, she mumbled something like "well that's my best song..." She faltered and looked up as Kurt approached. His breath caught mid-swallow. She was gorgeous. He held out his hand.

"It's a pleasure to meet you, Shannon." She stared at his hand, then slowly put hers into it. Her hand was tiny and smooth, but he forced himself not to hold too long. Looking directly into her breathtaking eyes, he forced himself to keep swimming and said, "I hope I get to hear you play again very soon." Then releasing her hand, he forced himself to turn away from her.

"You ready, Andy?"

"Yup, let's get to work." Andy started down the hallway to the side door. "See ya later, Shannon. Stay outta' trouble."

As Andy bent to tie his shoes, he said in a low tone, "Pick up your jaw, will you?"

"Dude, you didn't tell me she's beautiful." Kurt managed to whisper, still reeling from Shannon's effect.

Andy pulled open the door and let it close behind them before he replied.

"She's my sister, man! And I just re-met her." He stopped and turned around to face Kurt. "Hey, Kurt, did I ever tell you my sister Shannon is really pretty? I thought you should know."

Kurt rolled his eyes. "Okay, forget it."

"No, *you* forget it. She's off limits to you, pal."

Kurt threw his hands in the air. "Hey, what did I ever do? Man. A guy doesn't even get a chance these days."

Andy stopped again. His expression was serious enough to freeze pipes. "You're not what she needs right now. She's beautiful, sure. So are lots of other girls. Let it go."

Kurt stared at his friend. He tried to get what Andy was saying, but all he could remember were the tears Shannon had cried at the piano from those enormous blue eyes. "Okay, okay. She's out of my league, I get it."

Andy sighed. "It's not that, Kurt. Her mom just died, and she hates her dad. She needs time. You told me that yourself. She doesn't need a guy like you coming along and messing with her. Besides—if you had a younger sister, would you let me near her?"

"Are you kidding? No way!"

"Exactly. So hands off. If you want to be her friend, fine. But you better leave it at that, you hear?"

Kurt wasn't used to Andy being this serious, especially about a girl.

"Yeah, man. I—I'll leave her alone, okay?"

Andy nodded, looking satisfied. "Right, so this is where I'm at." He had already moved on to the topic of the desk as he pushed aside the drop cloth, and Kurt forced his brain to follow.

* * *

Shannon stayed in the living room after Andy and his friend walked out. She sat back down on the piano bench and stared at her hands' reflection in the shiny black fallboard behind the keys. She could still feel that large, rough hand warmly clasping hers. What had been his problem? He hadn't seemed able to look away from her. It was unnerving. She had been so startled by him, she couldn't even say right now what he looked like, aside from the fact that his hair was blond. The room had been a little dark, since she was playing without lighting. The song that boy had ruined was one she had composed for her mom's funeral. She and Laura had written words to it, and Laura sang it while Shannon played. She was amazed neither of them had broken down during the song. Somehow they had made it the whole way through. Not this time.

And of course whatever-his-name-was had come in right when she was crying. Yesterday she had *wanted* to cry. Now she couldn't seem to stop.

She wandered upstairs and found Laura busy texting her friends in Chicago with her new phone. Go figure. Last night Kevin had a cow, make that a whole dairy farm, because she had borrowed a phone to call Alan. Today when they got home, he gave them each their own cell phone. The man made no sense. She wondered if he'd get mad again if she called Alan. Good thing she didn't care.

She was disappointed when her step-father didn't answer, but she left a message, then dialed another familiar number and waited as it rang. First, second, third ring...

"Hello?"

"Todd!" She felt herself smiling the widest smile in days. Todd was 22 and on his own now, but he'd been a steady part of Shannon's life from the day she was born. His dad was Mom's first husband, but he had passed away when Todd was only two.

"Shannon? Is that you?" He sounded just as excited. "How are you? It doesn't seem like we said goodbye just yesterday. How are things? How's it going with Kevin? What about Andy?"

Shannon laughed, truly delighted to hear her big brother's voice. "One thing at a time. I've been better, but I think that goes without speaking. We went shopping today and got stuff we needed. Kevin's weird." She scowled. "I can't figure him out. Last night he wouldn't let us call Dad, and when we did anyway he got super mad—it was crazy. And then today he goes and buys us both our own phones."

"Wow. Really?"

"Yeah. He's generous but really on edge. I don't get it. But Andy is awesome. Not as good as you, of course."

He laughed. "Hey, I'm not worried, I know I'm irreplaceable. But I'm so glad he's there filling the void. When do you start school?"

"Tomorrow, I guess."

"You sound nervous."

"I am," she admitted slowly. "What if they are farther along than we were? Or using different textbooks? What if I fail, Todd?"

"Hey, you'll be fine. No doubt it'll be a struggle. I know school's been hard for the past few years, with—with Mom and all. But I know you can do this. Keep your eye on that date in June, remember?"

Shannon couldn't help but smile. "I'll try. Thanks, Todd."

"Hey, that's what I'm here for. You better call me, let me know how it goes. This is your new phone number?"

"Yup."

They spoke a few minutes longer before Todd had to run. When she put the phone down, Shannon felt like bawling her eyes out. Instead she crawled off her bed, knowing that running would be the perfect distraction. Her phone told her it was 7:00. Early enough for a quick jog down the long, winding driveway. She rummaged around in her shopping bags until she found a pair of yoga pants.

"What're you doing?" Laura was standing in the doorway with her phone in hand.

"Going for a run. Wanna come?"

Her sister curled her lips. "No thanks. I'm tired."

So was she, but she needed to exert herself somehow or she was going to have another meltdown. Quickly she changed, popped a new navy blue hoodie over her head, and tied on her running shoes.

"I'll be back soon."

Outside, a large black truck was parked in the circle, so she assumed Andy's friend hadn't left yet. Kurt, was it? She wondered what he and Andy were working on in the garage, but she really didn't care.

Soon she was breezing down the driveway, her feet pounding out a regular rhythm on the pavement beneath her. Bad for her knees, supposedly, but right now it felt amazing. She took a huge breath, letting the air expand her lungs. By the time she reached the end of the drive, her legs were starting to feel it. Man, she was out of shape. She used to run eight miles a day and barely feel winded. But she had been on the track team then. Last year she hadn't joined with Mom so sick.

The sun had set, so she turned around to head back. She didn't relish being alone in the dark, but it was peaceful. The trees rustled gently in the slight breeze, carrying chilly autumn air, and an owl began its nightly call off in the woods. It was all so different from the city.

She slowed her run and came to a gradual stop. Standing still, she let the night mountain air settle around her, wrapping her in its cool, dark embrace. She felt completely invisible.

She missed her mom.

Sudden and terrorizing loneliness seized her, and she started off at a fast run. She ran hard, as hard as she could up the steep incline. Her breath came in deep, ragged gasps. Why did her face feel wet? Salty water was dripping off her chin, and an anguished cry tore through the air.

Her foot came down on a large stick hidden by the dark and rolled backward, catapulting her to the ground. She landed hard on her right knee, then slid backward on the pavement as her upper body sprawled forward. She collapsed on the ground and slowly rolled onto her side, holding her knee, while her body wracked with sob after sob.

It hurt so bad, the hole in her heart left by Mom's death. She had cried in the months before her mom died, because they all knew what was coming. When her mom finally let go, was released from her terrible suffering, they were all relieved in some strange way. The battle was over, and life could go on. But then a few days later Kevin filed his petition, and a new battle began. Shannon hadn't even had time to think much about her mom's passing for the past few weeks. She hadn't shed a tear for Mom until now.

But now—now it was hitting. Shannon's heart was pounding, pulsing with pain each second that she lay on the driveway. Mom was gone. She would never see her again.

Mommy. Mommy. How could she be gone?

Mommy. Please come back, Mommy.

"Shannon?" A flashlight shined on her face, and she peered up through blurry eyes. How long had she been lying there?

"Shannon..." Andy's voice said again, this time soft and sad. "Come here, let me help you up."

She could hardly comprehend what was happening. All she felt was the constriction of pain, its vise-like grip on her chest and stomach and head. Mommy was gone.

Andy reached down and grabbed her under the arms with both hands and pulled her up like an infant. She tried to stand, but her leg buckled as she noticed searing pain in her knee.

"Andy, I think she's hurt!" The alarmed voice sounded familiar. Shannon strained to turn and see who was behind her, but it was too dark.

"Easy, Shannon. Here, sit back down." Andy tried to ease her to the ground, but she started to slip. Strong arms grabbed her from behind.

"Whoa, there. Let's go slow." It was a deep, gentle voice. He helped Shannon sit down. She still had no idea who he was. Everything was foggy in her head.

"Kurt, can you hold the flashlight so I can check her leg?"

"Sure thing."

Shannon let her head flop forward as tears continued to slide down her face.

"It's bleeding, but it doesn't look too serious. Shannon, what happened?"

* * *

Shannon didn't respond to Andy's question. Her head was bent forward, and Kurt heard terrible sobs ripping from her mouth. In the light of the flashlight, her whole form was shaking.

"Shannon." Andy tried again, gently touching her head. "Can you look at me?"

Slowly she looked up at him, and tears were pouring down her face.

"What are you doing out here?"

Shannon tried to answer, but she was shivering violently. Kurt realized that if she had been lying out there for long, she must be getting cold.

"R-r-r-r-unning." She took in huge gasps of air, breathing in jerky motions.

"And did you fall?"

She nodded, her teeth clacking as she wrapped her arms around herself. Kurt quickly threw off his wool coat and stepped forward to drape it around her shoulders, but she didn't seem to notice.

"Shannon, why are you crying?" Andy asked in the gentlest voice Kurt had ever heard him use, but it was still the wrong thing to say, because Shannon began sobbing ever so loudly again.

Rocking back and forth, she cried so bitterly that Kurt felt tears in his own eyes. She pressed her hand flat on her chest over her heart.

"Mommy." The word tumbled from her mouth in broken syllables. "It hurts...it hurts..."

Kurt couldn't take it any longer. "Hey, I'm gonna go get my truck so we can bring her back to the house, okay?" He was back in a couple minutes, setting the emergency break before jumping out.

It looked like Shannon had calmed down some in his absence, and she let Andy pick her up. He noted how small she was as Andy slid into the seat, cradling her in his arms. Kurt shut the passenger door and ran around to his side. A careful three-point turn had them heading back toward the house.

The porch light was on, Kevin waiting at the side door.

"What's wrong?" he demanded as soon as Kurt opened his door.

"Shannon fell and got a little hurt. Nothing too bad, I don't think."

Andy came around the side of the truck then, carrying the petite form in his arms.

Kevin opened the door wide. "Where's she hurt? Here, bring her to the couch in the living room."

Kurt followed them into the living room. Kevin threw all the pillows off the couch except for one, which he slid under Shannon's head. Laura came flying down the stairs, shrieking, "Oh my gosh, Shannon! Are you okay?" Kurt had met her earlier when she had come out to the garage, concerned that Shannon wasn't back yet.

Andy shushed Laura quickly. "She'll be fine." He looked at Kevin. "It's just her knee, Dad." Kevin was staring at Shannon's face, blotchy and streaked from crying. Tears were still seeping out from under closed eyelids, and her chest rose and fell roughly as she fought to bring herself under control.

"Why's she crying so much?"

Andy shook his head at his dad, mouthing "later."

"Her knee, Dad," he insisted.

Kevin bent to examine the injury. It looked to Kurt like she had landed hard on a sharp rock, and it had pierced the skin deeply. Then she must have slid, because little pieces of gravel were stuck all over in her skin.

Kevin dished out instructions to everyone in the room, and Kurt's assignment was to fill a zip-lock with ice from the freezer. When he returned from the kitchen, Kevin was spreading a towel underneath Shannon's legs on the couch to keep the upholstery dry and clean. Once he got the bleeding stopped, he began to pick the rocks out of her skin with small forceps.

Shannon's puffy eyelids popped open as she gasped with pain.

"Every time it hurts, Shannon, squeeze Andy's hand, okay?" Kevin looked to Andy for his agreement, and he immediately grasped Shannon's hand. She nodded with clenched teeth as Kevin dug deeper. Kurt saw Andy wince, but he didn't waver. When her dad spread a topical antiseptic over the wound, Shannon started crying again. Kevin placed a wad of gauze on the knee, then wrapped it with an elastic bandage. He pulled her amazingly intact pant leg down and gently put the bag of ice on top of her knee.

"There you go. All better." He patted her shoulder awkwardly.

Shannon released Andy's hand and looked up at him. "I went running so I wouldn't have a meltdown." She shook her head, her face mournful. "It didn't work."

Kurt bit back a laugh at her dry honesty. He saw that Andy was chuckling, too.

"Apparently not. But don't worry about that. You need to rest."

Kurt needed to leave. An hour ago. It was heading for 8:30 and statistics was calling his name. He nodded his head at Andy and gave a salute wave.

"Hey, thanks man," Andy called after him as he headed down the hall. "See ya tomorrow."

" 'Night." It was gonna be a late night for him. As always.

* * *

Andy offered to help Shannon upstairs, but she refused. Her knee burned like fire as she limped over to the stairs, but she was too humiliated to accept help.

She tripped on the second step, and before she could reach out her hands to steady herself, she was lifted off her feet and swung into the air. She turned her head, expecting to find Andy's face inches away—but it was Kevin. She hadn't been this close to him in more than nine years. Now he was holding her, and it made her want to flail her arms and legs and shimmy out of his reach. If she wasn't so exhausted, she might have. Instead she turned her face away, heart pounding, and blew out some air. He didn't look at her or say a word, only continued up the stairs with her dangling in his arms.

He eased her down onto her bed and walked out the door without a word.

Laura was already hovering over her, and Shannon had to shoe her away so that she could get ready for bed. Her knee hurt every time she took a step. She had just carefully climbed into bed a half-hour later and was about to turn off the table lamp when a knock sounded on the door.

"Come in."

Kevin appeared in the doorway and cleared his throat. "How are you feeling?"

She shrugged. "It still hurts."

He nodded. "It will for a while. I brought some pain relief for you. You'll sleep better with it." He hesitated, then crossed the room to her bedside, holding a glass of water and two little pills. Shannon accepted them, wondering why he cared.

He backed away toward the door quickly and cleared his throat again. "Well, I should let you two get some sleep. Our mornings start pretty early around here. Breakfast is at 6:45, and then we have to be at the school at 7:30 to get you girls registered for your classes. So—" He stopped and nodded. "I'll see you in the morning, then."

"Good night," Laura called from her bed, but Shannon simply watched him leave.

She eased back onto her pillow with a sigh after he disappeared.

"Shannon, what happened tonight?"

Shannon rolled over and faced the wall, her back to her sister. "I don't want to talk about it, Laura."

"But why were you crying?"

Shannon ignored the pesky questions, staring at the pink wall beside her. She didn't want to talk about anything right now. Didn't want to think about the way she had broken down. She had never felt so utterly and completely broken before. She hadn't been in control of her emotions. That scared her.

But her fright was nothing compared to her embarrassment. She wanted to shrink into oblivion at the knowledge that Andy—and his friend Kurt, of all people—had found her collapsed in a puddle of incompetent sobs. What had she even said to them in the driveway? She couldn't remember. She barely remembered them finding her. She only remembered slipping from Andy's grip and strong arms catching her from behind. And she remembered crying. Right in front of them. Crying all the tears from her broken heart that she had fiercely held in for three weeks.

* * *

Kurt focused on statistics for the next several hours. By 11:00 he was seeing double. And he still had to write a three page essay for comp. Only the rough draft was due tomorrow, but the better he got it the first round, the less time he'd need to spend on it later.

As he opened up a new document on his notebook computer, his mind wandered back to the events of the evening. In his head was a picture of Shannon on the couch. Her copper hair was a beautiful mess all around her head, and her face peaked out of the dark blue hoodie, revealing the delicate features he had failed to notice the first time. Fine eyebrows, a little darker than her hair, arched over her eyes. A small nose that turned up the slightest bit at the end accented her face, and her lips were full and soft. He had yet to see her smile, but he was quite certain she was perfect, tears and all.

She hadn't looked at him after they had found her tonight. Perhaps his presence had bothered her. Or embarrassed her. Maybe he should have left sooner, but he had wanted to help, and he definitely wasn't going to leave until he knew she was okay. She was a mystery to him—a beautiful, intriguing mystery.

"Essay." He said it out loud to tear his mind back to reality.

Andy had said he could only be friends with Shannon. For the life of him he didn't understand why, but he intended to be whatever he could to the girl he had met tonight.

Morning came too quickly, and he rolled out of bed with a groan. Four hours was not enough sleep, but it was better than some nights lately. He got ready in record time, forgoing breakfast. His schedule allowed him an early lunch. He survived.

He grabbed his book bag and headed toward the door, stopping at the coat closet on the way. He searched the hangers, wondering where his wool coat was.

"Shannon." He had placed it around her shoulders last night. She must still have it. He grinned as he grabbed his old green fleece. Now he had an excuse to see her again soon.

Chapter Four

Shannon looked around as she stepped into the kitchen. Kevin was alone at the stove. Looked like she was the first one there.

"How's the knee?" He didn't look up from the frying pan.

"Ugly. How'd you know it was me?"

Now he looked at her, smiling. "I would have heard Gabby, Daniel, or Andy coming the whole way." A series of bangs and scuffs above them proved his point. "And I've figured out your sister already. Always late."

That was for sure.

"Can I check your knee?" He turned down the fire under the frying pan and washed his hands. "Hop onto one of the barstools."

Shannon complied, too nervous about the day ahead to comment. She sucked in her breath when Kevin prodded her knee, pain shooting down her leg.

"You okay?"

"Sure. Just hurts."

He nodded. "I'm going to treat it with bacitracin and wrap it again. It's still pretty raw." He disappeared down the hallway and returned with a tube in his hand. Silently he pulled her leg out straight and put the ointment on, then wrapped a gauze bandage around several times. His touch was gentle, like a feather dusting her tender skin. He might be a crappy dad, but it seemed he had the doctoring thing down pat.

"There. We'll just do the gauze wrap today. That'll give you more breathing room." He turned toward the stove, and Shannon remained on the stool, looking at the bandage.

"Kevin?"

"Hmm?" He glanced back at her. "Did you need something else? We'll be eating in two minutes."

"No, I was just wondering… Is it going to heal? I mean, will it scar?"

He tilted his head back and opened his mouth, as if laughing, but silent. "Women. Is that all you care about? Yes, it will heal, Shannon, and no it won't scar. Give it time."

Shannon didn't know what to make of his reaction. "Okay. Thanks," she mumbled, sliding off the stool.

During breakfast she forced food into her mouth like a robot. Nausea stirred instantly. She just wanted to be home with Mom and Dad and Jaime. But there was no more home, and there was no Mom, and now there wasn't even Dad and Jaime. The same emotions that had overwhelmed her last night were stirring in her pulverized heart, and she knew she better stop herself before it was too late.

"May I be excused?" She pushed her plate away and charged from the table before anyone could speak. As she speed-limped through the living room, she noticed something grey crumpled on the floor by the couch. She paused and looked down at it. A coat? A memory flooded her mind. She was a puddle of tears in the driveway, and suddenly hands had wrapped that coat around her, squeezing her shoulders in the process. The same strong hands that had caught her when she slipped.

Kurt.

She groaned. Now she was going to have to see him again after her embarrassing debut. Just great.

After dropping Daniel at his daycare and Gabby at the elementary school, Kevin pulled into the high school parking lot. Shannon blew a slow, long breath from her lips as she climbed out of the van. She ignored the sting in her knee as she walked toward the building on one side of Kevin, Laura flanking his other side.

"If either of you need me for anything today, call my cell. I work in town today."

Shannon looked up at him with a frown. "Don't you always?"

He shook his head. "I wish. Only Mondays. I work at the walk-in clinic one day a week. The rest of the week I commute to Bristol, near the mall. I'm an ER physician at one of the hospitals."

She tried to focus on his words, not the butterflies having a wrestling match in her stomach as they neared the front doors.

"That drive must get old."

"It does. And sometimes I have to go down on the weekend, too. I was on call Saturday." He looked at her and held her eyes.

"That's why I couldn't make it to the airport. I'm sorry that upset you, but it couldn't be avoided."

Shannon looked away. "Oh."

"Anyway, we can talk about this more tonight. After dinner we're going to have a meeting to lay down some house rules."

"House rules?" Shannon echoed warily as he held the school door open. He followed them in and let the door clang shut behind them.

"House rules," he repeated, then pointed toward a door on the left. It read *Administration*.

A few minutes later, after Laura finished, Shannon settled in front of the registrar, Mrs. Nicholson, who was examining her transcript. It had just come over by fax from her old school.

"I see that school is a bit of a struggle for you, Shannon?"

Shannon reared back, indignant. She knew for a fact that her grades were better than Laura's, and this woman had made no comment to Laura.

Kevin held out his hand, and Mrs. Nicholson passed him the transcript. "Shannon, you're a senior. Don't you know how important grades are for college acceptance?" He squinted at the paper, then shot a look at her. "These grades are terrible!"

She felt like crying again. They didn't know how much she cared about her grades, that she was a perfectionist. They didn't know that for the past two years since Mom's diagnosis of stage 3 breast cancer, as Mom's health got worse and worse, Shannon had taken on the job of caring for Jaime after school. Mom was either too exhausted, at a doctor's appointment, or in the hospital. Alan was busy taking care of his wife. Shannon had come home from school every afternoon to take care of her baby brother, to make dinner, even to look after Laura. She hadn't had time or emotional energy for homework.

"I, um." She stopped and swallowed hard, fighting down her emotions. "I'll try to bring my grades up. It's been—hard. Due to my mom's—illness."

"Ah." Mrs. Nicholson nodded. Shannon didn't look at Kevin.

With no more mention on the matter, Shannon's schedule filled up with pre-calculus, English IV, American government, physics, P.E., art theory, and intermediate Spanish.

"SATs for seniors are in three weeks, and all seniors are required to take it. It's a bit late to apply, but I have connections. I'll give you the forms to take with you and fill out."

"Three weeks! I won't be ready by then!" Shannon's head was starting to spin. Nausea swirled.

Mrs. Nicholson sat back and drew her lips in a straight line. "Well you're just going to have to study hard and do the best you can."

"That's just—that's just great." Shannon took a deep breath and let it out in a loud puff. "I'm sorry, but it wasn't my idea to be here right now. I'm really stressed with all of this."

"Shannon..." Kevin's voice growled above her. "Watch your attitude. Karen?" He raised his chin at the registrar.

"Oh, I almost forgot. I understand you need to see the school counselor, Shannon?"

"What?" Shannon bolted up in her seat. "No. Who told you *that*?"

"Well, uh, I thought—"

Kevin cleared his throat. "Shannon, I suggested it."

"Wait, you told her that I need to see a shrink?" Shannon was so angry and humiliated she wouldn't even look at him. How dare he?

"Karen, could we have a minute, please?" Shannon waited until she heard the door close, then turned on Kevin.

"How *dare* you tell her I need to see a counselor? That's— that's not your business! If I want to see a counselor, I'll ask! And—and—and I *don't need to see a counselor*!" She knew she was yelling now, but she didn't care, as she glared at the man who was her biological father yet anything but her dad at this moment.

"Shannon, your mom just died. You're grieving deeply, and you've been uprooted to a new place. Clearly you have some deep-rooted...feelings...about me. I thought it would be a good idea." He reached out and touched her shoulder, but she jerked away.

He sighed. "I'm worried about you. Okay? I didn't suggest counseling to be mean." He leaned toward her. "I'm just trying to be a good father."

Shannon flinched at the word and faced him. "Well I didn't ask you to be my father. You forfeited that right a long time ago."

The stung look on his face told her she'd hit a nerve. "You know what, never mind. You keep crying in your room at night, fine by me." He stood up and went to the door. "Karen, we're ready to wrap this up."

The wide woman sat back down at the desk and looked questioningly at Shannon.

"No counseling."

The woman clicked her tongue, wagging her head. "If you change your mind, let me know."

Shannon ignored her. "Can I get my books?"

Kevin tried to say something, but she flung her hand up to say "enough."

She passed him by without a word and left. From her peripheral vision, she caught him swiping a hand over his face as he shook his head.

The morning progressed in an overwhelming blur. There was lots of confusion over her being a Conrad and curiosity about what she was like. She had no idea what was going on in any class. She and Laura hadn't been to school since the day before Mom died, and Claywood had started the semester a week earlier than Chicago. So basically she was a month behind.

Her last class of the morning was Spanish. A short blond woman greeted Shannon and rattled off something in Spanish, gesturing toward the seats. Shannon stared at her. She hadn't learned much from her previous Spanish teacher, who had basically been reviewing beginning Spanish for the first two months of school.

She blew air out of her mouth and pivoted toward the desks, which were filling up. A girl sitting in the front row smiled at her. She had a beautiful complexion, long dark hair, and eyes that matched.

"You're new, aren't you?"

Shannon took a step closer and stopped in front of her desk. "Yeah. And I think I'm in trouble with this class."

"Oh, come on. It's easy stuff. Here, have a seat." She moved her book off the seat next to hers.

"I'm not taking someone's seat?"

"Kyle usually sits there, so he can cheat off me. He'll get over it. Well, he might fail. But that'd serve him right."

Shannon laughed as she sat down. She liked this girl already.

"So what's your name?" the girl asked, looking her over. "I'm Stephanie Kallisto, by the way."

"Shannon. Shannon Conrad."

A slow smile spread over Stephanie's pretty face. "As in...Andy Conrad?"

"Yeah, he's my brother. Why?"

"Oh, nothing." Stephanie shrugged, coy smile still in place. "You look a lot like him."

Shannon wanted to deny that, since Andy looked an awful lot like Kevin, but she didn't want to be rude. "I suppose. Do you know him?"

"Well, yeah, sorta. Everyone knows who he is. He was the captain of the football team last year. I'll tell you a secret." She lowered her voice, leaning close. "In spite of his reputation, I've had a crush on him since I was a freshman."

Shannon frowned. What reputation did Andy have? She was afraid to ask. "Does he know you like him?"

Stephanie laughed. "Does he know who I am? I doubt it."

Stephanie helped Shannon get through the class period. They exchanged numbers with Stephanie's promise to call her later to see if she needed help with the homework.

After lunch, a quiet affair at a corner table with Laura, English IV was her next class, and it went by fairly uneventfully. At least Shannon didn't feel lost in this class. They were discussing a poem by John Donne in her textbook. But she found out right before class dismissed that they had been discussing the poem for three days, and a two-page analytical essay was due the next day. The teacher offered her one extra day of grace when she approached him after class. One day. She wanted to cry.

Her last stop was pre-calculus. It had been her biggest struggle back home. She went straight to the teacher and introduced herself. Mrs. Keller cordially showed her where they were in the textbook.

"If you're not in a rush after class, I can help you do a little catching up."

"That would be great." Shannon was relieved. "I have to wait for my ride anyway."

When she turned around, the class was almost filled up, but there was a desk in the front row open, so she claimed it.

She looked at the guy in the next desk. "I'm not taking anyone's seat, am I?"

He shrugged and smiled at her. "There's no assigned seating. You're fine."

Shannon was very glad for Mrs. Keller's offer to help once the class was underway. She had no idea what was going on.

"So, how'd it go?" Andy asked once they got settled into his car. His presence had attracted quite the ruckus, not just from football buddies who were still in high school. Shannon had noticed a lot of attention from the girls. Made her wonder about Stephanie's comment.

"Pretty good," Laura replied, settling into the front seat after Shannon had crawled into the back.

Andy looked at her in the rearview mirror. "How about you?"

She shrugged. "I'm behind in almost everything, but that was expected. I survived. I got to know this nice girl named Stephanie. I wonder if you know her."

He frowned as he pulled onto the street. "Stephanie who?"

"Stephanie Kallisto."

"Long dark hair? Really pretty? I remember her."

Shannon hid her smile. And Stephanie thought Andy didn't know she existed.

Just before their driveway they passed a large sign bearing the letters "J. Blake Acres," with a sketched logo of various trees in the background. The road beside the sign disappeared into the foliage, but Shannon could see the hills rising beyond the trees, and they were lined with neat rows of small pine trees.

At the house she headed upstairs, planning to tackle her homework. When she reached the top of the stairs, she heard crying. The sound led her to a room that had to be Daniel's. Little boy toys were scattered across the floor, and a big play train set on a table took up one corner of the room. The tiny boy was huddled on the bed, his shoulders shaking with sobs. Shannon glanced around. Kevin had said a babysitter would be at the house when they got back. Where was she?

"Oh, thank God you're here. You're the new sister, right?"

She jumped at the voice behind her. A girl a few years older than her stood in the doorway with hands on her hips. "Tell your dad that I quit. This kid never stops crying."

Shannon opened her mouth to respond, but the babysitter was already on the move. She dashed after her in time to catch sight of her sailing down the stairs. A moment later the side door slammed.

"Well, then." Shannon stood a moment, then returned to Daniel's room where the boy was still wailing. She stopped by the side of the bed and looked down at the rumpled form. He was her brother just as much as Jaime. As much as Andy or Todd. Why did it feel so different?

His wailing grew louder, and Shannon knew she couldn't leave him like this.

"Hey, buddy." She eased down on the edge of the little bed covered in stuffed dinosaurs, her knee smarting as it bent. She reached out and started to rub Daniel's back. He lifted his head to look at her. Tears covered his red face, and more spilled from dark brown eyes as he let out a hiccup.

"What's wrong, Daniel?"

"I want—" hiccup—"Mommy."

Shannon knew little about Daniel's mom, nor the circumstances of Kevin's recent divorce from her, but with his spotty marriage record, she could make some assumptions. She knew he'd cheated on Mom before he left her. Once a cheater, always a cheater. That's what Mom said. How Kevin had ended up with the house and kids in his latest divorce, she didn't know and didn't care to. But clearly this kid needed his mom.

"I'm so sorry, sweetie." Shannon pulled him into her arms like she'd done to Jaime a million times. Daniel was a year older, but not much bigger. Man, she missed Jaime. She'd been more mom than sister to him the last year. Surely he must be missing her terribly, too.

"I miss Mommy!" Daniel wailed as a fresh bout of tears cascaded down his drenched face. Shannon wrapped her arms around him, rocking him back and forth, humming a lullaby. He clung to her like a life-vest for a long time, and finally his tears abated, his breath ragged gasps as he calmed down.

He tilted his head back to look at Shannon. "When is Mommy coming back?"

The question hit Shannon with force. How many times had she asked her mom that very question after Kevin left them? Her heart began breaking for her half-brother, knowing all the confusion inside his head. She struggled to find something comforting to say, when he asked, "*Is* she coming back?" As he stared at Shannon with his huge brown eyes, Shannon felt a surge of anger toward Kevin. Had he not talked to his son at all? Even attempted to explain the divorce?

"I—I don't know, Daniel. I don't know if she's coming back."

That was all it took for Daniel to start crying again. Shannon held him close, and his arms clamped around her in a vise-grip. She let him cry another few minutes, then wiggled his shoulder and pulled back from him. Her chest was soaked, and the pattern of her shirt was imprinted on the left side of his face. She wiped his tears away with her finger.

"Are you hungry?"

He looked at her seriously for a second, then a smile started at one corner of his mouth. He gave a tiny nod.

"Alright!" Shannon popped off the bed, swinging him in her arms down to the floor. "Let's go raid the fridge, okay?"

He squinted up at her. "Are you really my sister?"

For some reason the words created a lump in Shannon's throat. She swallowed it away and forced a smile. "Yes, I am."

A grin exploded on his face, and he grabbed her hand. "Good, 'cause I like you, Shanny." The name smacked her in the face.

That was Jaime's name for her. Only Jaime. But somehow it sounded good coming from Daniel. She looked down at him with a smile and squeezed his hand.

"Come on, let's go!"

They made cookies and danced in the kitchen while they baked. By the time Kevin got home, Shannon had dinner ready and Daniel was playing quietly nearby with Hotwheels. Kevin had said the sitter was in charge of dinner. No sitter, no dinner. But not on Shannon's watch.

"Hi Daddy!" Daniel called from his spot on the floor by the breakfast bar.

Kevin frowned and didn't reply, his broad shoulders filling up the kitchen entrance. "What is he doing in here? For that matter, what are you doing here? Where's Natasha?"

"If you mean the flighty babysitter, she quit." Shannon turned her attention back to the pre-dinner dishes half washed in the sink. "I'm here because I'm hungry, and I figured I'm not the only one."

Kevin let out a swear word. "I can't believe she quit. Do you know how hard it was to find a babysitter?"

Shannon dropped the measuring cup she was washing and slammed her hand down on the faucet to shut off the water, swinging around to face Kevin.

"Would you watch your language? He's only four! Be decent!"

Anger shot across his face. "Watch the attitude, Shannon. I don't need it right now."

"I don't care what you need. I got here to find Daniel crying, alone, and I spent my whole afternoon comforting him, when I have three weeks' worth of homework to catch up on, and then I made dinner since your precious babysitter waltzed out the door, so what *I* need is a thank you!"

Kevin looked stunned, the anger evaporating. He came to stand beside Shannon and lowered his voice. "Why was he crying?"

Another lump suddenly lodged in Shannon's throat, and she had a hard time talking around it. "Because." She cleared her throat, her eyes suddenly welling up with grief. She would never see her mom again. "Because he misses his mommy."

Devastation worked its way into the lines in Kevin's face. Tired bags under his eyes demanded Shannon's attention against her will. She hadn't paid any attention to his appearance since her unfortunate arrival, but now as she looked at him, she realized his age was showing, whatever it was. She didn't remember. Only that his birthday was in November.

He was silent, staring at the floor, then he swore again, so softly she barely heard. He walked slowly to where Daniel had resumed his *vrooming* around the breakfast nook.

"Hey, Danny Boy." He squatted down and opened his arms. Daniel hesitated a second, then threw himself into his daddy's embrace. Shannon felt a veil of liquid settle over her eyes, and she blinked the moisture away. She wished she had someone she could throw herself at. She could use a hug, too.

Chapter Five

"Why don't you girls have a seat?"

Time to lay down the prison rules.

Shannon's dinner of beef fajitas had been a hit. Not a drop left. The cookies were gone, too. Kevin had summoned her and Laura to his office after clean-up. It was heading for eight o'clock now, and Shannon hadn't touched her homework. She tried to push down the panic that was clawing at her chest as she took a seat in front of Kevin's imposing desk, Laura beside her in another small padded chair.

It felt more like she was in the principal's office than sitting down for a chat with her dad.

He cleared his throat, resting his forearms on the desk. "First let me ask, how was school? Everything go okay?"

They nodded in unison, neither offering words.

"Do you have a lot to catch up on?"

"What do you think?" Shannon asked. "We haven't been to school in three weeks."

"Right." He rubbed his hands together. "Then I'll make this short." He leaned back, slowly settling into the depths of his chair. "Three things: curfew, dating, and housework."

"What?" Laura almost fell off her seat as she jerked forward. Shannon clenched her fists in her lap. This was going to be ugly.

"I won't have either of you gallivanting at all hours. You're both underage, and it's too easy for kids to get into trouble."

"Like what?" Shannon interrupted.

Kevin gave her a measured look. "I think you know what I mean." He switched his gaze to Laura. "The point is, Laura—I want you home by ten every night."

"Ten? Ten! Are you kidding me? I'm not a child!" Laura was on both feet, waving her hands in the air. Shannon had rarely seen her sister so agitated.

Kevin's blue eyes were unsympathetic. "Laura, you are fifteen years old. Why on earth would you need to be out past ten? At your next birthday we can talk about an adjustment, but I feel that ten o'clock is fair for now."

He left her sputtering and turned to Shannon. He studied her silently. "11:30."

"11:30?"

"I trust you. Don't abuse it."

Where had that come from?

"Now I'm serious about this curfew. After your first violation of more than ten minutes, you get another chance. If it happens again, I move your curfew backward half an hour. Which, for you—" He nodded at Laura—"would be 9:30."

She gulped back whatever she was about to say.

"Each time curfew is violated, I will move it back. I'm not opposed to a six o'clock curfew if need be. Of course, a complete grounding is always optional." He smiled with his mouth, but his eyes held a serious warning. "Are we clear?"

"Yes," Laura mumbled, barely audible. Shannon only nodded. He was such a control freak.

"Wonderful." Kevin paused to roll his shoulders, his back cracking loudly. "Next item, dating." He drew air into his mouth through his teeth. "I know you won't like this one, but it is what it is."

"Well then what is it?" Shannon knew her voice held a disrespectful tone, but she didn't care.

"You will need my approval before you date anyone."

Laura's foot slipped from where it had been propped on the edge of her chair and banged on the floor. Neither girl said a word. Shannon fought for control. For words. She had no words. This. Was just. Too much.

The silence stretched thin. Finally she looked at Kevin and said in a controlled voice, "It's not 1910, Kevin. Why do we need your approval? That's—that's archaic. Old-fashioned. Unreasonable!" Her voice was rising, and she took a deep breath.

A deep frown seized his face as he looked at her. "Number one, because I'm your dad, and I say so. Number two, because you're a girl, and consequences of bad relationships can be life-altering for you. And three, because standard of living and income of the majority is quite low around here, and I won't have you date just anyone. If anyone is interested in either of you, I need to meet him and find out about his family first to make sure he's acceptable for one of my daughters." He frowned. "I've half a mind to just say you can't date until you're 18, but I won't go that far yet."

"But that's not fair!" Shannon leaned forward, her hands spread wide in the air. "You get to decide if I can or can't date someone? That's *my* choice! We live in America! In the 21st Century!"

"Yes, and adulthood stills starts at 18. As long as you are my daughter and live in my house, I choose who you can date." Kevin spoke calmly, but Shannon didn't miss the challenge that voiced itself in his raised eyebrows.

"You choose everything for us, don't you? Where we live, who we date, what time we go to bed. Anything else you'd like to decide? Maybe my clothes for tomorrow?"

An exasperated sigh escaped from Kevin. He looked at them long and hard. Laura dropped her eyes, but Shannon held his gaze. "Look, girls. I'm simply trying to do what's best for you now that I am in charge of your wellbeing. Whether or not you think you should be here in the first place, you are, and I am your father, so I'm going to do whatever I must to take good care of you. I'm looking out for your best interest."

Shannon rocked her head back and forth. "If you really cared for our best interest, we'd be in Chicago with Alan."

He met her eyes in a flash, revealing more than just anger. She saw hurt. "You need to watch what comes out of your mouth, Shannon Conrad. I will not tolerate such disrespect. I am your father."

She didn't care if she hurt him. Right now she wanted to. As bad as he'd hurt her for the past nine years. "The only thing that makes you my father is a piece of paper. I might look like you, but I am nothing like you. I do not love you, and no matter what you try to control in my life, you cannot make me love you."

The stunned look on his face told her she'd hit her mark. He dropped his gaze for a moment and cleared his throat. Without looking up, he said, "Laura, you can go now. I need to talk with Shannon alone."

Laura looked at Shannon quickly, and Shannon gave a single nod, letting her know she'd be okay. When the door clicked shut, Kevin met her eyes. "Do you really hate me?"

It was harder to say now, when he was quiet with pain pulsing in his eyes, a mirror of hers. But she had never been able to lie, even to save a heart. "Yes."

He nodded and let out a long, noisy breath, scrubbing a hand over his forehead and down his face. All was silent for a moment.

"I'm sorry about the counseling thing this morning. I should have suggested it privately. I'm only concerned about you."

Shannon refused to acknowledge his sentiments.

He tapped his fingers on the desk top, staring into space. "I have a big learning curve, Shannon. Jumping back into your life after a nine year gap is proving difficult for all of us. I'm doing my best, but clearly I need to try harder." He looked at her. "It would make it easier if you would try, as well."

She still offered no response.

"Thank you for taking care of Daniel this afternoon. That was a very mature thing to do, and I really appreciated it."

She softened at the memory of Daniel's giggle over his flour explosions in the kitchen. "I didn't mind. He's a sweet kid."

Kevin's scratched his head. "I'm in a bit over my head with him and Gabby, too. Carmen stayed at home with them, and now trying to coordinate school and daycare and meals and laundry and, well, everything, is very challenging."

"Maybe you should have thought of that before you divorced her." The nasty words slipped out before Shannon could decide if she actually wanted to say them. Kevin's wounded face told her she'd poked his sore spots enough for one evening.

"Well, we can't go backward in life, only forward, so I have a huge request of you, Shannon. You have proven yourself extremely responsible already. It may take me a few days or weeks even to find another babysitter, which puts me in a bind. My job has been beyond flexible with me the past few months, but my coworkers have taken the burden, and I cannot continue to rely on them."

"What are you saying, Kevin?"

His shoulders sagged. "Would you be willing to take Gabby and Daniel to school and pick them up afterward? I was planning to give you the keys to the Explorer in the morning. I already added you to the insurance."

Shannon didn't know what to say. He trusted her that much? "Um, yeah. I don't mind dropping them off and picking them up. I suppose you need me to keep an eye on them until you get home?"

"Yeah." He cringed apologetically. "I know it's asking a lot when you have so much homework to catch up on, but I don't know what else to do." He opened his mouth, but quickly closed it, and Shannon knew there was more.

She sighed and rolled her eyes. "What else, Kevin?"

He chuckled humorlessly. "I'm that obvious, am I? I was going to talk to you and Laura both about this one, but I'll let you fill her in. I'd like you two to help out around the house as you are able. Gabby and Daniel both have a chore chart, but they aren't capable of all that much yet. The biggest things are laundry and cooking, some cleaning. I don't know how you managed to whip up such a delicious meal on such short notice tonight, but everyone loved it. If cooking is something you enjoy, the kitchen is yours."

Shannon saw herself being sucked into the housemaid roll rather quickly and did not see a way out. Someone did indeed have to do all of the aforementioned things, and being too responsible for her own good, she couldn't say no and live with herself, even though she would have no life. Hopefully Kevin found a replacement soon.

"Now, if we're agreed on this, can I look at your knee before you go do homework?"

"It's better," she insisted, rising to her feet. "Really."

"Please, Shannon." His voice was gently pleading, and she cracked a little.

"Oh, fine. You're the doctor."

When she came out of Kevin's office, her knee tingling, she heard footsteps on the stairs. Kurt appeared in the living room just as she rounded the corner, a cardboard box in his arms. She might as well take this opportunity to return the coat he had deposited on her during her hysterics. She grabbed it where she'd draped it on the couch and turned. Kurt stopped short with a smile.

An amazing smile. Shannon clenched the coat in her fist. How had she not noticed last night that he was incredibly attractive? She'd been too busy falling apart. He'd seen her like that?

She avoided his gaze, holding the coat out toward him. She had to say *something* to redeem herself.

"Thank you. It was really nice of you." He was silent, so she looked up to find him staring at her. His eyes were glowing with amusement. And...interest. She felt her face grow warm.

"Oh, no problem, I'm glad I could help." He had the deepest, dreamiest voice she'd ever heard, complete with a Southern drawl. He flashed her another movie-star smile but still didn't take the coat, and Shannon considered throwing it at him and running. Could he at least have been ugly? But no, he was as hot as a Hollister model. Even more. She closed her eyes briefly.

"I was a wreck last night." She peaked at him in time to see his exaggerated macho shrug.

"Hey, no worries. I end all my jogs with a good cry."

She cringed more than smiled at his attempted joke. Would the guy just take the coat so she could go hide? Her face was on fire.

"Don't be embarrassed," he said softly.

Was he reading her mind? She let her gaze stick a little longer. His eyes were the most unique shade of blue she'd ever seen. Dark, like blueberries.

"I've never lost anyone close, so I don't know what you're going through, but it looks awful. You must be missing your mom like crazy."

Tears sprang instantly to her eyes.

"I'm sorry. I didn't mean to make you cry again." The crestfallen look on Kurt's face rendered him instantly a little boy, and Shannon couldn't keep her lips from curving into a slight smile. She blinked the tears away.

"It's okay. I gotta get to my homework, though. Do you want your coat or not?"

He surprised her by laughing. She wasn't sure why, but she was glad. When she held out the coat again, he shifted the box to one hand so he could take it. She turned silently and headed for the stairs, but on the bottom step, she looked back. He stood transfixed, watching her with wide eyes. She offered a shy smile before trotting up the staircase.

Laura was sitting on her bed with arms crossed and lips drawn into a pout when Shannon entered the room. "What's got you so sunny? I called Dad, and he thinks Kevin's rules are completely unreasonable."

"You talked to Dad?" Thoughts of dark blue eyes and deep voices disappeared.

"Only for a couple minutes. He's putting Jaime to bed. He said to call back at ten."

Shannon looked at her watch. She'd never concentrate on homework until she talked to Alan. She couldn't wait to hear his voice!

* * *

Kurt had been waiting for that glorious smile since yesterday. As Shannon disappeared, he wanted to run after her and make her smile for him again. But even if that hadn't been a ridiculous idea, he couldn't have done it, because he was rooted to the floor.

Andy appeared out of nowhere and smacked Kurt on the back of the head.

"I saw that. You better watch yourself, man."

"Dude, I was just retrieving my coat. No thanks from you for being the gentleman last night and loaning it to the lady."

Andy shook his head, and Kurt knew his friend saw straight through him.

He had hours of homework waiting for him at home, but he had promised Andy he'd come over to help him move into the studio above his dad's garage. The addition of two sisters was good incentive, but he knew Andy had been wanting more space for a while.

It was after 9:00 when he got home, and as soon as he opened the door, he knew Mom was there. His mouth watered as the sweet aroma of baking swirled around his senses.

"Hey, Mom."

"Oh, hey!" She leaned over to give him a hug. "I didn't see you this morning. How was everything while we were gone?"

He shrugged. "Fine. Almost starved to death, but otherwise it was good."

"Well, no more starving. I'm back in full swing."

"So I smell." He made a big show of sniffing the air. "There's hope for me after all." He winked as he backed out of the kitchen. "I'm gonna hit the books. Late night for me tonight."

Mom turned away, her hands rolling quick balls of cookie dough. "Your dad wants to talk to you first. He's in the shop."

Normally Kurt wouldn't think anything of it. He and Dad sat down often to talk about business, and since his parents had gotten in late last night, they did need to catch up. But there was something off in Mom's tone of voice.

"Is something wrong?"

Her hands stilled for a split second, then rolled cookies even faster. She didn't look at him.

"You should go talk to him. Now would be good."

Kurt frowned and headed out the door, wondering what he'd messed up while his parents were gone.

Dad was in the woodshop office, sorting through a stack of bills. He looked up when Kurt pushed the door open.

Neither said a word. Kurt felt tension like summer humidity and obeyed when his dad pointed to a chair.

"Kurt." He didn't recognize Dad's tone. He shifted his feet nervously. "I found this in the bathroom upstairs." His dad held something out toward him on a tissue, and Kurt's face ignited with heat, not something that happened easily. "Had some company this weekend?"

Kurt heard it now, in his dad's voice. Disappointment.

He struggled to swallow. "I, uh, I—yeah. Don't really—know what to say." He studied the cracked cement floor.

His dad cleared his throat. "Was this your first time?"

Kurt's jaw was so tight he had to take some time to answer.

"No." He didn't dare look at his dad's face, but he heard the air blow from his mouth.

"Kurt, please don't tell me you make a habit of this behavior."

Kurt shrugged, unable to deny it. He heard the soft groan from his dad, and the sound of it pierced his heart, but he shoved it away.

"Kurt, don't you realize how wrong your behavior is? You're devaluing these girls. Girls deserve—"

"I've never done anything to a girl she didn't want," Kurt interrupted forcefully, finally meeting his dad's eye. "Girls are different now."

"Is that all you have to tell yourself to ease your conscience?"

Kurt glared at him. "Did you and Mom wait?"

Dad leaned his forehead into his fist. "No. We didn't wait. We should have. But at least we were serious about each other." He looked hard at Kurt. "I didn't spread myself around like mayonnaise in a sandwich shop."

Kurt felt anger and shame flashflood through him. He stood up so fast the chair rocked on its legs. "You know what? You've made your point. Now let me make mine: it's my life. I'm not forcing anyone to do anything against her will. End of discussion." He headed toward the door.

"It's going to catch up with you, Kurt," his dad's voice followed him out. "And you'll end up the one hurt the most..."

Kurt ignored him, slamming the shop door behind him and charging into the house. His mom called his name from the kitchen as he stomped through the living room, but he went straight to his room. Closing his door, he spun and slammed his fist into the white wall. Plaster crackled as it crumbled against his knuckles. With a sharp intake of breath, he pulled his hand back. It was bleeding. He groaned and slid down the door on his back until he hit the floor. Cradling the wounded hand in his lap, he leaned his head back and gazed at the ceiling.

There wasn't any truth in his dad's words, was there?

Chapter Six

"It's Shannon, right?"

She searched for the whispered voice and found herself gazing into eyes of melted chocolate. It was the guy who had told her there was no assigned seating yesterday. She nodded. Mrs. Keller was helping another student and for the life of her, Shannon had no clue what they were even supposed to be learning in pre-calc today. The formulas on the board swam before her sleep-deprived eyes in nonsensical Greekish form.

"Maybe I'm wrong," he said in a low voice, "but you seem a little lost. Do you need help?"

Shannon laughed humorlessly. "A *little*?"

While the hum of Mrs. Keller's voice continued around the room as she assisted other students, the helpful guy quietly explained and demonstrated the formulas until Shannon began to grasp the concepts. By the time Mrs. Keller passed by to check her work, Shannon was working independently. The teacher nodded down at her approvingly.

"I'm glad to see you're catching on." She smiled over at the boy in the next desk. "Thank you for helping her." He smiled back, and Shannon glanced at him in time to see dimples pop into his cheeks. He ducked his head modestly.

"No problem, glad to help."

After the bell rang, she was about to turn and thank him when Mrs. Keller called her name.

"Shannon, I compiled a list of possible tutors." She held out a piece of paper. "Unfortunately I don't have time to set one up for you, but I've included names of my six top students with their permission. I'm sure one of them will be willing to help you."

Shannon took the list. How was she supposed to know who these people were? And then what? Kneel down and beg for math help? How embarrassing! She forced a smile in Mrs. Keller's direction. "Thanks. I appreciate it."

When she got back to her desk, the nice guy was gone.

She stifled a yawn and headed out the door. Her morning had been crazy. Kevin had woken her before 5:00 because he'd been called into work early, so it was up to her to make sure everyone was ready on time. Gabby showed her true colors, refusing to get up. Shannon literally had to pick her up and wrangle her out of her pajamas and into school clothes. Eight going on 13 her eye. More like eight going on three!

Daniel hadn't been any jewel either, whining and crying the whole morning for mommy and then daddy. Shannon had forgotten to put orange juice out for breakfast, and Gabby threw a fit. Then she didn't cut Daniel's pancake into small enough pieces, and he wouldn't eat it. Laura got up late and was no help at all, and she completely skipped the breakfast Shannon had spent thirty minutes making. Andy downed his breakfast in two minutes flat and was out the door and down the driveway just as fast, with little words to spare.

Shannon had only slept three and a half hours after staying up until one a.m. attempting her homework. Which didn't seem to have helped much, looking back on her second day of school here. She rubbed her forehead as she waited beside the Explorer for Laura. The day wasn't over, either. She was on nanny duty now.

* * *

"How'd everything go?"

Shannon turned from the counter to find Kevin in the doorway. She bypassed his question, about to tell him he needed to go grocery shopping if he wanted her to cook tomorrow when she noticed the exhaustion lining his face. He leaned his back against the opposite counter and let out a loud sigh, then looked at her expectantly.

"You okay, Kevin?" She breezed past him with a stack of plates. He followed her into the dining room.

"Rough day in the ER. Lost three patients. One was only seven."

Shannon was speechless. Her day was nothing to complain about compared to that.

"So everything went okay?"

He must really want to know. "Yeah." She busied herself setting the table. "Daniel had fun playing out in the leaves when we got home. In case you notice any foliage in his hair."

Kevin cracked a grin. "I guess you must have joined him, unless that stick is there on purpose."

Shannon ran her hand threw her hair until it snagged on a twig. She shook her head. "He's a little hard to resist."

"Don't I know it," Kevin said with a chuckle. "Anyway, if dinner's ready, I'll go round up the troops."

"Where's Andy?" Shannon asked as she took a seat next to Daniel a few minutes later. She had set the table for six, but Andy's place at the foot of the table sat vacant.

"Working, I suppose, or out with friends. He runs his own schedule."

So Andy was in charge of his own life. And Shannon was the housemaid. That was...fair.

"Where'd you learn to cook like this?" Kevin broke the silence, reaching for seconds. The meal was disappearing fast. She'd made a potato and chicken casserole, seasoned green beans, breadsticks, and a salad.

Shannon shrugged her shoulders. "Mom taught me a lot, but when she got sick, I started doing all the cooking. There were some failures at first—"

Laura interrupted with a snort. "That's an understatement. I still remember my stomach growling at night after I couldn't eat your cooking."

"Oh please, you are so exaggerating!" Shannon glared at her sister, noticing Kevin's lips twitch into a smile.

"Well I guess you caught on eventually." He nodded at her. "The food is excellent, just like last night."

Before she could reply, the side door creaked open and shut with a careless slam.

"I'm ho-ome!" Andy's chipper voice rang out, and a few seconds later he appeared in the dining room. "Did you order out? It smells incredible!"

"Nope. We have our own gourmet chef." Kevin gestured at Shannon, appreciative smile on his face. "Warm some up, you don't want to miss it."

Andy heaped large servings onto his plate and disappeared into the kitchen. Shannon heard the microwave humming and Andy's cheerful whistle above it. She couldn't help but smile. Andy just had that effect on her.

He stepped back into the room a minute later, a dreamy expression on his face as he chewed, plate in hand.

"You know, Shannon, you could make money with this stuff. It's delicious," he slurred around another bite as he sat down at the table, tapping the plate with his fork. "Delicious."

* * *

"Hey, what time is it?" Shannon glanced around Stephanie's living room for a clock. She'd come over after dinner to get Spanish homework help. They'd done their fair share of chatting, too. Stephanie lived on a quiet street in Claywood.

"Almost 8:30." Stephanie dropped her pencil. "You need to go already?"

Shannon let her head fall into her hands. "I need to attempt my pre-calc homework. That class is going to kill me if this one doesn't."

Stephanie grunted. "Kudos to you for being in pre-calc. I can't even understand algebra II."

Shannon raised her head and gazed forlornly at Stephanie. "Well I don't understand pre-calc. It'll be a miracle if I pass. My teacher gave me a list of possible tutors, but how am I supposed to find one of them?"

"Who'd she recommend?" Stephanie looked more interested than she had all evening.

"I don't know." Shannon shrugged, then dug into her jeans pocket. "Here."

Stephanie scanned the list of names. "Oh, no. Not him. He's such a jerk." She muttered some more. "Stanley? He'll just want in your pants."

"Lovely." Shannon rolled her eyes. Maybe failing high school was the better option.

"Rachel. She's smart alright, but she's such a nerd, I doubt she'd be able to explain in human terms." Stephanie slapped the slip of paper onto the table. "I think you should go straight to Jesse, try him first."

Shannon blinked. "Who?"

"Jesse, oh I never know how to say his last name. Hang on, I'll track down a number for him."

Stephanie's fingers went wild on her cell phone. Almost instantly a hiccup sounded from the device.

"Bingo. My friend Jade knows everyone." She rattled off a number, and Shannon entered it into her phone. She picked up the piece of paper and read the last name on the list again. Jesse Kowalewski. What kind of name was that, anyway?

Gritting her teeth, she pushed call and waited. On the third ring, a weary-sounding female voice answered.

"Hello." It was not inviting. Shannon closed her eyes. She hated this. Really. Hated this.

"Um, hi, is Jesse there?"

"*Jesse!*" the voice hollered, directly into the phone.

With a cringe, Shannon pulled the phone away from her face as the woman continued yelling.

"Telephone!"

"Hello, this is Jesse," a warm male voice responded a few seconds later. It was in such sharp contrast to the first voice, Shannon relaxed enough to return the phone to her ear.

"I'm sorry to bother you this late, but Mrs. Keller gave me your name." She squeezed her eyes tight as she began her plea, wishing a sinkhole would appear and swallow her instead. "I just transferred to Claywood High, and I'm having trouble catching up in pre-calculus. She thought you might be able to help me. If you have time…"

"I can definitely make time," answered the cheerful voice. "You're Shannon Conrad, aren't you?"

She started with surprise. "How'd you know?"

He chuckled softly. His laugh reminded Shannon of a gently flowing brook.

"I only know of one new girl in pre-calc, and her name is Shannon Conrad. Why don't we meet up after class tomorrow to work it out?"

"Okay, sounds good." She felt relief coursing through her body. Maybe she'd get through pre-calculus with a passing grade after all. "Thank you!"

Stephanie grinned when Shannon hung up. "Jesse is genuinely a nice guy. He'll be a great tutor. He's in National Honor Society *and* on the football team, or at least last year he was. And he's cute, too." She lifted her eyebrows at Shannon.

That was the last thing she needed right now.

* * *

Kurt had been in a fog all day. He had slept fitfully for about two hours the night before, that was it. The only thing going through his brain was Dad's cutting words and every argument imaginable.

It was normal these days. Everyone was doing it.

No one "waited" anymore for the right person. That was just being a prude.

All the girls he'd been with had gone down willingly, if not eagerly. None had protested, so obviously it wasn't a big deal to them, either.

The list of excuses went on and on, all night long, until he was pretty sure he had exonerated himself. But he failed a quiz in every class that morning, and he hadn't been able to focus on work in the orchard and woodshop later. He and his dad had said little to each other, other than Dad asking why his hand was wrapped in a bandage. Kurt hadn't answered honestly. He'd fix the hole in his wall quietly.

His knuckles reminded him of his rash reaction every time he flexed his hand.

Now as he sat at his laptop, trying to concentrate on the essay revision he was supposed to have turned in today, his mind would give him no reprieve. He thought back to middle school.

He'd always been a flirt. By the time he was twelve, it didn't matter who the girl was, what she looked like, how she acted—if she was female, he flirted with her. It had started out innocently enough. In high school he had narrowed his focus to only the prettiest and most popular girls. He learned how to be smooth, and he never lacked for admirers. He never dated steady. He just made out with girls, and there were lots of willing candidates.

There were broken hearts and hurt feelings, too, but he never dwelt on those. Some girls were too emotional and had ridiculous expectations. Others… Well, others were easier; they knew how to give and take. One night when he was making out with one of those "others," things had gotten out of control, and they went farther than he had intended. Much farther. He crossed the proverbial line and never came back.

That had been more than two years ago. A lot had happened in two years.

Chapter Seven

"Headache?"

Shannon stopped massaging her temples to look at the nice guy who had helped her yesterday. She wished he could be Jesse.

She sighed. "Yeah, since last night. Hey, I wanted to say thank you for your help yesterday. You were a life-saver."

He smiled that dimpled smile again. "Not a problem. I was glad to help. So when's a good time for some real tutoring?"

"Wait—you're Jesse?"

He frowned at her before a smile slowly spread across his face. "You didn't know that when you called me?"

Shannon felt a laugh bubbling up her throat, and she let out an airy giggle. "Not a clue."

"Well, in that case," he said, his dimples deepening as he held out his hand. "Nice to meet you, Shannon. Jesse *Kowv-al-ev-ski.*"

Shannon slid her hand into his, and he gave a firm shake. "I don't know how I didn't put that together before," she confessed, feeling a bit embarrassed.

He laughed. It was the same wonderful laugh she'd heard on the phone last night.

"I guess I never did introduce myself, so that's my bad." The ringing of the bell drowned out his voice, and Jesse helped her again during class. Afterward he asked when would be a good time to get together.

"I go to work at 8:30 most evenings. Until then I'm free."

"Oh boy." She'd been thinking of evening tutoring. With babysitting and dinner prep, there wasn't much of a window for Jesse. "I don't know. I babysit my—my—" Why was it so hard to call them what they were? "My little brother and sister after school until Kevin—I mean their dad—my dad—" She stopped and scrunched up her face. She wasn't making any sense. "Anyway, I have to be at our house until like seven o'clock most evenings." She risked a glance at Jesse, expecting to see confusion on his face, but he only rubbed his chin.

"Well, I don't want to invite myself over…"

"No, no," Shannon rushed to reassure him. "You are more than welcome to come over before dinner, and we can study while I keep an eye on the kids. How's 4:30?"

"Perfect. I'll see you in about two hours then."

"Do you need directions?"

"Nope." He dropped his pre-calc book into his backpack. "I know where you live." He flashed a smile, showcasing those dimples she kept noticing. "No secrets in this small town."

* * *

When Shannon picked up Gabby and Daniel, they were both in tears. Daniel's care provider had no explanation, and Gabby wasn't talking. Daniel's wailing lasted until they parked in the garage.

"What is his *problem*?" Laura snapped as she jumped out of the vehicle. "Seriously. I don't ever want kids."

She stalked toward the house behind the running form of Gabby, who was still crying. Shannon stood outside the Explorer where Daniel was sobbing in his car seat. What she wanted was to sit down and cry, too. Instead she opened the backdoor and unbuckled him, unsure of her next move. He jumped out and threw himself at her, his arms immediately reaching around her neck. He buried his curly head in her shoulder and cried.

"You want to tell me what's wrong, Daniel?"

He peeked a look at her face, sniffling. "Well," *sniff*, "Jordie said," *sniff*, "that his mommy said," *sniff*, "that my mommy's not," *sniff*, "coming back." He turned his dark eyes up at Shannon, shiny with tears. "Is that true, Shanny?"

Shannon was appalled that parents in town were discussing Daniel's family situation with such frankness in front of their young children. Apparently they knew more than she did, though, and she didn't have an answer for Daniel.

"All I know is that you have a daddy who loves you very much. He's busy working hard so he can take good care of you. You just ignore Jordie or anyone else who says mean things like that. Besides, *I* love you, lots and lots." The shocking truth of her words made her stare widely into Daniel's trusting eyes. She wasn't sure how it was possible to love someone she'd only known since Saturday. But she did.

His face eased into a small smile.

"I love you, too, Shanny." He threw his arms around her neck again and pressed his wet cheek against hers. She hugged him tightly and lowered him to the ground.

"We better go inside, little boy. There are lots of toys to be played with in there!"

He giggled and swung her hand back and forth as they walked toward the house, shining a smile up at her as if he'd found a million bucks. Shannon couldn't help but smile back down at him, marveling at how resilient little kids were. She was really beginning to wonder what the story was with his mom, though. She knew Kevin could stoop awfully low, but he wasn't keeping her from their kids, was he?

Upstairs, she got Daniel settled with a coloring book while kids' songs played in the background. With a promise to come back soon, she ventured next door to Gabby's room. There was no response to her soft knock. She shifted back and forth on her feet. Consoling Daniel was one thing. He was four. Gabby was another story. She had no idea what to say to an emotional eight-year-old girl. Besides, she had homework to do. Mounds of it. And if these kids wanted to cry about missing their mom, well so did she. Even more so.

Taking a deep breath, she turned the knob and slowly pushed the door open. Gabby was lying face down across her bed, a teddy bear clutched under her arm.

"Leave me alone!" the angry, muffled words halted Shannon mid step before she could open her mouth.

"Okay. Let me know if you need anything."

Not ten minutes later a small voice interrupted her as she sat at the breakfast nook reading her English assignment.

"Shannon?"

Gabby stood in the kitchen doorway, teddy bear dangling from one hand, while the other hand rubbed red eyes. Shannon closed her book in surprise. She hadn't expected Gabby to actually change her mind. She pulled out the bar stool next to Shannon and shimmied to the top of it.

"Can we talk?"

Shannon bit back a smile at the grown-up sounding words.

"Absolutely. Want some hot chocolate while we talk?"

Gabby's face betrayed her with a smile that mirrored Daniel's. "Sure."

Soon more mommy-woes were pouring out of Gabby, along with excessive tears. It seemed Kevin hadn't explained anything about the divorce to his children, so there wasn't much Shannon could say. Anger burned in her neck. Kevin was a real piece of work as a dad. To all of them.

"I know you miss your mom a lot, Gabby." She put her hand on the girl's shoulder and squeezed. "I miss my mom, too. So maybe we can be here for each other?"

Gabby smiled slowly. "Okay. Does that mean you'll help me with my homework? I don't know how to do it."

It was an art project, and Shannon got so busy helping Gabby paint a garden scene that she jumped at the knock on the front door. She glanced at her watch. "It's probably Jesse."

"Who's Jesse?" Gabby followed her to the door and peered around Shannon as she opened it. Jesse stood waiting on the front porch in a dark red hoodie. Shannon noticed its worn appearance. Same with the jeans and shoes. There was nothing worn about his smile, though.

"Hey, Shannon." His dimples were deeper than ever.

"Hi, come in!" She swung the door wide.

"Who is he?" Gabby whispered, acting shy for the first time. She pulled Gabby in front of her, resting her hands on her shoulders.

"Jesse, this is my sister, Gabby. Gabby, this is my classmate Jesse. He's here to help me with my math homework."

"Oh." Gabby looked at him quizzically, then smiled. "Shannon was just helping me with *my* homework." She grinned up at Shannon. "She's real smart."

Jesse's smile slipped for a second. "I hope this isn't a bad time."

"Nope. Give me five minutes to finish with Gabby."

Jesse followed them into the kitchen and watched as Shannon touched up a few of Gabby's messy flowers.

"Think you can finish the rest, Gabs?" All she got was a nod, Gabby's tongue sticking out of her mouth's corner as she concentrated on painting a birdbath. Shannon shared a smile with Jesse, then nodded her head toward the kitchen table.

Before they could move, a wail sounded from upstairs.

"Shanneeeeeeee!"

A sigh escaped Shannon's mouth, and she looked apologetically at Jesse.

"That would be Daniel. I better go check on him."

"Can I come? I want to meet him."

"He's having a rough day, I'll warn you."

They went up the wide staircase side by side, Shannon feeling like a midget. Andy and Kevin were tall, but Jesse was even taller. Definitely a few inches over six feet. Of course almost anyone seemed tall next to her five-foot-four-inch frame!

She poked her head into Daniel's room. He was sitting on the floor with his back against his toy trunk, gazing at the door forlornly.

"You left me."

Shannon held back a sigh. "I'm sorry, sweetie, but I have to do homework. How about you play with some toys in the kitchen while Jesse and I do math?"

"Who's Jesse?" the little boy demanded.

"I am!" Jesse popped his head around the door frame.

"Oh." Daniel stared at him for a second, then his face split into his adorable grin. "Hi."

Jesse chuckled. "Hi." He crossed the room and held out his big hand. Daniel grinned bigger as he put his little hand into Jesse's and shook it like a man.

Once Shannon got Daniel settled at the table with a water paint book, she and Jesse dove into pre-calc.

"But I don't get why the y is there!" she was protesting more than an hour later when Laura stomped into the kitchen.

"When are we eating, Shan, I'm starving. Wait, who is *this*?"

Laura was assessing Jesse's looks, and Shannon could tell she liked what she found.

"This is Jesse, my math tutor."

"So you're like really smart with math, huh? Because, like, I could really use help with my math when you're done with Shannon." She flipped her hair with her hand, pulled out the chair on the other side of Jesse, and plopped down.

Jesse looked at Shannon questioningly. She clenched her teeth. Didn't Laura realize how obvious she was?

"I thought you were hungry, Laura. And when did you start caring about math?"

"When I realized there was a talented math scholar in the house," Laura replied in a silken voice, resting her chin in a delicate hand propped on the table. Her head was cocked to the side a little as she gazed adoringly at Jesse. Shannon allowed herself to pause for a moment and take a mental snapshot. Laura was beautiful. She looked just like Mom.

Jesse cleared his throat and smiled nervously. There were no dimples.

"Laura, seriously." Shannon was annoyed and embarrassed by her sister's flirting. "Back off. Dinner won't be till seven when Kevin gets here, so you might as well keep working on homework, or do me a favor and play with the kids for a while." Daniel had interrupted their studies continuously during the past hour and was in dire need of attention. At least Gabby had wandered off to entertain herself elsewhere.

Laura pushed her chair back and stood up with a huff. "You are so boring, Shannon." She stalked away, and Shannon shook her head and looked at Jesse.

"I apologize for that. I think..." She wasn't sure she should say this to a complete stranger. "I think she's looking for extra attention because she misses our mom."

He nodded thoughtfully. "Everybody reacts differently to grief. I'm sorry about your mom." She had a hard time looking away from his melty chocolate eyes.

"How'd you find out?"

"Well..." He seemed hesitant to own up. "Actually, I have government with Stephanie Kallisto, and—well, we were talking about you today."

"Oh, ah—okay." Why had they been talking about her? Her nerve failed her, and she didn't ask. Besides, if she stayed on the topic of Mom, she might cry again. "We should probably get back to pre-calc."

"Sure thing." Jesse demonstrated great patience as their session continued. Finally Shannon sat back, releasing a sigh. Daniel was asleep, head and arms flopped down on the table top. A string of drool led from the corner of his mouth to a little pool on the table.

"I gotta start on dinner." The kitchen stove clock read 6:13. "How much do you charge per hour?"

"Charge?" Jesse looked puzzled. "There's no charge."

"No, seriously, you just sacrificed a lot of your time, and I'm going to need your help regularly for a while."

"No. *Seriously.*" He echoed her words with a dimpled smile. "I won't accept money for helping you with pre-calc. I mean, we got tomorrow's homework done, and I brushed up on a bunch of concepts I was forgetting. So the bonus is mine."

Shannon looked at him skeptically. This guy was too nice. "Are you sure?"

"I'm sure." He grinned, stacking his math book and notebook. As he was sliding them into his backpack, footsteps thumped across the porch outside. Shannon expected Andy to appear, but it was Kevin who entered the kitchen first, with Andy and Kurt on his heels.

"I got off my shift early," Kevin started to explain, but he stopped mid-step. "What is *he* doing here?" His tone was deadly as he stared at Jesse, his face flaring an angry red.

Floored with confusion, Shannon felt her defenses rise.

"*He* is my pre-calculus tutor," she replied, an edge in her voice. "His name is—"

"I know who he is, and he's not welcome here."

Shannon was dumfounded, staring at Kevin. "What is your problem? Do my tutors have to go through your approval committee, too?"

"If you are going to bring them into my home, then yes. And *this* one—" he glared at Jesse—"needs to leave."

"But—"

"Shannon." Jesse's calm voice pierced Shannon's infuriated haze. He rested a hand on her shoulder. "It's okay, I'm going." As he passed Kevin, Jesse gave him a respectful nod. Shannon followed, shooting him a look of pure hatred, ignoring Kurt and Andy. Jesse stopped and sighed once they were outside, the door closed behind them.

"I'm sorry, Shannon."

"No, *I'm* sorry." Her humiliation burned brightly in the light of his sincere eyes. "He is a complete jerk." She growled in her throat. "I'm so embarrassed." When Jesse didn't respond, she studied him. "Do you know why he got so mad? I mean, he obviously knows who you are."

Jesse shifted on his feet, now refusing to meet Shannon's eyes.

"He doesn't like people who are—well, who are—poor." His brown eyes dropped to Shannon's again, and he said softly but without shame, "and he knows I'm poor."

"I see." Shannon dragged air into her lungs through her nose, trying to still her angry, swirling thoughts. She caught Jesse's eyes. "It doesn't matter to me if you're poor. Money's got nothing to do with brains and personality, and you've got both."

The dimples popped in, and he chuckled. "Thanks, Shannon. You're going to do great in pre-calc, okay? We'll talk tomorrow and figure out a better plan for this tutoring business."

Shannon watched him walk to his beat-up pickup. The passenger door was grey, but the rest was black with monstrous peeling patches and lots of rust. Clearly he wasn't joking about being poor.

Shannon stepped back inside with a slam of the door. Kevin was waiting for her in the kitchen. Thank goodness Daniel had disappeared, and Andy and Kurt, too. She wouldn't have to fight with an audience.

"Where's dinner?" Kevin asked before she could open her mouth.

She reared back. "Excuse me? I'm not here to talk about dinner. You were such a jerk to Jesse—someone who was kind enough to volunteer to help me with my hardest class!"

"Look, if he wants to tutor you, fine, but you'll do it elsewhere." Kevin crossed his arms over his chest and raised his chin, almost daring Shannon to oppose. She breathed deeply. Getting mad at Kevin hadn't worked so far. She had to stay calm.

"You know what, Kevin?" She spoke softly, narrowing her eyes at him. "Jesse might be poor, but I respect him more than I will ever respect you, and I barely even know him."

Kevin just shrugged, as if to say, "I don't care."

Shannon sighed. "Why did you make him leave? Please explain so that I understand."

Kevin frowned, stumbling with his words. "Well, he, uh, I—I didn't expect to walk in and, you know, see him—here. I know everyone in town, and I, well, I happen to know a bit about Jesse. He's—he's not from a good family."

"What's that supposed to mean?"

"He's from a very low-class family."

"Well he sure has more class than you," Shannon snorted, deciding calm was overrated. Kevin took quick steps toward her until he was only 10 inches away, his eyes blazing with fury.

"He is a loser just like the rest of his family, and if I ever see him here again, I will physically remove him. Am I clear?" He uncrossed his arms and swung a hand out toward the counter. "You going to cook or not?"

"Wow, and you call Jesse a loser." Shannon shook her head. "Do you have any clue how to be a father? You don't even notice that Gabby and Daniel are suffering, much less me and Laura. You'd rather just be nasty."

"What do you mean Gabby and Daniel are suffering?" His voice suddenly sounded thin.

Shannon opened her mouth to make a tart reply, but she couldn't. "They both came home crying today," she said softly. "They miss their mom." She choked on the last word before tears took over. "I'd do anything to see my mom again, but I never will. I understand if you and Carmen didn't work out, but Gabby and Daniel need to see their mother. At least she's still alive!"

She knew tears were streaming down her face, but she wasn't done. "If you really love them, Kevin, you won't keep them from their mother."

Kevin stood rooted to the floor with legs spread apart, arms held tautly at his sides, eyes staring unseeing at something above Shannon's head. She couldn't identify the emotion his face held.

When his eyes met hers, Shannon felt an electric current of shock.

There were tears in his eyes.

He made a sudden move toward the kitchen entryway, grabbing his coat from where he had draped it over a bar stool.

"I'll eat in town. Don't let the kids wait up for me," he said in a strange, strangled voice, and then he was gone, closing the door with a soft click.

All energy depleted, Shannon sank down onto the floor on her knees, rivulets of water trickling down her face.

The look on Kevin's face registered in her mind.

It was heartbreak.

Chapter Eight

Dinner that night was instant mac and cheese with a side of tears. Shannon reigned in her own just in time for another round of Daniel's and Gabby's when she attempted to explain their dad's absence. She had no idea their evening routine and limped her way through at Gabby's guidance. Good thing she'd practically raised Jaime the past two years, or she'd really be lost.

It was 8:30 by the time she tiptoed out of Daniel's room, where he had miraculously fallen asleep in her arms as she read a story to him. Then it was Gabby's turn, and she picked a long book and then wouldn't sleep. At 9:17 Shannon softly closed Gabby's bedroom door and walked into the sitting room. The light was on in the room she and Laura shared, so Laura must be working on homework—what Shannon needed to be doing. But the dining room and kitchen still had to be cleaned.

She returned to the kitchen to load the dishwasher and wipe the table before settling down with her Spanish vocabulary list. She needed to pass tomorrow's quiz badly.

She was concentrating so deeply on practicing the words out loud that the sound of a throat clearing made her almost jump out of her skin. She hadn't even heard the door open.

"Sorry, didn't mean to scare you." Kevin stood in the center of the kitchen, bulging plastic shopping bags dangling from his hands. "I brought groceries."

What was she supposed to say? *Thanks for filling your role as father and bringing home food for the table?*

"I'll just...put them away," he mumbled and turned toward the fridge. He came in and out several times, quietly restocking the kitchen and pantry. Shannon didn't say another word until he approached the table.

"What are you working on?" He pulled out a chair and sat down.

She looked at him warily. "Spanish."

"Oh." He paused, looking unsettled. "I actually know a lot of Spanish. If you ever need help."

"Really? How'd you learn?"

He hesitated, dropping his gaze to the table top. "Carmen taught me."

"Oh." Shannon knew Carmen was Latina, but she didn't know from which country. "Do you have a few minutes now? Because I don't know if I'm pronouncing these words right."

He scooted his chair closer, and Shannon ordered herself not to squirm. It was just Kevin. It was just…her… She couldn't make her mind say it. He wasn't her dad. Even if he was volunteering to help her with homework.

She tried to be subtle about scooting her chair away from him, but of course he noticed.

"Oh, sorry. I didn't mean to—to crowd you." His face was unreadable, set like a stone.

"You're getting the hang of it," he said as he stood, glancing at the clock half an hour later. "I gotta get to bed—and you should too."

Shannon looked up and gave him a small, if not confused, smile. "Thanks for your help."

"You're welcome." He looked very serious. "I haven't really checked to see how you're doing with school, and I'm sorry for that. Let me know if there's anything else I can do."

He headed out of the room, then turned back. "Oh, one more thing… Tomorrow afternoon Carmen is going to FaceTime with the kids. I'll log on to my account in the morning, but if you could turn on the iPad when you get home, I'd appreciate it. I'll let them know she'll be calling."

FaceTime was a start. They would see their mom's face, and that was more than Shannon would ever do. She looked at Kevin, feeling a sliver of respect. "Did you initiate this?"

He nodded, and there was a flicker of emotion that he quickly controlled. "Yeah, I called her. She said she will call around 4:00." He gave a brisk nod and turned to leave again. "Good night, Shannon."

"Have a good night, Kevin." She flashed a real smile at his retreating back. She felt victorious.

* * *

"So are you coming to the party Saturday night?"

Shannon looked up from her spaghetti to where Stephanie's snappy dark eyes assessed her. When Stephanie had introduced her to some of her friends the other day, one of the boys had invited her to a party he was hosting this weekend.

"I don't know. When and where is it, again?" She glanced at her watch. Ten minutes till the bell rang.

"Starts at 9:00. It's at Kyle's house. He lives on Ross Road. Just look for all the cars."

"What kind of party is this?"

"A classic Claywood High invitation-only party. You gotta come and see for yourself."

Shannon wasn't sure. She'd never been to a real high school party before.

When she walked into her English classroom after lunch, she saw someone familiar toward the front of the class. She hadn't realized Jesse was in her English class, too. He turned and shined a smile on her that could melt a glacier.

"I had no idea we were both in here!" she exclaimed as she approached him.

He laughed his wonderful laugh. "Me neither."

She paused to take a real assessment. Yesterday she'd been so focused on pre-calc that she hadn't let her mind dwell on what was right in front of her. But now she saw what Laura had seen.

Jesse's milk chocolate eyes were framed by thick lashes of the same color. His dark brown hair was short and just a little mussed. He was very tall, but not in an awkward, lanky way. The sleeves of his shirt were pushed up to his elbows, exposing well-defined forearms. Broad shoulders filled up the top of the shirt. Add in the persistent dimples, and a girl could get lost just looking at this guy.

He was still smiling at her, and Shannon quickly came back to earth when she compared Jesse's facial expression now to Kurt's look when she had given the coat back to him. Jesse was looking at her like...like a perky associate at the Walmart customer service counter, as if he was about to say, "Hi, how can I help you?" He was looking at her as her friendly math tutor and nothing more.

Trying to set his hotness aside, she told him that she couldn't have tutoring today, but she'd try to make it work tomorrow if he had a location suggestion.

"I'll think about it and let you know."

Back at the house, Shannon put out a snack for the kids the minute they walked through the door. String cheese and cucumber spears. Nothing fancy, but Gabby and Daniel devoured them. Laura lingered in the kitchen, eyeing the table hungrily.

"You can have some too, you know," Shannon said, popping a piece of cucumber in her mouth.

As Laura helped herself, Shannon studied her. She'd noticed her hanging around with various guys at school the past two days, and she was feeling some sisterly concern. "What was up with the way you talked to Jesse yesterday?"

Laura hardly reacted, giving a little shrug as she stringed her cheese. "He's hot. You weren't trying, so I thought I would."

Shannon stared at her sister, who ignored her. Either there was something wrong with Laura, or something wrong with her, and she didn't know which it was. She decided to change the subject rather than press further.

"Tomorrow I need to have more tutoring with Jesse in the afternoon. Kevin kicked him out of our house, so I'll need to meet him somewhere else. Think you can manage the kids for two hours?"

Laura made a face and called Kevin an inappropriate name. "I guess."

"Shanny, when are we talking to Mommy?" Daniel pulled at her pant leg impatiently. "Daddy told Gabby she's going to call us on the iPad so we can see her!"

Shannon smiled down at him, then looked for the time on the stove clock. "In about 20 minutes. I'll make sure everything's ready."

"Yay!" He jumped up and down and danced in a circle. "We're going to talk to Mommy! We're going to talk to Mommy!"

Gabby was too quiet as she finished her snack. She wasn't excited?

"I was hoping she'd come in person," she said quietly, eyes downcast.

Shannon got up and placed a hand on her shoulder. She didn't know what to say, not knowing where Carmen lived. Maybe she couldn't make it on such short notice. "Maybe she will next time. But for now you'll get to see her and talk as long as you want."

Gabby and Daniel had been waiting with the iPad in hand for ten minutes when four o'clock hit.

"Where is she?" Daniel bounced up and down impatiently.

"Your dad said 'around' four. Just wait."

But by 4:30, Shannon was having a sinking feeling in the pit of her stomach. Daniel's shoulders were slumping, and silent tears coursed down Gabby's face. Where on earth was their mother?

Five minutes later the side door banged open, and Kevin rushed into the room. He stopped short at the sight of the sullen trio gathered around the iPad. Shannon wondered what had brought him home so early.

"What happened?"

"She didn't call. You said she would call!" Gabby dove at him, slamming him in the gut. He deflected her with an "umph," and caught her before she slugged him again. "You liar!"

Shannon had never seen Gabby so mad.

Kevin ignored Gabby completely and pulled his phone out of his pocket. He walked down the hall, and before he reached his room, she heard his cold voice say, "Carmen."

It was mere seconds before shouting ensued, which became impossible to make out when his door slammed closed.

Daniel began sobbing loudly, and Gabby started off down the hall, seeming intent on interfering with Kevin. Shannon ran after her and pulled her to a stop.

"Oh no you don't. Wrong timing, Gabby."

The little girl fought and screamed before succumbing to tears, which turned to sobs as she clung to Shannon and babbled about her mom.

Shannon walked her back to the living room, where she collected Daniel and dragged them both upstairs. She put on a movie, ignoring their tears and questions. Once the yelling subsided long enough that Shannon thought Kevin might be off the phone, she ventured down the stairs, angry enough to butt heads with a goat.

Her heart pounded with anger and a small dose of fear as she lifted her knuckles to knock at Kevin's bedroom door. When he answered, she noted the utter despair written on his face, but she plowed ahead anyway.

"What was that, Kevin? You could have offered a little comfort to your kids or maybe an explanation, instead of jumping straight to an angry tirade with their mother who will probably be too scared to ever call again. You're a real jerk, you know that? She was probably running late or had an emergency, but I'll bet you didn't even let her explain, did you? She answered the phone, so you could have handed it to Gabby and Daniel so they could at least talk to her—but instead you drove her away! Do you think of *anyone* but yourself?"

Kevin looked her in the eye and cursed.

"You don't know anything about me, Shannon. You don't know anything at all."

Chapter Nine

It was the middle of the night when Shannon heard a bang downstairs. She squeezed her phone next to her pillow. 3:30. Was Kevin finally home? After cussing at her, he'd left the house. Thankfully Andy had shown up right after dinner, but he wasn't much help with all the tears and questions from her younger siblings. Getting them into bed had taken much longer this time. She'd gone to bed at 12:30, half of her homework undone, but she couldn't keep her eyes open another second. Kevin was still M.I.A.

She slid out of bed and glanced toward Laura's still form across the room in the semi-darkness. Apparently her sister was a deeper sleeper than she. Tip-toeing softly from the room, she was beginning her descent down the stairs when a string of slurred profanities assaulted her ears, followed by a sharp shushing hiss. She froze, not sure she wanted to know what the commotion was.

"Watch the wall, man!"

Shannon would know that deep voice anywhere, even in a throaty whisper. She scurried down the stairs until she saw a trio working their way across the house. Kevin staggered and sagged between Kurt and Andy, their slow progress illuminated by the hallway light behind them. More unintelligible slurred words blubbered from Kevin's mouth, and Shannon sank down slowly on the step with her fingers against her mouth.

Kevin was drunk.

She sat with tears sliding down her face until, many minutes later, Kurt and Andy re-emerged from the hallway leading to Kevin's room.

Just before disappearing past the living room, Kurt looked toward the stairs and stopped short. His head bent forward, as if squinting in the dark.

"Shannon?"

His rumbling voice propelled Shannon to her feet, and she galloped up the stairs two at a time and collapsed back into bed, watering the pillow with her tears. She ignored the soft knock a few minutes later and Andy's quiet voice, the image of her father, too drunk to even walk, seared into her brain along with every swear word in the English dictionary.

He didn't show face at breakfast, although Shannon saw no signs that he had left the house, and she was glad. She was pretty sure if she saw him right now, she would vomit all over him.

A loser. Her dad was a loser.

Andy came in for breakfast and tried to talk with her, but she pushed him off on Gabby and Daniel. They needed him more than she did.

In pre-calc she glumly told Jesse she couldn't study this afternoon either. No way was she going to leave Gabby and Daniel with Laura in their current state. He didn't press the issue, just offered an understanding smile.

Back at home she let Daniel drag her to his room to play with him. Gabby had vanished into her room without a word.

Daniel already had toys strewn across his carpet. Shannon plopped down on the floor with her back against the wall and picked up a chubby Fisher-Price person. Tossing it from one hand to the other, she wondered what to do about Kevin. He must still be in his room downstairs. His truck was parked in the garage, and a drinking glass was beside the kitchen sink that hadn't been there in the morning.

"I don't want to play with him, Shanny," Daniel whined, knocking the little toy man out of her hand. "Let's play with my train."

Shannon held back her sigh as she crawled across the carpet to where Daniel was setting up his wooden train track. The only place she wanted to crawl to right now was her bed.

After playing for an hour, she heard harsh coughing downstairs. She slipped to the top of the stairs, listening as the hardwood floor creaked under walking feet. Then she heard the kitchen sink running. Remembering Kevin last night so drunk he couldn't walk without help stirred up hot anger inside Shannon, and she trotted down the stairs while she had the nerve.

Kevin's door closed forcefully before she got to it, and she didn't pause before banging her fist on the door.

"Come in," his voice grunted.

Shannon pushed the door open, and a sour smell made her wrinkle her nose. Kevin sat on the edge of his bed, head in his hands. The room was a mess, and the man even worse. Pillows were scattered around the room, and one of the curtains lay in a pile on the floor. Kevin looked as disheveled as any Chicago homeless man she'd seen, and when he looked up, grey circles rimmed his eyes. His fiery hair was a disaster, and his hunched shoulder gave him such a dejected look, Shannon paused in pity.

He didn't make eye contact before he dropped his head back to his hands. "What do you want, Shannon?"

Her pity evaporated. "What do I want? I want to know what is *wrong* with you." He still didn't raise his head, infuriating her more. She plucked a pillow from the floor near her feet and chucked it at him. He didn't even flinch when it bounced off his arm. "You're a lousy father, you know that? And I can deal with that, but maybe Gabby and Daniel can't. They need you, and instead you're in here sulking about your ex, when it's your own doing! It's totally selfish that you divorced Carmen and made her move out, especially when you aren't taking good care of Gabby and Daniel. Why did you leave her? Why did you leave Mom? Why did you leave your first wife? Why do you always leave your wives, Kevin?"

His head finally snapped up, and there was fire mixed with tears in his eyes.

"I told you yesterday that you don't know anything, Shannon. You don't know a thing about my relationship with Carmen."

"Well then why don't you tell me so that I can understand?" Shannon's voice rose along with her frustration.

"Because it's none of your business!" he roared, jumping to his feet.

"It becomes my business when it takes over my life. I can't get any homework done because I'm being a mother to your kids, and then I wake up at 3:00 a.m. to see my father staggering through the house *drunk*!"

Kevin sank back down onto the bed and covered his face. He began to sob into his hands, his shoulders shaking. Shannon pulled away, slowly backing up until her legs hit the rocking chair beside the door.

Was he still drunk? She looked around for sign of a bottle or can, but nothing. He couldn't possibly still be feeling the effects of last night, could he? She lowered herself onto the chair, unsure what to do next.

He looked up at her with red eyes.

"Shannon, I didn't leave Carmen. She left me."

All the air expelled from Shannon's mouth. "But I thought—"

"You thought wrong. Carmen left me for another man."

Shannon raised her chin, the unexpected information little impacting her anger. "That's what you did to Mom. Now you know what it feels like."

His eyes strained with raw pain. "Yes...Yes I do."

Her anger started to recede like the tide at the broken-hearted look on his face. "Did you come home early yesterday on purpose, Kevin?"

He looked at his hands and nodded. "Yeah. I was hoping...I was hoping to convince her to come back. Thought maybe seeing the kids would change her mind, and she'd be more receptive to me after she talked with them." He clamped his mouth shut and worked his jaw as water trickled out of his eyes. "I've been avoiding the kids a bit because they always ask about their mom. And now I really don't know what to tell them." He shook his head, swatting at the tears snaking their way down his cheeks.

"She told me yesterday she wants nothing to do with me or with Gabby and Daniel."

Shannon took a shaky breath at the heartless words.

"She said...she said they are as good as dead to her." His voice cracked on the words, and he shot a pleading look at Shannon. "How can a mother do that?"

"Well," she responded slowly, "I guess it may seem more— unnatural—for a mother to reject her children. But there's nothing natural about a father doing it, either."

Kevin looked at her with a sorrow in his eyes that went deeper than any sorrow she'd known. He nodded, obviously catching her meaning, but he didn't comment. "What should I tell the kids?"

Shannon's mind rewound to the tall tales her mom used to spin to make her think Daddy was coming back.

"The truth. It'll hurt now, but less later. I wish someone had told me back then that you weren't coming back, so I would have stopped hoping and hurting."

Kevin sighed heavily. "I wronged you deeply, Shannon. You and Laura both. And your mother."

"Why did you leave her?" The question tour out again in an anguished whisper, and tears began trekking down her face. "Why did you leave us?"

Kevin tilted his head back, the lines in his face trenches of regret. "People tend to throw out what they don't value as they should. I learned too late that I hadn't valued the three of you for what you were worth. That's why I wanted your custody, Shannon—to try to make up for the past." His eyes dipped to the floor as he swallowed noticeably. "I understand if that can't happen, though."

He crossed the room to a tissue box and carried it back to Shannon, where she was huddled on the rocking chair. She wiped her face and blew her nose.

Kevin reached out a hesitating hand and squeezed her shoulder. "I'm sorry, Shannon. I am so sorry."

* * *

"Can you give me a ride to the game tonight?"

Shannon paused from tying on her running shoes. Laura was sprawled stomach-down on her bed with an Algebra book open, but clearly more interested in her phone than math. Shannon needed to do homework, but after that conversation with Kevin, she was afraid she'd end up putting her head on a book and bawling.

"What game?"

Laura looked at her like she was stupid. "Wow, you really are out of it. The football game. At the high school we attend."

Right. It was Friday night in October. Of course there was a game, even if she hadn't paid attention.

"I wasn't planning on going." She shrugged into a snug hoodie, tugging it down around her waist.

"You're so lame, Shannon. You can just drop me off . I'll find a ride home."

"Okay, okay. Fine." Man, Laura was getting so demanding. "I'm going for a run before I make dinner."

"Don't fall this time." It was sarcasm, not concern, coating Laura's words, but Shannon turned her back and headed out of the room. It was her first time running since her injury, but she was more focused on not crying this time than not falling.

After dinner, which Kevin attended much to Gabby and Daniel's delight, Shannon studied her closet. Just in case she ended up staying for the game, she didn't want to show up in her jogging clothes.

"Come on, we're going to be late!" Laura pulled on Shannon's arm a few minutes later, dancing on her toes. "You're so slow."

Shannon sent her a withering look. Laura was one to talk. She couldn't count how many times she'd been marked tardy at school in Chicago because of that girl. Mom was the only one who could make Laura punctual. Once Mom was out of commission, so was Shannon's attendance score.

"You can just drop me off in front of the school." Laura fidgeted in her seat nervously as they drove into town.

Shannon narrowed her eyes. "Are you meeting up with a guy?"

"No, why?" The answer was too quick.

Shannon shrugged and didn't answer. But she knew. "I might stay a while," she said instead. "I'll find a place to park."

The school parking lot was full, so she turned onto a side street. The sky was bright from the illumination on the football field.

"There's a spot!" Laura pointed to small space between a big pick-up and a car. Could she manage to parallel park decently? The Explorer was definitely larger than Alan's Ford Focus, the only thing she'd ever street parked.

"Whew." She let out some air after she safely moved the vehicle into park. She thought she was going to scrape the truck in front of her. Thank goodness she hadn't.

"See ya." Laura launched out of the Explorer and took off at a jog toward the school. The stands were visible from here, but a fence prevented direct access. Shannon couldn't remember the last time she'd seen Laura run. Whoever she was meeting must be really hot.

She snickered to herself and put her hand on the door to get out, then froze as a memory bombarded her without warning. The homecoming game last year. They had gone as a family. Laura's bimbo of a boyfriend was playing, and Mom had been cancer free for five months. It was a celebration. She could almost taste the pizza they'd eaten after the game. Two weeks later at a check-up, Mom's cancer was back. It never left again.

Shannon put her forehead on the steering wheel and sobbed. It wasn't fair. It wasn't fair that Mom had suffered so. It wasn't fair that she had lost her mom at such a young age. It wasn't fair that she had to live with jerkface Kevin now. None of it was fair. But it was reality.

She sat up and took a big sniff. Stared out the window at the football stands. Could she really make herself go out there? By herself? She didn't have anyone to sit with. Watch a football game alone? Mom would tell her to go. Tell her to make a friend. Shannon wiped her cheeks with the arm of her jacket, squared her shoulders, opened the door, and stepped outside.

"I was wondering if you were ever going to get out." She jumped at the voice. Kurt stood beside the truck she'd almost hit. How had she not realized it was his?

"Oh my gosh, Kurt. You scared me. How long were you watching me?" He had a knack for catching her at her worst.

He joined her as she moved onto the sidewalk. "Long enough to assume you weren't crying because your sister ran off without you."

Shannon snorted. "Hardly." She flinched when he had the nerve to elbow her arm.

"So what were you crying about?"

He was kind of pushy. Not necessarily in a bad way, but Shannon wasn't sure she wanted to open up to him.

"Just...you know. My mom." She bobbed her head, trying to ignore the lump glubbing up in her throat again.

"That's what I thought." His smooth voice was warm and gentle. "It's only been a few weeks, right?"

"Yeah." She cleared her throat. "Feels like an eternity. Feels like yesterday. Cancer sucks." She crossed her arms over her chest, as if she could shield herself from the pain.

Kurt was quiet. "For sure. I'm guessing you'll always miss your mom, but maybe one day the missing won't hurt quite as bad."

Shannon looked him full in the face, hoping the shadows from the street lights would mercifully hide the fresh tears in her eyes. "I hope you're right."

"I know the reason you moved here really sucks, but I'm glad you're here."

Shannon sucked in her breath, turning to look up the street. Anything but look at Kurt. He was just being nice, anyway.

"When you have time, I'd love to show you around my dad's orchard."

Why would he want to do that? Shannon forced the thought aside. "Wait, the one next to Kevin's house?"

He smiled. "J. Blake Acres, that's us. We have a Christmas tree farm and fruit orchard. Lots of other things, too."

"Like what?"

"Well we grow produce in summer and fall, and year round in a few greenhouses. My dad is planning more. We have a woodworking shop, a couple vacation cabins, and we also do landscaping and snow removal. My mom has a store in town."

"Wow. That's a lot. You do that all by yourselves?

Kurt got a laugh out of that. "Oh, no. My dad has a lot employees, and I help manage the farm. My mom runs her store in town, but she has workers and a manager, too. Seriously, you should come over and check us out."

It was his second reference to having her over. Shannon let herself wonder why this time. This guy was in college. There was no way he was *really* interested in her...right?

When she looked at him again, he was staring her up and down. Even in the murky dimness of the street lights, there was no masking the interest on his face as his eyes roamed her figure from head to toe, pausing in a few key places that should have made her blush. Her new jeans were tight, and he'd obviously noticed.

She'd caught guys looking at her before, but they had always been subtle and stopped when she noticed. There was nothing discreet about Kurt's perusal of her appearance however, and Shannon decided if he could check her out so boldly, she could do the same inventory without embarrassment.

She took stock again of his blond hair, just shaggy enough to give him a roguish look. It contrasted nicely with his square jaw and perfect nose. Those blueberry eyes snapped at her knowingly, and as for his physique, Shannon could clearly see the bulge of muscular pecs through his too-thin-for-fall Batman T-shirt exposed beneath an open leather jacket. He scored a perfect 10 on every item in the good-looks survey. He could have any girl he wanted. What was he doing standing with her?

Did he think she was pretty? Her pulse sped up.

"Your hair?" He broke their mutual observations with the question.

Shannon quirked her eyebrows. "What about it?"

He grinned, showcasing straight, white teeth. "I mean, is it natural? The color?"

"This?" She held out a thick strand, fingering it gently. "Sure is. Thanks to my dad."

"Well he had to be good for something." Kurt cocked his head as he examined her thoroughly, then nodded at her slow and special. "I like it. I really like it."

This time she did blush. He definitely thought she was pretty.

"Thanks." She dipped her head away, feeling like a child. "If you're wanting to see the game, we should probably head that way."

Kurt chuckled, and she wasn't sure why. They started slowly toward the school, side-by-side. Man, he smelled good. All musky and manly and… cinnamon-y. Her pulse was a thump-thump-thumping from his nearness.

"Can I give you my number?"

Shannon's head shot up. "Why?" she blurted before she could stop herself, and felt herself blush even more.

Kurt gave an over-casual shrug. "In case you ever need anything and Andy's not around." He held out his hand expectantly. "Here, let me put it in your phone."

Shannon hesitated, then unlocked her phone and handed it to him. His finger make quick work, but before he returned it, he hit call.

"And now I have yours." He winked at her as his phone started ringing in his pocket. Shannon frowned as she grabbed her phone back, feeling duped. If he really wanted her phone number, he could have just asked.

She pinned him with a stare. "How often does my dad get drunk?"

* * *

Kurt was stunned into silence by the blunt question. Clearly his method of obtaining her phone number had offended. He should have gone with his gut and just asked, but he didn't want to scare her. His usual finesse with females seemed to fail with Shannon. He should give up and move on to someone easier, but there was something about Shannon. Something deep that pulled him in. So deep that he was willing to wade the muddy waters of her daddy issues. Or try, at least.

"Andy didn't talk to you?" He breathed deeply of the wood smoke in the air. Somebody was cozy beside a fireplace nearby.

"No." Shannon's long copper hair swished back and forth as she shook her head. "I mean, he tried, but I didn't want to hear it then. I hadn't yelled at Kevin yet."

"You yelled at your dad?" Kurt started to laugh, then immediately stopped. "I'm sorry. That's totally not funny." He groaned. This was such a mess. "To answer your question, I think this was the fifth time he has gone out drinking since Carmen left him. It was the third time he couldn't make it home on his own. A couple times he drove home when he definitely shouldn't have. Twice Andy went to pick him up while I stayed at your house in case the kids woke up. I went with Andy the next day to pick up your dad's truck. This time since you and Laura were home, I went with Andy so I could bring your dad's truck back at the same time." That about covered it, right?

Shannon's head dropped until her chin touched her chest. "He's such a loser," she mumbled. Kurt wasn't sure if she was saying it to him or herself.

"He's hurting, Shannon. He loved Carmen a lot. Hurt people do stupid stuff sometimes."

Shannon jerked her head up and turned blazing eyes on him, her neck rigid. "Don't you dare defend him. I know all about hurt people. I lived through hell when he left us nine years ago. He's getting what he deserves."

Kurt shrank away from her fury, clueless what to say next. Everything he said or did was wrong. He hadn't felt this flustered by a girl in years. Normally girls fell at his feet. Not so this one.

They walked in silence until Kurt noticed Shannon was staring straight up at the sky. He glanced up. Even with the haze from the football field lights they were nearing, the stars were dazzling tonight.

"Beautiful, aren't they?"

Shannon stopped and sighed dreamily, her head tilted back exposing the world's most gorgeous neck. Stars held nothing on Shannon. There wasn't a word in the English language for her kind of beauty.

"Chicago was too bright to see many stars. This is...breathtaking!"

She breathed out the last word, and Kurt wanted to turn and tell her that *she* was breathtaking. Gorgeous. Stunning. Every word that came within a fraction of describing her. He clamped his jaw shut, knowing such a comment might not go over well right now.

They entered the school grounds and joined a throng of others heading for the stands. Kurt gave Shannon a sideways glance. What was it about her? From what he could see, her body was amazing, but plenty of other girls had lovely bodies. Her hair was definitely something special, and her eyes were magnetizing. Maybe it was the combination, or maybe it was something he hadn't yet identified, but he couldn't get enough of her.

"You got a place to sit?"

That was a backhand invitation if he'd ever given one. First the trick for her number, now this. He felt like such a school boy, but Shannon threw him all off his game.

She caught his intent, though, if he could judge by the color creeping into her cheeks. If she'd blushed outside under his obvious study of her features, he hadn't seen it in the dim street lighting. But the bright lights from the football field highlighted the pink tinge in her face now.

She brushed a hand through her hair, a self-conscious gesture he was sure. "No, that's alright. But thanks for asking."

He paused and looked at her seriously. "I meant what I said, Shannon. I wasn't just joking to get your number. If you ever need anything, even just to talk—please—let me know."

Her exquisitely blue-green eyes squinted at him, assessing his sincerity, and then she offered a small smile.

"Thank you, Kurt. I'll see you around." She turned and disappeared into the crowd.

Chapter Ten

Shannon slept in the next morning, relishing the badly needed rest. She hadn't stayed for the whole game. It had been tempting to accept Kurt's offer of a seat, but she wasn't sure about him yet.

When she padded downstairs around ten o'clock, she found a note on the counter from Kevin. He'd been called in to work. There went her relaxing Saturday.

The day flew by between tending to Daniel and Gabby and making brunch and a late lunch. Laura grabbed some food on her way out the door, heading "out with friends." Must be nice. To have friends, and the time to spend with them.

Shannon made a call to Alan, enjoying a few minutes talking with Jaime. Finally she got some homework done while the kids watched a movie. She was actually relieved when Kevin got home, greeting her quietly.

"Thank you, Shannon. Take the night off."

She could have hugged him. If he wasn't the dad she hated.

She was curled up in bed watching a movie on her phone when a text interrupted the scene. It was Stephanie.

Ur sister's here. Where r u? Party pooper.

Oops. She'd never told Stephanie she wasn't planning on going to the party. What was Laura doing there?

Shannon shook her head and tried to go back to her movie, but an unsettling tingle kept crawling up her spine. She tossed the phone aside, jumping to her feet.

She dashed into the bathroom and one glance in the mirror told her she couldn't show up at a high school party looking like this, even if it was only to find her sister. After a good fifteen minutes freshening up and a change of clothes, she examined her reflection in the full-length mirror. Same skinny jeans from last night, brown boots, and a dark blue shirt. The neckline dipped low. Mom had always made her wear a cami with this shirt, but Shannon didn't think Kevin would care, and she figured she was old enough to decide how much cleavage she wanted to show.

Kevin was in the family room playing a game with the kids when Shannon slipped by. She'd be back long before her curfew, and with any luck, he might not even realize Laura was gone.

Locating Kyle's house was easy enough because it was aglow with lights in every room, music blasting into the chilly night air. Shannon had to park a ways down the road due to the crowded street. When she reached the yard, people were clustered in groups, laughing and drinking, and she could see through the windows that the house was packed.

She swallowed nervously. She had never been to a party.

The front door was wide open, so she walked in and came to an abrupt halt. The house was crammed with people. How was she going to find Laura? She gave a slow pivot, considering leaving Laura to her own doings when she heard her name.

"Shannon!" It was the party's host, Kyle, with his friend Randy. "Hey, glad you could make it." Kyle pulled her farther inside by her arm. "Let me take you around. There's lots of people you should meet."

She tried to pull back, but his grip was like iron. She glanced at his other hand. Holding a beer can.

Randy slung his arm around her shoulder. "Come on, baby, I know you came here for me."

Panic welled in Shannon as she unsuccessfully tried to shrug Randy off of her.

"Randy, get lost. That's my sister you're messing with."

Shannon spun around, wavering with relief. "Andy! I didn't know you'd be here."

"Likewise." He snatched her out of Randy's reach and shuttled her into the next room, also packed with people.

"Have you seen Laura?" She had to yell above the music and loud conversation surrounding them.

Andy's eyebrows shot up. "She's here? Good luck finding her."

She sighed and turned away, but Andy grabbed her shoulder. "Be careful, okay? There's a lot of alcohol going around, and you look good." Shannon's face grew warm as his pointed gaze. She pressed her hand to her neckline and watched Andy disappear into the crowd. What had she been thinking? To come here, and dressed like this?

She fought her way into the next room, scanning the masses for Laura while ignoring several leering male glances. She spotted Stephanie in the hallway with her back against the wall. A guy faced her, his hands pressed against the wall above her shoulders. Shannon started to turn, not wanting to interrupt whatever *that* was, but Stephanie saw her and shoved the guy away.

"Shannon! You made it!" She grabbed Shannon and hauled her through a nearby door into a bedroom containing significantly fewer people than any of the preceding rooms.

"I'm so glad you came! This is the biggest party I've been to. Kyle asked his parents if he could invite a few friends over while they are out of town. I'm pretty sure they weren't expecting hundreds!" Stephanie giggled like it was the funniest thing ever. Shannon wasn't very amused. She was pretty sure his parents wouldn't be either, especially with all the underage drinking.

"You look fantastic," Stephanie chattered on. "You better watch out for the boys!"

Shannon made a noise of disgust in her throat. "Andy just rescued me from one."

"He's here?" Stephanie was already moving toward the door. "I just want a look. I haven't seen him in so long."

Shannon followed her out. "Did I tell you he does know who you are?" She had to raise her voice, but Stephanie stopped so suddenly that Shannon slammed into her from behind.

"*Ouff*," Stephanie grunted. "Wait, he does?"

"Yeah." Shannon rested her hand against the wall to steady herself. "I asked him, and he knew exactly who you were. Called you pretty."

Stephanie's eyes lit up. "If we find him, will you introduce me?"

"If you'll help me look for Laura next."

When they located Andy ten minutes later, Shannon's heart dipped to her toes and back. Kurt was standing beside her brother. She fumbled through an introduction before Stephanie adeptly took over and got Andy engaged in conversation. Shannon nervously turned to Kurt and found him at her side. He gave her a thorough once-over before handing her a glass tumbler.

"What is this?"

"Just try it." He was standing so close to her that she felt his leg brush her thigh. Finding it difficult to breathe, she brought the glass to her lips and took a taste. She drew back and coughed. It wasn't soda, water, or juice, and that didn't leave many options.

Kurt laughed just loudly enough to tell Shannon he'd been drinking, too. She thrust the glass into his hand and tried to stalk away. People blocked every possible escape.

"Shannon, wait." He grabbed her arm. Why did guys keep grabbing her arm tonight?

"I can't believe you! You saw Kevin. How can you be here drinking after—after *that*?" She wrenched herself away from him and elbowed her way through the crowd. Forget Laura. She was leaving.

She was almost to the front door when she noticed a couple making out in the corner. Mauling each other, really. She averted her eyes, inwardly tirading about the degrading behavior that resulted from intoxication. One foot was out the door when she heard a familiar giggle.

She whirled around and sought out her sister's gorgeous blond hair, finding it entwined in the hands of the guy in the corner. By the feet of the amorous couple were two tin cans. Not soda cans.

"Laura!" she shouted, jerking her sister out of the guy's arms.

"Hey!" The guy swore at her. "Who do you think you are?" He tried to grab Laura back, but Shannon bolted out the door, tugging Laura along with her. In her quick glance at the guy, he had looked at least 20 years old. Was Laura out of her mind?

"Shannon!" Laura protested. "I don't wanna leave yet!" She stumbled as she tried to pull out of Shannon's grasp and almost fell over. As a groggy giggle escaped her mouth, Shannon felt sick.

Laura was drunk.

Shannon marched her to the Explorer, where she pushed her into the passenger's seat. When she turned the key to start the engine, the dashboard clock lit up. 10:25. So Laura had blown her curfew, too. Great.

"Who was the guy almost in your pants?"

"He was not!" Laura answered in a whine.

"Well what was his name? He seemed very interested in you."

Laura hiccupped. "I don't know. He never told me."

Shannon sighed. This was a pointless conversation. How on earth was she going to get Laura inside without Kevin hearing? She could only imagine how furious he'd be to see Laura in this condition.

Fortunately the house was dark when Shannon helped Laura up the steps to the side door.

"*Shhh*. We gotta be quiet."

"What for?" her sister slurred loudly. Shannon clamped her hand over Laura mouth.

"Because you are past your curfew, you drunk fool," she said in a fierce whisper. "Now you either shut up, or I'm going to leave you out here."

Laura submitted and let Shannon lead her into the house. They crept up the stairs, Shannon holding her breath with every creaking step. Laura barely made it to the bathroom before she started vomiting. Shannon sank into bed and gave her pillow another shower of tears. Her life was a disaster. Disaster.

When morning dawned, she had such a headache it seemed she had been the one drinking. The sounds of Laura retching into the toilet throughout the night had repeatedly woken her from what little sleep her distraught brain would allow.

Thankfully Kevin didn't ask any questions when she appeared downstairs. It seemed he hadn't even realized both sisters had been gone. For once Shannon was glad for his negligent parenting.

After a jog and some time on the piano, Shannon dug into more homework in the kitchen. Andy showed himself around 11:30. She had heard him come in at four in the morning. Dark circles rimmed his eyes, but otherwise he seemed perfectly sober.

His appearance broke Shannon's concentration, and she decided to call Jesse to see if he'd thought of a neutral tutoring location. She left a message with a young-sounding girl who said she was his sister. Poor guy didn't even have a cell phone! He called her back a few hours later, enthusiasm revving like a car engine.

"Of course! I've been waiting for you to call. We can meet up in town at Nancy's Trading Post. It's a coffee-shop and deli, and they have free Wi-Fi. I always stop there for the Internet."

He didn't have Internet at home either? He hadn't been joking about being poor.

He gave her directions, and they decided to meet in half an hour. In the meantime, Shannon called Brittni. They hadn't talked since the night before she'd left Chicago. Catching up was a bit overwhelming. So much had happened in one week. It felt like an eternity already since she'd arrived in Virginia.

* * *

Kurt walked into his mom's store with a whopping headache. He had drunk way too much the night before. After Shannon ran away from him, he'd been so ticked that he downed a lot more alcohol. When the police arrived and busted up the party, he and Andy had left together with two girls in tow. To be honest, Kurt didn't remember much about the rest of the night. Including the girl's name. She wasn't from Claywood. Was it...Rhonda? Rebecca? Roxanne? It started with an R...right?

Kurt shook his head to clear it and headed toward the check-out counter. One of Mom's weekend workers, Ashley, was arranging some discount items on the shelf behind the register, and Kurt paused to admire her. She was a cutie.

"Oh, Kurt! Hi!" A deep blush spread over the girl's face when she saw him. That smitten look was a common reaction from girls in a 5-year radius of his age when they saw him.

Except for Shannon.

He frowned and walked away. He didn't usually pass up a chance to flirt with a female who was asking for it, but thinking about Shannon had ruined Ashley's opportunity.

He found his mom in the small second-floor of the store, muttering as she scribbled on her paper pad, her eyes on a line of candles on the shelf.

"Mom?"

"Just a second, Kurt. And that's...seven vanilla breeze." She looked up and smiled. "Sorry. Inventory time. Do you have the orchard delivery?"

"Sure do. Just wanted to let you know I'll be unloading in the back."

"Awesome. Thank you." She paused. "Did you get some rest last night?"

Kurt held back his sigh. Was he going to get a lecture from her, too? It was bad enough coming from Dad, but Mom usually let things slide. Then again, he usually didn't stay out till five in the morning.

"Yup, I slept," he answered quickly, looking away from her discerning eyes. "I'll go bring in the load now."

"Alright, honey." Kurt didn't miss the soft sadness in her tone. He glared at nothing in particular as he trotted down the narrow staircase. As he made his way through the store toward the back door, he noted how busy it was. This was the only coffee shop in town, and the only place that offered free Wi-fi, too, so it was usually bustling. Today was no exception. There were long lines at the barista counter and the deli. Several shoppers perused the shelves of canned goods from the orchard, others were looking around the bakery, and still more were in the produce section, picking through apples and pumpkins. With Halloween only two weeks away, pumpkin sales were exploding at both at Mom's store and at the orchard.

With his hand on the door marked "Employee's Only," Kurt took one more glance around, proud of his mom's flourishing establishment. That was when he saw a flash of fire among the customers and did a double take. Shannon sat at a tall table by one of the front windows, and across from her was Jesse Kowalewski. He'd been rather gleeful to see Kevin kick Jesse out of the Conrads' house a few days ago. What was Shannon doing with him again?

Jealousy made his skin tingle before guilt overwhelmed him.

Last night.

Her snarled words had been painfully true. Instead of having the sense to listen to her, he had wasted himself on more alcohol and some random girl.

Wasn't it always some random girl? That's what Dad had pointed out to him this morning. His dad had chewed him out when Kurt dragged himself from bed around noon. There was no point denying what had happened the night before, so when asked, he'd been honest. Yes, he'd been drinking, and yes, he'd spent the night with a girl.

"A different girl every time, Kurt? What happens when you meet a girl you actually like? One you want to keep? How are you going to be content with that? Are you going to be able to give up all the other girls in order to keep the one you love?"

Kurt didn't have an answer. He hated his dad for making him think about such a thing. There was no special girl so far, so why worry about it now?

His eyes trailed to Shannon again, bent studiously over a book. Wow, she was beautiful. And so—so—He couldn't put his finger on it, but whatever it was, it actually did make her one special girl.

She looked up then, straight at him. He swore his heart stopped beating.

She didn't offer him a smile, only looked at him as if trying to read his soul, her blue eyes nearly burning him.

Kurt froze. He didn't want her to know what was in his soul, but he couldn't tear himself away. She finally broke eye contact and returned to her book.

Then Kurt noticed Jesse was staring, too. At him. He assessed Kurt with a cool look on his face, distinct challenge in his eyes. Kurt sent a glare at him that could have cracked a canyon wall, then turned and slammed himself through the rear door.

* * *

It had taken only a minute after meeting up with Jesse to figure out that this store was Kurt's mom's. The J. Blake Acres logo was plastered around the store like wallpaper. She shouldn't have been surprised to see Kurt here, but she hadn't been ready. She was still mad about last night.

"You done with that one?" Jesse broke through her distracted thoughts. She found his gaze on her, those brown eyes so discerning and accepting.

She nodded, lowering her pencil to the table. "I didn't see you at the party last night."

"The one at Kyle's? How was it?"

Shannon crinkled her face with the memories. "Just a lot of drinking and stupid behavior." Kurt grabbing her arm. The nerve. She slammed her pre-calc book closed.

Jesse didn't say anything more for a long minute. "You look tired."

Shannon felt like weeping. "I. Am. Exhausted." How was it possible she'd only been here one week?

"So you've been here one week, right?" Jesse echoed her thoughts. "How are you doing?"

From anyone else that question would have sounded pushy, but not from Jesse. Compassion softened his face as he studied Shannon, and she had the urge to dump everything on him.

"Well..." Her voice cracked, and she swallowed and started over. "It's been one of the longest weeks of my life. I've had a lot of those weeks lately, but this one comes in near the top." He offered an understanding nod, and Shannon let it all flow out. "I still can't believe my mom is gone forever, and I'm stuck with stupid Kevin. I'm missing my step-dad and little brother like crazy. Now I'm pretty much full time nanny to two little siblings I barely know, while Kevin is hardly there. I'm way behind in school, and I have no life. I don't have time to sleep, and I have a million rules to follow set down by Kevin. Meanwhile my sister is making bad choices, and I don't know what to do. It just feels like my life is...out of control." She eased her fingertips along both temples, closing her eyes against the pressure.

"I've been praying for you."

Her eyes popped open, and she stared at Jesse, one eyebrow pulled low. "What?"

His dimples took a dip inward, and he chuckled. The best sound she'd heard all day. "When you sat down in pre-calc last Monday, I felt your hurting. I prayed for you that very minute, Shannon, and I have prayed for you every day since."

A lump formed in Shannon's throat. No one had ever said such a thing to her before. "Do you pray a lot?"

"Yeah. It's a habit."

"Why?"

He shrugged, his dimples glorious. "Why not?"

"Do you really think He hears?"

He gave a slow, deep nod that rubbed Shannon's heart. "I really do."

Now that was something to consider. "No one in my family is very religious."

"I wasn't raised in a religious home, either, but God got my attention last year, and my life hasn't been the same again. It's not like He worked some kind of magic and made everything right in my life. He made everything right in my heart, and that has made me able to handle everything that's wrong in my life."

Shannon didn't realize she was frowning as she worked at the question in her brain until Jesse's foot bumped her under the table gently. "What's on your mind?"

"Okay." Shannon lay her hands out on the table, palms up. "If God really listens and cares, why did He let my mom die? I've heard of Him described as a loving Father, but if that's true, He wouldn't abandon people the way my dad abandoned me."

Jesse took a long breath inward before slowly releasing it. "That's one of the most asked questions of God, and I don't pretend to have all the answers. I know we live in a sinful world, and things like cancer and death happen a lot. Sometimes God prevents it, and sometimes He doesn't. Sometimes we can see why, and sometimes we can't. But I do know that whatever happens, He is there by our side to help us keep going."

He splayed his fingers on the table and stared at them. So did Shannon. He had nice hands.

"I'm dirt poor, Shannon. If you saw my house, you'd understand your dad's reaction to me. I live in the worst trailer in the mobile home park. It's in…terrible shape. You can't imagine the condition." Shannon was startled to see his chocolate eyes swimming with tears, but he seemed to suck them back into his eye sockets.

"My dad is—out of the picture. Has been for several years. It's been really hard on my mom. She has manic depression. Can't work. She basically lies in bed all day, every day. Last year we got so bad that our electricity and water got cut. The only food we had was from food stamps. I was walking to school, which is two miles one-way. It was…really bad." His voice clouded with emotion. "I hadn't really ever asked God for anything big before. But I prayed and asked Him to help me find a way to take care of my family."

He met Shannon's eyes. "I'm eighteen, so I consider myself responsible for my family. I have fourteen-year-old twin sisters, and social services could help them, but I can't let them be split up. I had to keep us together. So I prayed. It was almost the end of last school year. A week later a fulltime job as night security at the lumber yard opened up. I never thought they'd hire a kid with no job history. But they did. And I knew that God had answered my prayer.

"I know that God hasn't provided extra for me. But He gives me exactly what I need every time. He gave me my sisters and a way to take care of them. He has never let me down, and I know that He won't. It doesn't mean it's easy. It just means He's right there by your side, going through the tough stuff with you."

Shannon was touched by his story, but she wasn't sure what God had given her to get her through. A jerk of a dad and two needy children? A wishy-washy sister?

She looked at the boy across from her.

A really nice math tutor. Who certainly didn't have time to be here with her.

"When do you work?"

"8:30 p.m. to 4:30 a.m. Sunday through Thursday, sometimes Saturdays. It's hard fitting in sleep and homework, but I am so grateful for my job. There's always sacrifices, like dropping out of the football team. The guys were really mad at me this year, but my family has to come first." He shifted his glance to her face. "Anyway, I wanted to encourage you. Sorry if it was too much."

Shannon tilted her head. "Not at all. Thank you for trusting me enough to tell me. That means a lot."

"Well, you know, we math tutors like to spill out our whole life stories to the unsuspecting recipients of our help." He grinned. Shannon smiled back, knowing they had just transitioned from tutoring to something more like friendship.

Jesse cleared his throat and pulled another book out of his book bag. "Want to study for the SAT?"

Shannon flopped over with a moan, her forehead on the table. She'd completely forgotten that test was in two weeks.

When she got back to the house, Kevin was in the kitchen making dinner. He asked where she'd been, and a heavy frown settled on his face at Jesse's name.

"Can't you find someone else to study with?" he asked, handing her a cutting board. Must be his way of asking for help.

"He was recommended as my best option, and I'd prefer to pass the class. Besides, I don't think anyone else would be willing to tutor me."

"Figures," he mumbled.

"What's your grief with him, anyway?" Shannon attacked a tomato with vengeance.

"We've already been over that, Shannon. No need to recycle that conversation."

She rolled her eyes and called him a name in her head that would have made her mom mad.

"We need to talk about college sometime soon."

"What about it?"

"Well, we need to discuss where you're applying and what you want to study."

She hadn't given much thought to college since Mom got sick. She had figured she'd be living at home during her college years, since Chicago had so many options. She had no idea what to study.

"There are some great universities in Virginia. Virginia Tech, UVA in Charlottesville, College of William and Mary..." He rattled on, but Shannon wasn't listening. She had no plans of going away to school until Laura could do the same with her, but she didn't think Kevin was ready to hear that.

When she didn't reply, he let the topic rest. They worked quietly side by side. They hadn't spoken more than courtesies since his whole Carmen breakdown.

He cleared his throat. Then again. Shannon looked up at him, but he avoided her eyes. Setting down his knife, he wiped his hands on a towel and moved toward the opposite counter.

"I, uh—I got something for you today. Gabby dragged me out shopping." He picked up a plain brown hardcover book with spiral binding. "It's not much." He held it out to her.

Shannon reached for it with her dry hand, hesitating. It was a journal. She didn't like to write.

"For drawing. Gabby said you're an artist. Thought you might enjoy keeping a sketch journal. Maybe it'll help with, you know, all the—the stuff you're going through." His lips twitched. "You can draw me with a dart board on my chest when you're mad."

Shannon didn't know what to say. She squeezed the journal in her hand, her pulse thumping through her thumb against the cover.

"Thank you. I—I'll use this."

He smiled, and Shannon noted the source of Andy's fabulous smile.

Chapter Eleven

"So what did you think of the party?"

Shannon looked up from her Spanish worksheet. Ms. Ellison had vanished to the back of the room helping a student.

"Umm..." Shannon didn't know what to say without offending Stephanie.

"Be glad you left," she whispered. "The cops showed up, and we got *buuuus*ted." She sang the last word loud enough to harvest a glare from the girl on her other side. "I'm surprised my mom let me out of the house this morning."

"The police took you to your mom?" Shannon gasped.

Stephanie laughed humorlessly. "The police *is* my mom."

Shannon felt her mouth form a silent *O*.

She couldn't find Laura after school, so she finally left without her. Her sister had been aloof since that stupid party. She wouldn't talk to Shannon about anything, and Shannon was starting to worry. Especially when she didn't show up for dinner. When Kevin asked where she was, Shannon couldn't make herself answer honestly. Because honestly she had no clue, and she knew Kevin wouldn't like that. She told him the only plausible thing she could think of—Laura had been asked to baby-sit in town. Mom would be crushed by her lying. But Kevin didn't question her story.

Thank goodness for the 10 minute grace period, because this time Kevin was still awake when Laura came creeping into the house at 10:07. She wouldn't answer when Shannon asked her where she'd been.

The next afternoon Jesse wanted to meet at Nancy's Trading Post again. Laura was a no-show after school like yesterday, so Shannon asked Stephanie if she'd be willing to cover her with the kids for one hour. She agreed on the slim chance that she'd see Andy.

"Oh my gosh, your brother's so hot," she groaned as Shannon drove to the elementary school to pick up Gabby. "We talked for like half an hour at the party. He is so funny!"

Shannon didn't reply. She wasn't feeling terribly amused with her brother the past couple days, in fact.

Jesse was waiting at Nancy's when she got there twenty minutes later. He smiled a warm greeting as she removed her coat and hung it on the back of the tall chair. As she hopped onto the seat, he pushed a steaming mug across the table toward her.

"What's this?" Quickly she noted there was only one. It had a giant swirl of whipped cream on top.

He ducked his head bashfully. "A gesture of friendship."

"Sure smells good," she said, leaning over to breathe it in. "Mmm, pumpkin spice latte?"

"They only have it in the fall. Nancy's puts Starbucks to shame with this one."

Shannon took a sip and had to agree. It was heavenly.

"You didn't want anything?"

He shrugged. "No, I'm good."

"You sure?" she pressed. He shook his head adamantly. Shannon narrowed her eyes.

"You only had enough money for one drink...didn't you?"

His eyes flickered enough to answer before he closed them. "Yes. And I wanted you to have it." He looked her in the eye. "So don't argue."

Shannon smiled and shook her head at him slowly. "I didn't peg you for stubborn. But I was wrong."

His dimples sank deeply into his cheeks as he laughed. "Did you ever! Let's get this pre-calc going, eh? I know you don't have much time."

Shannon sat back and looked Jesse over while he was busy setting up his textbook and notes. He was something else. Smart, attractive, and athletic, yet genuine, kind, and...religious? It was the oddest combo she'd ever heard of. But it sure was working for him.

That night she opened her new sketch journal and dated the top of the first page, it's blankness beckoning her to fill it. With a regular #2 pencil, she started to draw. A gentle face. With deep dimples on either side of his mouth. He looked nearly angelic when she was finished, and well, maybe he was.

* * *

The next afternoon Laura was missing in action again, so Shannon headed home. Laura hadn't gotten back till 10:02 the night before, but Kevin hadn't said anything. He looked surprised, in fact, as if he hadn't realized she was gone.

"Hey, let's go for a walk," Shannon suggested once Gabby and Daniel had devoured their snack of apple slices and peanut butter. She wasn't going to ask Steph to babysit again so soon, so a tutoring session was out.

An enthusiastic explosion rocked the room. Had they never been on a walk before?

"Can we take my wagon?" Daniel asked, jiggling up and down.

"Sure, sweetie. Where is it?" Shannon rummaged in the coat room for warm outerwear for the kids. The sun was shining brightly, but it was definitely cold out.

"In the garage," Gabby answered, struggling to wiggle her fingers into her gloves. "We take it in case Danny gets tired."

Shannon had noticed a distinct path through the woods behind the house a couple days ago, but now almost all the leaves were off the trees, piled onto the ground, and it was a little harder to distinguish.

She wrestled the wagon out of the garage and pulled it to the side of the house where the kids waited. "Do either of you know where that trail leads?"

Gabby nodded dramatically. "I do! It goes to Kurt's orchard! Can we go, please? Please?"

Surely she wouldn't run into Kurt if they just took the trail and came back. She wasn't ready to see him. Still didn't know what to say to him. What she felt about him.

"I don't see why not." She smiled down at Gabby, who was clapping her gloved hands in excitement.

"Yay! Come on, Daniel, let's go!" Gabby charged ahead, Daniel at her heels, while Shannon followed with the wooden wagon bumping along behind her. She relished the sound of leaves crunching to pieces beneath her feet. The smell of fall filled her senses, and she raised her face to take a big sniff. She could almost forget all her sorrow out here.

Daniel ran back and grabbed Shannon's free hand, swinging it back and forth. She smiled down at the pompom adorning the top of his hat.

"Geese!" he exclaimed. Honking filled the air, and they stopped and looked up through the bare branches where geese formed a sloppy V overhead.

"Where they goin', Shanny?" Daniel asked, leaning back so far he started to tip over. Shannon reached to steady him.

"They go south every winter. To stay warm."

"Oh. Why don't we do that, too?"

Shannon chuckled. "Good question, Daniel. Maybe because we don't fly."

"Oh." That seemed to satisfy him, because he took off running again. The leaves were so thick on the forest floor that they nearly reached his waist as he waded through them. He kicked his feet and sent a huge plume of orange and brown flying. The free-falling foliage twirled down, landed all over them.

"Come here, you little rascal!" Shannon grabbed him and gently dumped him on the ground. She and Gabby piled leaves on top of him until he was invisible. When he stood up, all they saw was a pile of dead leaves coming alive, and they collapsed into the leaves giggling.

"Man, I'm missing all the fun!" At the deep voice, Shannon was up and off the ground in one motion. Kurt stood a mere four feet away in a ridiculously casual stance, amusement flickering in his eyes. Her doubts about him melted into insignificance when she remembered she was littered in leaves.

"I didn't hear you coming!" Anxiously she brushed leaves off her coat, knowing her hair was hopeless. "What are you doing here?"

"You guys were making way too much noise to notice me," he said, winking at Gabby and Daniel. "In fact, I heard you all the way from the orchard."

"Are you serious?"

He laughed. "You're only about 20 yards from our property." He gestured down the path. "See that bend in the trail? That's where the apple grove starts. I was checking on the apple trees to see how they're handling the freeze when I heard the laughter and figured I should join in."

As she stood looking at Kurt, she couldn't help mentally comparing him and Jesse. Kurt was probably four inches shorter than Jesse, maybe 5'10" or 5'11". But he was so confident, so smooth, and the way he was looking at her was making her stomach feel all…seasick. She knew almost nothing about him, unlike Jesse, who had told her more than she knew what to do with. Jesse's looks were incredibly attractive, but Kurt's defined features, along with tan skin, those blueberry-blue eyes, and his sandy hair, made him the best looking guy she'd ever seen.

Her breath hitched in her throat as he walked right up to her and tugged a leaf out of her hair.

"Aren't you a sight for sore eyes," he joked as he discarded more leaves from her head.

She laughed, hating how nervous she sounded.

"Now that you're almost to the farm, it's a great time for a tour." He looked at Gabby and Daniel and raised his eyebrows encouragingly. "We have hot apple cider down at the orchard stand."

The kids turned on Shannon, begging to go. What could it hurt?

"I suppose so…"

Kurt's face drew up in a smug smile as he turned and walked with them. Just as he'd said, they reached the apple orchard in a few steps. Shannon wrinkled her nose at the scent of fermenting apples. Kurt laughed.

"That's what happens when apples fall to the ground and then we have a hard freeze. And then the apples thaw. Makes you want apple pie, doesn't it?" He poked her arm playfully. Shannon raised her eyebrows at him.

"That's—disgusting."

He laughed again as he herded them into a 1980-something Suburban parked at the end of a row between apple trees. The old beast roared to life, and Kurt pointed out the different varieties of apple trees as he slowly drove. Once they hit gravel, he picked up speed and shifted into second gear.

"We also have pear trees, but they're in the north sector. They look pretty much the same." He drove past a big log house built on a hill—"our house—" and made a right onto another road that took them up a steep hill through the woods. It broke into a clearing at the top, where four small log cabins stood, each a good distance from the other.

"These are the vacation cabins that we rent out."

"That's pretty neat. Do you get a lot of tourists?" It was Shannon's first question, and Kurt turned to her, looking way too happy that she'd spoken.

"Actually, we do, especially in the summer. There are so many parks around here, plus hiking and rock-climbing, so a lot of people vacation in southwestern Virginia. From May to the beginning of October these cabins are usually booked."

Shannon was impressed by the extent of the Blakes' business. Kurt's dad was quite the entrepreneur.

Kurt drove them back down the hill and took another road on the left. This one wound through the woods until the trees abruptly ended, and they were in the Christmas tree orchard. It stretched on forever before Shannon's eyes.

"There are a lot of Christmas tree farms about 20 miles south," Kurt said as he maneuvered over the bumpy dirt and grass road. "But ours is the only one around here, so we get pretty busy come December. We also ship trees to sellers in other places. One of our best sellers is in D.C."

"What kind of trees do you sell?"

"Fraser Firs, Virginia Pine, Eastern Redcedar, and Scotch Pine." He listed a few more, but Shannon honestly had no idea what the difference was. They drove down a row of pine trees in silence. She was intrigued by the neat rows. Some trees were tiny, others were just the right size for a living room. Some were so tall and overgrown, she wondered what they did with the unwanted monstrosities.

Soon they came out onto the main gravel road that seemed to cut the Blakes' property in half. Across from them Shannon saw a field dotted with orange.

"That's the pumpkin patch." Kurt gestured to the fallow fields behind the pumpkin patch. "That's where we grow other produce in summer. We've got a lot in the greenhouses, which you can just see over there." He stretched to point. "Pumpkins and apples are our fall crop, of course. This—" he pointed at a wooden building coming up—"is our orchard stand."

There were five cars parked in front of it, and the Suburban lumbered into the lot to join them.

"Can we get a pumpkin, Shanny?" Daniel asked excitedly as they walked into the little store. "Please? Please?"

Shannon glanced around. Although more rustic than Nancy's Trading Post, it sold much of the same orchard products. Bins mounded high with apple varieties, pumpkins, and gourds were forefront in this store, though. Enormous pumpkins of different shapes and sizes sat on the floor, and Daniel squealed with excitement when he saw one almost as tall as he.

The walls were lined with home canned goods, like apple butter, apple sauce, canned pumpkin, and pickled vegetables. Baked goods had their own table off to one side. Shannon examined the beautiful apple and pumpkin pies, assortment of cookies, and gourmet breads.

"Look, Shanny! Can I have this one?"

She spied Daniel waddling toward her with a large pumpkin in his arms. All she could see was it slipping and smashing into a million gooey pieces, so she dipped down and snatched it out of his hands. She held it up high and pretended to examine it.

"Hmm… Uh huh." She turned it one way, and then the other. "Daniel, I think it's perfect!" He beamed while Gabby danced with excitement behind him. "I don't have money with me right now, but maybe Kurt could put it aside for us, and I'll come back for it tomorrow?" She looked at him questioningly.

"Take it with you now. It's no problem."

"Are you sure? How much is it? I'll pay you later."

"No way. We have a whole patch of pumpkins dying from the frost. What's one more?"

Shannon looked at him under lowered eyelashes and said softly, "thank you."

Her stomach somersaulted at the intense look he gave her. He led them to the counter with hot drinks, and Shannon helped Gabby and Daniel fix their cups. When she turned around, Kurt pushed a Styrofoam cup into her hand. She forced herself to keep breathing as his fingers lingered on hers.

"I made you hot chocolate," he murmured, his face inches away.

"Thanks," she managed in a whispered squeak, willing her cheeks not to redden. Daniel's cry as he burned his tongue pulled her away, and she puffed in relief.

"I need to get them home and start working on dinner," she said once Daniel had calmed down.

"Sure thing." He drove them back to the edge of the apple orchard, where Daniel's wagon waited at the trailhead.

They were five minutes down the trail when she heard a shout behind them. She turned to see Kurt jogging after them.

"Hey, wait up!"

Shannon pulled Gabby to a halt and stopped the wagon where Daniel cradled the pumpkin in his lap. Kurt caught up to them, panting. He waved his cell phone.

"Right after you left, Andy asked me to come and help him with something. Mind if I walk with you?" He offered to pull the wagon and took the lead, chattering away with Daniel. Shannon was happy to lag behind and listen to Gabby. Kurt confused her until she didn't even know what she felt.

When they got into the yard, she saw Andy's car parked next to the garage.

"Andy, you in here?" He emerged from the back of the garage as she put Daniel's wagon away. "What are you always doing out here, anyway?"

He grinned. "Working on a surprise for Dad. You'll see at his birthday party."

"When is it?" Sad how little she knew about her dad. Just enough to make her not want to know more.

"In a week and a half, his 50th. I'm planning a big party. Which reminds me, can you take care of the food? I have no idea what to order or how much."

To be honest, she didn't want to do anything for Kevin. But to say so would make her look like a worse person than him.

"I guess... How many people are coming?"

"I dunno. Haven't finalized plans yet. I'll let you know."

Kurt walked in then, Gabby and Daniel following.

"Hey man, I didn't hear you pull up," Andy greeted him as they bumped fists.

"I walked. I met Shannon and the kids on the trail and showed them around the farm, so I decided to come back with them."

Shannon didn't miss the serious warning Andy's eyes gave Kurt, or the guilt that traveled across Kurt's face like a slow-motion film clip. What in the world? She furrowed her brow at the silent exchange. Boys. Aliens would be easier to interpret.

"I gotta go work on dinner. Feel free to join us if you're hungry, Kurt," she called over her shoulder as she prodded Gabby and Daniel toward the house.

To her surprise, she found Laura in the family room, slouched like a limp pillow on the floor in front of the TV. Her chin sagged morosely in her hand that was propped up by her elbow. Shannon felt sorry for her immediately.

"Laura?" she said softly, settling onto the floor beside her.

"Hmmm?" Laura barely seemed to notice her.

"What's goin' on, sis? You've been gone so much lately, and when you are here, you're so distracted you might as well not be." She reached out and touched her sister's arm. "I'm worried about you."

Laura looked at her, tears glistening in her eyes. "You don't understand."

"But I'd like to."

"Well, you can't." Laura turned back to the TV, shutting Shannon out. She stood up with a sigh. Laura was silent during the meal, but Andy and Kurt made up for it with their loud jokes and laughter. Shannon wasn't sure all their jokes were appropriate, especially in the presence of two young children, but she was grateful for the change of pace, especially since Kevin had texted to say he hadn't been relieved at the end of his shift and would be staying on until he was.

Shannon had made apple turnovers right before dinner, and Kurt and Andy ate them like there was no tomorrow.

"These are incredible!" Kurt exclaimed, making Shannon smile shyly. She left Andy and Kurt talking in the kitchen and went upstairs to get the kids ready for bed, which took almost an hour. She had homework in every class tonight, but dinner had to be cleaned up first.

She froze at the entrance to the kitchen. It was clean. Kurt was drying the counter with a dish towel. Shannon's mouth fell open in a silent exclamation.

"Are you okay?"

Shannon laughed and closed her flapping mouth.

"Yes, I'm okay." She cocked her head at him. "Thank you so much. I thought I'd have to clean up before I started homework."

Kurt looked pretty pleased with himself. "You're welcome." He replaced the towel on its hook and sat down on a bar stool. "Leftovers are in the fridge."

"You're amazing," she blurted out, then blushed. "I mean—never mind." He *was* amazing. She wouldn't take that back.

Kurt was grinning at her. "I'm sure you've heard it before, but you are one talented woman in the kitchen." She hadn't heard it put that way. His words warmed her belly.

"Aww, thanks."

"I bet my mom would give you a job. She's overloaded with all the baking."

She looked at Kurt in disbelief. "In case you hadn't noticed, I'm a little busy. I have children to look after, meals to cook, chauffeuring to do for the family, a sister to keep in line, loads of homework to keep up with—"

"Whoa, whoa!" Kurt held up his hands. "Forget I mentioned it." He looked at her closely. "Are you sure you can handle all that responsibility? I mean, not to mention that you've been here, what, a week and a half? Have you even adjusted to living here?"

Shannon felt tears coming, and she blinked rapidly. "No, I haven't, Kurt. Thanks for pointing that out." She started to walk out of the kitchen. "I think you'd better go. I have a lot of homework to do." She didn't want him to see her cry again.

"Ah, Shannon, don't go. I'm sorry! Man, I always make you feel worse. I never say the right thing."

She turned back and saw disappointment in his eyes.

"What do you want, Kurt?"

He flinched at her bluntness, but he crossed his arms and looked at her, almost challengingly.

"I want to stay here and do homework with you."

He did?

"Well alright then," she replied softly. She headed upstairs for her books.

"Did Kurt leave?" Laura asked when Shannon entered the room. She pulled out one of her ear buds, and Shannon could hear the music blasting from her side of the room.

"No. He's staying to do his homework with me." Shannon focused on stacking her books in her arms.

"He likes you."

She slowly turned, her pulse jumping. "How can you tell?"

Laura rolled her eyes. "You're so dumb with guys, Shan. Just be careful with him. He's a player."

Shannon stared at her sister. It was true. She *was* dumb when it came to guys. Laura seemed to read them much better. What did she mean that Kurt was a player?

"Don't worry, it's just homework," she said as she walked out the door.

"Just homework, oh please," she heard Laura muttering sarcastically behind her.

Downstairs she found Kurt kicked back in a kitchen chair, one foot propped on the chair across from him. He looked like he didn't have a care in the world. Or homework.

He'd walked here with them with the clothes on his back and his cell phone. That was it.

She sat down and frowned at him. "How are you going to do homework if you don't have any with you?"

* * *

Kurt opened his mouth to tell the gorgeous girl in front of him that suggesting homework had just been his scheme to spend more time with her. But before he could utter a syllable, Andy walked into the kitchen and stopped in surprise.

"I thought you'd left. Why are you still here?"

Kurt didn't like the hard edge to his voice. He scowled. Andy needed to cool it with the protective big brother act.

He gave Andy a dismissive look. "I'm going to stay and do homework with Shannon."

Andy looked at the table pointedly. "*What* homework?"

Kurt stood up. They needed to take this discussion elsewhere. He put his hand down on the table in front of Shannon, and when she raised her head to look at him, her indescribable eyes were full of questions.

"I'll be right back." He and Andy went out the side door to the porch, where each breath made a visible puff in the air. Kurt rubbed his arms with his hands, but Andy jammed his hands into his pockets and paced back and forth. He didn't say anything, so Kurt waited, ready when he did an about-face.

"What are you doing, man?" His tone held the most serious warning yet. "I told you to stay away from Shannon. More than once."

"Dude, calm down. I'm just being her friend like you said."

Andy snorted. "You wouldn't know how to just be friends with a girl if your life depended on it! I see the way you look at her, and it's not as a friend. You're trying to soften her until she's willing to hook up with you."

Was that what he was doing? Kurt wasn't even sure. He only knew something kept drawing him back to Shannon.

"But I really—I really like her," he said quietly.

"For real?" Andy's sarcasm was almost tangible. "And since when do you 'really like' her? Because I know who you spent

Saturday night with—and you seemed to 'really like' her. And it *wasn't* Shannon."

Kurt huffed defensively. "That's—that's different. You did the same thing."

"Yeah? Well the difference is I'm not sleeping with one girl during the night and hitting on my best friend's vulnerable sister during the day."

Kurt pulled his lips into a straight, firm line. He didn't like what Andy was accusing him of. But he also didn't like fighting with his best friend.

"What do you want me to do?"

Andy stared him down. "What I've said all along. *Leave. Shannon. Alone.* Got it?"

"Okay, okay, I get it." Kurt hated the whine in his voice. "I suppose you want me to leave now?"

"You said it, not me."

"Will you give me a ride?" He hated to grovel, but he didn't have a flashlight or winter coat for the long walk home.

Andy sighed and said with exaggerated patience, "Yes, Kurt, I'll give you a ride."

"Can I just say goodnight to Shannon?" He knew he was pushing it, but he'd told her he'd be right back, and he wasn't about to let Andy make him a liar.

"Thirty seconds," Andy snapped, and Kurt dashed inside with thoughts of pity for any children Andy might one day father.

Shannon had already busied herself in a book, but she jerked around when Kurt bounded into the kitchen.

"Sorry, Shannon." He forced away thoughts of how absolutely beautiful she looked. Her blue top matched her eyes almost perfectly and deepened the blond hue in her hair. And those lips...He wondered what it would be like to... *Focus, Kurt.*

"Something came up, and I gotta get home. Andy's taking me now. I really enjoyed...seeing you today." Oh that was lame, and so not what he wanted to say. "I hope you have a good night and get all your homework done."

He felt a hand grabbing the back of his hoodie, and before Shannon could say anything, Andy had hauled him out of the house.

Chapter Twelve

"Laura, please don't go!" Shannon tried one last time as she watched her sister pull loose pants and a coat over her costume.

"I'm not going to be a loser like you and stay home all the time. You should come with me."

"And risk getting caught sneaking out? No thanks."

"I've been doing it all week and haven't been caught yet." Laura eased the bedroom door open and slipped her head out to look. She glanced back one more time and mouthed "loser" before she silently disappeared.

Shannon groaned and fell back onto her pillow. It was Halloween, and her little sister was sneaking out to a costume party dressed as a rather slutty-looking bunny.

The past week and a half had been a nightmare. When Laura kept missing her curfew and it got moved all the way to 8:00 o'clock, she'd tried a new tactic. And it had worked. She came home after school and pretended to settle in for the evening. While Kevin was distracted, she sneaked out *after* her curfew. Shannon had begged her to stop, pleaded with her to tell her where she was going. Most of the time Laura ignored her. Tonight it had been obvious what she was up to.

Shannon felt guilty for letting her sister sneak out every night. She'd even lied to Kevin on several occasions when he asked if Laura was in her room. What else could she do without being a total snitch? At least Laura had been around in the afternoons to allow more tutoring sessions. She was getting along nicely in pre-calculus, thanks to Jesse, and they'd studied a lot for the SAT this week. Her results last year had been terrible. She'd taken the test two days after Mom's stage-four diagnosis. Now she was taking it a month after Mom died. She expected similar mediocre scores.

She forced herself to stop worrying about Laura and get some sleep. She'd need it tomorrow. The SAT *and* Kevin's birthday party. Which was worse?

She woke with a start when the doorknob clicked, and Laura's shadowy figure slinked across the room on tip-toes. The digital clock across the room read 2:07. It was the latest she'd pushed it. If

Kevin found out, she had a feeling they were both going to pay. He hadn't said much to her the past two weeks. Ever since he'd opened up to her about Carmen, he'd been polite but closed as a book on a library's shelf. He asked how she was and thanked her for meals and taking care of her siblings, but that's where the conversation ended. Shannon couldn't make herself excited about the party tomorrow, even for Andy's sake. He was having a hard time keeping it a secret, he was so excited. She couldn't figure out why he thought his dad was so awesome.

She rolled over and tried to go back to sleep. She felt groggy when her alarm rang. Laura was zonked out in her bed, heavy makeup smeared under her eyes. Shannon gazed down at her, wishing she understood her sister and hoping she could find a way to keep her out of trouble.

"You ready?"

Shannon jerked her head up from her locker where she had stashed a supply of pencils yesterday. Jesse was waiting with a warm, dimpled smile.

She gave a weary sigh. "No." She slammed her locker closed, wishing she could tell Jesse about Laura and ask his advice. But they had kept strictly to math ever since he'd bought her that drink. He was almost as closed as Kevin, although always friendly and compassionate. It was a confusing mix.

"You got this, Shannon." He surprised her by reaching out and squeezing her arm gently. "I'll be praying for you."

She hesitated, then smiled. "Thanks. I need it." In more ways than one.

Four hours and some change later, she staggered out of the high school with a headache the size of Mt. Everest. She was shaking from hunger after skipping breakfast, and her hand was cramped and throbbing from holding a pencil all morning. Preparing a party for Kevin was the last thing she felt like doing, but she'd promised Andy.

She made a detour to the grocery store to buy the last items for the menu. Andy had given her cash. He didn't know she was cooking everything herself. She had no idea where to order food around here—there were no real restaurants in town. She knew her food was as good as any restaurant, anyway, and she'd made a lot of things ahead during the past few afternoons while Gabby and Daniel were playing. Kevin wasn't home enough to even notice the extra dishes in the fridge and freezer.

When she got back to the house, there was no sign of life. Laura was gone again. Shannon knew Kevin had taken Gabby and Daniel to the Bristol children's museum at her urging. They were supposed to get back around 7:00. Since his birthday wasn't for another four days, he didn't suspect anything.

Andy's car was by the garage, as was Kurt's truck, so Shannon assumed they were finishing up their secret project for Kevin. Kurt hadn't said much to her since Andy had plucked him out of the kitchen that night more than a week ago. He'd been around plenty, like last night playing basketball outside with Andy, or two nights ago joining them for dinner. He'd thanked Shannon for the food, but that was it. She'd caught him watching her a time or two, but he never made any more moves, and Shannon wondered what had made him lose interest in her. It was bothering her a lot. But so was everything else in life.

"Andy?" She ventured into the garage. "You in here?"

"Yeah, just a second." He emerged behind a drop cloth hanging from the ceiling. "You wanna see it? We're done!"

Shannon *was* rather curious what Andy had been working on, so she followed him behind the dirty blanket. A beautiful wooden desk met her eyes. It had many compartments and was finished with intricate carved designs on all the edges.

"You made this yourself? It's spectacular."

"From scratch!" Andy beamed with pride, then gestured off-handedly at Kurt, who was touching up some spots with varnish. "It wouldn't be done if it weren't for this guy, though."

Kurt grinned but didn't look up.

"Anyway, did you need something? How's it coming inside?" Andy glanced at his watch, and Shannon let herself smile at his excitement.

"I just need some help putting the leaf in the table." She had already set up the dining room and living room to accommodate the coming crowd with extra chairs from the basement. A card table for gifts was near the front door, and another in the dining room for punch and dessert. All that was left was getting the extensions in the table.

"Oh, sure, I'll be over in a second." Andy didn't offer Kurt's help, and it almost felt like he was helping Kurt avoid her. Shannon swallowed back the hurt and sent another smile Andy's way.

"Thanks. I'll be in the kitchen."

By 2:30 she had the decorating done and focused on the food. She had never cooked for an event before and supposed she should be nervous, but she couldn't bring herself to care that much.

She could use more hands, though. It would be nice if Laura were there to help. Shannon had reminded Laura about the party last night before she'd left for her own party, so she assumed she'd be back in a few hours.

By 6:45 she was able to place a check beside everything on her menu. She'd made a lot. For starters, there was a fruit platter, vegetable tray, and mini spinach quiches. Bruschetta with freshly marinated roma tomatoes, baby green salad, and tomato bisque soup were the appetizers, besides French bread that she'd bought. Her entrée choices were pesto fettuccine with broccoli, orange glazed chicken and herbs, and braised short ribs with potatoes and mushrooms. The folding table was loaded with punch, coffee, hot apple cider, four dozen chocolate and vanilla petit fours, and a two-level chocolate birthday cake, decorated with a personalized message for Kevin. She even squeezed in candy and nut trays.

She was impressed with herself. It looked amazing. She'd never prepared so much food at one time before.

Realizing that guests would be arriving any minute and she was still in sweats and tennis shoes, she dashed upstairs and donned a short, slim-fitting black dress she had gotten at the mall when Kevin took them shopping, along with sparkly black five-inch stilettos. She'd blown her hair out yesterday, so she simply brushed it and swooped one side up with a comb, leaving the other side free-flowing. The look was completed with dainty, dangling gold earrings. After touching up her makeup, she hurried back downstairs, almost tripping in her tall heels. When she walked into the kitchen and found Kurt and Andy there, she thought she might have to pick Kurt's jaw off the floor and hand it to him.

"Shannon, you look *hot*," he croaked, then grunted when Andy soundly elbowed his ribs.

"It looks fantastic in here!" Andy interjected. "And so do you! I guess we better go change, huh?" He dragged Kurt out of the kitchen, and through the dining room, where he suddenly stopped. "Wait, did you *make* the food?" Shannon followed them into the room and nodded shyly. It did look stunning, her creations all lined up on the extra long dining room table in chafing dishes. She'd bought those, too.

"Unbelievable." Andy wheeled around to face her. "You are unbelievable." He threw his arms around her and gave her a crushing hug. "Thank you, Shan. You're going to make this so special for Dad." Shannon wasn't sure she cared one twit about that, but Andy sure was making her feel special. That was her first hug from anyone besides Daniel or Gabby in weeks.

The doorbell rang a few minutes later, and Andy played host, welcoming the first guests. His easy manners got the older couple laughing quickly. Shannon hung back, feeling out of place as more guests arrived. At the next knock, Kurt answered the door.

"Oh, hey," he said to the couple filling the doorway, then waved Shannon over. "Come meet my parents."

"Mom and Dad, this is Kevin's daughter, Shannon. Shannon, my mom, Nancy, and my dad, Jason."

Shannon shook their hands with a smile. Kurt was a blend of the two of them, with his mom's smile and eyes, but definitely his dad's build, tan complexion, and hair.

"Thank you for coming," she said. A timer started beeping in the background. "Oh, I'm sorry. I need to go check on that."

As she headed to the kitchen, she heard Kurt saying, "She made all the food herself. She's an incredible cook, Mom. Wait till you try her food. And she decorated this place, too...."

Her face warmed at his praise. He'd called her hot. She bit back a grin as she took the last item out of the oven and carried it to the dining room table where she studied Kurt's profile across the room. He looked very attractive in a fitted black dress shirt and tan slacks, a relaxed smile on his square face. Shannon's heart sped up when he caught her watching him. He gave a slow nod. What did that mean?

As the rest of the guests arrived in a steady trickle, Shannon couldn't stop glancing at the clock. Where was Laura? Kevin would be home any time. How could she be late for this?

"He's here, he's here!" Andy raced into the living room, shushing the guests.

"Andrew Lucas Conrad," Kevin's voice boomed down the hall the minute he walked through the side door. "Why are so many cars outside? You better not be having a party without my permission."

Andy met him in the hallway. "Sorry, Dad. Should I have told you?"

"Of course!" Before Kevin could explode, Andy pulled him into the living room.

"Happy birthday!" the waiting crowd chorused together.

Kevin's face registered shock before he started laughing. He took in all the people and decorations. Then he turned around to the dining room, where Shannon stood beside the table. He looked back at Andy.

"You are too much. Did you plan this?"

Andy grinned proudly. "Yep. Me and Shannon."

"I had no idea. Thank you. This means so much…" He choked up a little and coughed. "Well, well, my kids can make me cry." The guests all chuckled and started milling about again. Kevin moved toward them, then looked back at Shannon. "Can you bring Gabby and Daniel inside? I rushed in here to break up Andy's party." Andy laughed and threw his arm around his dad's shoulders.

The party progressed quickly with happy, hungry guests. Shannon glowed inside at each compliment she overheard about the food, everyone guessing which restaurant in Bristol had catered. If they only knew. She made sure Gabby and Daniel ate before hustling them upstairs to bed. Then she retreated to the kitchen, completely out of her element elsewhere. Kevin found her scrubbing out an empty pan.

"Shannon." It was probably the most gentle way he'd ever said her name, but she still focused on the dish in her hands.

"I'm absolutely astounded at you. I asked Andy which restaurant he ordered from. He said you made it all."

"All but the bread." She vigorously attacked a sticky spot in the bottom of the pan.

"Shannon, look at me." His voice was firm but still gentle. When she met his gaze, she softened at the pride shining in his eyes. "You amaze me. You can cook anything, balance an unreasonable schedule, you're an artist, a pianist, a runner—and you're more competent with Gabby and Daniel than many mothers are with their own children."

"I'm not really all that..." She didn't know how to respond to his admiration.

"Oh but you are," he said confidently. "I have given you so much responsibility because you continually demonstrate that you can handle it, and with precision. There's no way I'd leave Gabby and Daniel in your sister's care. Speaking of her, where is Laura?" He glanced around with a quizzical expression, and Shannon held her breath until he walked out of the room, but by the look on his face, she knew he'd be back. And he was, five minutes later.

"Shannon."

Not gentle this time. This was the regular Kevin. The rough Kevin.

"Where is Laura?" he rumbled.

She sighed and wiped the back of her hand across her forehead, tired. Of everything.

"I don't know." There. It was done.

"What do you mean? You always know where she is."

She wished that were the truth. No way to lie Laura out of this one. "Well this time I don't. I told her to be here." She faced Kevin and noted both anger and hurt. "I'm sorry, Kevin."

Andy popped into the kitchen with magnificent timing, dragging Kevin away to open gifts. Shannon stayed in the kitchen, trying to still her pounding heart. This wasn't over.

From what she overhead, Kevin loved the desk. The whole birthday party had been a success. Minus the fact that one of Kevin's own kids skipped it. Shannon blew out a puff of air.

Her whole family had skipped her last birthday in August. But that's what happens when your mom's hospitalized in the final stages of cancer. Who really cares about birthdays then?

She shook her head and turned the water back on, trying to clear the muddling thoughts crisscrossing though her brain.

It seemed like an eternity before guests started leaving. After Kevin thanked the last couple for coming and closed the front door behind them, Shannon forced herself to look at the clock.

11:01.

An explosion was imminent. No way Kevin was going to let this one go.

Laura was an idiot!

Shannon made herself as busy as possible putting leftover food away, wishing she could make herself invisible from the coming storm. Andy and Kurt were fooling around in the living room popping balloons, oblivious to the change in Kevin's mood as he stomped through the house picking up chairs.

"Shannon." Her jaw clenched as he came up behind her at the sink. "I've called your sister's phone five times; she's not answering. Where. Is. She?" His voice trembled with barely controlled rage.

Shannon shrugged. "I told you I don't know."

Kevin reached around her and slammed his hand down on the faucet, cutting off the water.

"This isn't the first time, is it?"

Shannon swallowed hard and turned around, forcing herself to meet Kevin's eyes. They were blazing with fury. "What do you mean?"

"Where was Laura at eleven last night, Shannon?"

Her legs trembled. "I—I don't know."

"And the night before?" When Shannon didn't respond, Kevin grabbed her by the shoulder, pushing her until her back dug painfully against the sink's edge. "Answer me!" he roared.

"I don't know," Shannon whispered, tears filling her eyes.

"How many times has she sneaked out and you didn't tell me?"

Tears rolled down Shannon's cheeks as she stared at the floor. "Ever since you changed her curfew to 8:00."

He let out a vile swear words and wrapped his large hand around her upper arm. "Three times I asked you where she was, and what did you tell me?"

Tears dripped off her face, and the kitchen was so silent she heard the splash on the floor. The silence ended with Kurt and Andy sliding into the room on their socks, laughing loudly. Kurt halted abruptly when he saw Shannon and Kevin, but Andy tripped over him, and they both fell down.

Kevin ignored them entirely.

"Shannon Conrad, you answer me right now." He twisted her arm until she whimpered.

"Dad, you're hurting her!" Andy exclaimed.

"Stay out of this, Andy," Kevin barked. "Shannon, this is your last chance."

Her voice wobbled as she said, "I told you she was upstairs in our room."

"You lied to me!" Kevin dropped his hand and turned his back, only to whirl around a second later. "How could you do that? I trusted you, Shannon!"

The words cut deep, and Shannon bowed her head, letting the tears flow freely. Kevin stalked out of the kitchen, and Shannon slid down the counter until her bottom hit the floor. She squeezed her face with her hands, taking three slow, deep breaths to stop crying. It took her a moment to realize Kurt and Andy were still in the kitchen, watching her. Andy stepped forward to offer her a hand and pulled her to her feet.

"Are you okay? What was that all about?"

"Nothing, I'm fine." She moved to the sink. "I need to finish these dishes."

"But Shannon—" This time it was Kurt.

"Just go!" she snapped, turning to glare at them both.

"Okay, okay." He put his hands in surrender mode and followed Andy out of the kitchen.

When Laura showed her face 45 minutes later, Kevin was waiting.

* * *

Shannon struggled to lift her mattress from her bed frame.

Whoever heard of grounding a seventeen-year-old?

She sighed and dropped her load, glaring over at Laura's motionless form across the room.

They were both grounded and phoneless for two weeks. She'd received the same punishment as Laura. Not fair.

There went her pre-calculus grade. Tutoring was off limits, too. And friends. As if she had any. Laura had experienced a complete meltdown in Kevin's office at their sentencing. She hadn't shown remorse until then, so Kevin didn't appear sympathetic in the least.

His anger at Laura was clear. Shannon wished he felt the same for her. But it was hurt and distrust he directed toward her, and that was harder to handle. Especially when he'd asked if he could even trust her to take care of Gabby and Daniel.

Laura was blaming Shannon for blowing her cover and refused to speak to her. Her sister had cried half the night.

Shannon decided it was high time she have her own space, so after attempting homework most of the day on Sunday, she started moving her belongings across the hallway into Andy's vacated room. But clearly she'd need help with the larger items.

Wandering downstairs, she scanned for options. Kevin would be last resort. He hadn't said much to her or Laura today, and she wasn't dying to speak to him either. A loud exclamation informed her that Kurt was in the house. She followed the sound to the family room, where Andy and Kurt were watching a hockey game. An intense one, apparently, the way they sat on the edge of the couch practically biting nails. She wouldn't bother them. She was embarrassed about the spectacle Kurt had once again witnessed last night. Bet he didn't think she was so hot sitting on her butt in tears on the kitchen floor.

She pivoted, ready to silently escape and resume her private struggle with the mattress when Andy said, "Need something, Shan?"

When she looked, he was still focused on the large screen TV, but Kurt's head swiveled her way. He was on his feet in an instant. "Hey there, you okay? What was going on last night?"

"Bro, maybe she doesn't want to talk about it." Andy pointed the remote at the screen and it went blank. "Game's over. Don't you need to get home?" He speared a direct look at Kurt, who shrugged.

"I'm in no rush."

Shannon hesitated, feeling tension rising between Andy and Kurt. Whatever was going on, she was almost certain it was about her. "Well, if either of you has time, I'm trying to move my stuff across the hallway, and I need help."

Kurt came just short of lunging toward her, but Andy's restraining hand closed as quickly on his shoulder.

"Kurt can't. He has to work. Right, Kurt?"

Shannon wondered at the hard edge in her brother's voice and his fingers noticeably digging into Kurt's shirt. Kurt's eyes darted to hers before nodding.

"Yep, I gotta go. Sorry, Shan. I'm sure Andy can handle it." Then he shot a glare at Andy, looking the most ticked she'd ever seen.

Andy followed her upstairs and offered his assistance, making jokes to lighten things, but Shannon stayed quiet. It seemed clear now that Kurt did have a thing for her, the way he popped up like a jack-in-the-box at her presence. Andy was the one trying to keep him away. The question was why?

Chapter Thirteen

"What do you know about Kurt Blake?" Shannon asked the question quietly as she and Stephanie worked on a Spanish worksheet together. Ms. Ellison was busy grading at her desk, and the sound of accented Spanish murmured around the classroom.

"Kurt?" Her tone of voice already said a lot. "Where shall I start? One of the best looking guys in Claywood—a fact he's well aware of. Last year he was student body president and football quarterback. His family is a big employer in town, pretty well-off, like your dad. Wait—shouldn't you know all this? He's Andy's best friend."

Shannon nodded. "He's around a lot. My sister thinks he likes me, but she said he's a player."

Stephanie snorted. "That's putting it mildly. From what I hear, he puts your brother to shame, which is quite a feat."

Shannon felt like she'd been slammed in the chest by a football. She took a slow breath. "So he—they—" She couldn't make the words come out. She didn't live in a bubble, and she knew it happened frequently, even in high school, but still...

Stephanie's voice dropped to the barest whisper. "They sleep around. Regularly, according to the rumors. Neither one has had a girlfriend, but I think that's the way they want it. Not to be tied down to one person." She made a face. "Personally, I'm not looking for a short-term thing like that."

Shannon grappled to accept the words, the information. *Andy* was like this? No. It couldn't be. She didn't want it to be. And Kurt? What of his attention? She closed her eyes in pain. Was he just trying to make her his next bed mate?

"It's one thing to do it with a boyfriend," Stephanie continued softly, looking so wistful that Shannon knew immediately Stephanie had done exactly that in the past. "I think it's totally another to do it at random like they do, although given the chance, Andy would be hard for me to resist..."

Their conversation left Shannon unsettled and to be honest, actually nauseas. She sat in the cafeteria with her sketch journal spread in front of her, hot lunch pushed aside. Another glance at the cute boy across from her at the next table, and she continued shading in his hair. He had an interesting face to draw, and she sure enough wasn't going to stomach food right now.

"Want me to introduce you?" Jesse's voice drew Shannon's head up with a frown. He nodded toward the boy. "I'll warn you, he's a bit younger than you."

Shannon cracked up and gestured for Jesse to sit down. "Please, no. If you introduced me to everyone I drew, things might get awkward."

"May I?" Jesse reached for her journal, and Shannon hesitated. It was almost more personal than words. Especially when Jesse filled the first page. Kurt dotted more than his fair share. Of course there were plenty of scenes depicting Kevin, but those were generally unpleasant.

She put her hand down on the book. "Only the previous two pages." Those were safe.

Jesse perused her work with interest. Today she'd sketched pretty much everything in the cafeteria, but the only face she'd detailed was the puppy-doggish freshman. Kevin would probably be shocked to know she'd already filled half the journal.

"Wow, Shannon, this is amazing." Jesse set the journal down and looked at her. "I had no idea you were such a talented artist."

Shannon turned her head shyly. He should see her paintings, then. If they weren't all in Chicago, along with her supplies.

"It's one of my true loves." Right up there with music and cooking. She did best when her hands were in motion. "By the way, I should let you know I can't have tutoring for the next two weeks. Long story short, Laura and I got in trouble and are grounded."

"Oh no! That's a bummer." Jesse offered a sympathetic slump of his shoulders. Shannon appreciated that he didn't ask what sort of trouble they'd gotten into. His forehead wrinkled as he seemed to be thinking very seriously. "I don't want to crash your sketching parties, but I'd be more than happy to go over pre-calc homework during lunch every day. I think we'd have enough time to eat, too, if you're inclined, that is." He dipped his head toward her uneaten lunch.

Shannon twisted her lips. Her life was a wreck. She could never explain it all to Jesse.

"You sure you want to eat lunch with me every day? I don't want your friends to feel ditched."

He offered a sad smile. "I already got ditched, Shannon. All my friends were football teammates. Like I said, they're not too happy I dropped football. Which is okay. I don't have much time for friends. But I always make time for lunch." A full smile filled his face now, along with those endearing dimples.

What else could she say? "Thank you!"

A few days later, after Shannon finished cleaning up from dinner, she sat down at the piano to play for a few minutes before tackling homework. Before she touched the keys, the bookshelf against the wall beside her caught her attention. The bottom shelf was filled with photo albums. A rather old-fashioned notion, and it made her curious. What was in them?

She slid off the piano bench and knelt on the floor, running her finger along the spines until she hit one that read *Gabby growing up*.

Pulling it off the shelf, Shannon gently opened it. The spine groaned stiffly as if it hadn't moved in a long time. The first page was full of pictures of Gabby as a newborn in the hospital. "Gabriela Lynchelle Conrad, November 22nd," the caption read. She was already turning the page when her eyes caught the digital date imprint on the photo. The year... No. Couldn't be. Wait.

Shannon hunched over and studied the date again. It really *was* the same year Kevin had abruptly exited her life.

Gabby was going to be nine in a couple weeks.

Kevin had left them nine years ago.

She rose to her feet slowly, the album dangling from her clenching fist.

She had been swinging when he'd come home the last time. It was warm and sunny, and the leaves on the tree where Laura played were still green. She had turned eight in the middle of August, right before she went back to school. Kevin had missed her birthday party. It was a few weeks later, and they had just gotten back from school and were playing outside. Must have been early September.

And Gabby was born two and a half months later.

She processed it numbly as she moved from the room and down the hall toward Kevin's office. She didn't knock, and he raised his head in surprise.

"Shannon? What's wrong?" He lowered the magazine in his hands to the desk top. Shannon slammed the album down on top of the magazine. She crossed her arms over her chest. She wouldn't cry in front of this jerk. She wouldn't.

"I always—" Her voice wobbled and she swallowed and started over, squeezing herself so hard it hurt to breathe. "I always knew you cheated on Mom, that you left her for Carmen. But I didn't know you left me and Laura for Gabby."

Kevin's face visibly drained of color as he stared at the photo before him. Shannon watched, waiting for him to say something. She'd always felt rejected. Now she knew she'd been replaced. It was far, far worse. Now that she understood, finally, the real reason her dad had left her, the pain was magnified ten-fold. Maybe a hundred.

Shannon felt no more anger toward him. Only hurt. Deep, twisting, intensifying hurt.

When Kevin met her eyes, his face was wracked with regret. "Shannon...I'm sorry." His voice cracked on the last word, and he dropped his head and wept. Tears ran down Shannon's face against her will, and she collapsed into the nearest chair. When Kevin regained composure, he looked at her with red eyes. "If I had known how much pain I would cause, there are many things I would have done differently in my life." He sighed. "I never wanted you to discover the truth, but it's rather simple math."

"Why—why did you leave us? I mean..." What did she really want to know? "I don't understand why you replaced us with Gabby, when you could have included all of us in your life. Did you not care about me and Laura at all?" Just saying the words burned a new hole in Shannon's battered heart.

"I loved you girls tremendously. Truly, I did. But Carmen has a strong jealous streak, and she pressured me to move on." His eyes flickered over Shannon's wet face. "That was very wrong, and again, I'm so sorry, Shannon. I know you felt forgotten, but you never were. I hope you believe me."

"Does Gabby know?" Shannon croaked, brushing with irritation at still-falling tears.

"No. Please don't tell her. She's been through too much already. Her conception wasn't her fault, and neither was yours."

Only when Kevin's face went slack with panic did Shannon register his words. Her heart iced over with dread, although she had no idea why.

"What do you mean?"

He shook his head too hard. Frantic. "Never mind. Bad word choice."

"What—what did you mean by that, Kevin?" she repeated slowly, struggling to draw air into her lungs. If he didn't explain himself, she wasn't sure she'd ever breathe normally again.

The room was thick with silence. Kevin closed his eyes tightly, gave a little shake of his head, then met Shannon's eyes head on. Her blood thundered in her ears so loudly she could barely hear him when he spoke.

"Your mother made me promise to never tell you. But maybe it's best you know now, rather than later. Before your mother, I was married to Andy's mother." He rubbed his nose with his pointer finger. "How much older is Andy than you, Shannon?"

She thought a moment. "Two years." What did that have to do with anything? Wait. Only two years? She turned widening eyes upon Kevin, and he nodded.

"That's right. Andy had just turned two when you were born."

"What are you saying, Kevin?" Was that her voice, shaking so brokenly?

"Shannon, when I met your mother, I was still married to my first wife." He cleared his throat, clenching his fists. "I had an extramarital affair with your mother."

Shannon sat in mute horror as the truth slowly washed through her mind, caving in what little was left of her world.

"Mom had an affair with you…when you were married?"

The shame on Kevin's face told all the details. Fresh tears cascaded as Shannon's picture of her mother crumbled before her mind's eye like a shattering mirror.

"Yes. She did." Kevin's voice was raw. "And when she told me she was pregnant and her parents had disowned her, I had to make a choice."

Shannon bolted ramrod straight in the chair, her identity wavering before her. "Tell me it isn't true!"

Kevin stared blindly at the open album in front of him. "It's true. I didn't actually marry your mother until after you were born." He slowly rose to his feet and came around the desk. Hesitantly he lowered his hand to Shannon's shoulder. "Your mother wanted it a secret because she didn't want you to feel unwanted, Shannon. Because—you weren't."

Shannon flung his hand away with both of hers like he was a disease and staggered to her feet.

She had been a horrible mistake. She hadn't been planned. She hadn't been wanted. Her entire existence was an accident.

Half blinded by tears, she fled the room, ignoring Kevin's pitiful call for her to stop.

She had been a consequence.

* * *

Kurt decided to drop by the Conrads' house on his way home. Andy had done an efficient job of keeping him away from Shannon lately, and Kurt was missing the sight of her. He knew his friend wasn't home, so maybe if he played it cool, he'd have a few minutes with Shannon uninterrupted.

He stepped into the kitchen first, the most likely space to find her. No such luck tonight. He turned around to leave just as she rounded the corner and collided into him. He caught her by both arms to steady her before he noticed the tears rushing down her cheeks. They instantly tore up his heart.

"Hey, what's wrong?"

"Nothing. Everything." She choked on a sob and tried to pull away. "I'm just looking for my water bottle." She jerked her head around, searching the room, but Kurt held on to her, pulling her closer. No way he was going to let her go like this.

"Shannon?"

She looked at him, her face crumpling with such intense heartbreak he felt it in his chest. "Why does life have to hurt so much, Kurt?"

He raised one hand and gently brushed the tears from her cheeks. "I don't know the answer to that, Beautiful." Seeing her like this was doing crazy things to his heart. He wanted to make her happy, to see her smile, hear her laugh, but he didn't know how.

She still gazed up at him with her sad, ocean eyes, and Kurt was a drowning man. His heart hammered as he took a step closer, pulling her to him until their bodies met. Her eyes widened as he slid one hand to her slender waist, and the other to the back of her neck. He lowered his head, and then his lips were on hers. He kissed her gently, trying to soothe away all the hurt. Tightening his arm around her waist, he pulled her hard against him, his other hand burrowing into the base of her silky hair.

Then she hesitantly kissed him back, and a tingling sensation shivered down his backbone. He felt her hands on either side of his face, and he knew he must be dreaming.

He was enjoying himself far too much when the hallway floorboards creaked with approaching footsteps. Slowly he pulled away, brushing his lips across Shannon's once more. A stunned expression highlighted her face. He smiled and winked, then hightailed it out the door. Andy was going to kill him if he found out.

* * *

"Shannon?" Kevin's form promptly replaced the space Kurt had just occupied, at a much farther proximity. "Please, can we talk some more?"

She pushed by him, ignoring him, and collapsed onto her bed when she reached her room. She had been conceived during illicit sex between her married-to-another-woman father and her home-wrecker mother.

Just when she thought life couldn't get any worse. Kurt had made her forget for a few minutes. But now the pain crashed, breaking over her, soaking into her.

She curled up in a fetal position, grateful she had her own room now. No wonder Kevin hadn't thought twice about leaving her. She hadn't been in his plan. She had been a huge mistake. That's all she was.

A mistake. She had ruined Kevin's life, and probably Mom's, too, and certainly the life of Andy's mom.

How could Mom have *done* that?

"Shannon." She hadn't even heard Kevin come in, but now he was easing himself onto the edge of her bed, his back toward her.

She slithered as far away from him as possible. "Go away. I *hate* you, Kevin."

"I made a mistake, Shannon. *You* are not a mistake. Do you understand the difference?"

"I don't want to talk." She rolled herself up until her chin rested on her knees, clasping her legs. "Leave me alone."

He studied his hands. "Do you wish I hadn't told you?"

Shannon closed her eyes. And be a living lie the rest of her life? Would that be better?

"I don't know," she groaned. "How many other lies have I been believing? Let me guess, Mom's entire family didn't really die before I was born." The word *disowned* rang a bell.

"Your mother's parents were pretty high-profile Catholics. Their tragically widowed single-mother daughter was a nice story for their political aspirations. Her unmarried pregnancy was not. The whole family disowned her."

"Who are they?" A mind-boggling thought, that Shannon had a family she'd never met.

"Does it matter?"

"I guess not." If they didn't want her then, why would they now? She frowned. "Todd must have known them. Did he buy the whole-family-died-in-a-crash story?"

Kevin massaged his temples. "I don't know what your mother told him. He never spoke to me about it. To my knowledge he doesn't know we were having an affair."

The word knocked the air from her lungs. Again. She held her head with both hands. "I *knew* it. I felt it the day you left, the way you dropped my hand. You regretted me, didn't you?"

"Oh, Shannon. I regretted what my choices did to my first wife and Andy—but I never regretted you. You looked so much like me and you acted so much like me—you *are* so much like me, even now. I knew if anyone could change my mind about leaving, it would be you. I could barely look at you that day."

But he'd left anyway. Because he'd never wanted her in the first place.

"I did love your mother very much, but I carried so much guilt with me from the start that we probably never had a fighting chance. She begged me to have another baby. She thought it would help if we had one planned, as a family. Instead of trying to make the best of things and do things right with you three, I kept myself away. I let my love for your mother slip away. That's when I met Carmen."

"How did you end up here?"

"Carmen was a nursing student at my medical office, so that caused a scandal. I was forced to resign. I'm originally from Virginia, only went to Chicago for med school. So I came back with Carmen to start over here."

Far away from her and Laura.

"How come you never looked back? Did we matter so little?" Her voice was a whisper.

"No, sweetheart." Shannon drew back at the endearment. "I was... *sick* with myself for all the mistakes I'd made. But I decided to put that behind me and focus on what I had now. I fell hard for Carmen, and I loved Gabby dearly." He searched for her eyes, but Shannon refused contact. "One reason I never attempted to contact you and your sister was because I knew it would draw me away from my new family. I was determined not to screw up this time. I told myself you girls were fine without me."

Hadn't she been? She didn't even know anymore.

"When I learned your mom had passed, I saw it as my chance to make up for the mess I made in your lives." His shoulders slumped. "If anything, I keep making it worse."

Shannon didn't say anything, then finally whispered, "I can't believe Mom started things with you when you were still married."

"Your mom was a wonderful woman, Shannon. Don't let one mistake ruin your good opinion of her."

Shannon sat up, her emotions spilling over. "One mistake? We're talking about *me* here! I wasn't wanted by either of you, and I forced you two together when you would have been better off apart."

"Shannon—"

"Enough, Kevin! *Leave me alone!*"

Kevin slowly backed toward the door, despair etched into his features.

"I'm sorry, Shannon. I really am very sorry," he said quietly, then closed the door.

Shannon curled herself in a tight ball and cried.

Hadn't Kevin done enough damage? Now he had taken the last thing she had to cling to.

Her mother.

Chapter Fourteen

Once her tears were spent, Shannon allowed herself to think about Kurt. She hadn't expected him to kiss her. It had been incredible. He was no novice, that was sure. She wondered how her response rated. Probably pretty lame since she hadn't had a clue what she was doing. She could still feel his hands in every place they had touched her body. And his lips... He'd tasted of cinnamon, just how he smelled. He must suck cinnamon candies all day in preparation of a chance with a girl.

Was that what she'd been? An opportunity?

She groaned and rolled over to bury her face in the pillow.

In one night she'd found out her Mom had had an affair with Kevin and she had been an unwanted baby, and Kurt had kissed her for whatever reason. Life couldn't get much more complex.

All she knew was she had always been unwanted, and tonight, wrapped in Kurt's arms, she'd felt more wanted than she knew possible.

She wished she could talk to Brittni, tell her everything, especially about Kurt. If only stupid Kevin hadn't taken away her phone, she'd call her right now, late as it was.

Flopping onto her back, she stared at the ceiling, shoving Kurt to the recesses of her brain.

Mom.

How could she?

Being an unplanned child wasn't the end of the world. Shannon had known friends who had been "oops" babies. But they had always been wanted. Whereas she wasn't even supposed to *be*. Her existence was a mistake, a symbol of her father's philandering and her mother's shameless disrespect.

Right now Shannon hated her mom every bit as much as Kevin.

She skipped school the next day. Made all the stops—daycare, elementary, high school—then turned around and came home. She didn't give a flying fig what Kevin would do when he found out. She spent most of the day watching TV and eating chocolate. She yearned to call Alan, but even if she'd had her phone, she wasn't sure if she would. What if he didn't know about Mom's affair? She didn't want to be the one to tell him.

After she did her afternoon round of pick-ups and gave the kiddoes a snack, she brought Daniel upstairs and put on a *Thomas the Train* video in the sitting room for him. She retreated to her room for homework, leaving the door cracked. Not ten minutes later it creaked open, and she looked up, expecting Daniel.

Instead it was Kurt, filling up the doorway with his broad shoulders. The sleeves of his grey long-sleeve T-shirt were pushed up to his elbows, exposing some of the most manly, muscley forearms known to mankind.

Shannon felt her face warming as he crossed the room to where she was sprawled on the bed. She didn't know what to say to him after last night.

"I sneaked away from Andy to check on you. I worried about you all night. You were really upset yesterday."

All she could do was nod. Her heart was pounding too hard in her chest for much else. She pushed herself up until her back was against the wall. Reaching out, Kurt ran the back of his fingers down her arm, and she couldn't stop the tremor that followed.

"Are you better now?" His deep voice sounded sincere as his dark eyes probed hers. Shannon needed to keep her head.

"Can I ask you a question?"

"Shoot."

She cleared her throat. "Why did you kiss me yesterday?"

A half-smile tugged at his lips, just smug enough to show he knew exactly how much his kiss had affected her. "Because you were crying, and I wanted to make you stop."

"Oh." So it had just been a diversion for her? A pleasant one, certainly, but was there nothing more to it?

"Why'd you kiss me back?"

His question hung in the air until Shannon tilted her head shyly. "Because it was my first kiss."

He jolted and stared at her face as if expecting a "just kidding." When she simply gazed back, his Adam's apple bobbed as he swallowed. His eyebrows rose and fell as he internalized something, then his face narrowed with purpose, and he put a knee down on the bed in front of her.

"So now I have a question." His voice was low, and he leaned over, planting his arms on either side of her. Shannon trembled at his nearness. "If I kissed you again..." His cinnamony breath fanned across her cheek. "Would you kiss me back again?"

She only took a split-second to make up her mind, raising her face to his.

"Yes." The whispered word left her lips, and Kurt's mouth immediately replaced it. The intensity of his lips gave her such a rush to the head that she could barely keep up. He was different than yesterday. Not rough, but...aggressive. She could scarcely breathe as he moved from her mouth to her neck, to her chest and back again. He slid his hands into her hair on either side of her head and groaned, a sound of want so strong it terrified her. Her body tingled as he pulled her against him and trailed his fingers up and down her back. She had never experienced anything this electrifying. The feelings coursing through her body were entirely new. And overwhelming.

His lips found hers again, and he gave her a passionate kiss that sent her head spinning out of control. She pulled back, needing some air. He was breathing heavily as he looked at her, his blueberry eyes glowing with desire.

Shannon drank in a deep, fortifying breath of air, wishing for space to think, but she was trapped in his arms.

"Why'd you kiss me that time?" she asked, leaning her head back as far as possible to see his face.

He considered her with a soft smile. "Because I like you. I really like you." The way he drawled out the *really* turned Shannon's stomach inside out.

"Oh." Had he really liked all the other girls he'd...been with? She wanted to ask but had a feeling that would make him mad. She hoped he wouldn't ask why she'd kissed him back again. 'Cause she didn't have an answer.

He leaned in and gave her a last, lingering kiss.

"I better go before Andy sends a K-9 unit," he sighed beside her ear and slowly edged away. "See you later." He dropped a kiss on top of her head as he stood, then backed to the door, looking at her longingly the whole time.

When he was gone, Shannon collapsed back onto the bed, feeling overwhelmed and slightly giddy. Kurt certainly knew how to escalate things quickly, and at this rate, she knew where he was headed. Her stomach tightened. Did she want that, too?

* * *

The slap of the basketball echoed between the house and garage as Kurt's fingers fell, missing the ball by a foot. He couldn't concentrate for anything after his detour to Shannon's bedroom. He bit back a smile remembering the way her body had trembled against his. She had yet to verbalize her feelings about him, but her reaction was strong.

Andy crouched to retrieve the rolling ball. "Dude, where's your head?"

Kurt shrugged it off, mumbling about being tired. If Andy knew, he'd slam the ball into Kurt's head. Then tackle him.

"Come on." Andy slapped him on the back. "Let's go grab a drink in the house."

He followed his friend into the kitchen, where they were greeted by a delicious aroma. Shannon was bent over checking the source of the fabulous smell in the oven, and Kurt admired her backside.

"What's for dinner, Shan?" Andy asked, searching the fridge.

"My own creation. I'm calling it broccoli chicken alfredo rice." She straightened and turned around, then froze at the sight of Kurt. Pink instantly tinged her cheeks, and Kurt hoped Andy was too busy guzzling iced tea to notice.

"Hey," her soft voice reached out to him, but he only winked until Andy headed down the hall for the restroom.

Shannon moved to the counter where a salad was half made and continued chopping at a celery stalk. Kurt followed her and leaned his back against the counter beside her.

She tilted her head to the side and shot him a shy glance. "You're welcome to stay for dinner."

Kurt stared at her beautiful face. Had he really just kissed her two hours ago? This ravishing girl?

He leaned as close to her as he dared, his voice a low rumble. "You're an amazing cook, but there's still nothing in this kitchen more tasty than you."

He knew it was cheesy, but her cheeks flamed with color just the same, and her eyes flickered to his face and away again. A soft giggle escaped her mouth before Andy's steel voice blasted across the room, "Shannon, can I have a word with you?"

Oh crap. Kurt didn't even look up as Shannon scuttled across the room. Krakatau was about to blow.

* * *

"Shannon." Andy's hard voice sounded just like Kevin. He drilled his eyes into her. "What did Kurt do to you?"

She hesitated, seeing Kurt leave the kitchen out of her peripheral vision.

"He kissed me."

She was surprised at the anger etched into Andy's face.

"Just once?"

"No..."

"You realize what he's after, right?"

She nodded, dropping her eyes.

"Have—have you ever been with a guy, Shannon?"

Humiliation made her dizzy as heat rushed to her face. She met Andy's eyes and saw only concern and protectiveness.

She shook her head.

Andy blew air from his mouth and rubbed his fingers down his chin. "You sure you want Kurt to be your first?"

She couldn't believe she was having this talk with Andy. If her face got any hotter, it was going to scar.

"I don't know," she said in a small voice.

Silence stretched between them.

"Shannon, don't."

She slipped a fist to her hip. "Why not? You think you're better than Kurt? I know you do the same thing."

He drew his head back, then lowered it. "No, I'm just as bad. What I mean is, I don't respect the girls who...who just...give themselves to me. But I respect *you*. If you give yourself away like that, for no good reason other than one night of fun, then that's all you are—one night of fun. But you're so much more than that."

Shannon stared at her brother, moved by his words. Boy, did she have some thinking to do. If only Mom were still...

Ugh. Mom.

Nope, she wasn't going there again.

* * *

Kurt waited in Andy's apartment for the impending volcanic eruption.

"Kurt!" He was roaring already. Andy jerked open the door and glowered at Kurt from the doorway. "I told you to stay away from my sister. You are never touching her again, so help me God." He slammed the door behind him and stepped right into Kurt's personal space.

Kurt backed up a step. "Hey, slow down. It was just a kiss, man."

"Yeah, well I know where all your kisses lead."

"She kissed me back. I didn't force her to."

Andy slammed his head into his hand with a groan. "You *do* know she's a virgin, right? I hate to talk that way about my own sister, but you leave me no choice."

This slowed Kurt down. "Yeah, I figured that out when she said it was her first kiss."

"Okay, fine, you gave her her first kiss. Let that be enough. Seriously. Shannon deserves better than a one-night stand, or even a two-week fling. She's been through enough junk. Do you have any idea how much more you would mess her up?"

Kurt jutted his chin out stubbornly. "I don't want a one-night stand with her, or a two-week fling. I want to date her."

Andy froze. "You want to *what* her?"

"You heard me. I want to date her. You know, go out with her."

"I know what date means, you idiot. Since when do you date?"

"Since I met your sister."

"And what if her version of dating does not include sex?" Andy spat out the question.

Kurt opened his mouth. He hadn't thought of that. "I'll...I'll respect that."

"Oh right." Sarcasm oozed from Andy's voice. "You're going to become abstinent to date Shannon?"

"Well... I, uh, don't...ah, mmmm..."

"Exactly. You'd either pressure her into it way before she's ready, or more likely, you'd be cheating on her all the time. You think I'm going to let that happen? My sister deserves so much more than that, Kurt. So if you don't want me to mess with your pretty boy face, then I suggest you stop messing with Shannon."

Andy stormed back out the door, leaving Kurt alone in his apartment alone. He groaned and flopped face-down onto the couch. He *had* been shocked when Shannon said their kiss yesterday had been her first. She had seemed hesitant, but not clueless. Letting reality sink in was taking some time. She hadn't been with a guy. At all. He knew he could never deserve her. But he wanted her just the same.

Chapter Fifteen

"I missed you yesterday," Jesse offered lightly, taking a bite of his sandwich. They were having lunch together as had become their custom that week. "Everything alright? You look sad."

Shannon blinked back tears. Everything was most certainly not alright. She moaned into her hands. "No. I really need advice from my mom. I feel lost without her." The bile of betrayal rose in her throat. "But now I don't know if I'd even talk to her if I could."

Jesse set his sandwich down. "Shannon, what's going on?" His voice was filled with concern. Should she tell him? He had proved himself a friend. She needed to talk to *someone* before she lost her mind.

"Oh, Jesse, it's terrible!" The words spilled from her mouth before she could stop them. She poured everything out, holding no horrific detail back from her discovery this week. The bell rang, signifying the end of lunch, but Jesse didn't flinch. Shannon felt her emotions bubbling to the surface and paused to pull herself together.

"How could my mom do that? I always looked up to her because she was everything my lousy father wasn't. But now I find out she was just as bad! *Now* what am I supposed to do?" She dropped her head down onto her arm where it was thrown across the table top. "I wasn't even supposed to be born."

"Shannon! Of course you were!"

"No, Jesse." She flung her head back up. "Haven't you heard anything I said? If they had made good choices, I wouldn't even *be* here. My whole existence is a mistake."

"Don't say that." Jesse's voice clogged with emotion. "*No one* is ever a mistake. God can take people's bad choices and turn them into something wonderful. Beautiful." He looked at her earnestly, and Shannon tried to grab on to what he was saying, sensing it might save her life. "Your parents made a mistake, and God turned it into *you*. You're a *miracle*—not a mistake."

She felt tears slide down her cheeks. "How do you know that?"

"Because God doesn't make mistakes." He sounded so sure, and Shannon wanted to believe him. But there was a first for everything, even God, right? Her doubts must have shown on her face, because Jesse leaned across the table intently.

"You're an artist. Do you paint?"

Shannon huffed a laugh. "Better than I draw."

"Okay, then don't tell me this has never happened: you're busy painting , diligently trying to keep all your different paint dollops separate on the palette, but two of them slide together anyway. And instead of a mess, they turn into a beautiful new shade that you never would have thought up. That's what you are, Shannon. A new shade of paint."

Tears poured down Shannon's face. Was that what she was? A new shade of paint? Destined to illustrate in a color no one else could?

Jesse reached across the table and squeezed her arm. "Do you have any idea how much God loves you?"

"No, but you're giving me hope."

The smile that lit his face could have won an award. "Good. Hey, we better get to class." He handed her a stack of napkins and cleared their trays while she mopped her face.

"Thank you for sharing with me," he said, looking down at her as they walked to English. "What advice did you need from your mom?"

"Well..." She nibbled her lip. "Maybe you can help. A neutral party may give better advice."

Jesse came to a standstill in the deserted hallway and turned around. "Okay."

Shannon suddenly felt awkward and knew she was blushing. "My brother has a friend who comes over a lot—"

"Kurt?"

"Of course you know." She laughed nervously. "Claywood. Small town. Yes, Kurt. Anyway, he said he likes me, and, well, he kissed me the other day, and it was my first kiss. I'm not sure what I should do or how I feel..."

She had rushed through the words, but she trailed off as Jesse's expression transformed, pure jealousy smeared on his face like engine grease.

He liked her!

He seemed to realize he'd been caught, because his neck started glowing, and he ducked his head. He coughed, then asked without looking up, "Do you know what kind of guy Kurt is?"

"Yes," she replied, barely audible even to herself.

"And...you're okay with that?"

"I don't know," she sighed. "That's why I needed to talk to my mom. That's why I talked to you."

He started walking again. "I can't tell you what to do, Shannon. That's a decision you have to make for yourself. I will only say that you deserve someone who's interested in what he can do for you—not just what you can do for him." Jesse's jaw clenched tightly, and Shannon knew he was more upset than he was letting on.

* * *

After a long Sunday clearing out the remnants of the pumpkin patch, Kurt was exhausted. He had come down with a cold a couple days ago, and his sinuses were badly congested. A cough had slowly moved down and settled in his chest halfway through last night, and he hadn't gotten much sleep after that. Today had been damp, drizzling on and off, and he had worked outside in soaked clothes for the past three hours. By the time he got home, his whole body racked with chills. His mom was in the kitchen making dinner when he slopped his way through.

"Kurt, you're drenched! Why did you stay out so long? You're already sick." She put her hand against his forehead. "And now you have a fever. Good job, kiddo."

He nodded miserably. "I better go change."

"Please, and put all those wet things straight into the washer. Then come back here. I've got hot soup and dumplings waiting for you."

He smiled in spite of the hammering in his head. Mom took good care of him. Two bowls of soup and three ibuprofen later, he was feeling a little better. Enough to head next door. Andy hadn't reached out to him since he'd chewed him out last Thursday, so he hadn't seen Shannon, either. And that was unacceptable.

He slipped through the Conrads' side door and found her as usual in the kitchen, cleaning up from dinner. Andy was bent over loading the dishwasher, his back toward Kurt. Shannon wore hot pink pajama pants and a cozy black sweater, her hair pulled up in a messy bun, and all Kurt could think of was sweeping her into his arms. But because Andy was there and Kurt valued his life, he threw her a wink instead and enjoyed watching her face turn scarlet.

"Hi," she said softly, ducking her head.

Andy whipped around. "Hey, man, I didn't know you were coming. We're just about finished, and then we can hang at my place."

"Oh, no rush." Kurt leaned against the entry frame, content to watch Shannon, but Andy had other plans.

"You sound sick, " he said, throwing darts at him with his eyes. "Maybe you should go home."

Kurt didn't have a chance to respond before Andy plunged on.

"Shannon, why don't you check on Gabby and Daniel? I'll have this done in a few minutes."

Kurt couldn't control his eye-roll. Andy was trying to get them as far from each other as possible. What a busy body.

Shannon didn't say anything as she headed toward where Kurt still stood. He took a step backward into the hall to let her out. As soon as she was past the entryway—and out of Andy's line of sight—he grabbed her hand. He just needed to touch her. Gently he rubbed his thumb back and forth across her knuckles, enjoying the softness of her skin. Looking into her eyes, more green than blue in the darkened hall, he felt the ocean current trying to pull him in.

She stood there looking at him with fascination—and fear. It hit Kurt that if she'd never been with a guy, this was totally new and possibly terrifying. He let go of her hand and reached to trace the side of her face with the back of his finger. Her tremulous smile assured him. She'd catch on. And he'd go as slow as she needed in order to keep her.

"Kurt, what are you doing to my sister?"

Shannon jumped back like a cricket in reverse at Andy's harsh voice and tore off into the living room. Kurt slowly reappeared in the kitchen, failing to meet Andy's eyes. He waited silently until Andy started the dishwasher, the rush of water signaling that the lecture was about to begin. Andy did an about-face and pinned him with a dark look.

He jerked a head toward the door, and Kurt followed him out and across the yard to the stairs on the side of the garage leading up to Andy's apartment. Kurt didn't say a word once they entered the small space, waiting on Andy.

"Kurt, you're not listening to me." He sounded frustrated as he pulled out a kitchenette chair and plunked down. Kurt sat across from him at the small table, hoping for a reasonable discussion. "You really like her? Or she's just your latest find?"

Indignation erupted inside Kurt—along with guilt—but he fought it down. "I really like her," he confirmed, holding Andy's gaze. Andy grimaced and shook his head, then stood abruptly and crossed the room to the sink, filling a glass with water. He downed it in a few seconds.

"Want any?"

Kurt shook his head. "No, I'm fine."

Andy jammed his body back onto the chair and leaned forward intently. "Look, man. Shannon's been through a lot, and lately it got even worse. It's not my place to tell you details, but I know she's feeling insecure, betrayed, and alone. It's natural she would be looking for someone to latch onto, and I swear, if that person is you—I'm just telling you now, if you take advantage of my sister—after all she's been through—you're choosing to end *our* friendship."

Kurt leaned back in his chair slowly. He felt as if he barely knew his best friend lately. "Dude, when did you become so... so serious?"

Andy leaned his forehead against his fist, his elbow propped on the table top. "Honestly, Kurt, seeing how my dad's actions have...have..." he snapped his fingers, finding the word, "*damaged* my sisters, well, it's made me think—a lot. About *my* actions." He shrugged, squinting at Kurt. "I don't know if I'm making sense. I only know I don't want to hurt people the way my dad has. He has too many regrets."

Kurt was at a loss. He hadn't ever thought as seriously about what he was doing as Andy seemed to be. He didn't *want* to.

Standing up, he paced around Andy's tiny studio, unable to stop the sigh that fell out of him. His life had never seemed complicated. Until Shannon. She had turned his world sideways, and he didn't know what to think anymore. Except that he wanted to spend every waking moment with her. If only he could.

* * *

When Shannon fled the kitchen, she was left with no doubt about why Kurt hadn't shown his face the past four days. She was just uncertain enough about where things were headed with him that she hadn't asked Andy to mind his business. Yet.

Maybe it was a blessing Kevin had taken her phone. And every other electronic in the house. She had no access to social media or any form of online communication during her grounding, and while not being able to talk to her faraway family members and friends was driving her crazy, she had a strong suspicion that Kurt would have been pursuing her via online venues. He was persistent, and so far Andy's ire hadn't done much to slow him down.

She was glad he'd come tonight. And scared. He wasn't giving up. She couldn't begin to describe the feelings he stirred in her. As if he had thrown her a lifeline, but she was afraid to grab on with both hands.

Brittni had always told Shannon she thought too much, but she now realized it might be because neither of her parents had ever thought *enough*.

Whatever she did with Kurt, she wanted it to be well thought out.

Whatever she did. Because right now she had no idea what that might be.

"I'm so bored I'm going crazy!" Laura's screech made Shannon jump where she had paused in the living room, consumed by her thoughts. Her sister stomped through the living room angrily. She'd been getting more unbearable by the day in the week since their grounding. "I'm going to lose my mind, and you'll have to put me in a mental institution. I hope you'll be happy then, Kevin!"

"You'll be fine, Laura," Kevin's calm voice came from the family room where he was watching television. "I'm not worried."

Laura flipped him off to his back.

"Laura!" Shannon gasped. "That's not nice!"

"Neither is he!" She whirled around. "Why'd you have to go and snitch on me, huh? Why couldn't you mind your business for once?"

Shannon raised her eyebrows slowly, narrowing her eyes. She'd had it.

"Mind my business? I covered for you for a week and half so you wouldn't get caught. I'd say it *was* my business. And I didn't snitch. You did yourself in by skipping Kevin's party. He's not stupid, Laura. If I hadn't lied for you in the first place, I wouldn't be grounded right now." She glared at Laura. "The whole world isn't about you, you know." She turned her back and took the stairs two at a time, slamming her bedroom door when she got inside.

A few minutes later a timid knock sounded, then Laura's wobbly voice through the door: "I'm sorry, Shannon. I'm sorry I've been so awful to you..."

Shannon scowled and opened the door. Laura's whole face was quivering as tears clogged her eyes.

"Please don't be mad at me. You're all I've got. We have to stick together."

"Oh yeah? Well I've been pretty much on my own for the past few weeks." Shannon crossed her arms, trying to harden herself, but it was difficult with Laura melting into a puddle in front of her.

"I know. I'm sorry. I'm just—" Laura wiped at her face and sniffed. "I miss Mom so much. It's hard to get used to her being gone."

Shannon ground her teeth together and looked away, thinking of all the things Laura didn't know. Should she shatter her view of their mom, too, or leave it intact? After all, Laura had been the wanted child, and she was suffering enough already.

She released a big sigh and dropped her arms. "It's okay. I know it's been a hard adjustment, and I probably haven't been as much help to you as I should. I'm sorry, too."

Laura threw her arms around Shannon and squeezed her hard. "It's not your fault. You're too busy."

Shannon didn't reply as she returned Laura's hug, happier than she was willing to admit to have her sister back on speaking terms.

She tossed and turned much of the night, tormented by uncertainty about Kurt. She still couldn't focus at lunch while Jesse talked her through pre-calc, which she had dismally misunderstood on Friday. She growled and scribbled frantically with the eraser as she made the same mistake for the fourth time.

"Shannon." Jesse's hand closed over her fingers, forcing her to stop before she rubbed a hole in the worksheet. His voice was frustrated but gentle. "Is there anything I can do for you?"

She looked up to find his ever-deep brown eyes searching hers with concern and—and a little something more. She knew he wasn't talking about pre-calc help.

"Oh, Jesse, I don't know..." She plopped her chin into her hands. Could she explain to him that she was trying to decide whether or not to give herself to Kurt, regardless of the results or his intentions? What did it matter anyway? Nobody cared what she did.

"Shannon, I care about you. You're my friend and—"

"Have you ever had sex?" she blurted, then felt an instant fever rise in her face. She covered her eyes with her hand, mortified, and gasped, "I am *so* sorry, I did not mean to ask that."

Jesse chuckled, and Shannon peaked at him through her fingers, unable to resist his laugh. His neck was red, but he answered evenly, "No, I haven't. Why do you ask?"

She slid her hand down to her chin again and clasped it. "I don't know. Seems like everyone's doing it."

"Not everyone. Less than you'd think in fact. But the ones who are get a lot of attention."

She swallowed hard and dragged her eyes to meet his. She knew exactly who he was thinking about. The same guy she was.

"Look, Shannon." Jesse's eyes offered complete acceptance. They told her that no matter what she chose, he was still going to be there for her. She was pretty sure he liked her, yet he wasn't condemning her for thinking about possibly getting involved with another guy. "It's not always easy to stand for what's right."

Shannon felt her forehead crinkle. She hadn't thought of what might be right or wrong. She just wasn't sure what she wanted.

"I don't get it. If no one else is worried about doing what's right, who's to say what *is* right?"

"God," Jesse said softly. There was something so sure about his eyes that Shannon felt chills shiver down her spine.

"God?"

"Of course. He's my creator. I'm accountable to Him for all my actions."

The bell rang, saving Shannon from a response. She was going to have to think on this one. Kevin sure didn't act like he was accountable to anyone for anything he did.

More confused than when she'd started the day, she decided to confide in Stephanie during P.E. about Kurt and Jesse both.

"Jesse's so old fashioned. Accountable to God? Give me a break. As if God really has an opinion about what we're doing." Stephanie lowered her voice. "Seriously, if you want to hook up with Kurt, that's nobody's business but yours. That's between you and Kurt, and it doesn't impact anyone else."

"But Jesse was talking about right and wrong—"

Stephanie laughed sarcastically. "That's for *you* to decide. No one else can tell you what's right or wrong for you!"

Shannon thought this over. "Yeah, but what if *I* think it's right for me to kill someone. Does that make it right?"

"Well now you're being ridiculous. Obviously that's wrong."

Shannon sighed. If some things were obviously wrong, then what about the things that weren't so obvious? She was still perplexed by the time pre-calculus started, sitting at her desk with her lower lip protruding in confusion. Jesse drummed his fingers on her desk to catch her attention. She found his dimples in place.

He tapped his temple. "Still thinking hard, I see."

Was she ever. Stephanie had said that if she had sex with Kurt, it would have no impact on anyone else. But was that true? She thought about Mom's decision to be intimate with Kevin once upon a time. She probably had thought something similar. It wasn't going to affect anyone else. But look at the train wreck that had followed. Still followed...

"Jesse, what do you do when you're confused about life?"

He shrugged casually as he settled into his seat. "I pray."

"Pray?" Shannon wasn't sure she'd heard right.

"Yep. Pray. God doesn't answer with lightning bolts, but sometimes He leads me to the answer in obvious ways. Other times He's more subtle. That's why you gotta listen."

Shannon stared at him. Who *was* this guy?

After class, he walked out to the Explorer with her.

"Does praying make you know what's right and wrong?" Shannon leaned her back against the driver's door, squinting up at him.

"Well..." He tilted his head in thought. "God's word makes those things pretty clear. But I do pray for God to keep me on track. It's easy to do something wrong and think it's okay."

Shannon cleared her throat. "Where does sex fall into this?" She willed her cheeks not to redden. It felt so awkward talking to Jesse about this, but she really wanted—needed—his answer.

"I believe sex should be saved for marriage. That's what God created it for."

He said it so simply. But it didn't seem simple. She thought of her dad. Her mom. Andy. Kurt. Stephanie. Myriad others who hadn't linked sex with marriage. Were they all doing something wrong?

"Shannon, I know that's pretty heavy, and you have…a lot… on your mind." He gently grabbed her shoulder. "But just remember, what you do—right or wrong—does not define you. Just like what your parents did, while wrong, does not define you."

Tears threatened her eyes "Then what does?"

"God." His grip on her loosened, but he held on. "God defines who you are—because He made you. There is nothing you can do to make Him love you more—or less. With human relationships, as you get to know someone, you grow to love them more. Not so with God—He loves you completely from day one. No matter what you do. There is nothing you can do to make God love you less, Shannon, and stop seeing you as the *perfect* shade of paint He created." Jesse's eyes shined with emotion as he squeezed her shoulder and let go. He took a slow step back. "I'll see you tomorrow, okay?"

Shannon watched him walk away, her mind reeling from his words. Was God really at the core of it all? The big and the small?

Chapter Sixteen

That afternoon Daniel started coming down with something. His forehead was warm, and congestion rattled as he snuggled against Shannon, falling asleep in her arms on the couch. She rested her chin on top of his head and closed her eyes. Grades had come out today, and her report card was dismal. Pre-calc had dropped to a low D without consistent tutoring. Ms. Ellison had given her an F in Spanish because she was behind. English was a D, too, just because she sucked at it. Everything else was a C, except art.

"Shannon." Her eyes sprang open at the deep voice. Kurt stood at the edge of the living room, gazing at her with Daniel in her arms, a tender expression on his face. "You are so beautiful."

Her face warmed as he came closer, butterflies of uncertainty fluttering inside her body.

"I came to drop off a bushel of apples. I set them on the counter." He gestured toward the kitchen. "Figured with your amazing culinary skills, you'd make good use of them."

"Aww, thanks," Shannon said softly, not wanting to wake up Daniel. "That was sweet of you." She debated what to say next, not sure she should voice her thought. Kurt just stood there, looking down at her with smoldering eyes. She could feel his desire tangibly.

He began slowly backing away, fists clenched at his sides. "I have to get back to work."

She tilted her head as she watched him and said exactly what she knew she shouldn't. "If you wanna come over later for dessert, I'll be sure to do something with those apples by then."

He gave her such a knowing look that she had to drop her eyes. "I'd *love* to come over later."

About eight o'clock Shannon decided to put away the crumb-topped apple pie she had made, half relieved, half remorseful that Kurt hadn't shown up. But as she pulled out the plastic wrap, the side door creaked open and closed. A few seconds later Kurt strutted into the kitchen, and Shannon felt her relief and remorse collide. Jesse's words spun through her head at a dizzying speed.

"There you are!" She hated the way her stomach was clenching up like a fist.

" 'Course! I wouldn't pass up a chance at your cooking." He winked at her. "Or a minute with you." He sidled up to her until his arm was touching her shoulder. As Shannon served up a piece of pie, her hand shook so much that the topping started to avalanche.

Kurt wrapped his hand around hers and helped her dump the piece onto a plate. "Girl, you need to *relaaaax*. I didn't know I make you that nervous." He straightened his shoulders smugly, then slung an arm around her neck and tugged her to the breakfast bar with him. Hopping onto a bar stool, he pulled the next one over and motioned for Shannon to sit. His thigh pressed against hers as he tested his first bite.

"This pie is incredible. Have you ever thought of going to culinary school?" He shoveled another fork-full into his mouth, closing his eyes with a satisfied sigh.

Actually, she'd thought of it a few times. Before Mom died. But now... She didn't want to talk about it. She shrugged her shoulder, brushing his arm. "Maybe. I have no idea what I'll be doing next year."

They sat in silence as he finished the pie. When he set his fork down, he looked at her.

"Where is everyone else?" The intensity in his blue eyes told Shannon why he was asking.

She could tell him that Kevin might be coming down any minute. That Andy was going to be coming in for some pie, too. But she told him the truth.

"Andy's in his apartment. Said he has a ton of homework and we won't see him till morning. Kevin is upstairs getting Gabby and Daniel ready for bed. He just went up. Laura's hibernating in her room as always."

"I see."

"You done with that?" She grabbed his plate and headed toward the sink, suddenly afraid. Why had she told him the truth? Why hadn't she said Kevin might be down any minute? That Andy wanted pie too?

He followed behind her, and then his hands slid around her hips. Her breath hitched at the intimate move as he pulled her so close that her back pressed snugly against his chest. Every nerve in her body screamed a response to Kurt's touch as he bent to shower a trail of kisses all over her neck. She smiled at the pure delight of the sensation, shivers descending down her back like rainfall.

Slowly he spun her around, kissing her neck until she was facing him. Her pulse raced recklessly as she wrapped her arms around his solid frame, enjoying the feel of his back muscles rippling beneath her hands. She looked at him when he straightened and found his eyes fierce with emotions. He leaned her back in his arms.

"I'm still sick. I don't want to get you sick."

That was her cue to get rid of him. But...

"I don't care." She was mesmerized by the hungry look in his eyes as his gaze dropped to her lips.

He stopped an inch from her face and murmured, "I know this is all new to you, so if I start going too fast, just tell me to slow down. I promise I won't hurt you."

He came down firm, tilting his head as their lips met. The result left Shannon's mind cartwheeling through space. Only this time, he didn't stop like the other times. He kept going and going until Shannon felt like she'd landed in a place she'd never been before and never wanted to leave. His fingers were trailing her face, down her neck and chest, and—

Kurt's hand was inside her shirt and touching her in a place she'd definitely not been touched before.

She pulled back quickly, embarrassed. "Too fast?" she squeaked, knowing her face was probably flaming.

"Okay, okay." He took a deep breath and retreated a step. He stared at her, a small smile playing across his lips. "I can't get enough of you, Shannon. You're good."

What he meant was, for having so little experience, she was catching on quickly. Which brought a rather unpleasant thought. Kurt had done the same routine with many girls. It probably didn't mean anything to him. He was just being patient until he could get what he really wanted. But did Shannon want that, too?

Honestly, she wasn't sure. She did love the feeling of being in his arms, like she was right now as he pulled her into a tight hug. He held her for a few minutes, gently rubbing the small of her back in slow circles. Then he tipped her head back, holding the side of her face with his hand, and gave her a tender kiss, one she happily returned.

"I need to go," he breathed as he released her slowly. He couldn't seem to let go of her hand, pulling her along with him to the side door. She followed him out onto the porch, where he turned unexpectedly and gave her one last and long, mind-altering kiss. Out of breath, she pushed him away laughingly.

"*Go*. Or I'll never get rid of you."

He grinned in his irresistible way and trotted down the steps. On his way to his truck, he turned around about five times, as if he couldn't bear to stop looking at her. Shannon shook her head. Men and their moony ways.

It was only after he had begun driving away that she looked up and saw Andy standing in the doorway of his apartment, arms crossed. She sucked in her breath. How much had he seen…exactly?

* * *

Kurt rolled his window down as he drove home, needing to air out his head. He may have pushed it a little far with Shannon tonight. He just wasn't used to going this slow, but he needed to be patient. It would happen sooner or later. And at the rate they were going, it would happen sooner *rather* than later.

He grinned as he remembered the way Shannon had responded to him. She couldn't resist him.

As he was pulling into the garage, his cell phone dinged. He put the truck in park and turned off the engine before picking up the phone. Not surprisingly, it was a text from Andy. He groaned, wanting to ignore it. *i saw that, man. ur not listening 2 me. i told u 2 stay away from her. i no its her choice, but dude, u need 2 give her space 2 figure this out. got it?*

He'd give her space, alright. So much space she'd be desperate enough to say yes to his next question.

* * *

After Kurt left, Shannon quickly put the pie away and headed upstairs. She had tons of homework, and all she could do was think about Kurt and kisses. Settling down at her desk, she opened her notebook and stared at the blank page.

A knock on her door startled her.

"Come in."

Andy appeared, and she instantly blushed and looked away.

"You were right in front of the kitchen window. I happened to be enjoying fresh air on my little porch. Something about the dark makes anything happening inside a lit room *really* clear."

Shannon flickered her eyes up at him. "So you saw everything?"

"I did." He sank onto the edge of her bed. "Shannon, I need to know if this is something you want. Because Kurt's not going to keep stopping. One of these times he's going to keep going. Is that what you want?"

Shannon swallowed hard at the lump in her throat. She was so confused.

"I don't know." It came out a tiny whisper, and Andy reached over and took one of her hands.

"I know I'm the last one who should be advising you. But I don't want you to get hurt or have regrets. Understand?"

She nodded.

He squeezed her hand and stood up to go. He paused at the door. "I asked Kurt to give you some space. I don't know how much he'll give. So I suggest you think on things pretty hard to figure out what you want."

She thought on it half the night and ended up more exhausted than ever by morning.

If she said no to Kurt, she was probably going to lose him. He'd move on to someone easier, right?

Why would she give her virginity to him? Just because he had given her her first kiss? It wasn't like he had given her anything special. It had just been another kiss to him. Another kiss in a long line of kisses with dozens of girls.

But he liked her. He'd said so. Was he being genuine?

She genuinely liked him. But that much?

She groaned aloud in government class and clasped her aching head. She'd already failed the quiz.

Jesse was deathly quiet during lunch, and Shannon made no attempts to break the silence. Why didn't he speak up? If he liked her, even a little, it seemed he would say something. Just tell her not to sleep with Kurt. Give her one good reason not to, and she wouldn't. But he said nothing.

Wednesday afternoon she called Todd and Brittni. She hoped Kevin had a long-distance plan on the house phone, but if he didn't, it'd serve him right for taking away her cell phone.

In hypothetical terms she described the situation to her brother. He was living with his girlfriend and had been for two years. Mom had never criticized his decision, and Shannon hadn't given it much thought. Seemed most people lived together before they got married, if they got married at all. It was no big deal. Except to Jesse with his weird ideas.

Todd left her confused. He, of course, had seen right through her words and asked if she was talking about herself. She couldn't deny it. His advice had been simple. If it's what you want to do, then go for it, but be smart about it. Use protection. If you're not sure, wait until you are.

He didn't tell her anything she hadn't already come up with on her own.

Brittni was even worse. Rather than caution of any kind, she started shrieking into the phone excitedly that Shannon was going to get laid. Shannon drew the phone back and stared at it. What was wrong with her?

She hung up no more enlightened than she had been before the two conversations. Like Andy had said, this had to be her decision.

* * *

Shannon settled down at the piano Saturday afternoon. It had been a long week. Tonight she'd get her phone back. Kurt's silence was killing her. Three days. It felt like three months. And she still hadn't figured anything out.

Plunking aimlessly at the keys until a tune started to find itself, she settled into the rhythm, making it up as she went. She'd been playing for twenty minutes when she heard a noise. She stopped in the middle of her song and swiveled around to find Kurt standing behind her.

"How long have you been here?"

"Long enough." He eased his hands onto her shoulders. "You play beautifully."

"Thanks." She smiled up into his blueberry eyes. Her heart started pounding as he slid onto the piano bench beside her.

"I've missed you," he whispered, then ran his finger along her hairline, tucking a few loose strands behind her ear. "Have I told you how beautiful you are?" He leaned in and kissed her temple. Shannon trembled at his touch.

"I was wondering if you'd go out with me." His voice was soft, his face hovering an inch from hers.

What was he asking her? "You mean, on a date?"

"Sure. If that's what you want."

Shannon was confused. She didn't think he did dates.

"What...what do *you* want, Kurt?"

"I want you to be my girlfriend," he said hoarsely, then leaned his forehead against hers. "Please say yes..."

She was stunned. From what everyone said, Kurt Blake didn't date girls. He didn't have girlfriends. He just hooked up and that was that.

Warmth spread through Shannon's body. She must be really special. Kurt was willing to give up all the other girls for her?

She forced herself to think as he began kissing her neck. She knew what he'd expect out of his girlfriend. On a regular basis. Something that Stephanie and Todd thought perfectly natural in a dating relationship. Something Jesse felt quite differently about.

Was it really wrong like Jesse said?

If her whole existence was a mistake, who cared if it was wrong?

Out of the corner of her eye, she caught sight of the painting above the piano. Bright splashes of color. Jesse's words seared her mind. A new shade of paint. She wasn't a mistake.

She scooted away from Kurt. She still wasn't sure if it was wrong or not, but she wasn't willing to take the risk. She wasn't going to go any farther until she was sure.

"Shannon, what?" Confusion creased Kurt's handsome face.

"I'm sorry, Kurt, but I—" she squeezed her eyes shut. *Say it. Just say it.* "Can't."

She opened her eyes to see hurt flooding into his.

"Well, why, why not?" he sputtered. "Did Andy say you can't?"

"No. He wanted me to make my own decision. I never meant to lead you on—"

"But you did!" He jumped to his feet, his face flushing a rare red. An angry red. "I know you enjoyed it. Don't try to tell me you didn't."

"I'm sorry!" She wanted to say that she liked him. That she just wasn't ready. But she was afraid he would push too hard for her to resist. "I'm sorry..."

"I don't understand, Shannon." He paced the throw rug behind the piano like a tiger in a cage. He was fighting hard to hide the hurt but failing miserably "You let me think you liked me." He jabbed a finger at his chest. "I deserve an explanation. Is there someone else? Maybe Jesse Kowalewski?"

Shannon drew back in shock. She hadn't seen that coming. "What are you talking about?"

Kurt scalded her with a look of scorn. "Don't play innocent. I know you eat with him every day."

"So you're having me spied on, is that it?" She stood up, hands on her hips.

"Oh yeah. I went undercover and everything." He glared at her. "No, actually, I have friends who still go to Claywood High, and word gets around fast."

"That's right, it does," Shannon lashed back. "Word about you sleeping with girls and how I would be, oh what, I don't know, number 125 this year? You think I'm interested in *that*? No thank you!"

She may as well have slapped his face. He looked stunned at her words.

Then he turned sharply and headed straight toward the front door.

He stopped and spun around. "It'll never work, you know. You and Jesse."

"This has nothing to do with Jesse. I've known what you wanted out of me all along, Kurt. I just didn't know what I wanted. Maybe I still don't, but I do know I don't want to be that kind of girl. I'm going to respect myself. Whether you do or not."

Kurt gave her one more glowering glare radiating with hurt.

"Boy, I read you wrong, Shannon." He stomped through the door and slammed it behind him.

* * *

Kurt jerked his truck door open and hopped inside, banging the door closed. He let out a mouthful of foul words as he started the engine. He'd never had a girl reject him before on account of the others. Shannon was unreasonable. What did she think, that he was going to spend his life waiting around until Miss Right magically fell into his lap? Yeah right!

He swallowed hard, not enjoying what he was feeling right now. He'd never been hurt by a girl before. He'd never let one close enough to make it possible.

This is why you don't date girls. This is why you've always done what you do.

Back home, he paced around his room. He wanted to punch something. Or better yet... A pleasant thought came into his head. Reaching for his phone, he searched through his contacts. "Amber Canton." He'd met her last week at the community college recreation center, and she'd flirted it up with him, giving him her number. He'd understood her suggestive looks, but his only thought for two weeks had been Shannon.

But now… Amber might be just what he needed.

Forcing thoughts of Shannon aside, he tapped call.

Chapter Seventeen

The moment Kurt disappeared, Shannon had the urge to run after him, take it all back. Instead she sank down onto the piano bench and slouched her face into her hands.

"What did I do?" she moaned.

"The right thing."

She jumped at Andy's voice and saw him descending the curved staircase. "Sorry, but I eavesdropped on the whole thing from the top of the stairs." He came across the room and opened his arms. Shannon let him envelop her in a comforting hug. "I'm proud of you, Shan. I know it wasn't easy."

"He looked really hurt." Shannon plopped herself back down. She felt sick right now. Had she done the right thing?

Andy rubbed his chin thoughtfully. "I was surprised he asked you out. I mean, he told me he wanted to date you, but I didn't believe he meant it."

Shannon blew out a big breath. "I hope this won't upset your friendship too much."

"Naw." Andy waved his hand. "He'll need to lick his wounds for a while. Probably won't see him around here any time soon. But since I work for his dad, I'll see him. We're guys." He shrugged. "We don't get hung up on stuff like this." He narrowed his eyes at Shannon. "Are you going to be okay?"

"Yeah." She smiled through her lie and quickly excused herself to her room. Kurt wanting something steady with her had thrown her for a loop. He must indeed have real feelings for her. No wonder he looked so hurt.

She sniffed, her eyes stinging with unshed tears.

Maybe his accusation held an element of truth. If she hadn't met Jesse, she probably wouldn't have turned Kurt away. She wouldn't have spent so much time thinking about whether or not she was willing to have casual sex, and if it was right or wrong. She would have gotten her first boyfriend a few minutes ago if it weren't for Jesse, and things would have just "happened."

This was when a parent would come in handy. A parent with a listening ear and sage advice. Shannon's eyes overflowed. That's what Mom had always been. But Mom had been hiding her dirty secrets, and now Shannon wasn't even sure she'd trust her mom's advice. She certainly wasn't about to ask Kevin's opinion. She couldn't decide if he'd feed her alive to Kurt or tie her up in her room until she was 30.

That evening as they were finishing dinner, Kevin returned cell phones to Shannon and Laura.

"Grounding's up," was all he said. Shannon hadn't said more than fragments to him since the story of his affair with her mom. He seemed respectful of her distance, only speaking to her when necessary. At least they hadn't argued for a week and a half. That must be a record.

After helping clear the table, Shannon wandered into the living room and curled up in a corner of the couch. She looked at the piano. She missed him already. The middle of her stomach ached with the feeling of loss.

She weighed her phone in her hand. Who would she call? Brittni? Todd? They'd want to know whatever happened with the guy she had told them about. And she had no idea how to tell them in a way they'd understand. Because she wasn't sure *she* understood.

She could call Alan, but of course they hadn't talked in two weeks. If she called him now, there would be too much to explain before she could get to what she really needed to talk about.

What about Jesse? Before she could talk herself out of it, she navigated to his contact. His home phone rang three times, and she was scrambling to think of a message to leave when a voice said, "Hello?" It wasn't him, and she almost hung up.

"Hi, is Jesse there?" she managed to squeak.

There was a pause, and Shannon could hear muffled words. "Can I ask who's calling?"

Maybe he didn't want to talk to her. They'd barely talked the last few days at school.

"It's...Shannon."

"Shannon!" Jesse's voice flooded the line in an instant. She could almost hear his dimples dipping. "Hey, what's up? How are you?"

"I'm—I'm good. I just got my phone back, and I'm not grounded anymore."

"That's great! Do you need help with homework?"

"No, I think I actually got pre-calc figured out this time." So why had she called him?

"Awesome! Hey, I'm going to church tomorrow morning. Want to come with me?"

Kurt wanted to sleep with her, Jesse wanted to take her to church. Could they be any more extreme?

"You can meet me there. Service starts at 10:30. It's the church on the square."

Shannon was confused about God. Maybe going to church would clear things up. If nothing else, it was a chance to get outside the house, which she hadn't done much for the past two weeks.

"Um, yeah, I guess…I could do that."

"Only if you want to." Jesse's warm voice assured her that he wouldn't be offended if she said no, but he sounded hopeful just the same.

"10:30?"

"Yep. You can park on the square, or there's a lot behind the church if you come up Elm Street."

"Alright." Quickly, before she chickened out. "Sounds good. I'll see you then."

"Can't wait!"

"Shannon." She turned at the sound of Kevin's hard voice. She hadn't even hung up yet, but he was heading her direction. "Who was that?"

Immediately her guard went up, a feeling she hadn't missed the past few weeks while Kevin was leaving her alone.

"Just a friend."

He scowled. "Any chance that friend goes by the name Jesse Kowalewski?"

"So what if he does?" She stood up and skirted around him, heading toward the stairs. She wasn't grounded anymore. She didn't owe him explanations.

"Wait a minute, we're not finished."

Pausing on the step, she looked at him, eyebrows raised.

"Was it Jesse?"

"Yeah."

He came to the stairs and stopped, crossing his arms over his chest. Standing on the floor, he was still taller than she was on the second step.

"It sounded like you made plans to see him tomorrow."

Shannon shifted her weight to one foot, sliding a hand onto her hip. "What, did you bug my phone?"

Kevin frowned at her. "No, Shannon, I heard you as I was walking by."

"Thanks for the heads up. I'll make sure to lock myself in my closet next time I want privacy." She turned, but before she had her foot on the next step, Kevin grabbed her arm.

"We're still not finished, young lady. If you understand pre-calculus, which I clearly heard you say, then you have no need to see that boy. When a boy and a girl make plans to go somewhere together, it usually ends only one way, and I'll not stand for that, Shannon."

"Jesse's not that way!" Shannon's face burned hot with anger. How dare Kevin think such a thing? "And neither am I! For crying out loud, Kevin, he invited me to his church tomorrow, and I'm meeting him there in the morning."

"Church? Well that's a new one. Nice cover. No guy in his right mind invites a girl to 'church,' for the fun of it. I know what he's up to."

"You don't have a clue what he's up to." Fury was trailing up and down Shannon's spine it a way it hadn't in weeks. "Just because you have no honor, doesn't mean no other guys do."

She left Kevin at the bottom of the stairs flapping his jaw around trying to come up with a response while she scaled the stairs two at a time.

* * *

Shannon's leg shook as she pressed the gas pedal. It was 10:27, and she had just pulled out of the driveway. She was going to be late. Turning around and going back to the house seemed like the best option. Who showed up late for *church*? Wasn't that like a sin or something?

She was still mad about last night. Kevin had followed her up to her room and lit into her about her grades. The jerk. As if she had time to keep up in school while acting as nanny, maid, and chef at home.

Nervous flutters pulsed in her abdomen as she neared the square. She hated going new places alone. Hopefully she'd find Jesse quickly.

The parking options along the square were all taken, so she drove around behind the church on the side street, like Jesse had suggested, and found a few empty spots at the back of the small lot. Sliding out of the Explorer, she took a moment to straighten her skirt and reapply her lipstick. She had been uncertain how to dress, and therein lay the reason she was late. She had tried on five different outfits before settling for a simple knee-length black and white floral print skirt and a fitted black V-neck sweater. The skirt flared out, contrasting nicely with her shiny black boots.

She paused on the sidewalk, debating where to go next. She stood near a back door, but a sidewalk led around the church to the front. She had just decided on the front when the back door swung open and an elderly man stepped out.

" 'Mornin', missy. You wouldn't happen to be plannin' on comin' inside, would ya?"

Shannon smiled shyly and changed her course. The man grinned at her with the few teeth that remained in his mouth, a white tuft of hair rising from the middle of his otherwise bald head. Offering his hand, he nearly crushed her small bones with his hearty handshake.

"I don't believe I've seen you here before," he crowed louder than necessary as he ushered her through the door.

"This is my first time."

"What's that?" He leaned closer to her. A woman who looked to be in her early 60s rushed over.

"Now Bob, don't you be frightening away the visitors. They're going to go deaf like you if you keep shouting at them." She sent a sweet smile Shannon's way. "I'm Betty. What's your name?"

"Shannon."

Betty gave her a dainty handshake, then gestured to the corner of the room. "You can hang your coat over there, sweetie. Do you need a place to sit?"

"Well, actually." Shannon paused as she shrugged the coat off with Betty's help. "A friend invited me. He probably saved me a seat."

They walked to the coat rack together. "Even better! What's your friend's name?"

Would she know him? "Jesse Kowalewski."

"Oh! *You*'re the one he's waiting for."

Shannon looked at Betty, surprised. "What do you mean?"

Betty hooked her arm through Shannon's and gently pulled her toward a set of stairs. "He's waiting for you upstairs. He told me he'd invited a friend, but he decided to go ahead and sit down when the service started." She waved her hand and laughed at herself. "Silly me, I was looking for a *male* friend. My head must be in the clouds about you young people!"

"Jesse and I are just friends." Shannon didn't want anyone thinking otherwise. Not right now. She was thankful when Betty graciously nodded and said nothing more. She guided her up a narrow stairway and into the church lobby. Pointing at the double doors, she whispered, "You'll find Jesse in there. He said he'd sit near the back."

Timidly, she pulled one of the doors open and slipped into the back of the sanctuary. It was small but full, and she didn't see Jesse anywhere, but a song up front distracted her as her love of music overtook her loneliness. Two women sang a duet, their angelic harmony stealing her breath away as they sang about the goodness of God. When the song ended and the parishioners burst into applause, Shannon remembered she was here to find Jesse. Someone shifted and she spotted him a few rows up. Dipping her head, she moved down the middle aisle and dropped into the pew next to him.

He offered a smile that put birthday candles to shame. "You made it!"

"Yeah." She rolled her eyes with a self-deprecating smile. "Sorry I'm late."

He shrugged. "You didn't miss anything too important—" He paused suddenly, and Shannon peered up at him. He was staring at her, taking her in, and then he met her eyes and ducked his head in his adorable way. He reached a hand to the back of his reddening neck. "You look really nice."

Shannon felt her lips curving into a smile as she whispered, "Thank you."

A man went up front and started to pray. While everyone else bowed their heads, Shannon looked around curiously. It was a traditional church, with an organ at the front and a lot of old folks in attendance. No contemporary instruments or technology. A giant fern splashed some color in front of the pulpit, and colorful banners with a Bible verse hung on either side of the platform. She guessed that less than a hundred people were in the sanctuary, and not many of them looked under age 50. What drew Jesse to this church?

The sermon was well underway before Shannon even had a clue what the pastor was talking about. He kept referring to Romans, and she wasn't sure if he was talking about people from Rome or, wait, was that a book in the Bible? She arched her back against the straight pew and let out a little sigh. Jesse leaned close to her ear.

"You doing okay?"

"Not really. I'm lost."

Jesse squeezed her arm and bowed his head, obviously praying, but for what, Shannon didn't know. Before she could wonder, the pastor's words caught her attention.

"When we love someone, we want to show them, right? So we do something to demonstrate that love. God is no exception. Paul says here that God loved us so much that He wanted to *demonstrate* that love. Just saying He loved us wasn't enough. He wanted to *show* us." The pastor leaned forward, gripping the sides of the pulpit with fervor. Shannon found herself leaning forward with him. What had God ever done to show that He loved *her*?

"That's what Calvary is about. God's tangible answer to our never-ending question, 'God, do you really love me? How much do you love me?' We see the arms of Jesus Christ stretched wide on the cross, and He says, 'I love you *this much*.'" The preacher swept his eyes over the congregation as he paused, then said softly, "He loves you just as much today. And tomorrow. And forever. And there is *nothing* you can do to stop Him from loving you."

A chill shivered across Shannon's skin, but it was quickly followed by a glow of warmth spreading in her chest. She couldn't explain it. She didn't understand it. But she liked it.

As people flooded out of the sanctuary, she stayed in her seat, Jesse at her side.

"So…how do you feel?"

She cocked her head and looked at him as she considered his question.

"At peace."

Jesse's dimples exploded.

"And I have no idea why, because I didn't understand much of the sermon. But the part about love at the end. That kinda got me. You know?"

"I *do* know. He loves you so much, Shannon. So much." Jesse said it with such meaning, Shannon felt herself believing him. He nodded his head toward the aisle, fabulous smile capturing his face. The church was mostly empty. "Should we go?"

"Yeah." She smiled up at him. Together they walked into the crowded lobby. They were almost to the stairwell when she saw a couple standing with Betty. Something about them was familiar, but she couldn't see their faces. As Jesse gestured for her to go first, she glanced back just as the man in question turned. Her heel caught, and she tripped a little. Kurt's parents came to this church? Mr. Blake nodded his head genially at Shannon. She felt her face warming, even though certainly Kurt's parents didn't know about his behavior, let alone hers.

"You okay?" Jesse looked at her closely as they descended the steps, and Shannon wished he wouldn't.

"I'm fine." *Oh please, just leave well enough alone…*

Thankfully he did, quietly walking her to the Explorer. "I'm glad you came," he said as she unlocked the driver's door. "During the sermon I was praying for you, that God would speak to your heart."

Shannon turned wide eyes on him. "That's what you were doing? Wow... I guess it worked." She was going to have ponder that one. Had God actually listened to Jesse's prayer? Sure seemed like it. Because it was like she'd gone from pre-calc to the piano the very second he bowed his head. Weird. Or wonderful. She wasn't sure which.

Jesse took a step back slowly, like he didn't want to go. "Wish we could talk more, but I gotta run. I visit a relative of mine every Sunday after church. He, well, he can't get out much."

As soon as she got home, Shannon unearthed her sketch journal. She hadn't added much to it recently, but now, with pencil poised, she imagined a cross with a man hanging from it. And it wasn't just any man. It was God's son, Jesus Christ. His arms were outstretched, held wide open not so much by the nails as by the boundless love He had—for her. Was it possible? She hoped so. *Really* hoped so.

* * *

"We saw your friend Shannon at church today."

Kurt's head snapped up so fast it hurt. He looked from where he sat at the table to his mom, rummaging through the refrigerator. "What?" He must have heard wrong. Shannon was consuming his thoughts so much, it wasn't unlikely.

"You know, Andy's sister?" Mom straightened up with hands full of various salad dressing bottles.

"At *church*?" Well Shannon was moving right along. To go from eagerly making out with him to landing in a church pew, Kurt was certain all the credit lay with Jesse.

Mom eyed him as she sat down at the table. "The way you sang her praises at Kevin's party, I almost thought you liked her. But what do I know?" She waved her hand dismissively, then looked hard at Kurt. "Shannon Conrad is a quality girl. If you don't move fast, you'll lose your chance, because you're not her only admirer."

"Nancy..." Kurt's dad touched her hand.

Kurt said nothing. He didn't want to give himself away. Wearing his heart on his sleeve once had been enough. All he'd gotten from it was hurt. He might go stark raving mad if he didn't start thinking about something other than Shannon. Nothing else would stick in his brain. Only she. Always she. Even during his time with Amber last night. Shannon. Shannon.

Shannon.

He didn't realize he'd groaned it aloud until both his parents looked at him.

"What was that?" Dad's eyes were sending Kurt a serious warning.

Kurt rubbed the side of his clenched fist on the table, then abruptly stood up, slamming his chair against the table. "I gotta go."

"But you didn't even touch your dinner!" Mom's voice was more alarmed than upset.

"Later, Mom," Kurt threw over his shoulder, rushing from the room.

"But—"

"Let him go, Nance," Dad's voice cut her off. "Let him go."

In his room, Kurt wanted to beat his head against the wall. This was ridiculous. How could one girl do this much damage? A girl he hadn't even slept with! Which was probably the problem. If she weren't so ridiculously stubborn. He ground his teeth together and cursed at Shannon.

Stupid Shannon.

He needed a distraction. A *major* distraction. One he'd used a number of times was named Carolyn, and she kept herself readily available for him.

He smiled and nodded, searching for his phone.

Yes, Carolyn would be the antidote for Shannon that he needed.

* * *

Shannon wasn't trying to eavesdrop. But the girl was standing right next to her locker talking to another girl.

"Guess who paid me a visit last night."

"Umm...Chris?"

"Nope. My favorite."

"Not Kurt."

"Yes, Kurt."

"Seriously? And you let him? Carolyn, you know how many girls he's been with."

The girl shrugged without remorse. "But he always come back to *me*. He was upset last night, and he says I have the magic touch."

"Yeah. Magic touch. I wonder how many girls he's used that line on."

The girls headed down the hall, disappearing into a classroom. Shannon struggled to breathe as she stared in their wake, somehow making herself start walking.

"Steph?" She slid into her seat in Spanish just as the bell rang.

"Hey, what's up?" Stephanie was digging in her purse, but when she looked at Shannon's face, she stopped. "What's wrong?"

"Please tell me there's more than one Kurt in this town..." Her voice shook.

"As far as I know, there's just one, Kurt Blake. Why?"

She sucked in a painful breath and shook her head. "Never mind. It doesn't matter."

But it did matter. She blinked and tears splashed onto the desk top as pain sparked through her chest. She'd been stupid enough to think that Kurt really liked her. That if he was hurt by her refusal, it meant he had true feelings. Now she understood. He'd only been after one thing from her. As soon as he realized he wasn't going to get it, he went to someone easier.

She sniffed and wiped her desk dry with her sleeve.

Was that all he had seen in her? Someone to sleep with? Was there nothing more to her?

After dinner that evening Andy helped her clean up while Kevin played with Gabby and Daniel.

"Kurt moved on fast." She managed to say it without emotion.

"Huh?" Andy looked up from spooning leftover sweet potatoes into a Tupperware container. "What do you mean?"

"He spent last night with a girl named Carolyn." Her chin started to quiver.

"*Carolyn*? Come on Kurt, seriously?"

"You know her too?"

"Of course. She's the biggest slut in the whole school." He rolled his eyes. "Kurt has always had a weakness for her."

"Sounds like they're a match made in heaven." Shannon slammed the trash can lid harder than necessary.

"You okay?" Andy asked softly, but she ignored him and turned her back, scrubbing a sticky spot on the counter with the back of the sponge. Andy pulled her back by one shoulder and peered at her face. Tears trickled down her cheeks.

"Ah, Shan." He folded her into a hug.

"I should have expected it, but I thought he really liked me." Her voice cracked, and she pulled away, mopping at her face with the back of her hand. She met Andy's eyes. "He asked me to be his girlfriend, Andy. Didn't that mean *something* to him besides— besides sex?"

Andy reached out and slid Shannon's tears away with his thumb. "This is why I told him to stay away from you. I knew he'd end up hurting you." He took her firmly by the shoulders. "I know it sucks right now, but trust me, you can do *so* much better than Kurt. At least you know for sure you made the right decision about him."

For *sure*.

But it still hurt like an ulcer.

* * *

"Kurt!"

Kurt sighed. Andy yelling his name and slamming doors had become too familiar. What had he done now?

He was in a corner of the wood shop working on a custom cabinet set. Andy had been over for work earlier. They hadn't said much yesterday or today. He'd been wondering how much Andy knew, and he had a feeling he was about to find out.

"Back here, Andy." He popped his head up and saw Andy standing at the front of the room looking around. He nodded his chin at Kurt as he walked to the back.

Kurt took one look at Andy's face and set down the sander in his hand. "What's up?"

Andy stuffed his hands in his pockets and glared at him. "Carolyn?"

Closing his eyes, Kurt swore softly. "Good grief, does the whole town know?"

"I really don't care. But Shannon knows."

Shame and guilt tackled Kurt like opposing players on the football field. He swallowed hard, unable to meet Andy's accusing eyes. He shrugged, trying to get control, forcing indifference.

"Why would she care, anyway?"

"You told me you liked her." Andy jabbed his finger sharply into Kurt's chest. "You lied to me, man. You lied to me!"

Kurt took a wobbly step back, his sternum smarting with pain from Andy's poke. "N-no, no I didn't! I really did like her. I *do* like her!" The words had scarcely left his lips before his mind betrayed him with a flashback of last night. And the night before. He spun around and groaned, aching for something to punch. He settled for his other hand, remembering in time that unlike his room, the shop walls were cinder block.

"Kurt, I want you to know that it wasn't easy for Shannon to turn you down." Andy spoke quietly to Kurt's back. "I saw the whole thing. It was a very difficult decision for her. To go from asking her to be your girlfriend to sleeping with someone like Carolyn one day later—that's a low blow to her, man."

Heavy silence settled between them as Kurt digested Andy's words. His shame was a living, clawing, strangulating force, trying to suffocate him. Unable to face Andy, he asked around the galling lump in his throat what he didn't want answered.

"What did she do?"

"She cried."

Yep, he'd always been good at making her cry. She already had enough to cry about. He hated himself for giving her more.

When he turned around, Andy was gone. Kurt paced back and forth. His interactions with girls had never bothered him before. Not really. Until now.

Acid burned in his mouth; his stomach churned; his head pounded. It felt like something was pushing at his skin, trying to tear him apart from the inside out. He kicked the wall and grunted as pain shot through his toes and up his foot. Swearing loudly, he swung around and came face to face with his dad, standing in the doorway of the shop office.

"Dad!" Had he been in there the whole time? Kurt didn't turn red easily, but he felt his face flushing now. "How—how much of that conversation—with Andy—did you hear?"

His dad looked at him, his eyes sad. "The whole thing."

Kurt let out a single syllable, emotionless laugh. "Yeah, okay..." He examined a crack in the cement in front of his shoe. When Dad's hand clasped his shoulder, he flinched.

"Let's go in the office." Dad propelled Kurt in front of him and pointed him to the brown swivel chair. Flopping into it, Kurt sprawled his legs out in front of him, slouching into the back of the chair. His dad pulled another chair from a corner and sat down across from Kurt.

"Son, I am...*very*...concerned about you." He reached out a hand to place on Kurt's knee. "Aside from the obvious emotional and mental consequences, there is tremendous physical risk to engaging in such...promiscuity."

The word cut deep in spite of the worry coating his dad's tone of voice. Kurt nodded and muttered, "I know." It was something he had chosen not to think about. He had always been careful and used protection, but he knew he was walking a precarious line.

Dad dug into his pocket and pulled out a scrap of paper. "I made you a doctor's appointment for tomorrow afternoon. I want you to go get checked out."

Kurt raised his eyebrows in question.

"I do not agree with your choices, Kurt, but I want to make sure you are healthy. I love you no matter how much your actions hurt me as a parent."

Kurt drew his fists up under his chin, forearms pressed together tightly. For the first time, he was starting to see himself. What his parents saw. What Shannon saw.

And he thought he might be sick.

A moan of despair rose up in him that he couldn't suppress. "I really screwed up this time, Dad."

Dad leaned forward, bending so he could look Kurt in the eye. "You really like this girl?"

He nodded slowly. "I do. A lot."

Dad gave him a look of sheer disbelief. "Then why did you go sleep with another girl?"

Kurt reared his head back in frustration, letting out a guttural groan of torture. "I asked her out, and she turned me down flat. I was hurt."

Dad let out a loud sigh. "I was so afraid something like this would happen. That's why I talked to you a few weeks ago. Remember, I asked how you would handle it when you met one girl more special than the rest? This was your way of handling it?"

Kurt slumped his head into his hands, paralyzed by a brain-muddling combination of self-pity, self-loathing and desperate self-justification.

Chapter Eighteen

"I'm sorry... Can you explain it one more time?"

Jesse's patience was admirable. Shannon was having the worst time understanding what they'd supposedly learned in pre-calculus class today. It just wouldn't connect in her head.

Nancy's Trading Post was busy as usual this Wednesday afternoon. Shannon glanced around from her perch on a tall chair, breathing in the delicious aromas. Maybe she would buy some fresh bakery bread to go along with tonight's dinner. She'd convinced Laura to stay home with Gabby and Daniel after school so she could get some tutoring, but she knew Laura wouldn't go so far as to make dinner, too.

"Okay, let's go over it again." She tore her eyes from the crowded room and back to the pre-calc book Jesse was shoving toward her. *Concentrate.*

"Yes, you got it, you got it!" A few minutes later, Jesse's excitement bubbled up into his hand for a high five. "Awesome. Now you'll get through the problems easily. Just watch."

Right he was. Twenty minutes later she had all of her pre-calculus homework completed, and she understood how she'd done it, too. Which was pretty impressive.

"I actually *get* it!" She beamed at Jesse. "Thank you!"

He laughed his wonderful laugh. "Always glad to help, Shannon."

She stacked her notebook on top of her textbook and was reaching for her pencils when she got the vague feeling of being watched. When she turned her head, her stomach attempted to scamper straight up her esophagus before landing in a heap back where it belonged.

There he was. Maybe 20 feet away. Standing just inside the "Employee's Only" door, leaning against the wall, arms crossed loosely over his chest as he stared at Shannon.

She couldn't help staring back, and her pulse floored like a race car, beating in her temples and throat. Remembering what Kurt had done so quickly after claiming to want her for his girlfriend, the hurt rushed in, along with tears to her eyes. His face blurred, and she broke contact by closing her eyes. She turned her face away sharply so he couldn't see the tears that her lids squeezed out.

"Do you want to go?" Jesse's gentle voice forced her eyes back open. She swiped at her cheeks and nodded, ignoring his questioning look. She wasn't going to stick around to buy bread with Kurt watching her.

She cringed at how quickly Jesse jumped to assist her with her coat. After insisting that Jesse had nothing to do with her rejection of Kurt, she could only imagine what he must be thinking. Although, after what he'd done with Carolyn and who knew who else by now, she frankly didn't care what he thought.

Jesse walked with her to the Explorer and stood as she tossed her backpack onto the passenger seat. When she faced him again, he looked troubled.

"Can I ask... No, it's not my business."

Shannon let out a small sigh. She owed him that much. "You're wondering what happened with Kurt?"

He squinted like he wasn't sure he did want to know, then nodded. "Yeah."

Shannon didn't look at him while she spoke, focusing on a cloud to the left of his head in the distance. "He came over last weekend—and he asked me out—to be his girlfriend. I almost said yes. But I didn't. I knew what that would mean. I'm still not sure where I stand, but until I'm sure, I'm going no farther. Especially with him." She couldn't suppress her shudder.

"He already moved on, didn't he?" Jesse's voice was too matter-of-fact.

She looked away again. He'd warned her. "I don't want to talk about it."

He didn't say anything else as she walked around the Explorer. She had already slid into the driver's seat when he caught the door in his hand.

"Wait, Shannon."

She raised her eyebrows in question.

His brown eyes were warm and sympathetic. "I'm sorry. I was insensitive. Obviously you're hurt."

She shrugged. "I'll get over it."

"I just want you to know how glad I am with your decision about Kurt. I know this is bad timing, but..." He smiled nervously, dimples barely denting. "I like you, Shannon."

Her wounded heart twitched at his words. She already knew that, but hearing it was a nice thing. She offered him a small smile, not really sure how to respond. Thankfully he didn't seem to expect anything.

"I didn't speak up sooner because it needed to be *your* decision. You didn't turn Kurt down for me. You turned him down for you."

It was true. Jesse had impacted her decision, but when she decided to say no to Kurt, it was because she respected herself — not because she wanted Jesse's respect. He had already assured her that she had it.

Out of nowhere, she was reminded of what Jesse had said about God. That He already loved her completely and nothing she did could ever make Him love her less. That was exactly how Jesse had treated her. It was that unconditional love that the pastor had talked about on Sunday. The love that Jesus had for her.

She tucked that thought into her heart. She wanted to think more about it later.

Jesse took a step back, suddenly yawning. "I gotta get going. Need to catch some sleep before work."

"When *do* you sleep?"

"Not often." He winked, as if it were funny. "From about 5:30 to 8:00 in the evening. Thankfully I can do homework in the security office, as long as I keep an eye on the monitors. I get off at 4:30 a.m. and go straight to bed at home. My first two periods are study halls, so I have an arrangement with the school not to come till third."

That was nuts. No wonder he was always tired.

She glanced at the dashboard clock. Almost 5:30. "Why did you agree to tutor me? You don't have time this!"

He quirked one eyebrow up. "I'd lose sleep over you any day, Shannon Conrad."

She shook her head as he closed her door. He smiled and waved, then broke into a jog toward his sad-looking truck. Shannon watched him climb in before she backed out of her space. Jesse was special. She'd never met anyone like him before, that was certain.

* * *

When Shannon's eyes went wide with pain that he'd put there, Kurt had stopped breathing. He didn't miss that swipe at her cheeks, either.

He had stopped by the Trading Post to ask Mom a question, and she wasn't even here. What were the odds Shannon would be instead?

He knew he should stop watching, but he couldn't tear his eyes away from where she and Jesse talked beside her car in front of the store. Jealousy flowed through him as Jesse followed her around to the driver's side.

He had no right to be jealous after what he'd done, first with Amber, then Carolyn. Not to mention all the girls before them. But none of that changed how he felt about Shannon now.

He stifled a groan and spun around, slamming himself through the employee door. His truck was parked out back. One of Mom's workers, a girl he faintly remembered making out with not that long ago, called to him from where she was stocking a storage shelf, but he ignored her as he trudged to the back door. Why had he never thought of the idiocy of getting involved with so many girls in such a small town?

He went home and checked the house, but Mom wasn't there either. Oh well. He needed to get back to the Christmas orchard, as they called it, where he had left Andy inspecting trees. The week after Thanksgiving they would begin cutting the best trees to ship out to their sellers and also to sell at the orchard stand, but they also needed to draw up a map marking out the best rows for each variety for the customers who wanted to cut their own. Personally he couldn't imagine ever driving up to some place and buying a tree that was just *there*. No, no. He would always need to inspect it first, compare it with all the ones growing around it, and have the wonderful satisfaction of cutting it down and hauling it away with his own hands.

He started back to his truck, but he changed his course when he heard the whine of a saw coming from the woodshop. He found his dad busy at work, bent over a table where a piece of plywood was secured in a vice. One end of the wood fell onto the floor with a *plunk* as Dad cut completely across it. He turned the saw off and inspected the edge he had cut, setting it down with a satisfied nod.

"Hey, Dad."

Dad's head whipped up. He lifted his safety goggles. "Hey, I didn't hear you come in. Thought you were out in the orchard with Andy."

"I'm about to go back." Kurt distractedly hit the cement floor with the heel of his work boot. He and Dad hadn't talked since Monday night after Andy had left. He wasn't sure what to say now.

"How was the doctor yesterday?"

Kurt coughed and cleared his throat, tugging at his coat around his neck uncomfortably. His dad sure knew how to come to a point quickly. "He didn't see any red flags. But he won't know for sure till he gets my lab results."

"When will that be?" Dad kept working, examining his cut without looking at Kurt.

"Tomorrow. He'll call as soon as he has a chance to go over it himself."

Dad nodded. "Why are you here, Kurt?"

Again caught off guard, Kurt hemmed and hawed for a few seconds, then clamped his dysfunctional jaw shut. Glancing around, he spied an empty five-gallon bucket in the corner, so he grabbed it and slammed it on the floor upside down, then lowered himself onto it. It wasn't very comfy, but he hardly noticed.

Why *was* he here?

"I saw her today," he blurted out before he could stop himself.

Dad set down the wood in his hand and came around to the other side of the table, standing in front of Kurt. "Shannon?" Kurt nodded. "And?"

Kurt looked up into his dad's eyes and groaned low in his throat. "I don't know, Dad. I saw how much I hurt her. For the first time I actually like a girl—*really* like her. And I totally blew it."

"Why do you like her?"

"She's amazing, Dad! In 17 years she has been through more junk than one person should in a lifetime, yet she is so strong. You should see her with Gabby and Daniel. She is compassionate and—and responsible. She's way more mature than her age, and boy is she a fighter. She knows how to fight for others, and she knows how to fight for herself. She feels things deeply and isn't afraid to show what she feels. Right now she is grieving badly for her mom but she is still holding herself together—and everyone else. It's incredible. She's beautiful, smart, and talented, but none of that has gone to her head. Like I said, she's amazing."

"Did you ever tell her?"

Kurt scrunched up his forehead. "What do you mean?"

"Those are some deep qualities you just mentioned. Did you ever tell her what you admired about her? Or did you just try to get her in bed?"

Kurt hung his head.

"That's what I thought." Dad bent and placed a hand on Kurt's shoulder. "Look at me, son." Kurt obeyed and saw a wealth of wisdom and sorrow in his dad's eyes. "The qualities you admire most about Shannon are what made her reject you. She respects herself. Maybe she did have feelings for you, but in any case, I suspect she didn't reject *you* so much as she rejected what you would have made her become."

Kurt considered this. It would explain why he felt like she had led him on and then suddenly spurned him. It would also make him feel like a whole new level of dirt for running straight to those other sleazes for comfort.

He blew a long breath of air from his mouth. "What do I do now, Dad? She knows that I...that I asked her to be my girlfriend one day and slept with another girl the next." She didn't know he'd slept with a different girl just hours after her rejection, and she didn't need to know; neither did Dad. Wasn't the day *after* bad enough? "I told her I liked her, but now she must think all I wanted from her was sex."

"Was it?"

"No!" Kurt groaned, burying his head in his hands. "I don't know what I wanted then, but right now I just know that Shannon is the most special girl I've ever met, and I don't want her out of my life. What do I do?"

Dad squatted down so he was below Kurt's eye level. "First, be a man and apologize. Tell her the way you treated her was wrong. Tell her how you feel about her, and apologize for not telling her when you should have. And don't add any expectations. Tell her simply because you want her to know. That's the easy part. Number two is proving to her that you've changed."

Kurt scowled and threw his hands into the air. "How do I do that?"

"Only truth can be proven, Kurt. *You* have to change. That will take time. Is she worth it?"

Kurt knew the answer without thought. "Of course. But how?"

His soul trembled at Dad's look of challenge. He wasn't sure he wanted to hear what was next.

"If you meant all those things you said about her, and you are going to tell her, then you need to be willing to back them up by waiting for her. If she's not ready now or doesn't trust you now, are you willing to wait until she is?"

Kurt stared at his dad, trying to translate what he was saying.

"I'm talking about starting over with a clean slate, Kurt. Abstinence. For one year. Shannon or no one."

Kurt gulped back whatever he was about to say. One *year*?

"Are you willing to give up all the other girls and wait for Shannon, even if it takes all year? If you're going to do it, you have to commit, or you'll be with another girl two weeks in. Don't do it just for Shannon. Do it for yourself. Learn to respect yourself—the way Shannon respects herself."

Kurt stared at him, wondering if Dad knew what he was asking.

Dad turned the saw back on, so Kurt left and found Andy in the Virginia Pines, measuring trees.

"Thought you got lost." Andy nodded at him. Their conversation the past few days had been stilted. Never in their five-year friendship had something come between them this much.

"No, man, I was just talking with my dad." Kurt pulled out his clipboard and marked the rows Andy had already completed. He wasn't ready to tell Andy what his dad had suggested. He needed to think more about it.

When Dad said Kurt would have to be committed, he had meant *committed*.

Chapter Nineteen

Kevin walked into the house just as Shannon was sliding garlic bread into the oven. She'd settled for a French loaf from the rinky-dink grocery store and doctored it up the best she could.

"Not possible, Mom. I told you last month."

Kevin shouldered his phone to his ear, a packet of papers tucked under his arm, his hands grasping bags of groceries. Not from George's Family Food Mart.

"No, I'm not avoiding. Just busy."

Shannon turned in time to catch his eyes roll to the ceiling as he hefted the grocery bags onto the counter beside her. She caught the word "embarrassed" from the other end, and Kevin snorted.

"Since when have I cared what my brothers and sisters think?"

He scowled at the response. "Apples and oranges, Mother. I've made myself clear. We won't be joining you this year."

As he passed by Shannon, she distinctly heard the words, "But it would have been splendid to reunite with Shannon and Laura."

She paused with her hand on the knife drawer. She vaguely remembered Kevin's mother. They'd called her Grammy growing up.

"Maybe next year, Mom." Kevin let out a weary sigh. "I gotta run. I'll call on Thanksgiving, okay?"

When the beep ended the call, Shannon busied herself selecting a knife for her cucumber salad. She peaked up and found Kevin leaning into the opposite counter, bracing his arms for support.

"Are you okay, Kevin?"

"Hmmm?" He looked up from studying the papers he'd brought with him. "I'm fine." He sounded anything but, but Shannon was going to be the last to push. They had barely spoken the past few days.

"Smells good." The smile he offered didn't come close to reaching his eyes, which trailed back to the papers on the counter.

"What's that?"

He was silent, and then his strangled voice said, "The final divorce decree. All it needs is my signature."

"Oh." For once, she wished he'd lied to her. "I'm sorry…"

He ignored her, so she went back to salad-making.

"What did your mom want?" she asked when the silence persisted.

"Our presence at her yearly Thanksgiving feast."

The memory bombarded Shannon so hard it nearly rocked her. "We went every year." She turned slowly and faced him. "I'd forgotten."

He nodded. "Well not this year. She's mad 'cause I haven't missed a year since, well, since the year Gabby was born."

The year he'd left them. The year he'd had an affair and a new child. Maybe his mom was on to something.

"Are you sure you're not avoiding them?"

His eyes blazed with sudden wrath. "That's not your business, Shannon." He gathered up the papers and stomped from the room.

* * *

"You interested in church again this weekend?"

Shannon looked across at Jesse. They didn't do pre-calculus at lunch so much anymore, but it had become a habit to eat together. No one tried to sit with them, and Shannon had a feeling people thought they were dating. Jesse hadn't made any moves since telling her that he liked her, and she was glad. To be honest, she was still hung up on Kurt, hurting and somehow missing him at the same time. But once she got over him, who knew what the future might hold.

"Gabby's birthday is on Sunday, and I'm planning her party." She offered an apologetic look. Gabby had dissolved into tears two weeks ago at the thought of not having a birthday party due to her mom's absence. Kevin looked so frantic that Shannon had volunteered for the job. For Gabby's sake. "Wish you could come."

"I'd love to." Jesse flashed his dimpled smile. "Sure would make for a memorable party. Years down the road… 'Remember the birthday when that kid Jesse got kicked out of my party? Dad just picked him up and threw him out the door!' "

"You retard." She chucked a crumpled napkin at him, laughing. "As if Kevin could pick you up and throw you."

"Hey, I'm not about to find out." Jesse was completely serious now. "Tell Gabby happy birthday for me. That's as good as it's gonna get."

Shannon's smile faded, realizing Jesse spoke the truth. He liked her. And she was…interested in him. But Kevin hated Jesse and didn't want her to be friends with him. Wouldn't even let him in the house. The likelihood of them ever becoming more than school buddies suddenly felt almost nil, a fact Jesse seemed keenly aware of.

Shannon sighed. "Ask me about church after Thanksgiving, okay? I do want to go again."

This smile could have served as a lighthouse in a hurricane.

Saturday night Shannon decorated the dining room and living room, putting her artistic flair to good use with pink and green streamers, Gabby's requested colors. Her chosen theme was spring flowers, and in spite of the frigid temperatures outside and the fall décor hidden beneath the faux flowers, Shannon cheerfully sprang into spring. Who was to argue with the logic of a nine year old?

She made a menu of Gabby's favorite Mexican dishes, keeping it simple and kid friendly. Gabby had invited 12 of her school friends, all girls of course. Boys were turtle soup, she said.

When she shut off the kitchen light at 11:00 p.m., she frowned. It was too bright outside. Going to the side door, she opened it and took a look outside. A thin layer of snow coated the ground, with more flakes steadily falling. It was beautiful.

Unfortunately it snowed all night and by morning there was almost a foot of snow. Gabby's face fell farther and farther as the phone began ringing after breakfast until every last one of her friends cancelled. No one was going to make it to the party.

"Hey, you've still got us, yummy Mexican for lunch, and a pretty darn cool room to eat it in, if I do say so myself." Shannon nudged her arm. "Let's go play in the snow."

Gabby hesitated. "Really?"

Shannon was happy to see the whole family rally behind Gabby and pile on the winter layers. Even Kevin came outside in ski pants and water-proof gloves, and soon it was all-out war. Andy, Shannon, and Gabby against Laura, Kevin, and Daniel. Shannon popped out from behind a pine tree and got clobbered in the face. Snow splattered into a white explosion across her face and eyes. She heard Kevin chortling—yes, chortling—and wiped the snow from her eyes, looking around for him. Her face stung from the sharp ice particles in his patiently made snow ball. He was doubled over with laughter, and Shannon stopped in surprise. She'd never seen him laugh so much before. And at her expense!

He straightened and held his hands up surrender-mode, still laughing. "I'm sorry, Shan. I didn't mean to hit your face. I guess I need to throw on your level."

"Ooooh, burn!" Andy exclaimed to Shannon's left. "You're not gonna take that from him, are you?"

Shannon didn't know. She was caught off guard by his use of her nickname. He'd never called her "Shan" before.

"I'd watch my back if I were you." The warning had barely left her frozen lips when she got smacked in the leg by a snowball from Laura. "Hey, what is this? Gang up on Shannon?"

Kevin cracked up again. "Yeah, apparently you have more than your back to worry about!"

"Hah-hah," she called out dryly, then ducked behind a tree, taking time to form a huge, smooth snowball. This called for stealth. She looked around for Andy, who had just taken aim and fired a snowball at Laura from behind the next tree. He winked at her and nodded. She waited until he had worked his way to the far side of the backyard, forcing Kevin to turn his back to Shannon. She saw her opportunity when he stooped down to scoop up a new handful of snow. Sprinting up behind him, she tackled him, knocking him face down into the snow. A surprised grunt came from him as he hit the ground, and he rolled over, only to be greeted with Shannon's snowball in the face. He sat up sputtering as all the kids clustered around him, laughing.

"Good one, Shan!" Andy high-fived her.

"Sorry, Kevin." She offered him a hand. "I couldn't reach you, so I had to, you know, take you down to my level."

He gave her an appraising look as he grasped her hand. She started to pull him up, but with one tug, he sent her toppling into the snow. Even she had to laugh, knowing she'd fallen right into that one. Flopping back, she spread out her hands and arms, moving them back and forth slowly.

"She's makin' an angel, Daddy!" Daniel called gleefully, clapping his hands. "I wanna make one too!"

When they finally headed into the house, frozen solid and covered in white powder, Shannon was surprised by how much fun she'd had. Even with Kevin. Who knew that was possible?

After a delicious spicy lunch, more games were played inside the warmth of the house, and they devoured cake and ice cream. Gabby declared it the best birthday she'd ever had.

"Thank you, Shannon!" She gave Shannon a tight hug as they cleaned up the streamers. "You're the best sister in the whole world!"

Shannon smiled and hugged her back. "You're not so bad yourself." Crazy how attached she was to this girl and her little brother. Kevin she could do without, but his offspring... Every last one of them, she was keeping.

***

Tuesday evening Shannon wandered up the wooden stairs outside the garage and tapped on Andy's apartment door. He opened it wearing boxers and a white wife-beater.

"Sorry." He grinned. "Busy packing."

She followed him into the small bedroom. "I heard you mention you're going to your mom's for Thanksgiving?"

"Yeah, she lives four hours away. I'll be back Saturday night."

Shannon frowned. "How did she end up in Virginia?"

Andy stuffed a pair of jeans into a yellow duffel and reached for a flannel top. "My parents are both from Virginia. They met in college. Mom moved with Dad to Chicago for residency. She wanted to move back to Virginia near her family after their divorce, but she couldn't since they had joint custody of me. I don't know if you remember that I used to split my time between them when you were little."

"I do, and I've wondered how you came to live with Kevin full time."

"Well, when Dad and Carmen moved to here to Virginia after... you know." Andy crinkled his face empathetically. "Anyway, my dad flew me here for Christmas the first year, and then my mom moved to Charlottesville, and I visited more often. When I turned 14, I told my dad I wanted to move in with him. My mom agreed because I was getting to be too much for her to handle." He shrugged with a small smile. "I guess I can be a trouble-maker."

"Why would you want to live with him? He cheated on your mom and screwed up your whole life!"

Andy sighed. "One thing you need to know, Shannon, my mom is extremely bitter over what my dad did to her. I got tired of that. Also, a teenage boy needs a dad. Living with my dad isn't always easy, but it wasn't bad until he and Carmen started having trouble. It helps that I'm so laid-back and just roll with things."

She shook her head. "I still don't see how you've handled life so well."

"Handled it *well*? Why do you think I have so many issues with girls?"

Shannon raised her eyebrows in agreement. "I've never heard you admit that before."

"Hey, I know I don't treat girls right. But it's the way Dad has treated them, so it didn't occur to me how wrong it was until I thought it was going to be done to my own sister."

Shannon dropped her eyes. That was a direct reference to Kurt. And she didn't want to talk about him.

She stood up, toying with the strap of his duffel. "I'm going to miss you the next few days. I'm very glad you live with us."

He tweaked her nose, and she met his sky blue eyes. "I'll miss you, too, Shan. You don't know what your coming has meant to this family."

She thought on his words as she lay in bed that night. What *did* she mean to the family? She had no idea.

* * *

"Shannon, do you have a few minutes?"

The mug of tea almost slipped out of her hand. She knew that voice. What was Kurt doing in her living room? Andy wasn't here, so obviously he'd come for her.

"Do you always have to just walk in?" She scowled, not looking up from Spanish. First night of Thanksgiving break, and she was studying. She was lagging on vocabulary lately. School had let out at noon and she'd spent most of the afternoon cooking for Thanksgiving dinner tomorrow. Kevin had worked today and was on call tomorrow, so who knew what would happen.

"I'm sorry." His sigh was audible. "If I'd called or texted first, would you have answered?"

She let her silence respond.

"Just a few minutes, Shannon, that's all I'm asking."

Finally she looked up. He was standing a few feet in front of her. Why did he have to be so attractive? Her heart pounded at the remembrance of his arms wrapped around her, his lips on hers. Then she thought of him doing all that and more with another girl. Lots of girls.

"Fine, but you won't change my mind."

"I'm not asking that." He took a hesitant step toward the couch and sat down, leaving a generous distance between them. He wiped his hands on his jeans, looking...nervous. That was something Shannon had never seen in him before.

He dug a folded piece of paper out of his pocket and opened it up, smoothing out the wrinkles. His hand shook. Shannon's breathing shallowed. What had he come to say that was making him this uncomfortable?

"I wrote you a letter." His voice was hoarse, so he stopped and cleared it a few times. "I'll give it to you to keep, but I'm going to read it to you first, because I want you to hear it from me."

He took a deep breath. "Okay, here goes. Dear Shannon, I am sorry for the way I treated you. I took advantage of your innocence and vulnerability, and that was very wrong. I am sorry." He stopped, trying to catch her eyes, but she dropped her gaze.

"I hope someday you can forgive me. I never should have started treating you like I only wanted one thing from you. Because that's not all I wanted. I won't deny that I enjoyed our moments of physical closeness." He cleared his throat again and took another breath. "But I should have told you how I felt about you before ever kissing you. I like you for much more than your looks, even though your beauty makes me stop breathing every time I look at you. I like you for more than being a good kisser — which you are. I like you because you are strong even though your whole world has crumbled around you, and you are strong enough to hold up the people around you, too. You are so talented, with cooking and playing the piano, and who knows what else. Gabby and Daniel adore you because you adore them and know just what they need. You care so much about the people you love. You feel things deeply and aren't afraid to show it, even if it makes people uncomfortable. I love your raw honesty, regardless of whether it's happy or sad." He looked at her again. "You. Are. Amazing. I wish I'd told you that before."

She met his eyes. They told her he was speaking the truth. He really did think she was amazing. Then why had he slept with Carolyn? *Why?*

Kurt shifted the paper from one hand to the other and coughed.

"I understand that you may not believe any of this, knowing what you do about me. I regret deeply the way I reacted to your refusal. I realize that me turning around and —" he gritted his teeth and took a deep breath, like he could barely make himself say what came next — "and sleeping with another girl right after asking you to be my girlfriend is not a good validation of my feelings for you. I know that my actions hurt you, and I am truly sorry. It was a stupid, selfish choice in a long line of stupid, selfish choices. It probably seemed to prove to you that all I wanted from you was sex, and when I couldn't get that, I moved on to where I could. And I am ashamed to admit the significant element of truth in that theory." He reached a hand to massage his neck, staring at the page as if he couldn't make himself go on. He met Shannon's eyes for a fleeting second, and she was struck by the complete vulnerability in his eyes. Something else she'd never seen in him before.

He cleared his throat again and relaxed the clenched hold he had on the paper. "I have developed a terrible habit of getting what I want out of girls, quickly, easily, with no strings attached. Or feelings. I had never truly had feelings for a girl until I met you. When you turned me away, it hurt me in a way I'd never felt before. I had no idea how to deal with it, and I chose the worst way possible. If I could undo that choice, I would."

He paused and drew in a long breath, held it in puffed out cheeks, then expelled it at once. He shook his head and said in a quiet, raw voice, "I practiced this, but it's...it's really hard for me to say it out loud."

She just waited while he rubbed his fingers across his forehead. He muttered something to himself, what sounded like, "You got this Kurt, just read it. Just read it."

He nodded and began reading again. "I know you've heard a lot of colorful stuff about me, and I have no idea how much is true or false. I do know rumors tend to grow, and I'm discovering my reputation has me sleeping with a different girl every night. I want to clarify that this is not the case. You said something about you being number 125 of the year." He stopped, staring at the page, forcing himself on. "I will be honest and admit that I've — I've been with — a lot of girls. I'm not counting, but it's nowhere near that number." His shame-filled eyes grazed over Shannon before landing back on the page. "I don't know if that makes any difference to you, but you knowing matters to me. Shannon, thank you for opening my eyes. I never saw a thing wrong with how I was treating girls until I realized how it looked to you. I don't know if this letter changes anything, but it is important to me that you know the truth, whether you believe me or not. I understand if you can't trust me right now, but maybe someday you will see that I mean every word."

He let the papers fall to the couch and slumped back as if exhausted. Shannon's mind was still grappling with everything he'd said. There were a lot of nice, meaningful things, but her brain latched onto his admission of all the other girls.

When he looked at her again, the shutters to his soul were wide open in his eyes. "Do you have any questions? Anything you want to say?"

"I don't mean to be rude, but about all the girls that you've, um, been with, isn't that kind of risky? You know what I mean?"

Kurt nodded, not meeting her eyes. Duh. Of course he knew what she meant. "It's plain stupid, that's what. I—I got checked last week, and my results came back." He sighed lightly. "I'm clean. I don't deserve to be."

"That's... good." Shannon didn't know what else to say. She needed to read his letter again and process it all. She looked down and traced her finger on the floral pattern of the couch, wishing he'd go away.

"Well..." He slowly rose to his feet. "I better get going. We're heading to my aunt's in the morning. Happy Thanksgiving, Shannon."

She raised her head and met his blueberry eyes.

"Same to you, Kurt." She paused, needing to say...something. "Thank you. For the letter."

He nodded, moving away. He paused at the entry way, and said in a voice barely a whisper, "I really am sorry, Shannon." Then he was gone.

Shannon reached over and picked up the letter. Everything he'd said was there. She'd had no idea he could write so well. The way he expressed himself on paper was beautiful and unlike anything she'd heard from him before. He seemed like a totally different person. And maybe he was. He had bared his soul to her today. She got the feeling it wasn't something he did often.

And why had he? She reread the paragraph where he listed all the things he liked about her. Obviously he'd thought about it carefully. She couldn't remember anyone ever saying so many glowing things about her at one time before. Her beauty took his breath away? And he thought she was strong, talented, caring, deep, and amazing? He really did like her.

She moaned aloud and threw her head against the back of the couch. Yes, Kurt had hurt her, but now he'd apologized. But along with his apology, he had turned over so many more rocks, she wasn't sure she could *ever* trust him. Yet she still had feelings for him. And then there was Jesse. She felt...*something*...for him. How could she possibly have feelings for two guys at the same time? Two guys who were complete opposites?

She felt more confused than ever. She couldn't help thinking of the continual string of girls in Kurt's life. What kind of scars did that leave on a person?

Then she thought of Kevin. And she knew the answer to her own question.

Chapter Twenty

"I've been wanting to talk to you about something."

Shannon looked over her shoulder. Kevin had ceased painting and was standing in the middle of her room with a roller brush hanging from his arm, dripping Spun Sugar onto the floor. She was glad they'd covered the carpet with plastic to protect it from the new cream color going on her walls. Thanksgiving had turned out pretty quiet since Kevin had been called in to work around noon. The four kids had eaten Turkey and stuffing together mid-afternoon and played board games. It hadn't felt much like Thanksgiving. Shannon was actually thankful that Kevin had Friday off to take them Black Friday shopping. It had been his idea for her to pick new paint for her room. He'd let her go all out and get a new comforter and curtains to match her new color scheme, which was contrasting tones of cream and burnt red. Tackling the walls was Saturday's project, and Shannon had failed to recruit any help besides her father. They'd worked in silence the past three hours, save for the Christian station playing from Shannon's phone. Kevin had raised his eyebrows at her choice but made no comment.

"Okay." She rested the small brush she'd been using around the door across the paint can and plopped down with a crinkle onto the plastic lining. Kevin didn't sit, but he returned the roller to its tray and crossed his arms, studying her from above.

"When I was in college and med school, I made my circuit through the ladies. Just hopped from girl to girl, never really settled down with one. I didn't have a clue what commitment was. Then I met this amazing girl named Danielle, and she blew all the other girls out of the water. I knew I wanted something special with her. Problem was, it's hard to go from having all the girls to only one and be satisfied. I was for a while, but it didn't take that long for my eyes to start wandering. Not because I didn't love Danielle. But because I loved myself more. I had learned to gratify myself without thinking of anyone else. That's how things started with your mother. That's how things started with Carmen."

Shannon frowned up at Kevin, wondering why he was telling her this. Not that she was surprised to find out he had been a ladies' man in his younger years.

"The reason I tell you this is not to make you think even less of me than you already do, but as a warning."

"What do you mean?"

"Okay, I'll confess. I overheard Kurt reading his letter to you."

"*Whaaat?*" the word spit itself out of Shannon's mouth before she could stop it. She felt blood rushing to her face as she remembered some of the things Kurt had said. "You, um, didn't hear the whole thing or anything, did you?"

Kevin gave her a measured look. "The whole thing. Start to finish. Yes, I was eavesdropping." He shrugged. "I've been a little concerned about you two. I'm not as oblivious as you think, Shannon."

She closed her eyes in hopes of melting into the plastic, wondering how much he knew.

"I'm not sure my kitchen is the most appropriate place to be gettin' it on with Kurt, but it's better than some other activities he had in mind."

"Oh my gosh." Shannon buried her face in her hands in utter humiliation. Kevin put a hand on her shoulder.

"I'm not trying to embarrass you. I—I wanted to say how proud I am of you."

She raised her head from her hands. What could he possibly be proud of?

"I can't think of anyone else your age who would hold the line you've chosen for yourself without serious parental pressure. I am so proud of you for staying firm." Kevin eased himself down to his knees before rolling onto his behind. "You should know that what Kurt did, writing and reading you that letter, took a serious amount of courage. It's one thing for a guy to brag to his friends about his nighttime conquests. That's how the male ego is fed, sick as it may seem. But for a guy to admit to the one girl he really likes that he's been with all those girls, and that he regrets it...that took a lot of guts." He sighed and drummed his fingers on his knee. "That being said, I want you to be careful with Kurt. His intentions may be good, even honorable, but speaking from experience, *wanting* to change and actually changing are vastly different. It takes a long time."

A long time. That's what it was going to be before Shannon trusted Kurt. It sounded like Kurt now was Kevin 30 years ago. And look at Kevin now. Shannon didn't want to end up being another Danielle.

"You don't have anything to worry about, Kevin."

He smiled at her, his eyes oddly alight. "I never thought I did. I really am proud of you, Shannon. I'm proud to have you —" He stopped suddenly and swallowed. "To have you for my daughter."

Something inside Shannon cracked at his words, and she stared at the floor, desperate to keep the tears from coming. Kevin didn't seem to notice, tilting his head back thoughtfully.

"I am amazed by the way you take care of Gabby and Daniel. It was Gabby who tore me away from you. And yet you have chosen to love her. The way you have taken Gabby and Daniel under your wing has touched my heart, and I will be eternally grateful. You have a beautiful heart, Shannon."

His words made her heart throb to the point of nearly bursting. Tears trickled down her face, and she didn't move to wipe them, for once not caring that Kevin saw her cry.

She couldn't explain why she was crying. She hated this man. His words shouldn't mean anything to her.

But they did.

* * *

"How's Shannon doing?"

Kurt and Andy were working together, dragging freshly cut Christmas trees over to the wagon to be taken to the orchard stand. Christmas tree sales were about to take off.

Andy glanced at Kurt with a slight frown at his question. They had carefully avoided her name, or even the hint of her existence, for several weeks now. Kurt hadn't seen her since he'd brought the letter nearly a week ago, so he had no idea what she thought of it. He'd given up torturing himself with questions. His Dad had been right about one thing. Change wasn't easy. In the last few days he had learned the meaning of the word temptation. Up until now, he'd never tried to resist anything, so he hadn't known what it felt like.

It sucked.

His dad was the only other person he'd shared his letter with. For four days before giving it to Shannon, he had labored over the letter like a course grade depended on it. If he put that much energy into his homework, he'd have As instead of Cs and Bs right now. The first draft had been pitiful. He'd lost track of how many times he had rewritten it. His freshman comp teacher would be shocked if she knew he could write like that when he put his mind to it. Dad had made him practice reading it out loud twice before he headed over to the Conrads' house.

He didn't know if Andy knew about the letter. He wanted to tell him, but he was afraid he wouldn't be able to live up to the expectations he was placing on himself. That's why he hadn't mentioned anything to Shannon about his one year commitment. Yep, he'd actually made it. Andy would be shocked, but he couldn't tell him. What if he failed? He almost had already, like twice. Better to surprise people by succeeding at something they weren't expecting than disappoint them by failing a set goal.

"Shannon?" Andy finally responded. "Hard to tell. I played football with her for two hours on Sunday, and she was quiet. She asked my dad yesterday if she and Laura could go to Chicago for Christmas. Of course he said no. She didn't get mad, but she seemed kinda depressed last night. Why do you ask?"

"Because I care about her, and I don't see her anymore." He thought that much was obvious.

Andy nodded. "Rumor has it you turned down two of Claywood's finest females this week," he said casually.

Seriously, this community was pathetic. Didn't people have anything better to do than gossip about his night life?

"Yeah, what about it?"

"Just made me curious. After what happened with Shannon." Andy lifted his eyebrows, asking for more information.

Seemed he didn't know about the letter. Kurt pressed his lips together to keep from spilling the beans and let the silence stretch as he and Andy tossed trees into the trailer. Andy grunted as he heaved a particularly large tree up high, then turned to Kurt.

"Look, man, I don't wanna pry. I respect your privacy." He shrugged. "I'm here if you need me, and I'm sorry if I haven't been the greatest friend lately. Shannon's my sister, but you're my best friend. I don't want anything to change that."

"No, man." Kurt paused to look Andy in the eye. "You *have* been a good friend. You don't gloss things over, and that's what I needed to...to help me see things clearly." That was as much as he was going to say, but it seemed to satisfy Andy.

"Good. How about we get these trees finished so we can play some ball?"

Now he was talking. He'd missed hanging with Andy.

* * *

December first arrived with almost two feet of snow. School let out mid-day Thursday, and Shannon barely got the Explorer home through the accumulating snow. Kevin got stranded in Bristol, but Andy made it home right before the power went out. It wasn't restored until Saturday. Friday was a snow day, of course, and Shannon spent most of her time trying to entertain her three younger siblings, and adding wood to the fireplace after Andy showed her what to do. Kurt showed up on a snowmobile late afternoon, and Shannon opted to hang out in her frigid room. She knew she'd have to face him again one day, but she wasn't quite ready.

Finally on Sunday she ventured out onto the now clear roads to meet up with Jesse at church. Betty patted her arm as they passed each other in the foyer.

"I am so glad to see you again, Shannon. If you ever need anything, you let me know, okay?"

Shannon smiled and thanked the sweet lady before following Jesse into the sanctuary.

"Betty's the reason I'm here," he whispered as she sat down beside him.

"What do you mean?"

"I'll tell you all about it sometime." He nodded at the group approaching the platform. "Right now it's time to sing."

Shannon had missed the congregational singing last time. She didn't know many of the songs, but with Jesse singing beside her, she had a strong lead to follow. His voice was wonderful.

Just like everything else about him, Shannon mused.

The sermon was about prayer. Shannon still hadn't ever prayed. The concept intrigued her. Prayer was Heaven's 911 line, the pastor said. He read several Bible verses about prayer, but Shannon wasn't used to the way the Bible was worded. The one thing that stood out was that God was like any other friend in that, to have a good relationship, she had to communicate with Him. He was unlike any other friend in that no prayer went unanswered.

"We can't *see* God in the process of answering our prayers. But in the Bible it promises that before we even ask God, He's already working on our answers. He doesn't need us to present our problems for Him to know they are there. He's all knowing—He already knows! But He needs us to present our problems to Him so that He knows we believe He is able to fix them. Prayer is our expression of faith. Prayer is our way of throwing ourselves on His mercy, admitting that we *cannot* do it on our own, acknowledging that God is our only recourse. God is *always* our only recourse."

Shannon considered the concept as she drove home. It couldn't hurt to try, right?

After shutting off the engine, she sat in the Explorer in the garage and bowed her head. She had no idea how to start.

"Hi, God? I don't know how to pray, and there's a lot about You I don't understand. But Jesse says You love me, and I'm choosing to believe him. So, if there's one thing You can do, please help me and my dad to get along. I really do want to have a better relationship with him, but I don't know how. Yeah, I guess that's it for now. Oh, a—amen."

She opened her eyes. That had been...weird. Not quite the way the pastor had described it. But somehow she'd been able to tell God what she'd never even told herself. She thought she hated Kevin. But somewhere inside, she didn't want to anymore.

Chapter Twenty-One

By the middle of the week, Shannon had said enough little prayers that she was starting to like it. In fact, she wanted more.

She paused beside the Explorer after school. Jesse had walked her out, and Laura was nowhere to be found. Shannon hoped she was making better friends this time around.

"Jesse, how do I become a Christian?"

He looked so stunned by the sudden question that at first he was silent. Then, as sudden as her question, his dimples popped in, and his face glowed with a smile.

"It's very simple. You ask Jesus Christ to come into your heart and life and to take out anything that shouldn't be there."

Shannon stared at him, barely daring to hope. She'd thought it would be some complicated ritual.

"That's all?"

"Yes. But don't underestimate it. It takes faith. Just because you give your life to God, it doesn't mean you will always feel Him. Sometimes you just have to trust. But it all starts by asking Him to take over." He squeezed her shoulder. "You won't regret it. Your life will never be the same again, Shan."

She mulled over his words as she drove home, picking up her siblings along the way. She wished she had someone else to confide in, but she could already predict the reactions of everyone in her life. If any of them thought God was as important as Jesse claimed, she would have grown up in church, right? And she wouldn't be going to church alone, right?

But then, Jesse went to church alone, too. So either he was on to something that his family didn't understand, or he was dead wrong. Shannon intended to find out. She was tired of lugging around all the weight in her heart.

The more she thought of it, the more restless she became. She paced around her room at home, feeling like something inside was chewing mercilessly on her heart. She was terrified.

What if God didn't answer?

But what if He did?

She nearly staggered to the ground, falling on her knees under the weight of it all. The weight of grief over losing her mother; the weight of loss from the shattered image of her mom; the weight of hurt and resentment toward Kevin; the weight of the tremendous responsibility he had dumped on her, to be in charge of the house and his two young children; the weight of the shame and rejection from knowing she had been a mistake from birth; the weight of stress over grades and her educational future; the weight of worry about her sister; the weight of missing Jaime and Alan and Todd.

She felt the weight. And she couldn't carry it a moment longer.

"Oh God," she whispered as tears began to seep from her closed eyes, "help me! Please take it all, and take me. I don't want to feel this way anymore. I want to be Yours."

Something like a healing wind blew through Shannon, touching every hurt. It was a life-giving hug, wrapping around her, not letting go until she could raise her head and smile through her tears, knowing God in Heaven saw her looking up at Him. She stayed kneeling on the floor, gazing upward, basking in the warm and loving presence of God. It was unlike anything she'd ever experienced, and then words came to her almost as a whisper in her mind, *I love you, My child, and I will never let you go.*

Her skin tingled with chilled bumps as she froze, overcome with awe. God was way bigger than she had thought. And right now, she felt incredibly small. Yet He had still heard her and reached down the instant she called. It was phenomenal. She sat quietly for a long time, shocked by the presence of God. She never wanted the feeling to fade. Gradually the intensity ebbed, replaced by a peace she had never known before. She smiled upward and whispered a thank you as joy bubbled up inside of her like a water fountain.

That evening during dinner, Kevin kept glancing at her. "What's got you so chipper, Shannon?"

She smiled. She couldn't seem to stop. The experience seemed too private, too intimate to share, but she would try.

"Well, I was feeling really overwhelmed about...everything." Kevin's eyes softened in understanding. "So I asked God to take it all. And...He did." It really *was* that simple.

Kevin's eyes went wide. "Well, um, good for you, Shannon." There was unmistakable wistfulness in his voice, but before Shannon could even wonder what it meant, Laura's snort sounded across the table.

"You're so weird, Shannon."

"Be nice, Laura," Kevin reprimanded with a scowl before he looked back to Shannon. "I'd like to talk to you after dinner."

"What did I do now?"

He threw back his head and laughed. "Can't I ask to talk to my daughter without indicating trouble?"

Shannon sighed heavily. "My track record isn't so good."

He was still smiling when he ushered her into his office a few minutes later, but he quickly sobered.

"I know you're not happy that I won't let you go to Chicago for Christmas. I didn't give my reasons at the time, but I'd like to explain. I'm really not a tyrant. I just really *do* want you girls here for Christmas. Not only because we are family now, but also—" His forehead creased with stressed furrows. "See, we always went to my mom's for Thanksgiving, and then Carmen's family came here for Christmas." His Adam's apple bobbed, and Shannon knew he hurt just talking about it. Half the time she forgot about the emotional pain he was in, because he didn't show it.

"Anyway, that obviously won't be happening this year, and it's going to be difficult for Gabby and Daniel. But they love you, Shannon. It's hard for me to admit, but right now *you* are the most consistent thing in their lives—not me. And they need you here this Christmas." His eyes pled with her to understand, to empathize, and his honesty turned her heart to mush.

"I'll make it a great Christmas for them," she promised.

Kevin shook his head. "That's not what I'm asking. Just be their sister. That's all they want."

Suddenly Shannon felt like crying, although she didn't know why. Thank goodness Kevin changed the topic.

"Tomorrow after dinner we are heading next door to select our Christmas tree."

That got Shannon's full attention. "Next door?"

He nodded. "I would love to have you come, so we can be a complete family. It's a tradition. But since it's almost guaranteed that you will run into Kurt, I'm going to leave that up to you."

Not for the first time, Shannon felt appreciation for the mature way Kevin treated her. When he felt like it.

"Thanks for the heads up. I'll let you know what I decide."

* * *

Shannon's traitorous heart thumped abnormally fast as she tried to ignore Kurt at the orchard stand. It was difficult, since he'd stopped in his tracks to stare at her the moment she walked in with her family. He was still staring as Kevin approached him, and Shannon turned her full attention to Gabby and the cute Christmas stockings that she was pointing to by the check-out counter. Kevin better not let on to Kurt that he knew about their would-be relationship. She'd die right here underneath the mistletoe.

Daniel was jumping up and down trying to reach a candy dish on the counter, and she picked him up, straining to hear any snippets of conversation across the room. It was rather crowded, but she heard Kevin say, "Just pick out your finest, and we'll be back shortly."

He herded the kids outside into the crisp air. Last week's snow crunched beneath Shannon's running shoes as she followed Andy toward the rows of Christmas trees. Still attached to the ground.

"Uh, what are we doing?" She trotted to catch up with Kevin. "It's pitch black out!"

"I know!" He actually grinned. "Isn't it great?"

Gabby bounced beside her. "It's our annual Christmas tree blackout!"

Kevin explained that every year while Kurt or his dad picked out their tallest and best tree for the living room, the family went into the orchard under cover of darkness and picked out a tree for the family room with flashlights.

"We never know what we have until we get back to the light." Kevin shook his head. "We've had a few monstrosities. But it's one of the kids' favorite Christmas traditions."

"My *most* favorite!" Gabby insisted emphatically.

Shannon laughed. "Well, I guess I have to experience it to understand. But I'm game!" Her breath left a visible trail around her, and she hugged her winter coat tighter. "Man, it's cold!"

"Supposed to get down to four degrees tonight," Andy supplied from behind. "We'd better hurry up. This is a good place to look."

Shannon had almost forgotten that Andy had inside knowledge of the orchard. This was her first time ever going to cut down a Christmas tree. Mom had an artificial one with pre-lit lights. It went up in a few minutes. Last year they hadn't had more than a miniature tree on the counter top. Mom had been admitted to the hospital a few weeks before Christmas and barely got home in time to celebrate the holidays.

Shannon shook off the morose thoughts and pretended to look for the perfect tree, although she really had no idea what she was looking for.

"I think I found one!" They followed Andy's voice and after much deliberation decided to cut it down. Shannon shined the brightest flashlight on the base of the tree where Andy was sawing while Kevin stood holding the tree steady.

"How's it coming?"

Shannon jumped at Kurt's voice, casting the beam astray. Where had he come from?

"Better focus on Andy, Shannon, or he'll saw his arm off."

The nerve. She sent a glare in his direction, hoping he could see it in spite of the dark. His throaty chuckle told her he had. And made her stomach flip.

Andy sawed through the final edge of the pine, and then he and Kevin picked it up and started walking. Shannon leaned her head back and her breath caught. It wasn't pitch black at all. It was a beautiful canopy of twinkling lights. The stars were resplendent! She knew she should keep walking or she was going to get left behind, but she couldn't tear her gaze from the spangled sky.

Footsteps crunched and stopped beside her and she knew without looking who it was. He said nothing as he joined her stargazing.

"Aren't they glorious?" she asked reverently. To think God had fashioned each one.

"They are." Kurt sounded reluctant. "We should probably catch up with everyone else."

They were alone in the dark with only the stars to witness. And he wasn't trying to take advantage. Interesting.

They began walking in silence, but Shannon tripped, bumping against Kurt as she caught her footing.

"I'm sorry, I'm sorry." She jerked away from him. "I can't really see." She'd given the flashlight back to Andy.

Kurt held out his arm like a proper gentlemen. "I know this place like my house."

Shannon hesitated, then slowly linked her arm through his. They both wore layers of jackets and gloves, but she still felt the electricity. What was it about him?

"So what are you planning to study in college?"

Shannon was surprised by the question. She wasn't sure whether Kurt was trying to start over in order to win her back or to prove his promised changes. But clearly he was after something. He still wasn't giving up.

"I don't know." She hadn't thought much about it yet. "I've considered music performance or culinary school. Maybe fine art. Kevin's pushing college apps down my throat."

"So you'll be going away?"

He sounded genuinely disappointed.

"I guess. What about you?"

* * *

Kurt let Shannon's question slosh around his mind for a minute before answering. They were nearing the stand. He didn't want this walk to end. He'd missed Shannon unmercifully, and he hadn't let himself hope for an opportunity like this to just be with her. Even for a few minutes.

"I'll probably do another year at community college. I do okay with grades, but I leave all the impressive education to my brother." What he meant was, he left all the success, all the right choices, all the impressing-the-parents to his brother.

"I didn't know you have a brother."

Kurt groaned inwardly. Why had he brought it up? "We're not very close."

"Oh. Where does he live?"

"He goes to Harvard's School of Law." Wait for it...

"Wow!" Shannon's voice filled with good impressions. "That's really cool!"

Yeah, or not. "I guess. Anyway, he'll be here at Christmas."

Their conversation died and he chanced a glance at her face. Still glowing. He'd noticed it the second she's graced the orchard stand with her presence. Something was different about her. He was very afraid her happiness might have something to do with a certain Jesse.

"So I was wondering, well—you seem different somehow than when I last saw you, or any other time, really. Is—is there a particular reason?" He held his breath.

"Different...how?" Shannon asked as she bobbed along next to him. They were desperately out of step, and he needed to slow down and match her stride, but if they went any slower, he was afraid of what he'd do to her that he'd regret. Like grabbing her face in both hands and kissing her smack on the lips.

He thought for a minute. "It's almost like you're..." He searched for the words. "You're glowing inside. And it's shining out of you."

"Wow." Shannon stopped and faced him, pulling her arm away from his. The light from the orchard stand reached them now. "That is the nicest compliment anyone's ever given me."

Man, he liked this girl. "So what's the secret?"

"God." She dropped the name so easily, Kurt wasn't even sure he'd heard correctly.

"Come again?"

"I realized how much God loves me." She smiled sweetly and with the halo of light bursting around her head from the stand's outside lights behind her, Kurt could have sworn she was an angel. "And it changed my whole outlook on life."

He scratched his head through his winter hat. Why were so many people in his life running to religion like it had all the answers? First Mom and Dad, now Shannon. Who next, Andy?

His only response was a low *hmmm* in his throat, and he kept walking. All he knew about God was a whole lot of *do*s and *don't*s, and not much fun.

Chapter Twenty-Two

"Laura! What's the hold up? We're gonna be late!" Seriously, that girl had made Shannon late for school three days in a row, and Shannon was sick of it. Marching up the stairs, she found her sister in the bathroom with the door closed. Shannon pounded her fist on the door.

"Laura Conrad! We need to be in first period in ten minutes, and we have to drop off Gabby and Daniel on the way. Come *on!*"

The door flew open and Laura staggered out, clutching her stomach. Her face was pale. "For your information, I think I have the stomach flu," she snapped, pushing by Shannon.

Rolling her eyes, Shannon followed. "You and your ailments. You said that *last* week."

Laura's "stomach flu" continued all week, and Shannon was starting to get worried. She thought maybe it was time to mention it to Kevin since he was, after all, a doctor, but then finals hit, and she was too busy studying to remember. Somehow she slid by in every class, passing, but barely. Thanks to some very late nights and good friends.

On top of exams was last-minute Christmas shopping and decorating the house. Kevin hosted a big shin-dig party on Christmas Eve every year, and he wanted the house immaculate. Shannon spent hours cleaning. Andy warned her that Kurt would be in attendance. She hadn't seen him much since their starry walk in the snow. He came and went with Andy as he had in the past and always sought her out to say hi. But that was it. She made sure of it.

The day before the party, she spent all afternoon baking. Kevin was having the event catered, so he didn't need any extra dessert, but what would Christmas be without baking? Shannon had special memories in the kitchen with her mom every year until last year. That's when she'd started baking alone.

She rolled the last fudge ball and slid the tray into the fridge, then headed upstairs. She hadn't seen Laura in hours. Her sister had been unusually quiet the past few days since school had dismissed for winter break.

"Laura?" Her bedroom door was closed, but when Shannon tried the handle, she discovered Laura curled up in bed asleep. Same as yesterday. Laura had always been a little lazy, but these days it seemed she did nothing but sleep.

Shannon shoved down the worry that was creeping up her throat. Laura was fine.

The next morning after breakfast, Shannon went to her room to change into running shoes, hoping to hit the treadmill in the basement, but she froze when she heard her sister heaving in the bathroom. Laura moaned and flushed the toilet, then returned to her room.

The axis of Shannon's world tilted.

Laura had been sick for three weeks now.

It was not the stomach flu.

She plowed into Laura's room without knocking. Laura sat on her bed sobbing with her arms wrapped around her middle.

"Laura, what's going on?" Shannon struggled to control the panic mounting in her chest. She breathed a prayer that didn't make a bit of grammatical sense.

Laura turned her ashen face toward Shannon, tears coursing down her cheeks. "I think I'm pregnant."

The word hit Shannon with the force of a football, even though she'd braced herself for it. "When was your last period?

"October."

"Oh, Laura," Shannon groaned, rubbing her palm on her forehead. "I didn't even know you had...*Ughhh*. Who did you sleep with?"

Laura's face crumpled, and she doubled over, weeping. "I don't know. There was more than one."

Shannon couldn't hold back the cry deep in her throat. Her sister was fifteen. *Fif. Teen.*

Laura sat up suddenly and grabbed Shannon's hand, squeezing it tightly. "I have to know for certain. Will you buy me a test? Please, Shannon. Today?"

Shannon swallowed hard, her chest heaving with emotion. Maybe—maybe Laura was wrong. There was only one way to know. "I'll go when I get a chance to sneak away. I promise."

Shannon finally came up with an excuse to run into town around four o'clock. She told Kevin she had to borrow a curling iron from Stephanie to do her hair tonight. It was a total lie, and she had a feeling she wasn't supposed to be lying as a Christian. But what was she supposed to say? Laura thinks she might be pregnant, so I'm going to the pharmacy to buy a pregnancy test so we can find out? Because that was the truth.

It only took her a few minutes to find the pregnancy tests at Rite Aid, and she just hoped nobody saw her that knew her. No curling iron could get her out of this one. Thankfully the store wasn't busy, since it was about to close for Christmas Eve, and she quickly selected a digital test for ten dollars. There were cheaper ones, but she wasn't going to risk the accuracy.

Back home she worked hard to convince Laura to get ready for the party first and wait until later to take the test. She helped her sister get ready before she turned attention to herself. She didn't feel much in a festive mood with Laura's condition, but her presence was expected downstairs shortly. Kevin had bought her a new dress online, and she had been looking forward to wearing it. Surprisingly he knew her taste. Deviating from typical holiday colors, her dress was gunmetal, halfway between silver and slate blue. It was a straight, fitted cut ending just above her knees, overlaid with lace and subtle sparkles. Sleeves reached just past her elbows. Best of all, it was comfortable. A loose, curly up-do completed the look, and when Shannon checked the mirror, she was satisfied if she ignored the worried lines marring her forehead.

A knock sounded on her door, and Andy popped his head in. "Dad's wondering if you can come downstairs and play piano for the guests who arrive early. The string quartet he hired isn't due for another ten minutes." Shannon nodded and stood, slipping into shiny black and silver stilettos. "Wow...You look great. I better go warn Kurt so he doesn't keel over when he sees you."

It was almost true. As she descended the stairs behind Andy, she spotted Kurt near the front door talking with a man. He turned his head, and his whole face went slack at her sight. Shannon's heart beat with the power of being a woman. When she reached the last step, Kevin appeared out of nowhere, cleverly intercepting Kurt.

"Shannon, you look absolutely stunning. That dress was an excellent choice, I must say."

She smiled at him. He looked quite dashing himself, and much younger than his 50 years. She wondered what he looked like inside, standing alone through this party for the first time.

She played Christmas carols until the real musicians arrived, at which point she happily melted into the sidelines. Laura sat morosely beside the fireplace, playing with the empty punch glass in her hand.

"What are you doing?"

She jumped, startled by the familiar deep voice that pulled her out of her artistic reverie. There were so many new specimens present that she'd busied herself with her sketch journal for the past half hour. Apparently her hiding place in the corner wasn't so subtle after all.

Kurt grabbed the journal off her lap without asking, and she yelped and tried to jerk it back.

He *tssked* and held it out of her reach. "Not so fast." He flipped pages quickly, and Shannon cringed. There were way too many sketches of him in there, and when he smirked, she knew he'd seen one. Her face warmed as he handed it back to her.

"Even more talented than you let on."

"You should have asked first."

"Why, so you could hide the pictures of Jesse so I wouldn't feel raging jealousy in my chest?"

She hadn't even thought of that. "There's more pictures of you than him," she said softly.

He smiled and sat down beside her. "I'm just joking, Shannon. You can draw anyone you like without my input." He cut her a glance. "But yeah, there are quite a few of me. Something you want to tell me?" He winked, and she knew he wasn't serious. "You look great, by the way."

So did he, in his pressed black suit, but she wasn't about to say so.

"Is your sister okay?"

Shannon followed his gaze to Laura, still beside the fireplace, arms clasped around her middle again, staring vacantly into space. She stood up. If Kevin noticed her like that, things could get unpleasant.

"Please excuse me, Kurt."

She stopped in front of her sister. "Laura." Laura's head jerked up as her eyes came into focus. They welled with tears.

"I can't stop thinking of it, Shannon. What if —"

"Stop it," Shannon hissed. "Do you want Kevin to see you like this and start asking questions?"

Laura sucked her lips in pathetically and shook her head, but more tears filled her baby blues. Shannon sighed. "Go upstairs. If he asks, I'll say you have a headache." It would be another lie, but that was better than the truth, for tonight at least.

She watched her sister drag herself up the stairs before she plopped down right where she'd been. The fireplace crackled and warmed her suddenly chilly limbs. The "what-ifs" started creeping up on her, and she blinked rapidly. Why was her life a constant nightmare?

"What's wrong?"

Shannon turned a glare on Kurt. "Are you following me?"

He grinned, unashamed. "Totally. I'm a fly, and you're honey."

"Oh, please." Shannon rolled her eyes, but she couldn't keep from smiling in spite of her tears.

"No seriously, to the guy who can't stop staring at you it's obvious something's really wrong with you and Laura. Are you missing your mom?"

Shannon blew a long breath out of her mouth. If it was Kevin asking, it would be easy to lie and say yes. But it wasn't Kevin.

"It's more than that." She pressed her lips together to keep her emotions inside. She was going to burst if she didn't say it. She lowered her voice. "It's extremely confidential."

Kurt's eyebrows dipped so low they nearly stabbed his eyes. "You have my word."

She swallowed hard. Why was she telling him this? Her voice dropped to a whisper and she leaned as close to his ear as she dared, hoping no one was watching.

"Laura thinks she's pregnant."

She felt more than heard his sharp intake of breath, and his eyes locked on hers for a few seconds before slowly closing in disbelief.

"I bought her a test today, but she hasn't taken it yet."

This time she heard the small moan in his throat. "I'd heard some things about her, but I didn't think the rumors were true."

Shannon slumped her face into her hand. "I didn't have a clue. I've been so overwhelmed with my problems that I neglected my own sister." Her voice cracked and she caught a sob, forcing it back down her throat.

"Don't blame yourself," Kurt's gentle voice rumbled beside her. "We all make our own choices." She supposed he knew that better than anyone. She excused herself from him, escaping to the kitchen to snack on her homemade cookies. She couldn't wait for this stupid party to end. When it finally did, she took a deep breath and dug through her dresser drawer where she'd stashed the pregnancy test. Holding the little box in her hands, she closed her eyes and begged.

Please don't let it be positive. Please, God…

Laura was lying down, with one arm thrown back on the pillow behind her head, eyes wide open and staring at the ceiling.

"Are you ready?"

The whole bed shook from Laura's trembling, but her sister nodded and pushed herself up. Shannon opened the box and handed her the plastic strip. They made brief eye contact, and Shannon saw a level of terror in her sister that she couldn't comprehend. She followed Laura to the bathroom and waited outside the closed door. It felt like forever, even though it was only a couple minutes.

"No, no," came the anguished moan, and Shannon barged into the bathroom. Laura sat on the closed toilet with tears flowing down her face. The pregnancy test lay on the sink counter.

"Please tell me it isn't true," she sobbed, rocking back and forth.

Shannon felt like she was suffocating. She stood frozen, staring at the positive sign, listening to her sister's heart breaking into pieces beside her, but she couldn't seem to do anything. She couldn't even breathe.

God, help us.

The plea came from deep within her, instantly ungluing her from the floor. She pulled her sister into her arms, rubbing circles in her back as Laura bawled on her shoulder. When at last she got Laura to her room, she knelt by her bedside, stroking her hair away from her face until she fell asleep.

Then she stole across the hall into her darkened room. She didn't make it to her bed, but slowly staggered to the floor on her knees. Covering her face with her hands, she wept.

Chapter Twenty-Three

Shannon awoke stiff and shivering. She pushed herself up, her body crackling and popping. Why had she slept on her floor? In her party dress?

A weight settled into her chest, and she remembered.

Laura was pregnant.

She dragged herself to her bed and gathered the blankets around her cold body.

What were they going to do?

The next time she woke up, sunshine was filtering into her room, and excited shrieks sounded from downstairs.

Slipping out of her dress, she donned fuzzy sweatpants and a warm sweater, wrangled her smashed hair into a sloppy bun, and padded down the stairs. Daniel and Gabby were so busy dancing around the tree in the family room, surrounded by a mound of wrapped gifts, that they didn't notice her passing by.

Last week Kevin had sat down with her to discuss plans for Christmas day. He wanted to carry on their tradition of cinnamon rolls for breakfast, so Shannon found a promising recipe online made with rapid-rise yeast. She'd never made cinnamon rolls before, so she hoped they would turn out. When she'd asked about dinner, Kevin got quiet. He said Carmen always made Puerto Rican food with her family. This year the Blakes had extended a dinner invitation to them.

"Shanny!" a little voice crowed behind her. She whirled around with dough covered hands to find a pajama-clad Daniel racing into the kitchen. "Did you see all the presents?"

"I sure did. I wonder if any of them are for you?"

His eyes went wide as he gasped, "I don't know!"

Gabby followed him into the kitchen and hugged Shannon tightly around the waist. "Merry Christmas, Shannon." Shannon returned the hug best she could. These two. Probably the only bright spots she'd see on this holiday.

She slid breakfast into the oven and was washing her hands when Kevin entered the kitchen, wearing a dark green and black striped button-up. Shannon paused to observe. She couldn't deny it. Andy had gotten his good looks from their dad. No wonder Mom had fallen for him all those years ago.

"Merry Christmas, everyone," he boomed with a big smile, swooping Daniel up into one arm. He gave Gabby a hug with the other arm, then moved toward Shannon. Was he going to hug her? Because he hadn't in nine years, and she wasn't sure she wanted him to. He must have sensed her resistance, because he stopped and put his hand on her shoulder, giving her a light squeeze.

"The cinnamon rolls look great. I didn't expect you to make them. Carmen always bought them from Nancy."

"Oh." Shannon shrugged. "Buying them never occurred to me."

He chuckled lightly. "Just like your mom."

An operation would have hurt less than his words, but Shannon shoved the feelings away. She had a sister in crisis.

As she scaled the stairs two at a time, memories with Laura flew through her mind at high speed. They'd been two peas in a pod when they were younger. It was only in the past few years they had pulled apart. Just how far, she hadn't realized until now.

Blood-shot eyes rimmed with dark circles greeted Shannon. She'd never seen her sister look so miserable. Sinking onto the bed beside her, she gave her a hug. Laura held on tightly.

Shannon didn't know how to ask her next question, but she needed to know.

"Laura, what happened?" She gently pried her sister's face off her shoulder. "I mean, how did this happen?"

"What kind of question is that? Only one way to get pregnant, Shan."

"I know that. But why? You've had boyfriends before and didn't sleep with them. Why now?"

Laura sighed, fidgeting with the blanket that was wadded into a knot in her fist. "When we first got here, I was so lonely. I missed Mom..." Her voice choked up and she paused to take a deep breath. "I missed her so much. You were busy and mad all the time, fighting with Kevin. I just needed Mom to pull me into her arms and hug me like she always did. But she wasn't here anymore to do that. So when I met a guy who wanted to do that...I let him."

Shannon slipped her arm around Laura's shoulders and squeezed.

"But it didn't stop with a hug. And it felt so good to be held, to be—to be noticed. I feel invisible around Kevin and Andy—and even you sometimes. So when he pushed for more, I didn't fight it. For a few minutes, I was his whole world." She raised her eyes to Shannon's, her lips quivering. "I just wanted to feel loved, Shan. Just loved. Don't hate me for that."

"Laura." Shannon took her sister's face in her hands and kissed her forehead. "I could never hate you."

"I hate myself," Laura whispered, tears overflowing and streaming down her face. "I'm such an idiot. When it was over, he was gone, and so was a part of me I never got back. It hurt so bad that he didn't care, that he had just used me. I thought the next guy would be different, and I still wanted to be held, to feel loved, so I let it happen again. And again..." Her voice cracked and she bent over, sobbing into Shannon's lap. Shannon's tears fell swiftly, dripping into Laura's hair.

When her sister sat up, she looked resolved, drying her face.

"I'm pretty sure who got me pregnant, because I only had unprotected sex once, but he'll never take responsibility."

"Shouldn't you at least try to talk with him? Or maybe Kevin could." If he didn't kill her first. "How are you going to tell him?"

"I'm not!" Laura gasped as if it was the most outrageous question she'd ever heard. "You're kidding, right? You think I'm going to tell him? He'll crucify me!"

"Yeah, but won't he be even madder if he finds out later? I mean, you won't be able to hide it forever."

Laura closed her eyes, and Shannon wished she'd used more tact. Her sister was under enough stress in the moment without thinking of the future.

"Listen." She seized Shannon's arm painfully. "You gotta promise me not to tell anyone. No one. You are the *only* person who knows, and it's gotta stay that way until I figure some things out."

Guilt slammed into Shannon. Why had she told Kurt the situation?

"I won't. I promise." If he told anyone, she was going to murder him.

Laura sank back down and buried her face in her hands. "I already barfed three times. I think I better stay in bed today."

"Unless you want Kevin to figure things out immediately, you're going to have to pull yourself together, sis. He's a doctor. If I tell him you're sick, he'll come check on you. Besides, it's Christmas. You can't stay in bed." Shannon tugged on her arm.

Laura groaned and flopped her head back down without reply.

Opening her sister's closet, Shannon skimmed the contents. When had Laura collected so many skanky outfits?

"Here." She pulled out a sparkly silver and black top. "Wear this with your new jeans. You'll look great in pictures."

She held her breath until Laura pushed herself up with a sigh.

"Okay, fine."

Shannon puffed out relief. Who knew how many times she'd have to repeat her pep talk today.

The day proceeded with opening presents, following by a late breakfast. Her cinnamon rolls were a smashing success. Shannon got many lovely things. Clothes, art supplies, music, electronics... Kevin was a generous father, and surprisingly discerning about her taste and desires, but Shannon could barely focus. Her eyes kept straying to check on her sister. So far Laura was holding it together. She'd caked on enough makeup to mask her misery.

Alan called, and Shannon kept it brief, mostly thanking him for the meaningful but inexpensive gifts he had mailed. She couldn't bear to pretend all was well with her step-father when it wasn't. She cherished her few words with Jaime. Man, she missed that kid. Todd had texted to say he would call later. He was spending the day with his girlfriend's family.

They were expected at the Blakes' no later than 3:00 for dinner, so Shannon went back to the kitchen. They couldn't show up empty-handed. Sweet and spicy glazed ham was her mom's Christmas tradition, and she couldn't imagine Christmas dinner without it. Or green beans with lemon herb butter, oven-baked baby red potatoes with dill, and candied sweet potatoes. That wasn't overdoing it, was it? Certainly the Blakes had other relatives at their home for Christmas. They needed lots of food. She threw in some leftover raspberry brownies just to be safe.

When they arrived at the charmingly rustic log cabin nestled amid towering pines, Kurt swung the door open before they even rang the bell. A large number of people were crowded in the living room, but Shannon ducked out with her large basket, following the smell of food. She needed to get the food to the kitchen. And avoid Kurt as much as possible.

"Mrs. Blake? I brought a few contributions for the meal."

The pretty blond woman spun around, oven-mitted hands flailing. "Oh goodness, you scared me, Shannon!" She laughed. "I'm racing against the clock here! Do you mind giving me a hand? Sorry we missed the party last night. We were picking up my parents at the airport."

"Oh, you didn't miss much." Shannon quickly unloaded her box of goodies onto the counter.

Mrs. Blake turned and froze at the sight on her counter. "Hun, you didn't need to bring all that! Although, I must say I am eager to try it. I still remember the food you made for your dad's birthday, and I can't tell you how many times Kurt has come home raving about your cooking."

Did Kurt talk about her that much? That was embarrassing.

When Mrs. Blake shoed her out of the kitchen a while later, Shannon peaked into the living room. Mostly full of people she didn't know, but Kurt was not among them, and that was all that mattered.

"Merry Christmas, Shannon." She paused and realized Mr. Blake was sitting on a couch she was passing.

"Hi Mr. Blake, merry Christmas." She smiled politely. A young man sat beside Kurt's dad, and she wondered if it was a cousin.

"This is my son Robert. I don't believe you've met."

His son? He didn't look a thing like him! Or anyone else in the family. Dark hair, dark eyes, and…short, she noted, as he stood up to shake her hand.

"Pleasure to meet you, Shannon. I've already heard much about you."

She wished she could say the same. "Nice to meet you, too." She would have tried to make a little more small talk, but Kurt appeared at that moment, headed in her direction, so she gave a quick nod and moved on. A swift glance revealed Gabby and Daniel sitting by the Christmas tree, so she headed in their direction. They were playing with the carved nativity set underneath the tree.

Shannon stared at the figure of a tiny baby nestled among hay in a manger. The artist's detail was minute. Honestly, she could understand why some people had a hard time believing in Christianity. But she believed. She *had* to. Without that belief, she had nothing to cling to. Without that belief, she didn't know how she was going to make it through the coming months.

Picking up the figure of baby Jesus, she held it in her palm, willing an answer to jump straight out of the manger. When it didn't, she squeezed her hand tightly around the hard, carved wood, closing her eyes against tears of despair. She jumped when a hand rested on her head.

"Are you avoiding me?" It was Kurt's deep voice, his tone low. She leaned to replace baby Jesus to his spot in the center of the nativity. Kurt squatted down next to her and reached out to finger a shepherd figurine with the fondness that only comes from a creator. If he had carved this set, he had a lot more artistic ability than Shannon realized.

"Do you believe?" Shannon asked softly, ignoring his question.

Kurt shrugged. "In Jesus? Come on. The whole God in baby form, growing up to die, rising again. It's a fable."

Shannon felt a pang of sadness. She sure hoped it wasn't made up. No, it couldn't be. She'd heard God's whisper.

"Did she take the test?" His voice was a whisper now. Shannon rolled her eyes inward, recalling how pushy Kurt could be.

She pressed her lips together and looked away, but not before tears filled her eyes.

"Hey," his voice softened like melting butter. "I'm only asking because I care. I care about you, which means I care about anyone *you* care about."

Shannon darted her eyes toward Gabby and Daniel, but they were absorbed in their play. "Positive." One word said it all. Kurt looked a little ill, but he recovered quickly.

"Are you *sure*? Those tests can be wrong."

"She's been sick for three weeks. You know, morning sickness." She hesitated, shy to mention something so private to Kurt. "And she's missed her period for two months."

"Oh." Kurt looked slightly embarrassed. "So then you're sure."

She nodded and repeated, "Positive."

Kurt studied her face intently. "How is she?"

"What do you think?" she snapped, then instantly shrank down. That had been too loud.

Silence hung between them before Kurt spoke again. "And you? How are you doing?"

Shannon wanted to be mad at his never-ending pestering, but when she looked up, ready with a snarky reply, she was stopped by the care brimming in his eyes.

"I don't know." Honestly, she didn't. She was still in shock. "I'm worried. Disappointed. Freaking out. So many things. She won't tell me who... you know. And she's refusing to tell Kevin."

"Can you blame her?"

No, she didn't blame Laura for not telling Kevin. But she had a feeling that whenever Kevin found out, he'd be blaming *her*.

"Promise me you won't say anything—to anyone?"

He looked down at her, his dark blue eyes betraying tender emotions. When he reached out and touched her cheek, she felt the spark of energy hum through her whole body. She hadn't forgotten what it felt like to be in his arms, but she forced herself to remember who this was. The guy she didn't trust. At all.

"Kurt?" The sharp tone rang out at the same moment Shannon leaned away. Kurt jerked his hand from her face, whispered, "I promise," and stood up. Jason Blake stood a few feet away, arms crossed as he watched his son. Kurt's jaw flexed when he held his father's gaze. Shannon had no idea what was going on between them, and she preferred it to stay that way.

When Mrs. Blake called them to the dinner table, a mixture of relief and disappointment sizzled through Shannon when she saw Kurt sitting on the other side of the table, not even across from her. Somehow she ended up in between an older woman who she assumed was his grandma, and his brother-who-didn't-look-like-a-brother. Robert was downright charming as he held Shannon's seat out for her even though Kurt was sending eye darts their way.

Laura was directly across from her, and Shannon tried to catch her eye. She was too busy staring at her lap to notice.

"Laura!" she whispered, and her sister gave her a tight smile and mouthed "I'm okay." Shannon was proud of Laura for holding it together so well. She doubted she would be performing this well if the roles were reversed.

During the meal Shannon couldn't help noticing the obvious differences and underlying tension between Kurt and his brother. Kurt was silent, actually, while Robert turned out to be quite the conversationalist. He kept the table captivated by his stories of mock trials at Harvard's law school. Mr. and Mrs. Blake seemed content to let him do all the talking as they watched with pride shining in their eyes. Shannon wondered if anyone else was catching Kurt's occasional eye-rolls at his brother's narratives.

"The ham is exceptional," Mr. Blake interjected into the conversation. "You made it, right, Shannon?"

She nodded shyly. "I'm glad you like it."

For the first time since the meal began, Kurt spoke. "Just wait till you try her desserts, Dad. You'll be begging for more. Especially her apple pie. Wow."

Shannon felt her face heat hot enough to bake said dessert, remembering what had happened after the last time she'd given Kurt apple pie. She couldn't believe he would bring that up right now! She glared at him until he looked down, but his annoying smirk told her what he was thinking about. She silenced a growl in her throat. No way was she going to trust him again.

Later on in the meal, she noticed that Gabby had stopped eating. Her plate was still full with entrees, but her fork had dropped in the middle, and she stared at her plate unseeingly. They were at opposite ends of the table, but no one seemed to notice when she got up and crept to Gabby's chair. Squatting beside Gabby, she put a hand on her back.

"Is something wrong, Gabby?"

Gabby turned toward Shannon, not quite looking into her eyes. "I miss my mom. She didn't send a present. She hasn't even called yet!" Big tears suddenly rolled down her face and plopped onto the table, and her voice dropped to a whisper. "I don't think she loves me anymore."

Shannon slipped her arms around her little sister and hugged her tightly. Gabby's feelings were an exact mirror of what Shannon had felt her first Christmas without Kevin nine years ago. She knew the pain of rejection well. Her mom had done her best to soothe her wounds, though. Perhaps Kevin could do the same for Gabby.

She reached for Gabby's chin and turned it in the direction where Kevin sat.

"You still have one parent who loves you very much, Gabby. I know it's not the same. But sometimes it's enough."

A sharp pain exploded inside her, so strong she nearly doubled over. Mom had always been enough. But now she was gone. In her distress over Laura's catastrophe, she hadn't thought about it. Her first Christmas without Mom. For the rest of her life. A shudder trembled through her body at the realization.

"You going to be okay?" she managed to ask. Gabby nodded.

"Yeah, I'm okay."

But Shannon wasn't.

* * *

He shouldn't have made that comment about pie. Judging by her face, he had sent himself spiraling downward in her good opinion.

Kurt had no clue how Shannon became more beautiful each time he saw her. He couldn't take his eyes off of her, even if she was mad at him. She'd left her red waves hanging loosely today, the way he liked her best. Her bright red off-the-shoulder top shimmered around her, showcasing one slender shoulder. Not just any red-head could pull off that shirt. But Shannon wasn't just any red-head.

He took a bite of a raspberry brownie, marveling that everything she touched came out delicious. When he looked up, she was crouched beside Gabby, giving her a hug. She moved away a moment later, in the direction of her place at the table, but then she paused, blinking rapidly before rushing out of the dining room. He glanced around. It didn't look like anyone else had noticed. Kevin was busy talking to his aunt, and Laura was toying with her fork, not eating anything.

Something was wrong with Shannon. He'd seen tears shining in those ocean blues of hers. He wasn't going to just sit here and do nothing.

He stood up.

"Sit down, Kurt," his dad barked. Apparently his dad had noticed. Too bad.

Throwing his napkin on his plate, he grunted an apology and left the table. His dad called his name again, but he kept going.

Shannon didn't know her way around his house, so she couldn't have made it very far. A quick check showed she hadn't gone to the living room, the nearest room.

A sniff caught his attention, and he followed it. Shannon stood in the hallway with her back to him, hugging her arms around herself. When a sob tore from her throat, Kurt couldn't stop himself from reaching for her shoulder. She whirled around at his touch.

"Leave me alone, Kurt. I want to be by myself."

Leave her alone? With tears coursing like a downpour? Not a chance.

He reached out a hand for her face, intent on wiping the tears, but she jerked away.

"Don't you dare try anything."

He definitely shouldn't have made the pie comment. "I'm just here because I care. Want to tell me what's wrong?"

She hesitated, then her face crumbled as she wailed, "I miss my mom." She sobbed harder and rocked back and forth, tightly hugging herself. Kurt felt helpless, but he didn't think she'd appreciate a forced hug. He racked his brain for ideas. Respectable comfort.

Yeah, he had nothing. Not his area.

She took a series of deep breaths and lifted a sleeve to mop her face.

"I'm a mess," she croaked.

"A little bit." He couldn't help smiling at her dry honesty as he peered at her blotchy, mascara-smeared face. She was still adorable. Speaking of adorable... "I may have a remedy. Not for the mess, but for the rest."

Shannon looked at him curiously.

"Follow me."

The fact that she did without question made Kurt's heart race. She trusted him more than she let on.

He led her into the laundry room. Shannon let out a squeal before he said a word and sprang to her hands and knees on the floor.

"So cuuuuute!" She scooped the tiny cocker spaniel pup into her lap. "When did you get him? Wait, is it a boy?" She checked. "Yep. What's his name?"

Kurt let out a happy laugh at her reaction. He wasn't sure who was more adorable, Shannon or the puppy.

"He was a Christmas present from my dad. My dog of 10 years died last year. I didn't think I would ever be ready for a new one, but this little guy..." He squatted down beside Shannon and scratched the puppy's ears. "He stole my heart immediately." Just like Shannon.

She hugged the dog to her chest, grinning brighter than the light. "I don't blame you. I'm smitten forever."

"So if I looked more like him, I'd have a better chance, huh?"

Shannon rolled her eyes at him. "Don't even go there, Kurt. Not today."

"Sorry." He laughed it off, shaking his head. "I named him Jefferson."

"That's cute, but for a dog?"

"Well my first dog as a kid was Washington, for George Washington, because I was obsessed with the revolutionary war at the time. So then my next dog I named Quincy. For John Quincy Adams, the next president. But Adams sounded just ridiculous, so I went with Quincy. I decided to carry on the presidential sequence, so this little one is stuck with Jefferson."

Shannon was outright laughing at him. "You are way more of a nerd than people think."

"And don't you dare tell." Kurt watched Shannon pour her love on one happy little pup for a few minutes before he cleared his throat.

"What do you miss most about your mom?"

Shannon's head jerked up and her eyes locked with Kurt's, and he felt her pain take a stab at his heart.

"Everything. She was my best friend. She was always there for me. Even when she was half-dead from chemo and cancer, she was still there for me in her heart. Sometimes I get so busy, I forget she's gone forever. Then when I remember..." Fresh tears overflowed from her eyes, and she smote her chest. "It hurts real bad."

Kurt eased onto his rump on the floor and slipped an arm loosely around her back. He was surprised when she leaned into him, her body shaking with sobs. Finally she pulled away.

"I'm sorry. It's just—"

"Stop it." He wanted nothing more than to pull her against his chest, as she was doing to Jefferson. "It's okay to cry." He was about to give another try at wiping her cheeks when Jefferson planted two paws on her chest and lifted his face to hers, licking her tears.

They both dissolved into soft laughter.

* * *

Shannon swiveled her head around when a sneeze sounded behind them. Kevin stood at the doorway, hand covering his nose.

"For pity's sake, Kurt. Can't you find a better place for this dog?"

Kurt chuckled. "You sound like my mom. I just got him this morning, and she's already giving him the eviction notice."

Kevin sneezed again. "Got a Kleenex around here?"

Shannon knew Kevin had a severe dander allergy. No medicine had helped after she and Laura got a puppy one Easter. They'd had to get rid of Max three days later. Broke Shannon's heart.

"He's allergic to animals," she informed Kurt.

Kevin's hand dropped from his face. "You remember?"

How could she forget?

She raised her chin, still wet from tears and Jefferson's tongue. "I remember everything, Kevin. I remember the day you left. I remember—" Her defiance melted as her chin quivered again. "I remember our first Christmas without you. For four months Mommy had been warning me that Daddy wasn't coming back. But I didn't believe her. I knew Daddy still loved us. He had to! I knew he would come back. I remember waking up Christmas morning and thinking this would be the day. This would be the day Daddy came back to us." Her voice broke. "But there were no presents from him. There was no phone call. There was nothing. I sat at the table and cried. Mommy held me. She soothed my tears. She told me she loved me. She was there for me."

She had always been there for her. *Oh, God, how will I survive without her?*

Shannon forged ahead. There was something she needed to say. Something she'd been able to live with when she'd had Mom. But now that she didn't, she wasn't sure she could live with it.

"Mommy told me that Daddy still loved me. But by the end of the day, I knew. He wasn't coming back for me. And he didn't still love me." She dropped her head and cried onto Jefferson's furry head.

A throat cleared, and feet shuffled, and she let Jefferson slip from her grasp.

"Shannon," her dad's dismayed voice came in a moan. He sank onto the floor beside her, pulling his knees up to his chin. Kurt had disappeared with Jefferson, and Shannon was glad.

She felt Kevin's hand on her back, and she flinched.

"Shannon." His voice was so broken, she risked a glance at him and was shocked to see tears snaking down his face. He took a hasty swipe at them, but she'd seen. "There is nothing I can do to undo the past. If I had thought about how much pain I would cause…" He groaned a sigh and shook his head. "But I can't go back. Only forward. I'm sorry I never came for Christmas that year. I'm sorry I never came to see you at all." Sorrow darkened his face. "I'm sorry for hurting you over and over and over."

Did he mean that? Shannon searched his eyes, mirrors of hers, and saw sincerity. A few of the broken pieces in her heart seemed to find themselves at that moment and bind together, and it was suddenly hard to breathe.

"I don't know if you will believe me, but I am so proud of you." He paused and swallowed. "I am the most sorry that you grew up believing that I didn't love you. It's not true."

She wanted to believe him. She *needed* to believe. To know her dad was proud of her. That he cared about her. That he loved her.

But if he meant those things, he wouldn't have left her, right?

She didn't respond to his words, and he sighed. "We should get back to the table. I'm sure the Blakes are wondering where we've gone."

Shannon rose wearily to her feet. The pain had faded to a dull ache vibrating in her heart. "I better clean up first. I probably look like the Grinch."

He actually laughed at that, then motioned for her to exit the laundry room ahead of him. She was already in the hallway when he called her name.

"Shannon?"

She turned around and raised her eyebrows.

"I just want to say—" He stopped and scratched the back of his neck, his faced scrunched in obvious discomfort. "What I mean is—" He closed his eyes for a second, then looked straight at her. "I love you."

She stared at him without blinking, her eyes slowly filling with tears. How many times had she dreamed those words from his mouth over the past nine years? She had no words of her own, but she nodded her head at Kevin, hoping he understood that she accepted his words. That she wanted his words. That she desperately needed his words.

He took a slow step toward her and pulled her against his chest.

It was her first hug from her dad in nine years.

Chapter Twenty-Four

Kurt barely made it to the table before Kevin did. He had stood outside the laundry room with Jefferson in his arms, unashamedly eavesdropping until he heard them moving toward the door. Then he'd shot down the hall like lightening, depositing Jefferson in his mom's craft room, crossing his fingers that the dog wouldn't destroy the whole room. He slid into his seat a few seconds before Kevin came into the room, enduring a bone-chilling glare from his father. When Shannon returned, she looked as fresh as a spring flower. Clearly she'd visited a mirror and worked magic with water and Kleenex. But it was more than that. She looked happy. He'd missed the ending, but no doubt something wonderful had just happened between her and her dad.

Several hours later as the Conrad family was getting ready to leave, Kurt pressed a small gift bag into Shannon's hand.

"What's this?"

He shrugged, trying to look casual. "A gift from a friend. Open it."

Her hesitation was obvious, but curiosity won as she dug through the tissue paper he had painstakingly folded until it sprouted perfectly from the mouth of the red bag. She pulled out the bundle of cloth and let it unravel in her hands. He'd seen the turquoise scarf in a store window next to his community college. He hadn't been sure she'd accept it.

She fingered the soft fabric, running her hands over the edging of gold threads.

"It's beautiful."

"It'll look even better on you."

When she rose on her tip toes and placed a kiss on his cheek, he forced himself to stand stock still. His dad was watching a short distance away.

"Thank you." Her eyes were warm on him. "You're a good friend."

If only he could be more. "Merry Christmas, Shannon."

The next few days flew by with his house full of family. Kurt kept as busy as possible working in the shop or on the farm. Anything to keep him away from Robert. The only thing he had felt toward his brother in the past seven years was resentment. Getting into arguments with Rob would only hurt his mom. He'd rather work his butt off.

* * *

"Shannon, what is wrong with your sister?"

Years ago when Shannon was watching Laura's soccer game in 6th grade, a stray ball had slammed her in the head. She hadn't seen it coming, and suddenly her whole head went numb, her vision black. She'd tumbled to the ground. She'd probably have done the same now if she weren't sitting.

"Wrong?" she croaked, her voice cracking on the "o." Kevin had appeared with no warning, staring down at her where she sat in the family room sketching Jefferson.

Life had been a roller coaster for the past week. She couldn't describe the emotional high she'd been on since Kevin's declaration. Who knew such a simple phrase could heal so much brokenness?

At the same time, Laura's condition was threatening to destroy her newfound joy. She certainly didn't feel the peace from God she had felt before Christmas underneath the burden of Laura's secret. Alan kept calling to talk with them, but Shannon always came up with an excuse to jump off the phone as soon as she could. Laura flat-out refused to speak with him. Shannon kept praying for a miracle, but she couldn't expect God to make Laura un-pregnant. Laura was keeping to herself, which honestly wasn't anything unusual. She'd thought Kevin hadn't noticed.

He tilted his head toward her challengingly. "Yes. Something is wrong with Laura, and I'm sure you know what it is. Please tell me."

Shannon's heart pounded. This was her dad. He'd apologized for all he'd done wrong. He loved her. The sudden longing to be honest with him nearly overwhelmed her.

If she was honest, Laura would never trust her again. If she lied, Kevin would never trust her again.

Oh, God. Why is this so hard?

Telling him was the right thing. But she would lose her sister, her only remaining link to Mom.

Time stood still.

"It's not all that." She'd made her choice. "It was painful going through Christmas without Mom. Laura's having a hard time coping. She'll be okay, but right now she's trying to get a grip." If it weren't for the galling lump of lies in her throat, she might actually convince herself. Kevin certainly looked convinced.

"Oh, well I'm glad that's it. I was getting worried. She's been so quiet. You think she'll be okay soon?"

She dug her hole deeper. "Oh yeah. Don't worry. She talks to me, and she's going to be fine." God forgive her, but that was the biggest lie of all.

Kevin left her after that, and Shannon bee-lined it up the stairs. Tears stung her eyes. How could it be so painful to tell a lie to her dad?

"You've got to tell him!" She barged into Laura's room without knocking.

Laura lowered the book in hands to her lap. "Tell who what?"

Shannon slammed her rear end onto Laura's bed, making Laura bounce. "You know exactly what I'm talking about! I just told a huge lie to cover your butt, and Kevin is never going to forgive me when he finds outs."

"Since when do you care what he thinks?"

"That's none of your business." Shannon trembled with anger and guilt. She took a deep breath, trying to calm herself. "Laura, don't you think he needs to know? So you can see a doctor and make sure everything is okay?"

"I can't tell him. I do feel bad keeping it from him. But I'm so scared of what he'll do."

"But—"

"No! You promised! You can't tell anyone!"

Shannon examined her hands in her lap.

"Kurt knows."

She felt Laura turn sharply toward her. It was quiet for a moment.

"That's okay. He won't tell."

Shannon was surprised by her response. Maybe Laura understood Kurt better than she did.

"I don't know how you resist him if you like him that much."

Shannon groaned loudly. "I don't want to talk about that. Please, Laura. Just think about telling Kevin? He'll find out eventually anyway!"

Her sister was on her feet in an instant. "And I decide when he does! So just keep your mouth shut if you love me."

Shannon squeezed her eyes tightly. This wasn't fair. She had to get out of here. Before she either screamed her frustration in Laura's face, or the truth in Kevin's.

When she returned downstairs in her jogging clothes, she heard the gun-popping and tire-squealing of an action flick. Sure enough, Kurt and Andy were lounged back on the family room couch, focused on the hotrods zooming across the screen. Shannon sneaked by and out the door, layered only with a windbreaker. She'd be sweating soon enough. Thankfully it hadn't snowed since before Christmas, and while the ground was still a dirty white, the roads were clear.

She ran hard. If only she could sweat out the guilt for lying to Kevin. The panic she felt building in her chest about Laura. The despair she knew only God could cure. If only running would cure it instead.

Almost two hours later she crested the last rise in the driveway, barely dragging her feet. As she neared the side door of the house, it opened and Kurt emerged.

"Shannon! What are you doing? It's freezing out."

She nodded, too weary to even speak. "Just—had to—run," she panted, leaning over to brace her hands on her legs.

"There's a treadmill in your basement, you know."

"I know." She took several slow breaths before straitening.

Kurt frowned, examining her closely. Certainly she was a sight. All sweat and grime and flushed flesh. Lovely.

"Are you okay?"

She shrugged. "No. My dad told me he loves me last week, and today I lied to him about Laura." Now why had she blurted that out? Why was she always telling Kurt more than she should?

His head tilted sympathetically. "You've got a lot on your plate. It's too bad you can't confide in your dad, but I guess that's Laura's call."

She nodded, blinking back tears. Time to change the topic. "You going out tonight?"

"For New Year's Eve?"

" 'Course. Going to a party, getting drunk, grabbing a girl." She drawled out the last word, and Kurt visibly cringed.

"Not this year. I told you I was going to change. I keep my word."

"We'll see." She softened her skepticism with a wink and took another step toward the door. "Happy New Year, Kurt."

"Shannon, wait."

She turned around to find him nervously shifting from one foot to another, his hands in his carpenter jeans' pocket.

"Can I ask you a question?"

Oh boy.

"Sure."

"When I asked you out, did you turn me down because you didn't like me?"

She crossed her arms across the front of her lime green jacket. "You know my reasons, Kurt."

"So did you like me?"

"Does it matter?"

"I just want to know. Please?"

Shannon hesitated. "I liked you a lot." And liked him still. But she wasn't going to admit that.

He was silent. When she met his eyes again, they were tender enough to warm her from inside out. "I can't get you out of my head no matter what I do, Shannon."

"Sorry," she whispered with a smile. "G'night."

He nodded his chin. " 'Night, Shan. Happy New Year."

Chapter Twenty-Five

"Not good," Laura moaned, clutching at her stomach. She'd been hiding her morning sickness miraculously well, but Shannon could only imagine how miserable she felt. Apparently the smell of the hot lunch had set her off.

She squeezed Laura's hand. "Take a deep breath."

Her only response was another sickened moan, and then Laura dashed away from the lunch line and ran out the cafeteria door. When she returned, Shannon pulled Laura into the line right in front of her just in time to get meatloaf slopped onto a plate. Laura's face was the color of ash as she tried not to gag.

"Is she okay?" the grumpy-faced server asked, staring at Laura with flaring nostrils.

No. She's fifteen and pregnant.

"Yeah, she's fine." The lie came too easily for comfort.

"Shannon! Over here!" The voice came as they were making their way through the crowded seating area.

Shannon looked around and her eyes landed on Jesse's dimpled smile. He bounded from his chair and headed their way. She hadn't seen him in two weeks, and she had missed his ever-cheerful presence.

"How've you been?"

He flashed his dimples, hesitated, then grabbed her to his chest in an eager hug, nearly spilling her lunch. He only held her for a few seconds, but she felt his heart hammering. When he backed away, a crimson hue was creeping up his neck and into his face.

She looked at him in surprise. He'd never done more than touch her shoulder before. He looked embarrassed, but he maintained eye-contact and said, "I've really missed you. You have no idea how glad I am to see you."

Well actually, she was getting a pretty good idea...

"I'm happy to see you, too."

"You two love-birds going to just stand here, or are you going to sit down?"

Shannon felt her face turning red as she glanced at Laura. Her sister was examining both of them with eyebrows raised in dry amusement.

Jesse chuckled. Oh, that laugh of his. It always made everything better. "Now that you mention it. I was saving you a seat." He nodded at Laura. "You're welcome to join us."

Laura waved his words away. "Don't wanna crash your party. I'll—" she threw her thumb over her shoulder—"sit over there." She smiled knowingly at Shannon, her face still pale. "See you later, sis."

Jesse led Shannon to his table and sat down. He paused while reaching into his lunch bag.

"Look, I know it's not my business, but is something wrong with your sister?" His face was so concerned, Shannon had to bite her tongue to keep from spilling the truth. She looked into his melted chocolate eyes, trying not to let herself melt down.

"I—I wish I could tell you, Jesse, but I can't. I gave a promise."

He nodded slowly. "Is she okay?"

Even a white lie to Jesse seemed so wrong. "No." Her voice came out a whisper, and she shook her head. "She's not okay."

"I'm sorry to hear that." Jesse assessed her, slowly chewing his sandwich. "How are you? How was your Christmas?"

"It was okay. Up and down." More like catastrophic and phenomenal. The highest of highs and the lowest of lows in the span of one week.

"I see. I wish I could help more."

"You do." She smiled up at him. "Just by being you. How has your Christmas break been?"

"Well I worked almost every night and caught up on a lot of sleep during the day." He shook his head. "Working nights is killing me, Shan. I don't know how I'm going to keep it up and still graduate."

They talked until the bell rang.

"Ready for more fun in pre-calc?" Shannon's voice betrayed her misgivings as she gathered up her trash.

"Oh yeah. Second semester. It's gonna be fun." He flashed his dimples at her dismayed face. "Don't stress about it. I'll be there to help you."

"What would I do without you?"

He stood gazing at her, then smiled sideways, only one dimple showing, and asked shyly, "Can I have one more hug?"

Shannon's heart rate jumped. She'd spent so much time and thought on Kurt over her break, she'd almost forgotten about Jesse's feelings for her. "Yes. You may."

With a chuckle, Jesse opened up his arms, and Shannon leaned into him. His arms closed around her, holding her to his chest. He was so tall, her head rested right on his heart. It was racing again. But this time he held her longer. She heard him swallow hard, and then his hold on her relaxed.

"We better go." His voice was suddenly hoarse. He cleared his throat and stepped away from her. "Time for English."

"I saw that," Laura said the moment Shannon reached the Explorer after school. "I don't know what you did to make two of the nicest and best looking guys in Virginia both head over heels for you, but Shan, you got a mess on your hands!"

Did she ever.

Later that week Shannon invited Stephanie to come over Friday evening. They hadn't hung out in weeks, and Shannon was missing some quality girl time. Laura kept herself holed up in her room most of the time.

They were chatting while painting their nails when a soft *tap tap* sounded on Shannon's bedroom door.

"Shannon? You in there?"

"Coming." She opened the door. She didn't know Andy was home. "What's up?"

"I was wondering—whoa, I didn't know *you* were here." His gaze landed on Stephanie, and something instantly changed in his body language. "It's great to see you, Stephanie. I came up to see if you ladies would care to join me and Kurt in watching a movie." Before Shannon could explain that she and Steph were about to do facials, Stephanie answered for her.

"I would *love* to. That sounds wonderful. What do you think, Shan?"

"*Suuuu*re," she drawled dryly, but neither of the two noticed as they threw flirty glances back and forth like a game of catch. So much for girl time.

"Fantastic. Why don't you come downstairs with me, Stephanie, and help us choose a movie while Shannon cleans this up."

She was on her feet faster than a popping jack-in-the-box.

By the time Shannon got to the family room, everyone else was seated. The couch was made to comfortably fit three, and Andy was at one end with Stephanie cozy beside him. Kurt had taken the other end, leaving a narrow space for Shannon between him and Stephanie. Butterflies erupted in her stomach at the thought of sitting so close to him. But where else would she sit? She gave him a piercing glare as she squirmed into the seat, hating and loving the way she was pressed against his side.

As *The Mummy* began, she closed her eyes. There was a reason she hadn't seen it before. Horror was not her cup of tea. But since it had been Stephanie's pick, Andy insisted they watch it.

Man, she was tired. She'd been up crazy late last night doing homework, and her stupid brain never let her sleep, anyway.

A yawn devoured her face before her head listed and landed on something firm.

A loud gasp from Stephanie startled her awake, and she cracked her eyes open. When the pillow underneath her shifted, she realized she'd been sleeping on Kurt's shoulder. Her neck exploded with fire when she tried to quickly jerk her head up.

She groaned and dragged her head up more slowly, reaching a hand to rub her neck.

"That wasn't too comfortable for me, either." Kurt's joking whisper tickled her ear. She moved to apologize, but he put a finger against her open lips. "Don't say you're sorry." She tasted the salt on his skin, especially since he was slow to move his finger away. Her stomach flipped sickeningly.

Maybe she should sit on the floor.

"Here, let me make us both more comfortable." In one smooth move he lifted his arm up and slid it around her, clasping his hand on her thigh. Now her shoulder overlapped his chest, and she could lean her head back against the front of his shoulder. His chin grazed the side of her forehead.

"That better?" his voice purred against her ear. A shiver involuntarily shimmied through Shannon. All she could do was nod. She needed to scramble out of his reach immediately, but she couldn't make herself do it.

His hand slowly edged upward, toward her waist.

"Cut it out," she whispered, but he had the audacity to wink at her.

"What, you don't like it?" he whispered back, a rakish grin on his face. "How about this?"

Shannon flinched as his fingers slid underneath the bottom hem of her shirt and trailed along her bare stomach.

This had to stop. She brushed his hand away and stood up quickly before she lost her nerve. She didn't say a word as she left the room, not letting herself look back.

He caught up with her just outside her bedroom door.

"Shannon." He groaned her name and grabbed her arm. "I'm sorry."

She turned to face him.

"Look, I know that was out of line. Please forgive me."

She let out a noisy breath of air. "Okay, fine. Don't worry about it. But I'm not going back down to that horrible movie." She couldn't suppress her shudder, and Kurt grinned.

"I didn't peg you for a horror girl."

She crinkled her nose. "No, thank you."

He was staring at her with a soft expression on his face. "I love when you do that with your nose."

"Whatever. Why are you still staring at me? What do you want?"

"You."

Her breath caught as he stepped directly in front of her and grabbed her by both wrists. "I know why you turned me down the first time, Shannon, and I get it. But I gave them all up for you.

You stopped me in my tracks, and I don't ever want to go back to that. *Please...* Give me a chance?"

Shannon's heart pounded, and she looked away, knowing if she looked into Kurt's blueberry eyes, she would say yes.

"I—I don't know."

"Will you think about it?"

The clock on the wall behind them ticked like a time bomb until she took a shaky breath and risked a look in his eyes, brimming with hope.

"Okay. I'll think about it."

The next afternoon while she was cooking dinner, Kurt popped his head into the kitchen and winked.

"Still thinking?"

At her look of death, he shrank back quickly. "Sorry. My dad keeps telling me I'm too pushy. I guess he's right again." Well whatever he was, he was hard to resist. She gritted her teeth as he came closer and reached his arms as if to pull her to him but then stopped himself. "I'm totally crazy about you."

Shannon held herself rigid, desperate to keep herself from melting into his ready embrace. She backed up one step, then two. "I still don't have an answer, okay?"

He looked a little stung, but he nodded and wished her a good evening before vanishing out the door. Shannon sank back against the counter.

She almost skipped church the next day. Seriously, who went to church to meet one guy while considering dating another? But she hadn't gone in weeks, and her soul was craving that connection with Higher Powers she'd felt enough times to leave her always wanting more.

Jesse greeted her with a warm smile and side-hug. Shannon squirmed beside him. Maybe she shouldn't have come after all. She certainly couldn't concentrate on the sermon and didn't feel the presence of anyone or anything except her nagging conscience.

After the service, Jesse walked with her to the Explorer. As she fumbled in her purse for her keys, he stilled her with a touch to her elbow.

"What's wrong, Shannon? Something's been bothering you since you showed up."

She sighed dramatically. Why did he have to read her so well?

"You're not going to like it."

A pained look pinched his handsome face, but he shrugged. "Go on."

"Kurt asked me out again."

Jesse crossed his arms over his chest slowly, but he didn't look surprised. "And?"

Shannon sagged against the Explorer. "I didn't give an answer. I said I would think about it."

Hurt sprang across his face before he skillfully smoothed his features into a mask.

"You still like him, then."

Shannon felt like a heel. "I'm sorry," she muttered, turning away.

Jesse pulled her back by the shoulder. "Don't leave me like that. I'm not mad at you. I don't expect you to like me just because I like you. Sometimes we can't help who we develop feelings for. If you like Kurt as much as I like you, I understand that this is a very hard decision to make."

Shannon had the impulse to throw her arms around Jesse in a bear hug, so relieved that he understood. "I feel so torn. I do like him a lot, don't ask me why, but I also know what a relationship with him is going to involve sooner or later." She looked him bravely in the eye. "I also don't want to hurt you, because I do care about you, Jesse."

He smiled, his dimples barely a dot. "Don't you worry about me, Shannon. God always takes care of my heart. All I want is for you to decide what's right for you. Or if you're up for it, let God decide, and trust His choice."

Shannon swallowed hard. She knew without an in-depth Bible study where God stood on this.

"Hey." Jesse dipped his chin to get her attention. "I'll be praying for you."

And she needed it.

* * *

"Kevin?" Shannon peaked around the door into his office Monday night. "You got a few minutes?"

"Of course." He pushed away the laptop on his desk, gently lowering the screen. "What's going on?"

"What's going down is more like it, and that would be my Spanish grade." She flopped into a chair. "Help!"

He chuckled and came around to sit beside her. When the preterite verb tense was beginning to make sense to Shannon, she sat up straight. "Thank you so much. I'd be lost without you."

The smile that lit his face warmed Shannon all over. "Any time. How are things going?"

She considered his question. What did he want to know? He wasn't much for small talk.

"What I mean is, are you still thinking about it?"

She frowned. "About what?"

He flickered one eyebrow upward. "Kurt."

Shannon couldn't stop her mouth from dropping open as way more warmth than wanted flooded her face. Before she could think of a response, Kevin saved her the trouble.

"Before you accuse me of bugging the walls, let me explain that I was supervising Daniel in the bathtub the other night when Kurt followed you up. I couldn't help but hear what he said. And what you said."

Shannon looked away. How was it that Kevin seemed in tune with every detail of her personal life, yet utterly clueless about Laura? She sighed, prepared for a lecture when she met his serious blue eyes again.

"Look, Shannon. We've talked about Kurt before. We both know more about him than either of us cares to. Obviously you do have significant feelings for him. I'm not going to forbid you from dating him, although I very much want to. You have a good head on your shoulders, and I have no doubt you will make the right decision. But I want you to think very, very carefully about this."

Shannon took a shaky breath. "I am."

"Good. I'm not trying to overreact or control. Just trying to be a good dad."

Her eyes welled up at his words, although she couldn't have said why. "Thank you."

He tapped her chin. "I trust you."

A confusing mix of emotions tumbled through Shannon as she left the room. He might trust her now, but whenever he uncovered the truth she was hiding for Laura, she wondered what would become of his trust.

And she still didn't know what she was going to do about Kurt.

Later that week, she was dusting the bookshelves in Kevin's office when cracked black leather binding caught her attention, faded gold letters spelling *Holy Bible*. Her fingers hovered near the spine. She'd never touched a Bible. There was always one in the seat back in front of her at church, but she'd never worked up the nerve to pick it up. Gently she hooked her index finger over the top of the binding and pulled it out. She rested the book reverently in both hands and examined the cover. It was so worn, it was soft to the touch, and in the bottom right corner in dull lettering was *Kevin T Conrad*.

This was Kevin's Bible? That was an ending she never would have guessed.

She felt a little bad for not knowing what the *T* stood for.

After dinner and homework, she pulled the Bible from her top desk drawer where she'd carefully stashed it and started flipping through the flimsy pages. Myriads of notations and underlines dotted the pages, and she *hmmmed* out loud. The mysteries about her dad continually abounded. Apparently he had at one time been quite familiar with the words of the Good Book, but he didn't seem to care one twit about them now.

She slowly paged her way through the various books, many of which she'd heard of, but there were some—she paused at Nehemiah—that were new titles to her.

Her mind wandered as she aimlessly turned pages. Jesse had been quiet all week, and she'd been too preoccupied to care much. She spent most lunch breaks watching Laura across the cafeteria pretend everything in her life was hunky dory, when Shannon knew it was all an act to cover her catastrophic secret. She couldn't stop worrying about her sister. Even Kurt had slid to her back burner, since he'd given her some much needed space. She knew he wouldn't stay away forever, though.

Her eyes suddenly stopped on a page. The title said Psalm 23. It sounded vaguely familiar, so she began to read.

> *The Lord is my shepherd, I shall not be in want. He makes me lie down in green pastures, he leads me beside quiet waters, he restores my soul. He guides me in paths of righteousness for his name's sake. Even though I walk through the valley of the shadow of death, I will fear no evil, for you are with me; your rod and your staff, they comfort me. You prepare a table before me in the presence of my enemies. You anoint my head with oil; my cup overflows. Surely goodness and love will follow me all the days of my life, and I will dwell in the house of the Lord forever.*

The sweet sigh of God's presence wafted through Shannon, and she closed her eyes and soaked it in before re-reading the passage. The officiant had read it at her mom's funeral service, but she hadn't paid much attention then. But now she could actually feel herself there, resting in the soft grass beside a gurgling brook, safe with God. Her wants supplied. Her needs cared for. Her future secure.

Could it be so? She studied the passage. Walking through the valley of death. Eating in the presence of enemies. It wasn't always a watercolor painting. But it still said to fear no evil, that goodness and love would always follow. And that was because God was leading down a path of righteousness.

Maybe righteousness wasn't always safe. Maybe it wasn't always pretty or friendly or comfortable. But it did lead to a permanent future in God's presence. And that was one place Shannon wanted to be.

"Oh, God, thank you. Thank you for this beautiful poem that you gave to…to whoever wrote it. I don't even know. I still don't know much about You, and even less about your Bible, but I do know You love me. Thank you for loving me. I love You, too." Tears pricked her eyes, and she blinked against the overwhelming love wrapping itself around her. "Please, God, help me to follow your path of righteousness. No matter what. I want to have the kind of rest this poem describes. But even more, I want to be with You."

She sat in the warm, wonderful silence for a few more minutes before whispering, "Amen."

She wasn't quite ready for Kurt when he showed up the next evening. He sauntered into the kitchen while she was spooning leftover baked ziti into a glass storage container. She stopped and just looked at him.

"Hi." They'd texted a few times over the past week, and he'd made no mention of his question. Was it too much to hope he'd keep it that way?

"Hey. We need to talk, Shannon."

Yep. Too much.

She sighed and opened her mouth to respond, but before she could make a sound, he grabbed her by the waist and kissed her. She was so surprised, she started to kiss back. A moan rose in her throat. She'd missed this...

He pulled away, just enough to nuzzle her nose and drawl in his deep, husky voice, "I've missed you."

He slid his arms around her, his lips finding hers again. She was powerless to stop him. She didn't want to.

But when his hands crept into her back pockets, she knew she had to.

She tilted her head away from him enough to break contact and felt his hands relax their hold behind her.

"I want you so bad, Shannon." His voice was horse, his body shaking with desire.

Shannon backed away slowly. She kind of wanted him, too. Her body flashed hot at her admission. Man, this was hard.

She squared her shoulders and met his blue eyes. "You'd really take it that far with me?"

Shame, guilt, affection, and desire played bumper cars across his face, but he didn't look away. "Yes."

God, help! "You know where I stand on that."

He groaned and threw his head back. "Oh come on, Shan. Don't be such a prude! I like you. I *really* like you. Sex is a natural thing to do with someone you like."

Was that true? She took a deep breath and puffed it out slowly. *He guides me in paths of righteousness.* The words from last night's Psalm flashed through her mind.

"So did you 'really like' all the other girls you've slept with?"

He coughed at the unexpected question and paused, scowling.

"No, I didn't have feelings for them. But I don't do that anymore. I've changed, Shannon."

True. He had changed a lot since she'd met him.

Strength, God. I don't want to hurt him. But I'd rather hurt him than You.

This was it. No going back after her next words. She swallowed the tears that threatened. She could cry later. She'd already gone through this with him once; what was another round?

She crossed her arms over her chest to keep her heart in place and closed her eyes. She wasn't sure she'd say it otherwise.

"You have changed, and I admire that. But I'm not going to date you. So please stop asking."

When she opened her eyes, his indescribably attractive face was frozen in shock. He gave a small shake to his head as if to clear the fog. "Did I hear you right?"

Shannon squared her shoulders. "Yes. I do like you, Kurt, but I'm not going to be more than friends with you. I'm asking you to respect my boundaries. No more flirting. No more kissing. No more touching. No more anything. No more."

His eyes darted about wildly as pain rushed into them, his jaw clenched tightly. When his Adam's apple bobbed up and down, tears flooded Shannon's eyes. "I'm sorry, Kurt."

He threw a foul word in her face before he spun around and strode from the room.

Chapter Twenty-Six

He'd done exactly what he had promised himself he wouldn't.

Glancing at the sleeping form beside him, Kurt sighed. It wasn't Shannon.

So much for one year.

He closed his eyes, unwilling to think about Shannon any more. She'd made her choice. Now he'd made his.

Light exploded in the room, and his eyes popped open as he bolted upright in the bed. He almost vomited at the sight of his dad standing in the doorway.

"Kurt Joseph Blake, what is going on?"

Kurt didn't answer. As Victoria sat up blinking in the sudden light, she hugged the blanket to her bare chest. It was obvious what had gone on.

With a vehement groan, Kurt threw himself back onto the pillow. Something slapped onto his head. His pants.

"Get dressed. Now." Dad reached down and picked another article of clothes off the floor, flinging it forcefully onto the bed. He pointed at Victoria. "You, too." He turned his back in the doorway, but he didn't leave. Victoria scampered out of the bed and threw herself into her clothes. She didn't look at Kurt, but he could see humiliation glowing on her neck.

He took a deep breath and let it out slowly before climbing into his jeans. He'd never felt this embarrassed in his life.

And Dad was a whole new level of mad. Kurt was scared. He hadn't felt scared in a long time. His shaking hands could barely zip his pants. Who knew where his shirt was.

Dad cleared his throat loudly.

"Victoria, are you fully clothed?"

Kurt's face went slack. Dad knew her name?

"Yes, sir," she choked out.

Dad turned around and looked at her where she stood staring at her feet. "You'd better call someone to pick you up. Kurt and I are going to be a while."

"Yes, sir." It was a whisper now. Grabbing her coat, she fled from the room without a glance in Kurt's direction.

He bent down to look under the bed, still searching for his shirt, when his dad's feet stopped in front of him.

"Kurt." Dad's outstretched hand held the shirt. "Put it on." His tone was rough, his words clipped, and when Kurt looked up, he saw fury in his dad's eyes. He swallowed hard and straightened, grabbing the shirt out of his dad's hand.

"Sit," Dad barked as soon as Kurt's head emerged through the neckline. Kurt sank down on the edge of the bed, tugging the shirt down to cover his torso. He raised his eyes to his dad, who was towering over him with his legs spread apart, his arms crossed tightly over his chest. His fingers were drumming his bicep repeatedly as he stared Kurt down.

"I'm sorry, Da—"

"Don't." Dad cut him off with one word. "Don't talk to me, Kurt. I don't want to hear your pathetic excuses. No. This time I want you to listen to me."

Kurt nodded, dropping his eyes to the floor.

"Look at me, Kurt. I want you to look at me when I speak."

Kurt obeyed, but he wanted to close his eyes against the distaste he saw on his dad's face. The disappointment.

"This is my cabin, Kurt. This is a part of my business. *My* business. Not yours. It is not for you to use for your selfish, immoral pleasure." Dad opened and closed his mouth several times. "I can't believe you, Kurt. You picked up a girl and brought her to one of my vacation cabins to—to have sex with her! What is wrong with you?"

Kurt opened his mouth to reply, and say what, he didn't know, but he didn't have to figure it out, because Dad snapped, "I'm not done. Victoria Anderson is the daughter of one of my friends. This could affect *my* friendship with him. But you never think about anyone besides yourself, do you?"

Kurt felt his chest rising and falling roughly as he struggled to breathe, but his dad still wasn't finished.

"I happen to know that Victoria's boyfriend broke up with her last week and broke her heart. That's why you knew she'd be easy prey for your sick games." He shook his head. "You disgust me, Kurt."

The words sliced through Kurt with such pain his breath stopped completely. He thought he would choke. He might even cry if he hadn't long ago trained himself never to let tears anywhere near his eyes.

"I'm sorry, Dad, I'm sorry," he croaked, unable to face his dad a second longer. "Are—are you gonna fire me? Or kick me out?" His mind raced in panic. What would he do if his parents turned him away?

A heavy sigh came from Dad, and he settled a hand onto Kurt's shoulder.

"No, Kurt. We won't throw you out of the house. And I'm not going to fire you just yet. But some things are going to have to change. I thought they had..." He trailed off as he sat down next to Kurt. "What happened, son?"

Kurt lowered his head and told Dad everything that had transpired with Shannon. She was really done with him. There was nothing more to hope for. Yes, he'd known about Victoria's boyfriend dumping her out of the blue last week. He knew they'd had a physical relationship and she could probably use the comfort. He admitted how low he had stooped.

"But what's the point, Dad?" He threw his hands in the air in frustration. "Shannon is not going to come around even though she likes me. What is the point of depriving myself when she doesn't even care that I am?"

"You're still not getting it, Kurt." Dad leaned forward so he could see Kurt's face. Kurt swallowed and forced himself to meet his dad's eyes again. "It's not about Shannon. It's about the fact that you view girls like a vending machine. You want to push a button, get exactly what you want, and walk away when you're done. I don't know where you ever got that idea, but it is totally wrong." His dad paused to let out a long breath of air. "Kurt, when you are intimate with a girl, what is it about for you?"

He didn't realize his dad was waiting for an answer until the silence stretched long. He knew it was just about sex. That's all he wanted out of these girls. They were a means to an end. A source of fleeting pleasure.

"Do you understand the meaning of the word lust?"

Kurt's eyes closed at his dad's second unanswerable question. He hated that word. Lust. It sounded so base. Uncivilized. Animalistic. Like he was a dog acting on instinct, and all the girls were in heat.

The blast of truth nearly knocked him from the bed. That was exactly how he was.

"I want you to think about Shannon for a minute." Oh, but that was so painful. "Think of all the things you told me you admire in her. Remember your list? Those are qualities that deserve love, not lust. You should be seeking out ways to cherish her, not use her; give to her, not take from her."

Kurt let the words wash through his mind. Love. Cherish. Give. Fine verbs to be sure, but he had no idea what they really meant.

"You know, your mother is the only woman I've ever been intimate with. Some people may scorn that, but I think it is incredibly beautiful. To me, she's perfect. She is my only standard of love and beauty. That's something you'll never have, and you can't undo that—but it is not too late to make a change for a better future."

Kurt sat in silence, forcing himself to be totally honest. His intentions toward Shannon hadn't changed. He did have feelings for her that he'd never had before, but he still wanted the same thing out of her that he'd wanted from all the others. He'd told her he'd changed. It was almost laughable, it was such a lie. He hadn't changed a bit. And the problem was, he didn't know how.

"How did you know I was here?" The idea of taking Victoria to the vacation cabin was extremely stupid. But it wasn't the first time he'd used this cabin for such purposes. Man, he really was sick.

"Andy called the house trying to find you. He said you disappeared while he was in the bathroom, and you weren't answering your cell phone. I asked if you'd had a run-in with Shannon, and he thought you probably had. I drove all over town looking for your truck. I hoped to find you before you broke your pledge. Thought maybe I could talk you out of it. But I was too late. This was the last place I thought to check."

Kurt sighed. He had a dad who cared. That was more than many of his friends could say. He wished he weren't a continual disappointment to this good man. He wanted to change, for that reason alone.

"If I'm going to change, it has to be for more than Shannon. Once she hears about this…" He shook his head. "She'll never look at me again."

"I don't think she'll know unless you tell her. Victoria was so embarrassed, I don't think she'll be telling *anyone* about tonight."

True enough. Neither would he.

"Do you want to change, Kurt?"

He looked at his dad.

"Do *you* want to change? For you?"

For the first time, he really did, and not for Shannon's sake. He could already feel the weight of guilt and shame for what he had just done. What he had done so many times. He hated himself for it.

"I do, Dad, but I don't know how." He was fighting tears for the first time in five years. It took letting go of all his pride to say the next words. "Will you help me?"

Dad gently placed his arm around Kurt's back. "Now we're getting somewhere."

* * *

It had been four days since Kurt had left her in the kitchen blinded with tears. Four long days of more tears, a lot of Psalms, and a lot more of wondering if she'd made the right decision. She hadn't told Jesse yet. They hadn't even been eating lunch together, and her pre-calc grade was slipping. By Thursday she decided it was time to mend that particular fence.

"Hey Jesse," she greeted him as she sat down beside him in pre-calculus.

He was silent at first, then slowly straightened his spine. "Shannon. How have you been?"

There was something unspoken in the simple question which he didn't dare ask. She made herself look at him. No one quite carried his heart in his eyes like this boy. His chocolate eyes were a swirl of emotions. Hurt. Fear. Denial. Concern. Affection. Hope.

"I said no." She said it softly, staring at his face to see if he understood.

The whites of his eyes went wide. "Y-you did?"

Maybe her silence had made him think the opposite.

Jesse slumped his face into his fist in weakened relief. "I thought—I figured—when you stopped eating lunch with me—" He breathed out of rounded lips, obviously too overwhelmed for words. "Why didn't you tell me?"

The bell rang, and further discussion had to wait until later. For the first time in weeks, Jesse walked Shannon to the parking lot. He was quiet until they reached the Explorer, where he faced her.

"I've been going crazy. I imagined...the worst...going on between you and Kurt."

Shannon's face flushed at the intimation, and she hung her head. "I'm sorry. I should have told you sooner. It wasn't an easy thing, and I needed time to process."

"Understood. Just know I am so happy with your choice, Shannon. I'm here for you any time you need me." He reached a hand to her shoulder and squeezed, his dimples dazzling. "I've missed you."

Shannon smiled up at him honestly. "Me too."

The following week was a busy one, with a research paper due, a pre-calculus exam, and a Spanish presentation. On top of everything, Kevin pulled Shannon aside one evening to discuss her grades and hand her a stack of college applications.

"Shannon, you can be anything you want to be. I know you've got it in you to get straight As if you choose to."

She knew she could. If she didn't have the stress of losing her mother, reuniting with her bipolar father, mothering her younger siblings, shouldering the burden of Laura's secret, and dealing with her emotions over two boys at once—if all these things were factored out, she just might have straight As.

Most of the applications required an essay, so she had to put them off for the next weekend, during which she devoted herself to selling herself to colleges she couldn't care any less about attending. Some were in Virginia, a couple in Tennessee and North Carolina, one in Washington, D.C., and one in New York City, of all places. As if she would go there by herself. Kevin must have lost his mind. If only Chicago weren't so far away. There were any number of colleges there she'd be happy to attend, but she wasn't about to go that far from Laura.

* * *

"Smells great, Shannon."

She looked up from the stove, wiping her hand across her forehead. Was it hot in here, or was it just from standing over the stove?

"I didn't hear you come in." She smiled at Kevin, trying to ignore the dull pain in her forehead. The past three days her dad had helped her study Spanish every night in preparation for a big exam yesterday. He had been very patient and helpful.

"Guess what?" She dashed across the room to where she'd set the graded test on the counter, flashing it in his face. "Check it out!"

She had been getting along record-well with Kevin lately. It's not that they were sitting down every night and having deep conversations; there wasn't really light talking and joking, either. Shannon couldn't have explained what was different in their relationship. It was more the feeling inside her about him. She hadn't told him that she'd ended things with Kurt, but she was pretty sure he knew anyway. He always seemed to know. She wondered again how he could be so incredibly, annoyingly discerning about her and so utterly oblivious to her sister's dilemma. In a way she couldn't wait until he found out, even though she knew it wouldn't be a pretty scene.

His most impressive Conrad smile filled his face at the red *A* in the corner. "That is fantastic, Shannon!" He unexpectedly swept her up into his arms for a tight hug. "I am so proud of you."

Her heart glowed at his words, and she returned the hug. "Thanks, Dad."

He pulled away, staring. "What did you say?"

Shannon smiled faintly. She hadn't said it intentionally, but when it came out, it sounded right. "I said, thanks…Dad."

He reached out and touched her face, then grabbed her into another crushing hug. "I love you, Shannon," he said roughly, his voice catching. "I really do."

"I know." Her eyes pooled up with happy tears. "I know."

* * *

"Are you feeling okay?"

Shannon lifted her spinning head from her hands. It felt like it might split into pieces at any given moment, and her skin was hot and clammy.

"I'm fine." She wasn't, and she knew it. She had tossed and turned all night with a fever, but she hadn't mentioned it to anyone. Life must go on.

Jesse narrowed his eyes but said no more. When they both stood up with their lunch trays, Shannon swayed back and forth until Jesse dumped his tray on the table and grabbed her.

"What's wrong?"

"Just dizzy," she murmured, clinging to his arm.

"You're burning up." Jesse's hand pressed against her forehead. "Maybe you should call your dad."

Shannon shook her head, but that only made the room turn sideways. "I'm fine," she repeated, hoping saying it would make it so. "But…would you walk with me to English?"

An endearing grin filled his face. "Don't I always?"

The afternoon was unbearable. Shannon fainted in P.E. and had to sit out the whole class. She didn't even try to keep up in pre-calc.

"Please go to bed as soon as you get home," Jesse urged as he walked her out to the Explorer. It was a pleasant, warm day, the sun shining brightly, but the glare hurt Shannon's eyes so badly, she almost had to close them. Oh, the pain in her head…

"I'll try to." A car in need of a new muffler roared by, and she cringed. Loud noises were grating on her nerves, too. "You go on, I'll wait for Laura. I'll be fine, Jesse. Really." The look on his face told her he didn't believe a word of it.

"Call me when you get home?"

She tried to smile, grateful to see Laura hurrying toward them. "Okay."

Picking up Daniel and Gabby had never seemed to take so long. The road swam before Shannon's eyes as she tried to navigate the way. What felt like hours later, she dropped her backpack on the hallway floor and stumbled to the living room, collapsing onto the couch. Gabby, Daniel, and Laura hovered over her, asking a million questions, but she didn't understand a word they were saying. She…just…wanted…

Sleep.

* * *

Kurt frowned at the name lighting up on his cell phone.

Jesse Kowalewski. Why was Jesse calling him? And why was he still one of his phone contacts?

"Hello?"

"Hi, Kurt." Intense deja vu washed over Kurt, but he wasn't imagining that this had happened before. It had many times, back when he and Jesse were friends. Good friends.

"Sorry to bother you," Jesse was saying, "but I'm calling to see if you'd be willing to check on Shannon when you have a chance, the sooner the better."

It took a minute for Kurt to get his jaw to function. "You're asking *me* to check on Shannon?"

"Look, she's really sick. I asked her to call me when she got home, but I didn't hear from her. She's not answering her phone. So I called the house, and Laura answered, so worked up it's hard to say how bad Shannon really is. I'd go myself, but I don't want to push the boundaries where my welcome is concerned. Under any other circumstances I would not ask this of you, but please…"

Kurt was a guy. He could only process one thing at a time. And there was a whole lot going on here he needed to compute, as quickly as possible. First of all, he had the feeling Jesse knew more about him and Shannon than he would prefer. Second, Jesse's voice was filled with worry, and Jesse didn't worry easily. Third, Jesse liked Shannon. If Jesse was worried about Shannon, then Kurt should be even more worried. Because he liked Shannon way more than Jesse did. Fourth, Jesse had guts. To respect Kevin's barrier even when the girl he liked was sick, and then to ask the other guy who liked her to go to her? But he really couldn't expect any less from Jesse.

"Sure thing, I'm on my way right now. How sick was she earlier?"

Jesse described her symptoms. It sounded like the flu to Kurt, but when he heard the word "fainting," he picked up the pace, jogging down the stairs into the garage. He was absolutely not ready to see Shannon.

"Okay, I'll go see how she's doing and give you a call back." Kurt still couldn't quite believe Jesse had just called him as he hopped in his truck and revved it to life.

His dad had kept a tight rein on him the past few weeks. He called it accountability. Whatever it was, it sucked to no end. Kurt felt like a small child again. "Where are you going? Who are you going with? When will you be back?" If that wasn't bad enough, his dad randomly called his cell phone to check on him throughout the day. Every night they sat down to talk, and Dad wanted to know everything. What Kurt was doing when he was alone, what he was looking at online, even what he was thinking about. *Everything.*

Kurt had gone to Victoria to apologize a couple days after their rendezvous. She had been mortified like his dad had predicted, but she didn't let Kurt take all the blame. Kurt had no intention of touching a girl for a very long time. Unfortunately good intentions did little toward changing inclination, desires, and habits. Bad habits. This whole "changing" process was going to be slow and painful.

He parked next to the Conrads' garage and let himself in through the side door.

"Laura?" He stepped into the living room. She was sitting on the floor next to the couch where Shannon lay. Kurt stared at Shannon. She was beautiful. So. Beautiful.

Popping up off the floor, Laura rushed toward him. "Thank goodness you came, Kurt. I don't know what to do. She won't answer my questions. I'm not even sure she's hearing me. I tried Andy, but he's not picking up."

Kurt lowered himself to his knees beside the couch. Beads of sweat pooled up above Shannon's lips and lined the sides of her face, dampening her hair line. Her body was shaking with chills, but when Kurt placed his hand on her forehead, all he felt was intense heat. Too intense.

Her eyes fluttered open, and she squinted up at him through pain-shuttered eyes before her lashes closed again. She tried to say something, but only her lips moved, and Kurt was pretty sure it was his name she mouthed.

"Any idea where your dad would keep a thermometer?" He wasn't panic-prone, but he'd never felt skin that hot.

Biting her lip, Laura shook her head. "No, but I'll look in his bathroom." She scampered down the hall, and Kurt watched, noting she still looked as slim as ever. No one would have guessed she was more than three months pregnant.

When she returned with a thermometer, Kurt gently opened Shannon's mouth and slipped it inside. An eternity later, it beeped. 104.3. Shoot. That sounded too high.

"Do you have your dad's work number?"

It took a few minutes for the Emergency Room receptionist to track down Kevin, but at last his voice filled the line.

"Dr. Conrad? This is Kurt Blake."

"Kurt? Why are you calling? Did something happen?"

"Shannon's sick, and one of her school friends asked me to check on her. She's burning up. Her temp says 104.3. She's practically delirious."

He hissed through his teeth. "Whoa. Uh... I'll head home as soon as I can. But in the mean time, try to get that fever down. Who else is there? Did Andy go with you?"

"Laura's here. Haven't seen Andy all day."

Kevin was silent a moment. "Really. That's interesting. He told me he was going to be working all afternoon with you and didn't know when he'd be back."

That *was* interesting, considering he'd told Kurt he wasn't able to work today due to a big homework load and would be home all afternoon and evening studying.

"Anyway," Kevin went on, "right now I need you to get Shannon into a cool bath. Keep her in there until that temperature comes down at least to 103."

Kurt gulped. He was supposed to give Shannon a bath?

"Laura, start filling a tub with cool water," he bellowed the second he hung up. Her look told him he must be crazy, but she ran straight for Kevin's room. Kurt knew the master bath had a Jacuzzi tub.

He stood over Shannon, waging a war with himself. He knew he needed to hand this job over to Laura. But he didn't want to. Suddenly her eyes opened, clear and blue, and she looked straight up at him. At this moment she trusted him. He couldn't betray that trust.

Scooping her up in his arms, he carried her down the hall to Kevin's room.

"What are you doing?" she asked, her voice barely a whisper. Her head rested heavily on his shoulder.

"Your dad wants you to take a cool bath." He carried her into the bathroom where Laura was swishing her hands in the filling jet-stream tub. He set her down on the wide ceramic edge. "Laura's going to help you."

Shannon nodded and closed her eyes, immediately slumping over toward the water. Kurt sprang forward to steady her.

"Laura, you're going to have to support her and help her undress and get in there."

"I can't! I'm not strong enough."

"Well you're going to have to be. I can't help. I'll be right outside the door, though."

"Kurt, it's an emergency. No one will blame you—"

"Don't tempt me, Laura," he raised his voice angrily, whirling around and dashing out the door before his mind changed. He closed the bathroom door and paced around Kevin's bedroom. This was definitely not what he'd had in mind when he'd asked his dad for the afternoon off.

His pocket started vibrating. Dad. Of course. How on earth was he going to explain himself? But if he didn't answer now, he'd have an even bigger hole to climb out of tonight.

"Hey, Dad."

"Son, what's going on? I thought you were staying home to study."

He bit back a sigh at the feeling of chains around his arms and legs. He'd always been independent. Being micromanaged was not an easy fate for Kurt Blake to accept.

Briefly he detailed what had happened, starting with Jesse's call. "Please believe me, Dad. Laura is helping her with the bath right now. I'm waiting in another room, but I'm not leaving until Kevin gets here."

Kurt cringed at the weighty silence on the line.

"I believe you. But you better be out that door the minute Kevin arrives."

Kurt let out the breath he'd been holding. "I will."

It took 45 minutes for Shannon's temperature to come down. Kurt found Gabby and asked her to get some fresh clothes for Shannon, since her old ones were doubtlessly soaked in sweat. When the bathroom door swung open, Shannon appeared in black leggings and a bright green long-sleeve T-shirt, supported on either side by her younger sisters. She offered Kurt an exhausted, quivering smile.

"Do you want me to carry you?"

Her hesitation was obvious, but she nodded. For the second time in an hour, he picked her up. Her skin was still hot to the touch. He loved the feeling of her in his arms, though. But no, he forced that thought away, gently settling her down on the couch.

"Thank you, Kurt," she murmured, closing her eyes instead of looking at him.

"Rest. Your dad will be here soon." No sooner had the words left his mouth than the side door slammed, and Kevin bounded into the room.

"How is she?"

"Temperature is down slightly, but it's still a high fever."

Kevin nodded and pulled open a pharmacy bag in his hands. Kurt took his cue to leave.

As he began backing out of the living room, Kevin looked up from where he was bent over Shannon.

"Thank you, Kurt." Gratitude flashed across his face. "I'm sorry if I put you in a difficult situation." He raised his eyebrows. "I know everything that's happened between you and Shannon."

Everything? Embarrassment almost knocked Kurt into the wall. He leaned his shoulder against the drywall for support, taking a shaky breath. When he forced his eyes back toward Kevin, the doctor still watched him, a look of understanding on his face.

Kurt pulled his lips into a frank grimace. No point in denying the truth. "Yeah, well, I gotta get home, promised my dad…"

On the way home, he called Jesse.

"Thank you. Thank you a million times over," his old friend said. Kurt wanted to retort and say that he hadn't done it for Jesse. But instead he said, "No problem." When he got home, Dad was waiting for him. He took one look at Kurt's face and jerked his head to the kitchen.

"Come on, let's sit and talk."

Chapter Twenty-Seven

It took Shannon a full two weeks to get back to her normal self. The Super Bowl came and went, during which she hid out in her room, feigning a relapse. She could hear a familiar deep voice chuckling downstairs . Even though she had faced Kurt a week ago, she had been out of her mind with fever. That didn't count.

Later that week Kevin rapped on her door while she was studying. She smiled up at him as his frame filled the doorway. He'd taken very good care of her while she'd been sick. It was pretty handy having a doctor for a father, especially when he was turning into such an attentive dad.

"So, Valentine's Day is this weekend."

Shannon raised her eyebrows. "And?"

"Do you have any plans?"

She wasn't sure if this was a nosy question or not. "No." She didn't. She'd been hoping Jesse might plan something. She'd thrown out a few hints lately. But they seemed to bounce right off him.

"Good. I'd like to take you and Laura to dinner."

A slow smile spread across Shannon's face at the idea. A Valentine's date with her dad. "That sounds nice."

Only when his shoulders dropped, releasing tension, did Shannon realize he'd been nervous to ask.

* * *

No one could understand why Laura turned down Kevin's invitation tonight. Shannon had gotten mad. She didn't understand. Laura wasn't close to Kevin the way Shannon had become. They hardly fought anymore, and Laura had overheard Shannon call him "Dad." She certainly wasn't ready to do that yet. Then again, she hid herself away in her room every evening, while Shannon actually spent time with their dad. No wonder they were building a relationship. Laura was jealous, but she was afraid to be around Kevin much. With his discernment, it wouldn't take much for him to discover her sins.

Her cop-out was that she had a lot of homework to catch up on. Which wasn't a lie. Her grades were the worst they'd ever been. At this rate, she was going to have to repeat her sophomore year. If she was even in school next year.

Tears threatened to come, but she blinked them back. She'd given in to tears too much. Crying wouldn't help her figure anything out.

As soon as Kevin's taillights disappeared down the driveway, Laura looked down at the crumpled paper in her hand. It contained the number she'd swiped out of Shannon's phone this morning while Shannon was cooking. Now all she had to do was work up the courage to call him.

With shaking hands, she dialed the number.

"Hello?"

"Kurt?"

"Yesss…" He drew the word out uncertainly. "Who is this?"

"This is Laura. Conrad."

The silence hurt Laura's ear, and she realized she was holding her breath.

"Laura…" he finally said wearily. "What do you need?"

Oh, she hated being a burden, and of all times. Not just a Saturday night, but Valentine's Day, too. She'd counted on him being too loyal to Shannon to be out with another girl tonight, though. Looked like she'd judged him right.

"Is there any way you can drive me to town?"

He was quiet again. "Why?"

She swallowed. She wished she'd told Shannon. "I—I need to—talk—to someone."

More silence. "Would that someone be the father of your baby?"

Now it was her turn to be quiet. How did he know so quickly? "Yes," she whispered.

Oh, that silence was going to make her go deaf. Then, finally.

"I'll take you. What time?"

She had to swallow her relief in order to answer. "After 7:00." Matt worked until 6:30 on Saturdays. "Don't tell anyone. Especially not Andy."

Kurt heaved a large sigh. "Is he there?"

He wasn't, so Kurt agreed to pick her up at 7:30. Good thing Kevin had hired a babysitter before she decided to stay home. Denise or Cherise or whatever her name was currently lay tangled in a pretzel with Gabby on the Twister mat.

The ride into town was silent. Laura asked Kurt to drop her off at the Sunoco on the north of town. She didn't want anyone seeing where she went, and Matt only lived two blocks from the gas station.

She slid out of his truck, barely glancing at him. "I'll be back soon." It was cold and dark outside, and she was shivering by the time she spotted the small, grey house. The outside light was on, but Matt's car was in the driveway, so he must be home. She took a deep breath, shut her eyes, and thumped on the door with her gloved fist. She was about to knock again when she heard the lock turning.

When he opened the door, an onslaught of memories slammed into Laura. She hadn't seen him in so long.

"Laura," he said slowly, stepping outside and shutting the door behind him, his face surprised and a little wary. They stood together on the front step, shivering in the cold. Laura could barely make herself look at him. Man, she had really made a mess of things.

"What are you doing here?" Matt interrupted her shame-filled thoughts.

"I'm here because—I'm pregnant, Matt." Saying the words aloud was awful enough. Seeing the shock on his face was worse. Heavy silence hung between them before Matt spoke.

"And you think it was *me*? Laura, I'm not trying to be rude, but I know I'm not the only guy you slept with."

If only shame could kill...

"No, but you're the only guy who didn't use a condom." She took a deep breath to gather courage. She willed him to believe her. "R-remember that time? When—when you didn't have one, but you didn't want to stop and so...." She trailed off and looked up at his face. He wouldn't meet her eyes. "It only takes once."

She barely breathed as she waited to hear him acknowledge the truth. But he crossed his arms and cast a doubtful look at her.

"I don't think it's fair to peg this all on me when you were messing around with other guys. You can't prove it. And besides." He took a step closer and grabbed her upper arm, speaking into her ear, "I'm 20 years old, and you're 15. You're below the age to consent. I could go to jail." He stepped back and shrugged. "And I have a girlfriend now. I'm not about to screw that up. I'm sorry for your—situation. But…" He let his refusal hang and simply shook his head.

Laura tried hard to keep the tears at bay, but they rushed into her eyes anyway, and Matt sighed. "I think you better go now, Laura. I gotta head out in a few anyway."

She turned away silently, too numb to say anything. As she wandered down the sidewalk toward the gas station, she battled feelings of hopelessness. She gave up the fight against tears, no matter how pointless they were. If Matt wasn't going to help at all, she was on her own. Kevin was no dummy, and he would figure things out soon. Her next step had to be telling him.

* * *

Laura probably thought she'd been subtle by having Kurt drop her off at Sunoco, but she wasn't considering that he'd grown up in this town. He knew everyone. Especially the guys. Guys like him. And only one such guy lived near that gas station

True to her word, Laura was back in less than twenty minutes. Kurt had been studying by the inside light of his truck, growing colder by the second, but when Laura came into view, he turned the key in the ignition and blasted the heat. Her dejected gate announced that the visit had not gone well, and when she climbed inside the truck, tears were trickling down her face.

"Are you ready to go home?" he asked.

She sniffed and wiped at her face. "I guess." The despair in her voice tugged at his heart, just like it had on the phone when she'd solicited his help. Man, he was getting soft.

"What happened?" As if he didn't know. A few months ago, if one of the girls he'd slept with had come to him pregnant and claimed he was responsible, he'd have turned her away in a second. Because he knew most of those girls had been with other guys. Just like Laura had.

"I told him I'm pregnant and that I know it was him, and he doesn't believe me." Laura buried her face in her hands, sobbing.

Kurt exhaled, rubbing his forehead. He left the truck in park. Obviously they were not ready to go home.

"Laura—" Kurt paused, trying to make his voice as gentle as possible. "Are you certain you know who got you pregnant?" When she nodded, he pushed further. "Look, I'm not trying to be judgmental—I have no room for that." She raised her head. "But you've been with more than one guy, right?" Another nod. "Then what makes you sure it's this guy?"

She drew her lips together nervously, then spoke in the tiniest voice imaginable. "Have you ever had unprotected sex?"

Kurt cleared his throat and rubbed the back of his neck. Was he really having this conversation? With Shannon's sister? "Once or twice." He was beginning to understand.

"Would you believe that I only had unprotected sex once, with one guy?"

He felt sad for Laura. "Yes. But he probably won't."

"He doesn't." Her words were soft, accepting. "I need to see a doctor and find out exactly how far along I am. I know even with protection, stuff can happen, but if I'm right about how long I've been pregnant, then I'm right about the guy. I wasn't with anyone else for a few weeks then."

"Did you really like him?" Kurt put the truck in reverse and backed out of the parking spot. Laura seemed to be pulling herself together now.

She let out a cynical laugh. "Sure did. I don't know what I was thinking, though, 'cause he's too old. It never would have lasted. I can't believe I thought he actually liked me for more than sex..." She trailed off, her words tainted with sorrow.

Kurt had difficulty swallowing. How many girls had he made feel that way?

"It's Matthew Burke, isn't it?" He pulled onto the road and glanced at her in time to catch the almost imperceptible head nod in the beam of the street light. "I won't tell anyone."

"I know."

If only Shannon trusted him as much as her sister did.

"Don't you think it's time to tell your dad? You just said you need to go to a doctor. I'm sure he'll be upset, but he does need to know."

"I don't know how to tell him. I'm—I'm scared of him."

"Maybe if you write out what you want to say to him first. Then ask him to listen while you read it." Like he'd done with Shannon.

"I'm not a very good writer, or anything else really, but thanks for the suggestion." Laura was quiet. "Shannon said you're an amazing writer."

"She did?"

"Uh huh."

He must be glowing in the dark from the second-hand praise. Shannon had endured a lot from him. The least he could do was help out her sister. "I'll help you write a letter to your dad if you want."

"You'd do that? Man, you really *do* like Shannon."

He bit back a smile. Laura had seen right through him.

* * *

"How's your curry?"

Shannon looked up mid-bite. The ride to Bristol had been quiet, as had their meal so far. The Thai Bistro Kevin had chosen was packed with a mix of starry-eyed couples and others who looked more like they were completing a duty.

"It's delicious. Thank you for taking me here...Dad." The word always stuck on her tongue just a little. Only once had it rolled off naturally.

"You're welcome. You deserve it. Your work ethic is very strong."

Like yours, her heart replied, but she couldn't quite get the words from her mouth.

"Shannon, I owe you an apology."

She paused with spoon in hand, panang curry dripping into her bowl. "For?"

Kevin rested his fork on the table beside his almost-gone pad Thai. "Working you too hard. I placed unrealistic expectations, demands, and responsibilities on you that has led to severe lack of sleep and stress. It was not fair of me to place so many burdens on you that they would deplete your immune system."

Shannon shook her head. "It's not your fault I got sick. It's flu season."

"My fault? No. But I could have—*should* have—taken better care of you. I will be advertising for a full-time nanny next week."

"Really?" She turned hopeful eyes on him. "You mean it?"

"I mean it."

"Don't get me wrong, I adore Gabby and Daniel, but I'd love to have more time to focus on school."

He smiled and resumed eating. "Understood. Have you given any more thought to what you might study in college? I saw you marked all your applications as undecided."

Shannon propped her elbow on the table and leaned her cheek against her fist while she chewed. She stared at her glass of iced tea for answers, but it was silent. "I don't know, Kevin." His name slipped out. "I haven't had time to think about me. I can cook, play piano, create art—and I enjoy those things. That's as far as I've gotten. I'm always too busy taking care of other people to know what *I* want out of life."

"Do you enjoy taking care of other people?"

Did she? Jaime flashed through her mind. During the second year of Mom's illness, she had taken almost complete care of her little brother, and she didn't regret a minute of it, even though she'd had to drop track and friends and even piano lessons.

She thought of Daniel and his big brown eyes and darling hugs. Of Gabby and her attempts to act grown up and brave and like she wasn't hurting over her mom's absence. Of Laura...Oh, Laura. She'd let Laura down.

"Look at me, Shannon." Her dad's voice was gentle, so she obeyed, meeting his blue eyes, serious and tender at the same time. "Culinary skills, music performance, and fine art are all wonderful things. No doubt you could go very far in any of them, because you are incredibly talented. But I want you to look a little deeper inside, and see what I see."

She couldn't keep staring at his eyes, so she dropped to studying the diamond pattern on his black and white tie.

"I see someone who cares. Do you know how rare that is in today's world? You care about more than yourself. You care about others. I have watched the way you care about Gabby and Daniel, when you didn't even like them at first. It's easy to care now, but you didn't always love them, and yet you cared about them anyway. Because it's who you are. I don't know how, but you even care about *me*."

Her eyes darted back to his before she could stop them.

"You have something the world needs, Shannon, and that is compassion. If you decide to pursue culinary school, or music or art, I will support you one hundred percent. But I am asking you to consider what else you might be able to do. What else you might be passionate about. There are endless careers that revolve around service—teaching, social work, the medical field, just to name a few. Not only would you contribute invaluably to such a field, I think you would also find it more fulfilling than you can imagine."

His speech left Shannon's mind reeling, and she reached slowly for her glass to take a sip. Kevin saw all that potential in her? Knowing that he believed she was capable of so much made her want to reach for something higher than she'd thought of before.

"I will—" She paused to clear her throat. There was suddenly a catch. "I will consider what you said. I want to make you proud."

His smile was one of fierce fatherly pride and affection. "You're something special, Shannon Conrad. I hope you know that."

She was pretty sure if her heart glowed any brighter, she'd catch on fire.

* * *

"Laura?" Shannon trotted up the stairs as soon as they got home. It was late. Kevin was in the kitchen paying the babysitter, who'd already put the kids to bed. No sign of Andy anywhere. He'd barely shown his face the past few days ever since Shannon had happened upon him and Kevin arguing.

"I don't understand what is happening to you," she'd heard Kevin say, his voice laced with frustration. "It's not like you to lie to me. Where *were* you?"

"It's none of your business," had been Andy's surprisingly tart reply. Shannon had never heard him talk like that to Kevin before. She'd scuttled off quickly, but she was still wondering what it was all about.

"Hey, Laura?" She pushed Laura's bedroom door open. A lump under the covers moved around until a blond head appeared. "I'm sorry. Did I wake you up?"

She shook her head. "No. I couldn't sleep anyway. How was it?"

Shannon shrugged, feeling awkward. She knew Laura didn't have any sentiments about Kevin like she did. "It was nice. Wish you'd come." She dropped onto the bed beside her sister and looked closer. Laura's eyes were too red.

She reached a hand to run through her sister's thick locks. "I love you. You okay?"

Fresh tears filled Laura's eyes and spilled down her cheeks. "While you were gone, I talked to the guy who got me pregnant." Her eyes revealed deep, resonating pain. "He doesn't believe me because he knows I slept with other guys. I was so stupid, Shan! So stupid..." She sniffed "I wish I'd told you back then, but I was hurting too much. So I just kept going back to those stupid guys."

Shannon stroked her sister's hair back from her face, her heart aching until bitterness filled her mouth. "Will talking about it now help?"

"Maybe." Laura laced her fingers through Shannon's. "The first guy's name was Alex, and he was drunk. So was I."

"Oh Laura..." Shannon's heart broke for her sister. Why hadn't she tried harder to reach out to her sister in the fall? She'd known something was wrong, but she'd been too busy with her own problems.

Laura took a shaky breath and looked at Shannon. "I hardly even remember it, Shan. I barely remember giving away my virginity." New tears sparkled in her eyes.

"Maybe it's better that way."

Laura closed her eyes. "I'd do anything to have it back." She squeezed Shannon's hand tightly. "When I realized what I'd done, I was sick. But since I'd already done it, I didn't see the point of stopping. Maybe I didn't care anymore. I lost something I could never get back. Alex came back for more a few times, and it felt good while it lasted, but then he moved on. Realizing he didn't even care about what I'd given him broke something inside of me, so when I met Matt, I didn't think twice about giving in to him. I didn't think I'd end up falling for him." Her wistful smile told Shannon that Laura still liked the jerk, whoever he was. "I was stupid enough to think he really liked me, but as soon as he got tired of me, it was over. It hurt so bad, all I wanted to do was find something to take away the hurt. Ethan was next..." She stopped and met Shannon's eyes. "The hurt is so much worse now than then."

Tears splashed onto Shannon's lap from her own face, and she put her arms around her sister.

"I'm so sorry. I let you down, sis, so much."

"It's not your fault." Laura's voice was a whisper. "But Shannon—I'm scared." Her grip tightened. "And I'm worried. I think I might have...a problem." Her face crumpled up again, more tears sliding down her cheeks in an impatient rush.

Shannon bolted upright. "You mean like an STD?"

"Yes," her sister squeaked, covering her face with both hands and sobbing.

A million thoughts cascaded through Shannon's mind, fighting for prominence, and the winner was this: "Laura, you've *got* to tell Kevin."

Winning control over her tears, Laura nodded. "I'm going to. Kurt's helping me."

"*Kurt?*" Shannon couldn't have been more surprised as she stared at her sister.

Laura wouldn't meet her eyes. "I should have just asked you, but I took his number out of your phone this morning. He drove me into town tonight while you were gone so I could talk to Matt. He knows everything. He offered to help me write out what I need to say to Kevin."

Shannon rubbed her face in her hands, her brain overwhelmed.

"He's not as bad a guy as I thought at first," Laura said. "At least he's *trying* to clean up his act, you know?"

Oh, she knew. She hadn't been totally delirious when he'd made the decision to leave her cool bath in Laura's hands. *Don't tempt me, Laura.* She remembered that flinty determination in his voice, even if her eyes had been too shuttered by pain to see his face.

It was nice of him to help her sister. She had the urge to call him right then and there to thank him. Of course she wouldn't, but she was getting a feeling. It was small, but it was just a little bigger than gratitude.

It was respect.

Chapter Twenty-Eight

"How was Valentine's Day for you?"

Shannon considered Jesse's question on Monday in the lunchroom. Yesterday she'd seen him at church, but she'd decided to take Gabby and Daniel with her for the first time, going early so they could attend Sunday school. They'd loved it, but they'd also kept her too busy to talk with Jesse much.

"It was—good." She smiled, remembering her dinner with Kevin, but seeing Laura sitting alone at the farthest table in the back of the room, facing the wall, twisted her heart. She'd noticed her sister's social circle at school shrinking over the past weeks, but this was the first time she'd seen Laura by herself.

"Sorry, do you mind if I eat with my sister?"

Jesse turned to look and found Laura with his gaze. "Looks like she needs you." His warm brown eyes were sympathetic. "One question before you go." Suddenly his dimples smoothed out and he cleared his throat. "Do you have any plans on Saturday?"

"No. Whyyy?" Shannon drew the words out, her heart suddenly thumping. She didn't miss the red glow creeping up his neck.

He shrugged casually. "I want to show you this cool place where we can go for a walk or a run."

Shannon wasn't sure if he was asking her on a date or not, but since she enjoyed spending time with him and didn't get to do it often, she wasn't going to get hung up on technicalities. She offered him her best smile. "I'd love that!"

Saturday afternoon found them driving south on back roads in Jesse's rusty-bucket of a truck. The only instructions he'd given were to dress warmly and bring her running shoes if she wanted. She had no idea where they were going, but she trusted Jesse with her life. He hadn't brought it up again since asking her on Monday except to confirm it yesterday. She was confused by the fact that he had admitted, more than once, that he liked her, but he didn't try to initiate more than friendship with her.

After crossing the Interstate on an overpass, he turned onto a road that led into dense foliage. So many evergreens and mountain laurel filled the forest that the landscape took on a dark green color, rather than the leafless winter that surrounded Shannon's house. The road twisted and turned tightly, following a river on one side, lined by high rocks on the other.

"This is beautiful!" Shannon noted a narrow bridge spanning the river. "Is there a trail here?"

"Welcome to the Virginia Creeper Trail." Jesse pushed the brakes gently and signaled a right turn for a small pull-over, big enough for two or three cars. "It's an old rail bed that was transformed into a bike trail. I did the whole thing once, around 30 miles, but this section is my favorite. There are a lot of bridges built where the old train trestle crossed the river back and forth. It's pretty and peaceful." They both got out of the truck, stepping into the bright sunshine. It was one of the warmest days they'd had all winter. Perfect for a stroll in the woods. "I thought we could walk a while, or even run if you're up for it."

"If I'm up to it? Keep up if you can!" She took off at a sprint. In seconds she heard Jesse's feet softly striking the ground as he caught up.

"You forget who you're running with," he proclaimed, not sounding the least bit winded. "I was a star member of Claywood High's basketball, baseball, football *and* soccer teams for three years. Not to mention all of my elementary accomplishments."

Shannon laughed at his boasting as he fell into step beside her. "Do you miss the sports?" It was hard to talk. She hadn't gone running much lately, and she was sadly out of shape.

"You have no idea." His tone was nostalgic, but he flashed his usual grin. "All part of growing up, I guess. Some aspects are better than others. Like spending time with you. That's pretty nice." They jogged for a while, bantering back and forth until he tugged on her shoulder, slowing down.

"Hey, let's walk for a bit and enjoy the view. This is one of the prettiest spots."

"Wow, this trestle is curved!" Shannon marveled at the long, gently curving bridge they stood upon. "I've never seen anything like it."

"It's unique all right." They walked to the middle and stopped to look down at the rushing water. The river was full from melted snow, gurgling and hissing below them.

"Shannon?" Jesse's voice broke through her water-filled reverie, and she tore her eyes away from the frothy water and found him looking at her with a serious look on his face.

"Yes?"

His dark eyes had an intensity she'd seen before, but not in him. He hesitated a moment, then took a step closer and grabbed her by both shoulders, his hands trembling slightly. He slid his hands down to her upper arms and squeezed, pulling her up on her toes, and lowered his head until their lips met. His kiss was soft and tentative, and he broke away quickly. When Shannon looked up into his chocolate brown eyes, they were glowing.

Well, this was definitely more than friendship.

His next kiss was more curious, like he was gently pushing a door open to find out what was behind it. It lasted longer, and Shannon's tummy tightened while her heart beat out a staccato rhythm.

When Jesse pulled back again, he was smiling, dimples firmly in place. "That was my first kiss." Shannon cringed internally. Kurt had been hers, and Jesse knew that. He pulled her into a close embrace. Shannon reached up and found his face, taking it in both hands, and kissed him. *Really* kissed him. When he finally pulled back, gasping for air, he looked at Shannon with wide eyes.

"Wow."

Kurt *had* said she was a good kisser.

Shannon almost slapped herself. That was her second thought about Kurt in a matter of minutes, and she was here with *Jesse*. Would she never be rid of that boy?

Jesse started walking again, and Shannon matched his stride. When he nudged at her hand, she opened her palm to him, and he twined his fingers through hers. She gave his hand a contented squeeze. She liked this.

On the ride home she noticed Jesse getting quiet as they neared Claywood. By the time they passed the high school, he was completely silent, and if she said anything, he only grunted. A terrible feeling sank through her gut. Had he decided so quickly that he didn't like her? Maybe she really wasn't everything Kurt had said. Maybe he'd just been buttering her up to get her into bed. Maybe—

"Shannon, I'm sorry. I shouldn't have done that."

She hadn't even noticed they'd come to a stop at the bottom of her driveway.

"What?" she whispered.

"Kissed you. Held your hand. Any of it."

"Why not?" She gathered all the courage in her heart, along with her fledgling feelings for Jesse. "If you'd ask me out, I'd say yes."

He turned to her with a confusing mix of joy and heartbreak on his face. "Well now Shannon, that means a lot. Thank you. But your dad is never going to let that happen."

Shannon frowned, crossing her arms. "I'm actually getting along very well with him. You might be surprised. He's changed."

"Has he?" Jesse started creeping up the drive. "Or have you?"

Shannon was still stuck on the meaning of his question when they crested the hill and pulled up to the side of the house, the setting sun splashing color across the siding. Before she could utter another word, the side door flung open and Kevin marched down the steps.

"What in tarnation is going on? Where have you been?" He jerked the passenger door open and yanked Shannon from the truck. "What were you doing with this boy?"

"We—we—we were just hiking!" Shannon shot a wild look at Jesse who had come around to stand at the front of his truck, but he returned with an "I-told-you-so" look and stuffed his hands into the pockets of his worn jeans.

Kevin shoved Shannon toward the house and took a menacing step toward Jesse.

"You get lost, Jesse, and don't show your face here again. And stay away from Shannon!"

Shannon stood away from Kevin and watched Jesse's truck disappear down the driveway before she turned on Kevin. She hadn't felt this mad at him in...months.

"What is *wrong* with you?"

He let out a loud breath and ran a hand over his face. "You guys caught me off guard, and I just kinda lost it."

Shannon inhaled sharply through her nose, her nostrils flaring. "What exactly is your problem with Jesse?"

"He knows what it is, so let that be enough. Believe me, he knows better than taking you out and whatever else you let him do to you." He turned accusing eyes on Shannon, and she felt the wound acutely.

She lifted her chin. "He wants to date me."

"No way." Kevin's tone was deadly.

Shannon shook her head. "You didn't forbid me from dating Kurt, Claywood's biggest heartbreaker, yet you go into a rage when I come home with Jesse, who probably has the most integrity in town? You have some twisted standard." She turned to leave, but Kevin grabbed her arm.

"You want to know what's twisted? I'll tell you what's twisted. Jesse's father used to be my best friend. And now he's in jail. The honorable Jesse didn't tell you that, did he?"

Shannon stared at Kevin without blinking. Jesse's dad was in jail?

* * *

Jesse flexed his hands on the steering wheel as he drove the five minutes to the trashy trailer park he'd called home for the past four years. By now Shannon probably knew the truth about his dad. He didn't know why Kevin hadn't told her before. Probably because it was an embarrassment to him.

He never should have touched Shannon when he knew he couldn't make her his girl.

"Did I rush things, God?" he asked aloud, maneuvering around a pothole. He'd hadn't been able to resist her in the woods, just the two of them. His need to give her a tiny clue how he felt had overruled his head—which was over heels in love with her.

Her kisses had been earth-shattering, and he'd feel like the king of the world right now if he didn't know she'd learned to kiss like that from Kurt. He felt a new understanding as to why Kurt kept coming back to her, though. He could honestly say he liked Shannon for who she was on the inside, and he'd liked her for that long before he'd done more than touch her on the shoulder. But kissing her had turned something on inside of him that he was quite sure had been better left off a while longer.

"Exactly how much did I just mess things up, God?" he groaned as he pulled into the short driveway next to his trailer. He loathed this place and the fact that he couldn't provide something better for his family. Who had he been kidding, thinking he could have Shannon? She practically lived in a mansion, and he in servants' quarters.

He should have listened to his dad. When he'd told him he liked a girl, he had cautioned Jesse to take it slow. Then Jesse had told him whose daughter she was, and Dad had basically said "good luck," with a healthy dose of sarcasm.

"What's wrong with *you*?" Jasmine demanded when she saw his face. His sisters were in the living room playing Boggle, slouched into the middle of the saggy couch. It always dumped its occupants to the center if it didn't swallow them up in the gaping crevice where the back met the seat. They couldn't afford cable or Internet, so most of their entertainment was in the form of games and books and home improvement projects. Well, Jesse was the only one doing the latter. A quick glance in the kitchen told him the faucet still dripped obnoxiously, and the light fixture above the kitchen table dangled more precariously than yesterday. Wallpaper was shredding from the walls; the linoleum was chipped and stained. Looked like he needed to spend a little more time on home improvement. As if he had any more time...

He waved off her comment, shaking his head. "Nothing. How's Mom? Any better than this morning?"

Jasmine looked at him. "What do *you* think?"

He sighed. Everything was going from bad to worse. Mom's mental health, Jasmine's attitude lately, now his friendship with Shannon.

"Well I'm gonna check on her, then head to bed early while I have the chance."

His mom was asleep in her room, but the bottle of pills on her nightstand caught Jesse's eye. It seemed like she had to take an entire pharmacy of medication to keep her depression from killing her.

Crawling under the covers, he curled up tight in his floppy bed, fighting off shivers. They couldn't afford to keep the heat on at night, and it was barely on during the day, either. When the chills subsided, he rolled onto his back and stared up at the water-marked ceiling above him. The wall above his bed gaped open with a hole, and the room smelled strongly of mildew.

His dad had been a college buddy of Kevin's. They had both gone to medical school together in Charlottesville. Jesse hadn't known much of this as a child, but he'd learned a lot in his prison visits with Dad. Dad and Kevin had kept in touch after Dad moved to southwestern Virginia and Kevin went on to Chicago. Later when some scandal had forced Kevin to resign his job— Jesse was sure it must have been his affair with Carmen—his dad, the ever loyal friend, invited Kevin to join his private practice in Abingdon. Jesse didn't know why Kevin had chosen to settle in Claywood. Probably because it was small and not nosy. He wished.

Gabby had been born a few weeks after Kevin showed up in his world. Since the dads were best friends, the families did a lot together for a few years.

Jesse sighed and rolled over. That's when Dad had ruined everything. Abusing his privilege as a doctor, he began writing unnecessary prescriptions, not only for a few friends, but also for himself. When Kevin discovered that he was addicted to Vicodin and Codeine, he chose to look the other way. But then one day—a day Jesse would never forget—one of Dad's patients died as a direct result of him being under the influence of drugs. That's when life as Jesse had always known it spiraled out of control and never came back.

Dad was convicted on a number of drug-related charges, as well as involuntary manslaughter. He was fined thousands of dollars for medical malpractice that his insurance refused to cover, and his medical credentials were permanently revoked. His sentence was 25 years. He'd almost taken Kevin down with him, too, but he was saved by his lawyer. Jesse didn't know all the details. Something about Dr. Conrad being on probation, and then he decided to specialize in emergency medicine and go on as if he'd never known Martin Kowalewski. Jesse and his mom and sisters had been forced to move to Claywood when their house in Abingdon was foreclosed. Couldn't keep up with the mortgage without Dad's income. Jesse shuddered, wishing he could forget that day, too. A distant relative owned a mobile home in a trailer park in Claywood and offered to help out. They'd been here ever since. No one in town knew Jesse's past—except for Kevin and Andy. And Kurt. But that was another story.

Warm sunlight spilled through Jesse's cracked window shade, waking him with its brilliance. One glance at the clock had him hopping out of bed. He'd slept late. He had needed it, since he rarely slept for more than three hours together. But he wasn't going to make it to Sunday school this week. Hoping Shannon would be at church, he showered quickly and was out the door in twenty minutes. Miraculously there was a free parking spot by the curb directly in front of the church, and he jogged across the small lawn, springing through the front doors and nearly plowing someone over.

Of course it was Shannon, and they both froze and stared at each other. She broke eye contract first when Daniel tugged on her hand.

"Are we gonna sit down, Shanny?" he whispered, pointing at the sanctuary doors. She nodded and then looked up at Jesse again. "Do you—do you want to sit with us?"

He shouldn't. He almost wished she hadn't kissed him the way she had yesterday. His world had been cock-eyed since then, and he was still trying to set it right-side up. That red lipstick on her lips today wasn't helping one bit. Sitting beside her would be too painful.

"No, I don't think so, Shannon." The hurt that traveled across her face took a fisted swing at his stomach. "I want to talk with you after church, though, if you have a few minutes."

He caught up with her in the parking lot after the service where she looked like she was attempting to evade him.

"Shannon. Give me a minute. Please?"

She didn't reply, didn't even look at him as she unlocked the Explorer and put the kids inside. He waited, knowing she would turn. He wasn't ready for the tears glistening in her eyes when she did.

"Why didn't you tell me about your dad?"

She was standing a few feet away from him. All he wanted was to take her face in both of his hands and kiss her. But he knew that he couldn't. Well, that he shouldn't. That he *wouldn't*.

God, what did I do?

"I'm sorry I didn't tell you. Do you think it's easy to tell people that—that your dad is in—that he's in prison?" He looked down, feeling the familiar tears pricking behind his eyelids. He hated how easily he cried. It wasn't a very masculine trait. "I was 14 when my dad was arrested, went on trial, and went to prison. It was…" Words were inadequate to describe the hell he had lived through four years ago. "It was devastating. My dad, my hero, turned out to be a drug-addict, and I'm sure your dad told you the whole story." Risking a glance at Shannon, he saw her pretty head nodding. "It's been really rough since then, and there's never a *good* time to tell someone, 'oh, by the way, my dad's in prison for manslaughter, among other things.' I just…" He shrugged and looked her in the eye again. "I didn't want you to think badly of me." Like Kevin did. Like Andy did. Shannon probably didn't know Andy used to be a close friend. But Andy would never tell her that.

"I'm sorry. I should have been up front with you a long time ago."

"That's okay." Her soft, understanding voice caressed him, and he yearned to hold her in his arms. "You visit your dad every Sunday, don't you? The relative who doesn't get out much?"

"Guilty as charged. My mom has a fit of depression if I mention his name, and my sisters won't have anything to do with him. I'm the only one willing to visit. And besides, he's the reason for who I am today."

"What do you mean?" Shannon squinted at him quizzically.

"See, there's this sweet little lady named Betty who does Bible studies at the prison. During my dad's second year there, she studied with him until he gave his life to Christ. My dad repented and confessed to God, Shannon, and even though he's going to be in prison for a long time, he's more free today than before he was behind bars. He wanted his family to share in his new joy, so he sent Betty to me."

"The Betty who goes to this church? One day you said she was the reason you were here!"

"That's the closest I came to telling you. But I couldn't get up the nerve, and you never asked later, so I just...didn't." He shrugged apologetically. "My dad is a changed man, Shannon, and God used Betty to bring both him and me to the cross. My mom and sisters still want nothing to do with God, but I keep praying. In the mean time, I visit my dad every Sunday, and we have our own Bible study, since we can't go to church together."

Shannon looked at him with a tender, melty look that had him itching to pull her against him again.

"I'm sorry about yesterday, Shannon. I wasn't planning to do that. I know I can't ask you out. But I like you very, very much."

She smiled in a way that lit up her eyes. "I like you, too."

His heart did a dance.

"Kevin doesn't have to know," she said quietly.

Jesse dropped his head against the temptation. She wasn't making this easy. Did she have any idea how hard it was for him to turn her away right now? He might as well push her straight into Kurt's waiting arms. "I can't do that. And neither should you."

Her lips softened into a small pout, but she nodded.

"Your relationship with your dad has come a long way since you got here, and I would never forgive myself for interfering with that. We'll just keep being lunch friends, okay?" That was so not what he wanted...

She stared at him. "How do you do that? How do you accept...*everything*...like it's easy?"

Easy? She didn't have a clue. "A lot of prayer, Shannon. A lot of prayer." He took a step back. He needed to get away before it became obvious how absolutely not easy this was. "I'll see you tomorrow, okay?"

Walking away from her was one of the hardest things he'd ever done.

* * *

Four days later, Shannon was still struggling not to let resentment take over her feelings for her dad. A lot of prayer, Jesse had said. So far it wasn't helping much. She and Kevin hadn't talked much since Saturday. Given the history, she understood why he wasn't keen on the idea of her going out with Jesse. But it wasn't fair to either of them.

When Laura volunteered to clean up after dinner on Thursday, Shannon hugged her and ran upstairs to take a quick, hot shower. She had a lot of homework awaiting, but she hadn't had time to read the Bible in a while, so she grabbed the thick book and carried it down to the kitchen. She intended to keep Laura company while she finished loading the dishwasher, but Kevin was still in the room, sitting at the small kitchen table with tax forms spread in front of him. Shannon hesitated, then slid into a chair across from him.

He grunted. "Never thought I'd say this, but reading that looks a whole lot better than filing taxes."

Shannon smiled. "When did you get this?" She tapped the soft leather cover.

"It was a gift for my 12th birthday," he replied without pausing to think. "A gift from my dad."

Shannon stopped mid-page-flip. She'd never heard anything about her grandfather. "What happened to him?"

Kevin batted her words away like a fly. "Not something I want to talk about."

"Oh." She kept perusing her Bible, but her mind lagged behind. Her dad was always a mystery.

She was still working her way through the book of Psalms. It was slow going, since she wasn't much of a reader, and she tended to re-read each psalm several times to deepen the impact.

She found her page marker at Psalm 60 and began reading.

O God, you are my God, earnestly I seek you; my soul thirsts for you, my body longs for you, in a dry and weary land where there is no water. I have seen you in the sanctuary and beheld your power and your glory. Because your love is better than life, my lips will glorify you. I will praise you as long as I live...

Her eyes welled up as her soul filled with the longing these verses described. She was dehydrated, and God was the only source of water. She wanted to want Him more. She read again, *because your love is better than life*. That's what Jesse understood. That's how he could accept the unacceptable. Because he knew that God's love was better than anything in this life, so, by the love of God, he could handle the loss of anything in this life.

Shannon trembled. She wanted to experience God in that way, but it terrified her. She had to be willing to trust God on a level she didn't yet understand.

She looked up at her dad, busily scribbling on one of his forms. She should have told him about Laura right away. She should have trusted God with the outcome.

Good thing Laura was about to turn herself in to Kevin's mercy. She'd told Shannon this afternoon that Kurt was reviewing the final draft of her letter tonight. Tomorrow was D-day.

Shannon eyed her sister bending over the dishwasher, allowing her eyes to linger on her subtly thickening waist. It was a small bump, but no one would think anything of it if they didn't know the truth.

Laura tried to close to dishwasher, but the door didn't latch and sprang back down, hitting her in the belly. She jumped back and cradled her stomach protectively. It was the most beautiful, motherly thing Shannon had ever seen her sister do.

"Laura Sarah Conrad!"

Shannon jerked her head back to Kevin and found him staring at Laura. Not at her face, but at her midsection. His face was turning the beet red that clashed with his hair.

The lie was over.

He knew.

He stood so fast his chair flew across the room as he charged toward Laura. She shrank back against the counter. Shannon opened her mouth in a silent scream when Kevin's hand slapped her sister across the face. A small whimper escaped from Laura as she cowered before their father, trembling with rage.

After a slew of swear words shouted from his mouth, he grabbed Laura's chin and jerked it up.

"You look at me and answer me, Laura. *Are you pregnant?*"

"Yes," she said in a whispered squeak. "I'm pregnant."

Suddenly he spun her to the center of the kitchen, and shoved her shoulder so hard she crashed onto the floor.

"No!" Shannon screamed from her seat, frozen in horror at the scene happening before her.

Kevin ignored her and placed his foot on Laura's belly where she was crumpled on the floor.

"You little whore."

Shannon gasped at the heartless words spitting out of his mouth. Laura struggled back onto her feet as tears poured down her face. She crossed her arms over her chest. Shannon could see her shaking from here. She didn't know what to do.

"How long have you been pregnant?" Kevin demanded, his face contorted with rage.

"Around four months."

He lunged at her, grabbing her by the shoulders. "When were you planning to tell me?" he roared. "After the world knows?"

Laura sobbed so hard she was barely understandable. "I was planning to tell you tomorrow, okay?"

"Tomorrow? Right." He swore again. "Four months... Four months ago was October." His face twisted up like a screw. "So that's what you were up to all those late nights, huh? Sleeping around like a slut."

Laura's shoulders hunched at the words, and Shannon felt the wound inside herself.

"And which of your boyfriends is responsible for *this*?" He jabbed at her belly.

Her mouth opened and closed twice before she wrenched herself out of his hands and ran from the room.

"Laura Conrad, we are not finished!"

When she didn't return, Kevin turned and advanced toward Shannon.

"How long have you known? How long, Shannon?" He grabbed her arm and hauled her out of the chair. "Answer me!"

She'd known all along it would go down like this. But in the past few weeks when she'd felt so close to him, she'd had this little fantasy that he'd be nice about it. Calm. Understanding. Forgiving. Boy had she been wrong. And it hurt. Worse than he'd ever hurt her before.

"I've known since Christmas Eve." She was amazed at the calm sound of her voice.

"*Why didn't you tell me*?" he screamed, shaking her violently with every drawn out word.

"Because I knew how you'd react!" Her calm façade dissolved as her heart braced for the hurt that was coming.

"You lied to my face! Point blank! You know why I believed you when I asked you what was wrong with Laura? Because I trusted you. I gave you a second chance after your escapade in the fall, lying for your sister. And now you've done it again." He laughed savagely. "Last time. I will *never* trust you again, Shannon. Never."

When she'd made the choice to lie to him, she'd known what it meant. But hearing the words from his lips broke the dam inside, and she started crying.

Kevin paced around the kitchen, head in his hands. "I can't *believe* this. This is bad. This is so bad. There goes my reputation, up in smoke. What are people going to *think*?" He turned a hateful glare on Shannon. "You girls are just like your mother. Irresponsible, promiscuous tramps dragging unwanted babies into the world."

Shannon felt the bite of his words across her body like an ant attack. "Is that what I was, Kevin? An unwanted baby?"

"I didn't say that."

"No? Why don't you just admit that you wish Mom had given me up?" The muscles in his jaw jerked back and forth. "Or better yet, that I had never been born, and you wouldn't be saddled with us now?"

"Watch your mouth, Shannon Conrad," Kevin warned, but she plunged on.

"Do you know how much Laura is hurting right now?" Shannon came closer to her father. "Do you think she *wants* to be in this situation? It takes two people to make a baby, Kevin, and the jerk who got her pregnant won't even own up to it. And you want to pin all the blame on her? Do you know how scared she was to tell you? What she needs right now is to be loved in spite of her mistakes. What she needs is someone to take her to a doctor to make sure everything's okay. What she needs is her dad to give her a hug and tell her she is going to get through it because he is going to be there for her every step of the way. What she needs is a parent! But you have no idea how to be one!"

He took two quick steps and slapped her face on one side, then the other, hard enough to send her stumbling backward. "Don't talk to me like that!"

Shannon stared at him in stunned silence, and he glared back. She felt the last pieces of her heart crumble, and her face followed suit. Unwilling to let Kevin watch how much he'd hurt her, she left all the crumbs of her heart on the kitchen floor and started running. He called after her, but she didn't stop. Nearly blinded by tears, she tore the door open, jumped off the porch, and sprinted down the driveway. She ran and ran, heedless of where she was. All she felt was the pain in her chest squeezing so tightly she couldn't gather enough oxygen for her lungs.

That, and the ice cold wind on her bare arms.

Chapter Twenty-Nine

She didn't know how long she'd been running when it started to snow. The wet sting against her cheeks and arms slowed her steps, but she didn't stop. Where would she go? Not home.

It picked up quickly, the white flakes swirling around her in a dizzying dance. Her feet slipped on the slick asphalt as a truck rumbled up behind her. She heard male laughter as it passed, but she didn't bother looking.

A few minutes later she clenched her teeth against the shivers, squinting into the blinding snow. She must be almost to town. Could she make it somewhere warm?

Another truck approached from the opposite direction, or was it the same one returning? Shannon didn't care. It passed slowly, then stopped, then began backing down the road toward her. Her heart beat fast. What did the driver want? She almost wished whoever it was would kidnap her and spare her from ever seeing Kevin again. But that would leave Laura to face him alone, and she'd fight to the death to prevent that.

The truck ambled back until the window fell in line with Shannon. She stared straight ahead, running as fast as her Toms would allow, her heart pounding with terror.

"Shannon?" The deep voice was such a relief, she missed a step and slipped, skating across the drifting snow and landing in the ditch. The fallen snow burned against her arm. Why had she been wearing a short-sleeve T-shirt at home in the dead of winter?

She was still struggling to right herself when a figure appeared out of the whiteness. He scooped her up like a baby and set her on her feet beside the truck.

"What the heck are you doing?" Kurt lifted his cell phone to cast a ray of light. Her body was convulsing from the cold. He stared for a second, took in her attire, and let out a nasty word, but somehow it didn't hurt the same as when Kevin said it. He jerked the zipper down his coat and shrugged out of it like a lunatic, throwing it around Shannon. Nothing had ever felt so wonderful. She barely noticed as he picked her up and placed her inside his truck.

"I don't know what is going on, but I am taking you home," he said the minute he jumped into the driver's side and closed the door.

"No!" Shannon's hand was already on the doorknob, ready to bail, but her frozen hands wouldn't pull the darn thing. "I'm not going home."

Kurt paused. "Well, you can't stay out here. You're nearly frozen. I guess we can sort things out at my house."

Shannon didn't say anything as Kurt continued down the road, his wipers swishing back and forth rapidly against the white onslaught. She only cared that the heat was blasting at its highest setting, and she wasn't going home to Kevin.

When they made it to Kurt's house, he parked his truck in front of the shop. "Sorry, garage is full right now. Come on inside." He jumped out of the truck, but Shannon took her time moving her numb limbs out the door. She slid slowly to the ground, but the instant her feet hit the ground, they slid in every direction at once.

"Whoa, there." Kurt's hands promptly grabbed her waist. How had he gotten around to her side that fast? "You okay?" He removed his hands quickly, but Shannon still felt their warmth seeping through her. He offered her his hand and tugged her across the walk and to the front door. He closed the door behind her, and she stood huddled on the landing of the split-level house, willing her body to stop shaking. That's when she finally looked at Kurt and her eyes popped open.

"Do you normally wear just a wife-beater under your coat?"

He chuckled, a shaky sound due to his own shivers. She hadn't noticed what he was wearing when he'd shared his coat. Again. Seemed they'd come full circle.

"Now there's the Shannon I know and like." He winked. "No, I don't. Do you normally go jogging when it's ten degrees in a T-shirt and whatever you call those flimsy excuses for shoes on your feet?"

Shannon looked down. She was dumb. She could have died out there.

She shook her head and met Kurt's eyes. "Thank you." Her eyes strayed to his arms, still puckered in tiny goose bumps. Mercy, he was ripped.

She rolled her shoulders to relax her cold, tight muscles. "So what *are* you doing in that undershirt?"

He shrugged his ridiculously muscular shoulders. "Just finished up a rousing game of ping pong in the garage at my birthday party and had to run a buddy home. So I threw a coat on and went. Never imagined finding you out there."

Shannon stared at him. "It's your birthday?"

Another shrug. Dang, what did he do to get a body like that?

"Tomorrow. Sorry I didn't invite you to the party. No girls allowed."

Shannon smiled at the elementary phrase. "That must be where Andy was."

"Yeah but he left early. Said he had to study."

She lifted her eyebrows. She hadn't seen a trace of Andy all evening.

Kurt frowned. "He didn't come home?"

She shook her head, too weary to reply. Shivers kept racking her body no matter how hard she tried to keep them at bay, and the effort was exhausting her back. She slumped over a little. "Can I sit down somewhere?"

"Of course." Kurt sprang forward. "Sorry. We need to warm you up. You better have a good explanation for this one."

"Kurt?" Another voice filled the space, and Shannon looked up to find Mr. Blake standing at the top of the stairs. "What's going on?"

"Umm." Kurt glanced at Shannon. "I'm not sure. But Shannon needs a place to hang out for a bit."

Mr. Blake assessed her, and she squirmed under his study. He gestured for her to come in, and she dragged her tingling feet up the stairs, strangely comforted by Kurt's hand on the small of her back propelling her forward. He led her to a chair in the living room, then disappeared, calling, "I'll be right back. Let me grab a shirt."

Shannon melted into the soft armchair one vertebrae at a time. What was she thinking running off like that? Kurt must think she was absolutely nuts. It wasn't his first time to rescue her from a run, either. She tried to wiggle her toes and fingers. How in the world had she run that far like this? She must have done almost four miles.

"Can I get you anything, Shannon?" She jerked her head up. Kurt's dad was still in the room.

"No, I'm fine. Thank you." She forced her teeth not to chatter, immensely relieved when Kurt popped back into the room, this time a cozy-looking white sweater settled around his torso. Shoot, he looked good in anything.

He squatted down in front of her. "Need anything? Hot drink? Blankets? Anything to make you comfortable so you can tell me what in the devil's name you were doing running along the road in a blizzard dressed for a picnic?"

Shannon swallowed hard. Was he going to make her talk in front of his dad? She nodded her head ever so slightly in Mr. Blake's direction. "Please, Kurt," she barely whispered. Kurt gave her a long look.

"Be right back." He crossed the room and talked in a low voice with his dad. Shannon closed her eyes. This nightmare was far from over.

* * *

Shannon had noticed his athletic physique. Several times, Kurt was sure. He'd been lifting weights for four years, but the past few weeks he'd upped the ante. Basically, whenever he had urges to return to, ahem, past behavior, he worked out instead. It'd been Dad's suggestion, of course, and Dad was his spotter. In the last couple days he'd started noticing the results, especially in his arms. But that didn't really matter now. What mattered was the serious look in his dad's blue eyes.

"I don't like it, Kurt."

"I know, but she's not going to tell me what's going on with you standing there."

His dad growled in his throat and crossed his arms. "Okay, fine, but take her to the kitchen. It's safer."

Less intimate, he meant. His dad wouldn't trust leaving him in the family room alone with Shannon. He wasn't supposed to spend time alone with any girl. That was rule number one for this abstinence boot camp he had subjected himself to.

"Okay. Kitchen."

"Make her a drink, I'll send your mom in with a blanket. Keep it short, alright? I'll call Kevin and let him know she's here."

Kurt returned to Shannon, who looked like she'd wilted right into the floral pattern on the chair.

"Think you can stand back up? We can talk in the kitchen."

She nodded, suddenly looking uncertain. "Can I see Jefferson?"

Kurt winced as he led the way to the kitchen. "Let me check. Pick a spot."

He bounded out of the kitchen and nearly plowed over his mom coming up the stairs. Right. He was supposed to be in the garage helping clean up from his party.

"Mom! Great, it's you. Shannon's here and she asked for Jefferson. I know you banned him from the house, but I don't want to make her go outside again because she nearly froze to death out there and—"

"Just go get the dog, Kurt. Your father told me about Shannon. But make sure he doesn't destroy my craft room again!"

"Thanks, Mom." He dashed out the door and trotted across the lawn to the shop, where Jefferson ran to his feet.

"Come on, boy. Shannon needs you." The growing dog jumped into his arms, and Kurt jogged carefully back to the house. The snow was getting thick. Mom handed him a blanket as he passed through the living room, and he found Shannon sitting where he'd left her. She was still shivering violently, staring at her hands in her lap.

Her eyes came into focus when Kurt dumped Jefferson into her lap.

"Oh my goodness, you're getting so big," she crooned to the dog, immediately burying her face in his fur. Jefferson happily licked her face and snuggled against her chest.

"Can you stand up again, Shan?"

She obeyed without looking at him, lifting his dog in her arms as she rose to her feet. Kurt wrapped the blanket around her, squeezing her shoulders gently before easing her back into the chair. He made hot chocolate in the microwave, then dragged another kitchen chair over and sat down facing Shannon, so close that his knees were straddling hers. He paused and thought about what his dad might have to say about that and scooted back a few inches. He watched silently as she clung to Jefferson like he was a life vest.

Only in the glow of the overhead light did he notice the red marks on her cheeks. It wasn't from the cold. Protective rage barreled through him as he gently reached out and cupped her cheeks.

"Who did this to you?" Whereas cold had caused his body to tremble not long ago, it was anger that now shook his frame.

Tears spilled down her cheeks, wetting his hand. Her grieving eyes met his steadily as she said in the softest voice, "my dad."

It took a while to get the story out of her, and it didn't come coherently. After bits, pieces, and chunks, Kurt had a pretty good idea of what had happened. Even he flinched when Shannon repeated the names Kevin had called Laura.

He didn't say much. He didn't have much to say. Just asked enough questions to keep her talking until it was all out.

They sat in silence as Kurt tried to digest what had happened. He'd known Kevin would be mad, but to be slapping his daughters around? That was going too far.

"Have you been teaching Jefferson anything yet?" Shannon's question pulled his thoughts to the present. To Shannon, here in his own house.

"Trying. He's too hyper. But I taught him a few tricks. Want to see?"

They spent the next forty-five minutes playing with Jefferson, and soon his furry pal had Shannon laughing. Kurt wouldn't mind staying up all night coaxing Jefferson to roll over if that made Shannon happy.

"How's it going?" Kurt's head jerked up. Dad was standing in the doorway. He stifled a yawn with his lips. "It's getting late."

Kurt glared at him. Now was not the time for obvious statements. They all knew it was late, but some things were more important than sleep. Like Shannon.

She looked embarrassed as she stood up, the blanket slipping from her shoulders. "I'm so sorry, Mr. Blake. I'm embarrassed to impose on you like this, but please, can I stay here a little longer?" She clasped her hands together in a pitiful plea. "I just can't go home yet."

Dad gazed at her, and Kurt clenched his jaw. *Please, Dad, don't send her away.*

"You may stay here as long as you need, Shannon. Your dad knows where you are."

She visibly shrank. "He does?"

Dad nodded. "I thought it was right to tell him."

"Oh."

"Come on, Shannon," Kurt took her by the arm and gently pulled her back to where they'd been sitting on the floor. "I didn't show you how Jefferson chases his tail yet."

His dad disappeared, and they carried on with their dog show until Jefferson became tuckered out. He curled up in Shannon's lap and shut his droopy eyes. She lovingly stroked his head until soft snores puffed from his mouth.

"I never said thanks for what you did when I was sick." She glanced at Kurt with a small frown on her beautiful face. The face that Kevin had slapped. Oh, he was mad. "How'd you know to come?"

"Uh..." He knew his mouth was hanging open as he searched for an answer, but the only thing he came up with was the truth. "Jesse asked me."

"What? How—?" She cut herself short, her face incredulous.

Kurt chewed his lip. Obviously Jesse hadn't told her about their history, and he wasn't sure he was ready to tell her that Jesse used to be one of his best friends but had ditched him because he didn't approve of his womanizing ways. Or something like that. "You know, old football teammates. Guess he dug my number out of somewhere." It was sorta true. Right?

"Oh." She still looked confused. "Well, at any rate... Thank you."

He shrugged. "I didn't do much. But I was glad to help."

She smiled faintly, reminding him of all they'd gone through. "I know."

"Oh, I just remembered something." He left her with Jefferson and trotted to his room, returning with a folded sheet of lined paper in his hand. "This is the letter Laura wrote to your dad. I already reviewed it, and it's good. She's a terrific writer. I was too busy getting ready for my party to get it back to her earlier today." He dropped his head, feeling awful. "If I had made that effort, things may have gone differently tonight."

"No." Shannon reached out and touched his arm. "It's not your fault, not even a little. Laura should have told Kevin much sooner. And I shouldn't have lied to him. But we both made those choices. Thank you for at least trying to help Laura. That was...really nice of you."

Something about her voice was different, and he looked in her eyes and—*gulp*. Call him crazy, but he was almost certain he saw respect.

"It's almost midnight." Her tired voice broke into the quiet, and Kurt let out the breath he didn't know he'd been holding. Thank goodness. He'd been about to say something stupid.

"I know. You ready?" He hated for her to go back to Kevin.

Gingerly she eased Jefferson from her lap and stretched up to her full height, her knees cracking.

"No. But I can't stay here, can I?"

"Wrong person to ask, Shannon," Kurt said dryly. He'd let her live here, and she knew it. "Come on, let's get you home."

His mom was still reading by lamp-light in the living room, and Dad was sitting at her feet where she played in his hair with the hand not holding her book. It was nice of them to sacrifice their sleep for Shannon. She sincerely thanked them and followed him back out to his truck. Their short ride was a quiet one, and as they pulled up in front of her house, Kurt's hand was already on the door handle when Shannon spoke.

"Can I ask you a question? It's…really personal."

Oh boy. "Nothing's off the table for you, Shannon. Shoot." He reached his hand up to turn on the dome light. "Just in case your dad's watching. He doesn't need anything else to get worked up about."

He knows everything about you, by the way."

"Terrific. Carry on."

Shannon laughed, then instantly sobered. "I'd just like to know what made you the way you are. I understand why Andy messes around with girls. He has had no model of functional relationships, thanks to my dad's example. But your parents seem to really have it together, so…what happened?"

Kurt swallowed hard. She had to ask that. He wasn't sure he even knew.

"There are times," she continued, "like tonight, that I feel you genuinely care about me very much. But there have been other times, like the last time you asked me out, that I felt like all you wanted me for was sex."

Her words almost made him gag. "I'm sorry I made you feel that way," he said hoarsely. He sighed against the repulsive truth. "Sometimes it was probably true."

"Why? Why did you start sleeping with so many girls, Kurt?"

A long silence ensued as he thought about himself. How *had* he come to this?

It had started a long time ago, really.

"Remember meeting my brother Rob at Christmas? He's adopted. My mom's labor with me was really bad. We both almost died, I guess, and her uterus was so damaged, she couldn't have any more kids. When I was four, my parents began thinking about adopting a baby. They worked on it for a couple years, but it was really slow. I was eight when they met Rob. I don't even know how they found him, but the adoption went through, and before I knew it, I had a new big brother. He was 12. I've never known why they chose him. I thought they wanted a baby. He and I never clicked. It started out with normal jealousy, I guess.

I'd been the only child for eight years, and suddenly all the attention was poured onto this new kid."

He paused, the memories rolling back. All the times he wanted approval, acceptance, attention, and it seemed his parents didn't even notice him or his accomplishments. "Rob was better in school than I was. I've pulled Cs at best most of my life. Rob came along and got straight As. He was a hard worker. My mom taught him how to cook, and he made dinner at her side every night. When he was in high school, he took an interest in politics, and he and my dad would have all these political discussions. He was good in sports, too, which was my only strength. Junior year he was student body president. Senior year he was class president. Member of debate team. Member of every sports team. Yearbook. Drama. You name it, he was in it, probably leading it. He could do everything right. Everything but get a girl. I still remember when I was a freshmen and he was a senior, this girl sitting next to me watching him speak up front at a school assembly commented that if he had my looks, he'd have all the girls in town fighting over him."

He leaned back in the driver's seat and absently ran his finger in a circle around the steering wheel.

"I was already a flirt. Some things just come naturally." He let out a dry chuckle. "That comment got me thinking. I decided to see just what kind of attention I could get from a girl if I tried. And boy... I found the one thing I was *good* at.

"While Rob was away at college—political science/pre-law at University of Tennessee—my parents went down to visit him pretty often on weekends. They always came back singing his praises. You'd'a thought he could walk on water. They didn't even come to my games at school, and they were always on my back about my grades. I guess I started using girls as my defense mechanism. Like, at dinner when my mom gushed about Rob's latest feat, in my head I'd be saying, 'yeah, well I made out with so-and-so today for twenty minutes, so obviously she appreciates me even if you don't.' I guess that's how it started. I liked how it made me feel. I finally found something I was good at to boost my confidence."

He stopped, blowing the air out of his mouth slowly. Words didn't usually tumble out of him at the rate they were right now. He'd almost forgotten who he was talking to.

His phone started buzzing. Dad. He was probably wondering what was taking Kurt so long to bring Shannon home. He pressed ignore.

"Toward the end of my sophomore year my parents were gone one weekend, visiting Rob. And..." His voice started to shake. "I brought this girl home to hang out, and things went farther than I intended. Like, way farther. You know..." He swallowed hard. "And it—it felt good." A big understatement, but he wasn't about to delve into the sordid details. "So things just went...from there." Rob had flown through college with high honors, graduating with his bachelor's in just three years, while Kurt struggled through his junior and senior year. What had begun as a way to keep his self-esteem up had turned into a habit. Maybe even an addiction. That's what Dad said.

He cleared his throat. "How...how much more do you want to know?"

"That's enough," Shannon said quietly. Kurt looked at her for the first time in five minutes. Her hair had been in a knot at the back of her head all evening, but sometime while he'd been talking, she'd let it loose. The copper strands swirled around her face and down her shoulders in such a fashion to almost knock Kurt off his feet, and he wasn't even standing.

He took a deep breath. Who was he kidding? She'd made herself clear enough times. "Sorry if that was too much."

She shook her head, finally looking at him. Oh, his heart. She was seriously the most beautiful thing he'd ever seen.

"No, it wasn't. Thank you for your honesty. I guess that wasn't easy."

Not hardly. "Anything for you."

She smiled. "I'm sorry I can't be what you want. But I'll always be your friend, Kurt."

And he'd always want more... "Same here, Shan."

"Have you told your parents what you told me?"

"What?" he exclaimed. "Are you kidding?"

"Well, if they know about your—history—they might be wondering why, too. They need to know how they hurt you, because they probably don't realize it. Even if it's just to get it off your chest, I think you should tell them."

"Maybe," he said slowly, his mind racing at the idea. What if he did? How would they react? Would they understand? What would it accomplish? Anything?

"I think you should tell them tonight. While you've got your nerve up. If you told me, you can tell them."

Ah, man. She was the best. He longed to pull her into his arms and hold her. If only...

"I better get inside. He's waiting." Her voice suddenly sounded broken, and Kurt looked toward the house. Kevin's form filled the doorway, both hands on hips.

"You want me to go in with you?"

"No. I'm not scared of him. Just hurt."

"I'm sorry he keeps breaking your heart. You deserve so much more."

The eyes she turned on him were watery. "Thank you, Kurt. Happy birthday."

"Night, Shannon."

He didn't wait to watch her reach her dad. If he saw any manhandling, he was afraid what he might do.

"What took so long, and why didn't you answer your phone?" Dad was interrogating him before he even got halfway out of his truck. His dad was in his face, but Kurt stayed calm.

"I was talking with Shannon. Where's Mom? I know it's late, but I really need to talk with both of you."

His mom had already gone to bed but thankfully was still awake when Dad checked. He felt bad to drag her back out, but if he didn't say it now, he never would.

He sat down in the living room, and they followed suit, watching him. He clenched his fists on his thighs to still their shaking. This was even harder than he'd thought.

"First I want to apologize for any embarrassment I've caused. I never wanted to be a source of shame for either of you."

Mom started reaching out a hand to correct him, but Kurt said, "Please, let me finish. Shannon asked me tonight why I am the way I am. And this is what I told her." He repeated the story, adding or removing details as needed. He didn't blame them. He'd made his own choices.

By the time he finished, Mom was crying. She folded him into a hug. "I'm so sorry, sweetie. I never meant to hurt or neglect you. You always seemed so strong, never expressed a need. I must have been blind. You will never be an embarrassment to me, I promise you that." She stepped back and dabbed at her face with her pajama sleeve. "I've been somewhat shocked by the things your dad has told me, but they in no way changed how much I love you." She placed her hand on his cheek affectionately.

"Thanks, Mom," he muttered. "I love you, too."

Dad still hadn't said anything, so Kurt looked at him warily. He came down on one knee in front of him so he could look Kurt in the eye. His face was filled with pain.

"I don't know what to say, son. We should have explained the circumstances behind Robert's adoption to you a long time ago. He had endured extreme abuse and needed tremendous emotional support. He blossomed under our attention, way beyond anyone's expectations. We were thrilled by his progress. You didn't ask for attention, and Robert did. Like your mother said, maybe we became blinded by the fulfillment we got from seeing the difference we were making in his life. I had no idea you were hurting so much from it. I should have been more aware. Please forgive me."

Kurt couldn't ignore the true regret in his dad's eyes, and he knew his dad was already blaming himself for what Kurt had become. "I forgive you."

"If it means anything to you, I think you have real talent for leadership, and I would be confident turning over full management of the farm to you tomorrow."

It did mean something. It meant a lot. Kurt nodded, unable to speak around the enormous lump obstructing the air in his throat.

"If I haven't said so before, what you are doing—being willing to turn yourself around, accept help, and admit you're in the wrong—takes a huge amount of courage, and I am very proud of you, Kurt."

Dad pulled him up on his feet and wrapped his arms around him in a tight embrace.

"Son, I love you."

Kurt buried his face in his dad's shoulder and cried for the first time in five years.

* * *

"Don't you ever pull a stunt like that again." Kevin grabbed Shannon by the shoulder as she came through the door. She tried to squirm away, but he propelled her into the kitchen, where he swiped his thumb across both of her cheeks.

"Better put some ice on that one," he grunted, turning to dig in the freezer for an ice pack. Wrapping it in a towel, he pressed it into her hand. "Go to bed."

She posed to leave, then fished in her pocket and pulled out a crumpled piece of paper.

"Here's the letter Laura was going to give you tomorrow." He didn't reach for it, so she let it flutter to the floor.

"There you are!" her sister gasped, bolting up in bed when Shannon entered her room. "Why'd you leave? Where were you?"

Shannon's conscience smote her as she gazed at her sister's bloodshot eyes in the dim lighting of the night table lamp. She should have stayed here with Laura.

"I'm sorry, sis." She kicked her shoes off her aching feet. She could barely walk. "I had to get away. Kevin..." She took a deep breath, but the tears started again anyway. "He..." She couldn't go on, bursting into tears, and Laura wrapped her arms around her.

"I know, Shan," she sniffed. "I know." They cried together until they fell asleep.

Chapter Thirty

"Come in." Expecting Shannon, Laura didn't glance up when the door opened after a soft knock.

"Laura."

Her head snapped up at Kevin's hard voice. He'd hardly spoken to her in the past week since he'd discovered her secret. Even yesterday when he'd picked her up early and taken her to the doctor. The ride to the nearest OBGYN in Abingdon had been silent.

Her baby's heartbeat was the most terrifying and amazing sound she'd ever heard. The doctor had confirmed she was 18 weeks pregnant. Matthew Burk's baby for sure. Not that she'd ever doubted.

Kevin towered above her bed, looking down at where she was curled up trying to read some story for English that didn't make a bit of sense.

"Dr. Swanson called me today."

Instant nausea.

"You tested positive for Chlamydia."

Bile slid to the back of her throat as she closed her eyes and took a panicked breath of air. "What does that mean?"

"It's one of the most commonly contracted sexually transmitted diseases. It is easily treated with antibiotics. Unfortunately it is the most dangerous STD for a pregnant—girl."

The disdain in his voice was duly noted.

"She wants to see you again Tuesday before she decides what medication to prescribe." He looked mad, disgusted, embarrassed, and concerned all at the same time. Laura supposed the concern was a good thing, but she still wanted to crawl under the bed to hide from his disappointment.

"I'm sorry, Kevin," she squeaked.

He sighed heavily. "Not as sorry as you will be, believe me. Four o'clock on Tuesday. I gotta go make some calls and find a sub at the hospital."

Laura twisted her lips tightly as she watched him exit her room. She created so many problems for him. For everyone. Her hands clutched at her ever expanding abdomen. What kind of life was this baby going to have? Was it even fair to bring it into the world?

She squeezed her eyes, but the tears came anyway.

"God?" her voice quivered softly. Shannon prayed a lot. She'd seen her and tiptoed away, not wanting to interrupt. Laura didn't know how to pray, but man, she was desperate. "God, I need help," she whispered before dropping her face into her hands and bawling.

* * *

"Man, you're really starting to bulk up. Been lifting?"

Kurt popped his head through a fresh T-shirt. The shoulders were tight. He nodded, running his hand through his shaggy hair. He felt great after a long run with Andy and a shower. The snow had finally melted off the roads yesterday.

"Yeah, my dad and I have been working out together."

"You haven't been going out much."

Kurt flickered his eyes to meet Andy's. Parties and girls, he meant. "Trying to make some new habits." At Andy's look of surprise, he said mildly, "You were the one who got me thinking that way. Remember?"

"Oh. Right." The way Andy was looking around the room and at anything but Kurt made Kurt decide it was time to fish.

"How are your sisters?" He hadn't spoken to Shannon since he'd rescued her from the snow. Not that he wasn't desperate to, but his dad had forbidden him on pain of work probation if he didn't keep his distance.

Andy shrugged. "I don't know."

"You do know Laura's pregnant, right?"

Andy rolled his eyes at him. "Of course. My dad's still steamed about it."

"So you haven't talked to Laura or Shannon about it?"

Andy looked down.

"Ditching them as much as me, huh?"

Now his head shot up, sky blue eyes blazing. "What are you talking about?"

"Remember when Shannon got the flu? You told me you had to study that day. Said you'd be home all afternoon and evening. But when I checked on Shannon, you weren't there. And then Kevin said you'd told him that you'd be working with me all afternoon and evening and didn't know when you'd be back. Ringin' a bell?"

Andy crossed his arms over his chest, looking ticked.

"And then there was my birthday party. You left early to 'study.' But you weren't home for the big showdown with Laura, now were you? That's just two occasions of several that you've lied to me lately. It's not my business to know every detail of your life, but I take exception to my best friend not being honest with me."

Andy was silent. He shifted back and forth on his feet before finally meeting Kurt's eyes. "I've been with a girl."

Duh. "Which one?"

"Uh… Stephanie."

"Stephanie? Shannon's friend Stephanie? That Stephanie?"

"Yes, that Stephanie," Andy said with a scowl.

Kurt studied him a minute. "You sleeping with her?"

Andy rolled his eyes. "What do you *think* I'm doing? Sitting on a park bench holding her hand?"

"Does Shannon know?"

"No, and it's not her business, so don't you dare tell her."

Kurt groaned. "Dude, you know her mom's a cop, right?"

Andy sent a withering glare his way. "She's 18, Kurt."

"Okay, just looking out for you, bro." Kurt knew he had no room to criticize Andy. "How long has this been going on?"

"Since that day Shannon got sick. But Steph's had a crush on me for three years." Andy grinned, looking smug. "She was easy to convince."

For some inexplicable reason, Kurt felt sad. What Andy said made perfect sense. If a girl was willing, why not? He'd thought the same way for a long time. But now it somehow sounded very distasteful to him.

"So it's just sex," he said, remembering when his dad had asked him the same thing.

Andy sighed dramatically and looked around for a place to sit. He opted for Kurt's bed, sprawling onto his stomach.

"It's more than that." His words were muffled against Kurt's pillow before he rolled onto his side. "I like her. She's so..." He pursed his lips as he thought of the word. "Uncomplicated. Being with her, even just hanging out, is fun. Easy. Relaxing. She's happy to just be with me. She's not pushing for commitment. She's okay with what we have right now without trying to force me to make it more."

So basically it was just sex to Stephanie, too. Or she was so desperate for love that she would take whatever she could get. Whichever the case, Kurt felt sick. Was that really how he had treated girls for two plus years?

"So..." He began slowly, unsure how far he should push. How far he had a right to push. Wait, he didn't have any right. But he was going to push any way. He always did. "You're not going to date her. You two are just going to hang out, have sex, and not worry about the day after tomorrow."

"You're one to talk," Andy grunted, heaving himself off the bed and heading toward the door. "See you later."

"Andy, wait."

He stopped but didn't turn around.

Kurt wanted to tell his friend everything. About his one-year commitment. About the changes he was trying so hard to make. About his dad drilling and grilling him, day in, day out. He *needed* to tell him. But he just wasn't ready. He still wasn't sure it was going to work, and he needed some evidence before he told anyone. Especially before he told Shannon's brother.

"You're right. But I'm just trying to understand. Neither of us has ever had anything long-term, and I was just wondering..." He shrugged his hands in the air. "Just wondering how you're feeling about it."

Andy sighed and faced Kurt. "Fair enough." He raked a hand through his messy auburn hair and wandered back over to the bed, plopping down on it. "I don't really know *what* to do. Like I said, I do like her, and I don't want to play with her feelings. But after seeing what my dad has gone through with Carmen, I'm not about to commit to anything serious. Since she's not asking for that, I'm planning to keep going and play things by ear. That way I can back out easily if needed." He finally looked at Kurt. "That's pretty bad, isn't it?"

Kurt didn't reply. It was. But he understood. "Hey, man. It's your life. Just remember, you would *kill* me if I treated Shannon the way you're treating Stephanie."

Andy's face reddened as he stood. "I know. I know. Hey, look, I'm sorry I didn't tell you."

Kurt clapped him on the shoulder. "It's all good, man. I get it. I'd ditch you for Shannon any day."

"Keep dreaming," Andy's taunting voice floated down the hall as he left.

Kurt grinned and popped a cinnamon hard candy into his mouth. He'd never stop.

* * *

Shannon could barely keep her eyes open the following Monday. She'd been up late on the phone with Alan the night before. They hadn't talked in ages since she'd stopped answering his calls. But when her phone rang last night, she'd picked up. He was relieved to hear her voice and devastated by her news. He cried when she told him about Laura.

She'd had to push Laura hard to get her to talk to their step-dad, but once she relented, she spent the next 20 minutes sobbing into the phone. She didn't tell him about the STD test.

It had been a long week. Turned out Laura had an intolerance for erythromycin—the medication prescribed for the Chlamydia. She had vomited violently since Wednesday when she started her first dose. She'd stopped the medication on Saturday and was waiting for a new prescription that hopefully wouldn't kill her.

What killed Shannon was seeing her sister in so much pain. Physical and emotional. Kevin was being such a jerk. He must have the coldest heart south of the Arctic Circle.

Stupid Kevin. She slammed her locker shut after switching books between classes, paying no heed to the gossips beside her until she heard the name "Laura Conrad."

Her head snapped around, her eyes landing on two freshmen. The one who had just said her sister's name looked at her with wide eyes, her mouth forming a silent "O."

"You were saying?"

"Oh. No. Never mind."

"No, please, continue. I'd like to hear what you were saying about my sister."

The girl visibly gulped. "I didn't start the rumor, I swear. It's all over the school that she's pregnant."

"*No.*" The word moaned aloud by itself. This wasn't happening. Please, someone pinch her and tell her this wasn't happening. *God, no.*

"Well, is it true?" the second freshman blurted, probably drawing courage from the terminally ill look on Shannon's face.

She hoped Laura would forgive her for telling the truth this time. She was done lying. "Yes, my sister is pregnant."

As she walked away, low voices spread the nasty news down the hall. She felt like she might lose her breakfast.

"There you are!" Finally she found Laura during the lunch period. She'd spent most of it searching for her. There was no way she could eat.

Laura looked up blankly from a corner of the library, tears snaking down her cheeks in rivulets. Her red eyes declared that she'd been crying a long time.

"I'm so sorry, hun." Shannon folded her sister into a hug. "I guess you couldn't hide it forever."

Laura nodded against her hair. "Kylie asked me on Friday point blank if I was pregnant. I decided to be honest. I begged her not to tell anyone." She sniffed. "Some friend."

The remainder of the day Shannon waded through the most putrid gossip she'd ever endured. She felt devastated by the heartless words her classmates were throwing around about her sister. Nothing worse than Kevin had called her, but who cared about that jerk face anyway?

The rumors continued to escalate, and by her last class period, Shannon had lost whatever food was left in her system. Just before pre-calc, the principal approached her wanting to know where Laura was. Apparently she was skipping classes. He didn't mention the rumor, but his eyes were troubled enough that Shannon had no doubt he'd heard.

She sat at the back of the class. Jesse looked over his shoulder at her questioningly. Dear Jesse. He probably hadn't picked up on the rumors yet. He was far above even the worst gossip.

The second the final bell rang, Shannon shot out of her seat. Laura was already waiting for her at the Explorer, tears cascading from her eyes.

"Take me home, Shannon, please," she sobbed as Shannon reached her.

Shannon was halfway into the driver's seat when she heard someone calling her name.

"Wait, Shannon, wait!" It was Stephanie, jogging across the parking lot with her backpack bouncing up and down on her back, dark hair fanning out behind her head. Shannon slid out and closed the door as Stephanie came to a stop in front of her, panting heavily.

"Oh my gosh, Shannon. I heard what they're saying. Andy — you never said a thing. It's true?"

She nodded. They'd just hung out last week, and it had been so hard to keep up the secrecy. "I didn't feel it was my place. But it's true."

"Wow." Stephanie sighed and shook her head, then reached over with uncharacteristic compassion and gave her a hug. "I'm sorry. I don't know what else to say, but I'm here if you need a friend. Let's get together again soon." Touched by the first kind words all day, Shannon murmured a misty-eyed thank you.

Kevin was in a foul mood when he returned from work. Gabby and Daniel knew something was up, since Laura had been crying all afternoon and Shannon had mostly stuck with her sister. Even an incredibly quiet Andy was at home.

"It's everywhere." Kevin's grim voice sliced through their silent half-eaten dinner. "The whole town knows."

Laura dropped her empty fork with a clatter and bowed her head until her chin hit her chest. Loud sobs soon shook her form, but Kevin only stared across at her with cold eyes.

"I hope you're satisfied, Laura. I haven't been this humiliated in a long time."

Not since your affair with Carmen, huh? Shannon forced the smart reply back down her throat. Oh, she hated him...

* * *

Laura cried herself to sleep that night while Shannon stroked her hair. When her breathing finally evened out, Shannon slipped out of the room and crossed the hall. She had a long list of homework, but how was she supposed to concentrate? She sat at her desk staring for a while, then pushed her chair back. For some reason she always felt closer to God sitting on the floor.

She let out a slow breath, silently begging God for help in short phrases.

Her phone rang, and she grabbed it to find the name *Kurt* lighting up the screen. She paused. He usually just texted. Which he hadn't done in...a while.

"Hello?"

"Hey, Shan." His deep, rumbling voice was the most comforting sound she'd heard in a while. "I—I heard. I just wanted to check on you and Laura."

A warm rush of emotions flooded Shannon. He was a sweet guy.

"Are you okay?"

She was quiet, fighting tears. "No."

"And Laura?"

"What do you think?"

A frustrated sigh puffed into her ear. "I wish I could do more. Or anything at all."

"Thank you for caring."

"Of course. You know the drill. If you need anything..."

Shannon felt a smile forming on her lips for the first time all day. "You always say that."

She could almost hear his grin. "And I always will. 'Night, Shan."

Her smile slipped as she hung up. She was starting to count on him always being there. But one day he'd give up and move on. That would be a painful day.

***

The next day when Shannon exited the food line, she spotted Laura sitting by herself at the farthest table in the lunchroom. All her so-called friends had abandoned her.

"Hey sis." She slid in next to her sister. "You doing okay?"

Laura nodded, but Shannon didn't miss the tears she hastily wiped. "Yeah. I'm surviving."

Shannon reached out her hand and gently rubbed Laura's back, shooting a silent prayer heavenward. Two masculine hands appeared across from her, bracing on the table. She looked up and into Jesse's solemn eyes.

"Can I join you?"

She bobbed her head. When he sat down, he was quiet for a few minutes, like he was deep in thought. Finally he looked at Laura.

"Is there anything I can do for you, Laura?"

Laura pushed a smile through her lips. "Not unless you can roll back time. Thank you, Jesse. You're a really nice guy. I wish more guys were like you." Her voice cracked, and Shannon knew she was thinking of the guy who'd gotten her pregnant.

Jesse turned his dark, chocolate eyes on Shannon, filled with true regret. "I wish you'd told me."

So did she. She wished she'd done a lot of things.

"Now I understand why you've been so burdened. How's your dad with this?"

Shannon looked down at the watery mashed potatoes on her tray. "Not good. He just found out two weeks ago. I lied to him about it. I've known for almost three months."

Jesse sucked air through his teeth. "That long?" He was quiet. "Wouldn't you be mad, too?"

Shannon slowly sank her head back. Why did Jesse always have to be right?

"Yes, but that doesn't make his—his cruelty okay. You have no idea how nasty he's being."

He made a cringing face. "I can imagine. I know him better than you think."

Right. She'd forgotten.

"I'm just saying, who knows how far an apology might go? Maybe nowhere, but it won't hurt you to say it."

She *did* regret her lie. "I know lying was wrong."

"It must have been a hard choice. Tell him that. Say you're sorry. And while you're at it, might not be a bad idea to say something similar to your other Father. You know, the One Who loves you unconditionally."

Right again. Only Jesse could have made her see that.

"Maybe I will." She tilted her head at him. "Thank you."

His dimples dove deep as he gazed at her, his eyes softening into warm puddles. He was remembering kissing her. She just knew it. Especially when he closed his eyes and gave a little shake to his head. Keeping it clean. That was Jesse.

"I've missed you," he said softly as he stood up. "I'll leave you two alone. But I'm here for both of you. Remember that." He looked at Laura, then held contact with Shannon's eyes for a long moment.

"You know he's in love with you," Laura said when he'd gone.

Shannon sighed. "Something like that."

* * *

"You can't skip school just because you don't like the gossip. You should've thought of that before you slept with all the boys in town." Kevin slapped his hand down on the counter, and Shannon flinched. He'd been berating her sister for the past five minutes after finding out she'd stayed home today. Yesterday she'd skipped most of her classes anyway. Shannon had found her hiding in the bathroom twice. So when she didn't come down this morning, Shannon left without her. She was worried Laura might have a nervous breakdown if she had to endure another day of Claywood High slander. It was vicious. Unmerciful.

Like Kevin.

"I don't know what to do with you, Laura." Her sister was sobbing in front of him. "Go." He waved his hand like she was a fly. "Get out of my sight. If you ever skip school again—you won't forget it."

Shannon trembled at the threat. She remembered the force of his palms against her face. They were quite capable of more, she was sure.

He stalked out of the kitchen after Laura disappeared, and Shannon slowly followed. Tomorrow was Friday. Thank God. Hands down the longest week of her life. And she'd had plenty of long weeks with Mom.

She watched as Kevin dropped onto the living room sofa and threw his head back with a groaning sigh. When he didn't move, she timidly approached him. Jesse's words pushed her forward. It was the last thing she felt like doing.

"Kevin?"

His head snapped up and he glared at her. "What, Shannon?" His sharp tone said more than his words. Shannon felt something like sorrow shoot through her. They'd been close not long ago. She'd called him Dad. Would she ever again?

"I just want to say… I'm sorry for lying to you about Laura." Her voice was almost a whisper. "I didn't want to hurt you. But I *couldn't* hurt her."

The anger in his eyes drained like a sink. He gave a rough nod. "I know, Shannon. I know."

Then he stood up and quickly walked away.

* * *

Stephanie came over the next evening, and Shannon was glad for the company. Kevin had been silent since her apology, and Laura kept mostly to her room at home. Andy rarely showed his face these days. Sometimes Shannon just needed a distraction.

They were watching a movie and snacking on salt and vinegar Pringles when Stephanie's phone made a ridiculous sneezing sound that Shannon recognized as her text alert. Diving for the phone where she'd thrown it on the floor, Stephanie scanned the message and popped to her feet.

"Oh my gosh, there's an emergency, and my mom said she needs me ASAP." She cast big apologetic eyes toward Shannon. "Sorry to run out on you like this, but I know you understand." She gave Shannon a quick hug and disappeared faster than Shannon could react.

Bewildered, Shannon hit the power button on the remote and the screen went dark with a snap. She'd had a perfect view of the phone screen when that text came in. It hadn't been Stephanie's mom. It was Andy.

She jumped up and hurried into the kitchen, leaning over the sink to look out the window.

There was Stephanie, just reaching the top of the stairs to Andy's garage apartment, her dark hair flinging about her head as she glanced around. When the apartment door opened, the light pouring out revealed Andy with an eager grin. He planted a kiss on her lips, pulled her into his arms, and the two vanished inside.

Shannon gripped the edge of the sink tightly. They'd only been watching that movie for 15 minutes. Something similar had happened each time Stephanie had come over lately, but Shannon had been too overwhelmed by life to think much of it. It didn't take any wondering to conclude what a boy like Andy was doing in his apartment with Stephanie. How long had this been going on behind her back?

Anger pushed her toward the side door, and she marched across the yard and up the stairs. Not bothering to knock, she barged through Andy's door, and he and Stephanie parted with a gasp. They'd been kissing, Andy sans shirt.

She just stared at them. Andy dropped his head and massaged his neck, his entire face glowing bright red. Stephanie, however, crossed her arms and raised her chin.

"Don't look at me like that, Shannon."

"You used me, Stephanie." Shannon said the words softly, on the verge of tears as her anger merged into hurt. "You didn't want to be my friend—you wanted Andy. You've been lying to me. How could you do that?"

Now Stephanie's eyes slid downcast, her shoulders slumping with them.

Shannon turned to Andy.

"So this is why you don't even care about Laura."

He looked up now, his forehead wrinkled in protest. "No, I care—"

"And you don't care about me. You just care about yourself, don't you?"

The silence was thick.

"Just like our dad. It's gone really well for him. You have a bright future ahead." She turned to go.

Groaning, Andy swore and grabbed her arm. "Shannon, wait."

She looked him in the eye. "No, I'm done here. You let her use me, and you lied to me. I don't need that."

This time he didn't call after her as she left. The tears were falling by the time she reached the last step. Kevin didn't care. Andy didn't care. Stephanie didn't care. Did anybody care about her?

She looked up at the black sky just in time to see a shooting star streak across the dark expanse between two trees. It disappeared behind the foliage in the blink of an eye, but Shannon felt the dazzle in her heart. Her heavenly Father cared. He'd sent that star just to tell her so. She wasn't alone.

And Laura needed to know that she wasn't either. Shannon picked up the pace, trotting upstairs to her sister's room.

"Hey, you okay?"

Laura's face was pale as paste. Shannon touched the back of her fingers to her forehead. Hot. Tears trailed down Laura's face, and she reached her arms around her midsection, moaning in pain.

"I keep getting these awful pains," she gasped through clenched teeth. "The past couple hours it's been getting worse."

Shannon put her hand over her eyes, wanting to shut out reality. "Have the pains been coming more often?"

"Yeah." Her voice was weak.

Shannon felt lightheaded.

"And the pain has been getting sharper?"

Suddenly Laura started sobbing. "Yes… And I'm bleeding!"

The room was spinning so fast, Shannon wasn't sure if she was standing or falling. "How heavy?"

"Really heavy!"

Shannon swallowed back her panic and took off across the room at a run.

"Where are you going?"

"To get Kevin, you moron."

"*Why?*" Laura sounded incredulous at the idea.

"Because you're in labor!"

Chapter Thirty-One

Laura stared blankly at the white hospital wall, her hands lying lifeless at her sides.

Lifeless, like her baby. Her baby boy.

She should be relieved.

But she wasn't.

"It's my fault, Shannon," she whispered dully when Shannon made it to the hospital in the late morning. "It's all my fault." Her cheeks were dry. Her tears had bled out along with her baby, and there was nothing left inside.

Shannon smoothed the hair away from her face in that endearing motherly way she didn't realize she had.

"Don't say that."

"It's true. It's because of the STD I have. I did research."

Shannon gently shushed her. "You need to rest, Laura. Just close your eyes and rest."

Laura obeyed, but she knew she would not sleep.

* * *

Shannon found Kevin in the hospital waiting room flipping through a sports magazine. His eyes weren't even focused.

"Kevin?" He looked up at her, then nodded his head to the seat beside him. They sat in silence a minute, and then Shannon repeated what Laura had just told her. "Is it true?"

A deep sigh vibrated his body. "Possibly. Chlamydia in pregnant women can lead to premature labor. In Laura's case, she was too early in her pregnancy to have a fighting chance of the baby making it."

"But hasn't she been taking meds to get rid of the Chlamydia?"

"When she reacted to the first prescription, we had to wait for a second one. Besides, I have no doubt the Chlamydia had already done its work. It's for the best, you know."

"How can you say that?" Shannon exclaimed. "Laura's devastated!"

Kevin glared at her. "I wasn't going to let her keep the baby. She'd have been more devastated then."

Shannon shook her head. "You really have no heart, do you?"

"I do," he said tightly. "But I also have a brain. Even you must know that whether she kept the baby or not, neither was going to be easy. It's just better this way."

Maybe so. But he didn't have to be cruel about it.

* * *

It was Wednesday evening before Kurt made himself get into his truck and drive over to the Conrads' house. He'd known about Laura's miscarriage since Saturday morning when Andy called him to let him know he couldn't make it to work. He had stayed with Gabby and Daniel while Shannon drove to the Abingdon hospital. Kurt had sent her a text saying something totally lame like, "Sorry about what happened to Laura." She hadn't texted back, and he still didn't know what to say. He only knew if he really cared, he had to show his face.

The downstairs of the house was mostly dark when he got there, so he hesitantly went up the stairs, following the sound of childish voices. He found Shannon in the bathroom shared by Daniel and Gabby. She sat on the closed toilet seat, chin resting dejectedly in her hands as she watched Daniel splash around in the tub.

"Hi Kurt!" he exclaimed, and Shannon swiveled her head around. She offered a half-smile with absolutely no heart, not saying anything. She wore the scarf he'd given her, and she looked amazing, but he didn't mention it.

"Hey, buddy! What do have there?" Kurt tore his eyes away from Shannon's beautiful face and eyed the plastic boats that bobbed around in the soapy water with the little boy.

"This is my yacht club!" Pride shined in Daniel's eyes. "Shannon told me that fancy boats are called yachts and that they have clubs. I've never been in a club, so I wanted to have my own yacht club."

"I see," Kurt said with a chuckle. "Do you have a favorite yacht?" He squatted down beside the tub, his shoulder brushing against Shannon's knees. He felt her hand on the back of his shoulder.

"Do you mind watching him for a few minutes?"

"Not at all." He smiled over his shoulder. "Where's Kevin?"

She shrugged. "Not home yet." Kurt looked at his watch. It was after 8:00. What was keeping Kevin? Surely he was needed here now more than ever.

When she returned, Daniel's tub time ended, with much protest from the self-proclaimed yacht club president, but finally he was dried and jammy-clad.

"Let me put him to bed and I'll be out," she said softly, and Kurt settled into an easy chair in the sitting room at the top of the stairs. He was glad she left the door open to Daniel's room so he could relax to the sound of her reading *Goodnight Moon*. He marveled at her voice inflexion, rising and falling at just the right times in the story. How did she do it? How did she carry on and on? How did she give of herself, when he knew she had nothing left to give? When her heart was broken?

"Kurt?" Her sweet voice brought him back from his world of questions, and he opened his eyes. "Oops, did I wake you?"

"No. Not quite. Your bedtime story *almost* worked."

The first real smile of the evening crossed her face, quickly. He noted the fine lines of exhaustion pulled at her eyes.

"Andy's not around?"

Now she gave him a tart look. "If that's who you're looking for, he's right above the garage, but he might be a little busy."

Only the slight catch in her voice betrayed her.

"I'm sorry, Shan. I wanted to tell you, but..." He let out a noisy breath. "When did you find out?"

"Friday night. Right before I discovered Laura in premature labor. It was a great night."

He swallowed, wracking his brain for words. Stupid Andy. He had plenty of words for his friend right now. Ditching his siblings for Stephanie, when they all needed him more than her.

"Are you drawing? Or—" He stopped to think. What else made her tick? "Or playing piano?"

She shook her head, her gorgeous hair rustling against her cheek. The cheek he dearly wished to stroke. *No, focus Kurt.*

"I'm just worried about you," he said softly.

She tilted her head with a small smile. "Thank you. I'm okay. The only thing holding me together is God."

He didn't hold any stock in that, but whatever worked for Shannon.

"But thanks for the reminder about drawing. I need to do that." She moved away from him, across the room. "Laura could use some company." He couldn't ignore the pleading in her eyes as she looked back at him, and he rose to follow her into her sister's room. The sorrow in the room was almost palpable. After five minutes Kurt had the sensation of being choked. Laura lay on her bed, curled into the fetal position, staring vacantly. Shannon was talking to her sister, but really she was just babbling to fill the silence. Finally she stopped and looked at Kurt in desperation. He had to at least try.

"Laura?"

No response.

He tried again. "Laura?"

Her eyes flickered in his direction, and he took this as recognition.

"Is there anything you need, Laura?"

Her lips formed a word, but no sound came.

"Can you repeat that, Laura?" He put his ear close to her face and finally heard the miniscule, anguished voice.

"Matt."

Slowly he straightened, an awful squeezing sensation gripping his heart. Shannon looked at him questioningly, and he knew she hadn't heard. He just shook his head. He had to get out of here before he started banging his head against the wall. This must be what mental institutions felt like. Or, or funeral homes. Too much sadness for one person to absorb. He couldn't handle it.

He bolted from the bed and walked out of the bedroom without a word. He was halfway down the stairs before he heard Shannon calling him.

"Kurt?"

He looked back and found her right behind him.

"What's wrong? Are you going?"

So much confusion filled her face. Confusion, pain, and exhaustion. It wasn't fair. Man, why was this world so messed up? Why did people like Shannon and Laura have to suffer for the, the...the evil things done by people like Matt and Andy and Kevin and...and him?

"Sorry, I gotta run." He threw the words over his shoulder as he skipped the bottom step and rushed from the house. He revved his truck engine more than necessary and threw a little gravel turning around, but he didn't care. He drove into town aimlessly until he passed a house lit up like a lighthouse, the street crowded with cars, and remembered Riley's party. He'd been invited, but parties were not a part of the turn-your-life-around regimen prescribed by Dad.

He touched the brake pedal. Oh, he wanted to go in there. Drink enough alcohol to clear his mind of Laura and miscarriages and Shannon's sad ocean eyes.

A girl walked out the door of Riley's house just then and stared right at him. Raised her hand and waved him over. Carolyn. No. *No no no.* He wasn't going that route again. She headed his way, and he had the urge to throw the truck into park, but instead he hit the gas for all he was worth, not caring how loud his tires squealed. He didn't slow down until the end of the street, and that was a rolling stop. By then he knew where he was going. He was about to pay a visit to Matthew Burke.

* * *

The next evening Shannon was unloading the dishwasher while fuming to herself about Kevin's absence for the third evening in a row when the doorbell rang.

The *front* doorbell.

"Who in the world?" She scurried into the living room, ceramic plate still in hand. She flipped on the porch light and unlocked the door, curious who might be standing outside at nine o'clock on a Thursday evening.

She examined the tall young man standing before her. "Can I help you?"

"Uh, uh, yeah...I'm here to see, uh, Laura," he mumbled, avoiding her eyes.

Shannon stared at him as her mind flashed months back to an image of Laura standing in the arms of a passionate man.

"Can I tell her who's here?"

The guy took a deep breath, so big that his coat rose and fell with his shoulders. "Matt."

Unconsciously her mouth fell open. The puzzle pieces drifted together, but it took her mind's eye a minute to see the complete picture. The guy Laura had been making out with at that awful drinking party in the fall...the guy who looked at least five years older than her...the guy who had gotten her pregnant...the guy who refused to take responsibility...the guy who was standing outside her door in the freezing cold...All one guy.

She ushered him in, directed him to the sofa, and then somehow got up the stairs without tripping or dropping the plate still in her grip.

"Laura?" Her sister was sound asleep. Gently she shook her. "Laura."

"Hmmm?" Laura sleepily replied, opening her eyes. "What's a'matter?"

Shannon bit her lip. "Well, I'm not sure, but...Matt is here."

Laura's eyes widened so far they seemed to swallow her face. "Oh." She said nothing else for a few seconds, then cried, "I look awful!" and fled to the bathroom.

Five minutes later Shannon sent Matt up to Laura's room, nervously pacing the living room floor until she heard footsteps creaking above her. Matt retreated down the stairs, nodded toward her, and slipped out the door. Shannon rushed up the stairs and into Laura's room.

"That was...quick." As she sank down onto Laura's bed, she searched her sister's face. Tears were running down her cheeks, but somehow she looked better than she had in weeks. She smiled through her tears.

"He apologized for everything. He said when I came to him, he knew the baby was his, and he said he is sorry for making me go through everything alone. He said sorry that I lost our baby, and for hurting me and using me. He said he should never have slept with me in the first place, and that he should have been more careful, too. I told him about the Chlamydia, and he is going to get tested. He took all the blame, Shannon." She shook her head slightly, wonder filling her face. "I never thought I'd hear him say that!"

Shannon reached out and hugged her sister. "Then why are you crying?"

"Because." Laura pulled back from the embrace "I had been hoping all this time that he would come back to me, and he made it clear he will not." She shrugged with one shoulder. "I always knew loving him was unrealistic. But I kept hoping. I guess now I can stop."

"Oh, sweetheart." Shannon hugged her again. "You are very brave."

Chapter Thirty-Two

"Are you sure, Laura?" Shannon eyed her sister doubtfully the next morning when Laura appeared at breakfast, a resolute expression on her face. "You could just wait for Monday."

"I've missed enough days. I'm going to school." She glanced down at her jeans, hugging her now-flat tummy. "I...I hope the kids, you know, leave me alone..."

Shannon sighed. Laura better not count on that. But she was stronger than she realized. Look at her, five days after a miscarriage, still pale and puffy-faced from too little food and too many tears, and of her own volition she was choosing to return to school. Kevin didn't deserve such a daughter. Pushing away that troubling thought, Shannon smiled at her sister and reached to squeeze her hand.

"I'm proud of you. Now you better get some food in you."

The day dragged by. Jesse offered genuine words of encouragement, but Shannon was growing immune to them. She wasn't sure how to carry on without a dad at all. It was as if he'd just given up on them. She hadn't seen him since Sunday. She heard him come in late every night, and he was gone by the time she put breakfast on the table every morning. No notes, no text messages. Nothing to check on her or Laura. Or even Gabby and Daniel. They were all suffering.

"My day went okay."

"Huh?" Shannon looked at her sister as they walked side-by-side to the house, Gabby one step ahead, Daniel already having run into the house. "Oh, Laura, I'm sorry. I'm so distracted I didn't even ask you how things went." She'd been too busy thinking in circles about their dad.

"I understand. But anyway, it went okay. I mean, people made comments. About me having an abortion." She rolled her eyes, but the hurt was evident. "I knew they would. But most just ignored me. Which is better than comments."

"I'm glad, Laura." Shannon meant it. She was shocked at the tremendous difference ten minutes with Matt made for her sister, and she was very grateful for whatever transformation had spurred the man to apology and responsibility. "You're looking much better." She smiled encouragingly at her sister, and Laura returned the smile.

"Thanks. I better get busy on homework. I'm only behind by like...two weeks." She shook her head and scooted ahead of Shannon inside the door. Shannon watched her go, pride gripping her heart. Laura was pretty amazing.

Finally Friday night Kevin showed up as Shannon was setting the table.

"What's for dinner?"

"Well hello to you too, sunshine. To what do we owe this honor?"

His eyebrows flickered upward. "You better watch it. I am in no mood to put up with your nonsense."

Laura drew short in the entryway when she saw him, and Kevin turned. He sized her up silently, then turned back to Shannon.

"I trust you girls are staying out of trouble. Learning from your mistakes." That was aimed at Laura, obviously.

"Of course. I'm not sure the same can be said about you, though."

His face tightened. "I thought we had moved beyond this type of disrespect, Shannon."

"Me too. I thought we had moved on to better parenting, but I guess not."

That earned her a slap across the face that sent her spinning into a chair, knocking it over.

"Who would want to be at home around you?" Kevin roared. "Get out of here. Go to your room! I don't want to see your face again tonight. You too!" He stabbed his finger toward Laura. They exchanged a look, and then Shannon lowered her head and following her sister from the room. They passed a wide-eyed Gabby and Daniel on their way but didn't say anything. She was trembling with rage by the time she reached her room. She hadn't eaten, but he'd made her lose her appetite anyway.

She tried to stay out of his way all weekend, but any time their paths crossed, it didn't go well. What had happened to the dad who'd claimed to love her? Had it been that fleeting? She couldn't wait for Monday to go back to school and especially for him to go back to work. If this was the new normal, she wasn't going to last.

God, help.

* * *

Kurt checked his phone. 9:18. It seemed unconscionable to go to bed this early only half way through spring break. Shouldn't he be partying somewhere tropical? Isn't that what college kids did during spring break?

He sighed. Not this college kid.

He was bored. He'd spent all day working on the farm, overseeing the things his dad usually did. Mom and Dad were gone on a three-day business trip, and his dad had left Kurt in charge. He enjoyed the responsibility, but it certainly did make him exhausted. He yawned loudly.

Maybe he *should* go to bed.

The doorbell rang.

That was odd. Few people ventured all the way up the Blake's long, sometimes treacherous driveway. And *never* at this time of night.

Again the doorbell ding-donged, over and over. Growling in irritation, Kurt heaved himself off his bed and trotted across the living room and down the stairs. Barely had he gotten the deadbolt unlocked when the door flung open into him, revealing an unexpected sight.

"Hi, Sugar," Carolyn purred, flouncing into the doorway and pushing herself against him. She kicked the door shut behind her with a slam. "Thought you might be lonely tonight. Or bored. Home all alone. Poor baby." She was massaging his chest with her magical hands.

Kurt gritted his teeth. He *was* lonely. He *was* bored. He was missing his old life, too.

She smelled so good. Why did she have to wear that perfume?

She led him like a puppy to his room. She'd been there before.

She began her usual routine, while Kurt responded mechanically, as if he were watching himself from above, knowing he should stop what was happening below, but frozen, unable to do anything.

Maybe he didn't *want* to stop it. Yes, that was it. He *wanted* this to happen.

But not now. Not here. Not with her.

NO!

This had to stop. Now. But how? He wasn't strong enough. He wanted her.

Help! The cry shot through him, then from somewhere came his voice.

"Hey, Carolyn?" The words sounded sluggish. "Give me a sec, okay?"

"Sure, baby, do whatever you need to be ready to enjoy me."

Her words gave him instant nausea, and he fled the room as casually as he could. Hurtling down the stairs, he felt shivers run across his torso. Where had his shirt gone? He dove into the coat closet, stripped a flannel jacket off the hanger, and wrestled into it.

Run. Run. Run.

The only words ringing in his head.

So he ran. Stuffed his feet into some random shoes by the door, grabbed a lumpy coat his dad must've had for 30 years, and ran.

Four years in high school track had not been wasted.

He ran hard until he reached the orchard store, where he had left the Suburban a few hours earlier. The keys were still in his jeans' pocket, and his pants were still, thankfully, on his body. With a jerk, he opened the door and revved the giant to life, sending gravel shooting through the air as he escaped.

A few minutes later he found himself at the Conrads' house. He'd barely seen Andy this week, although he too was putting in extra work hours at the farm. Andy had been mostly working in the new greenhouses, while Kurt had been from one side of the farm and back again every hour. Maybe Andy was home now. Kurt needed someone to talk to. Man, he missed his dad already.

There was no answer to Kurt's knocks at Andy's apartment door. Maybe Andy was in the house. He'd check. He certainly couldn't go home anytime soon.

The side door was unlocked, so Kurt let himself in. It was after 10:00 by now. Maybe everyone was in bed.

No, someone was up. He followed soft voices and laughter to the family room, where to his surprise, Shannon and Laura were playing tennis on the Wii, both in pajamas and fuzzy slippers. They were adorable.

So caught up were they in their game, Kurt was able to lean against the entryway and watch them unnoticed. Shannon was losing. Badly. But Kurt didn't miss the shine on her face as she watched her sister swing the remote high over her head. Kurt's roiling emotions slowly settled and calmed, and his body relaxed as he watched the sisters competing. Before long, the game ended with a sound victory for Laura.

Laura started with a small gasp when she turned around.

"Good grief, Kurt, you scared me! How long have you been there?"

Shannon whirled around with wide eyes, her face instantly flushing. She looked down at her pajamas and self-consciously tugged up the neckline of her tank-top. Kurt looked away, embarrassed. He'd never felt embarrassed by seeing any part of the female body before. But Shannon was pure. And he didn't want to do anything to make her feel differently.

He glanced up to see her settling a hoodie over her head.

"You're pretty good with the tennis," he said, nodding at Laura.

She laughed and shrugged. "It's just the Wii. In real life, I'm even better." She flashed a smile. Everything about her seemed fresh. Healthy. She was drastically improved since last week. "Well, I'm headed to bed. Nice to see you, Kurt. Night night, Shan." She blew her sister a kiss and disappeared, leaving Kurt standing an awkwardly far distance from Shannon, who stood like a statue.

He took a few steps closer and stopped. He'd left so abruptly last time, no wonder she was wary of him. "I thought you'd all be in bed. I was just checking if Andy was in here. Any idea where he is?"

She shook her head. "No. I haven't seen him today." Then he was still spending all his spare time with Stephanie. Poor Shannon. She looked more tired than normal, which was difficult to imagine.

"Oh. Just needed some fun time with Laura?"

"No, I was going to work on homework, but she asked me to play with her, and I couldn't turn her down. We haven't done something like this in…a long time." Vulnerability spilled across her face, and she dropped onto the sofa. "You can sit if you want."

He bit back his smile at her backhand offer and came around to sit beside her.

"Laura seems a lot better," he mused aloud.

Shannon nodded excitedly. "She is! Kurt, it's amazing! She is doing…amazing!" she repeated, her face shining again. Kurt loved how much she… how much she *loved*.

"What happened? Last week I was pretty worried when I saw her."

"Me too. But you'll never believe it! The next day, Matt came!"

"He did?" Shock jolted through Kurt. Matt had actually come? "Wow," he breathed out the words, trying to remember what he'd said that may have spurred Matt into action. Who cared? Only thing that mattered was that it had worked, and now Laura was coming back to life. "I didn't think he actually would."

"What do you mean?"

"Huh?" He'd said that out loud. Woops. "Oh, nothing."

"Wait." Shannon narrowed her eyes at him. "Did you talk to Matt?"

Honesty was always his best course with Shannon. "Yes. Yes, I did."

With no warning, her eyes welled up with tears, and she moved as if she would hug him, then pulled back. "Thank you so much." The fervency of her whispered words made her voice shake. "You worked a miracle."

His breath caught on her words, but he shrugged. "I just wanted to help, that's all."

Her eyes shined at him like the moon outside that had guided his steps here. "You have no idea how much you helped."

He wanted to capture her words and keep them safe somewhere.

"Seriously, I can't thank you enough. I don't know—can I thank you with cookies? There's a fresh batch in the kitchen."

He grinned. "You think I'd ever turn that down?"

She laughed. A glorious sound he'd not heard from her in a long time. "I'd stay and chat, but I desperately need to get some homework done, and it's late."

Was it safe to return home yet? Carolyn didn't give up easily. He'd have to take a moonlit drive.

"No problem. I'll lock the door on my way out." He stood and took a step toward the kitchen. "Shannon, if you ever need anything—anything—please tell me. I'll do everything in my power to help you."

The planes in her face softened into something like wistfulness, but she merely nodded and left the room without a word.

***

The next afternoon Shannon was building a Play-Doh castle at the breakfast nook with Gabby and Daniel when Andy sauntered into the kitchen.

"Hey guys, what's up?"

His casual greeting exploded the room into chaos as Gabby and Daniel both bolted from their seats and charged for Andy. Daniel climbed right up him, excited cries filling the air. Gabby, however, stopped short in front of her big brother.

"Where have you been?" she demanded, little hands on little hips, glaring up at him. If he looked any more sheepish, wool would have sprouted on his face.

"Been busy."

Shannon studied him. His face was a little too rosy. "Why are you here?" They hadn't said more than casual greetings since she'd confronted him and Stephanie.

"Kurt threatened to fire me if I didn't come home and relieve you." He shot her a chagrin-filled look. "I'm sorry for not being around. I'm also sorry for—" His eyes shifted to the young ears. "Can we talk later?"

"Sure."

"Oh no!" In all the ruckus, someone had knocked over their creation and it had broken into colorful pieces. Tears filled Daniel's eyes. "My *castle!*" he wailed, dropping his head into his hands. Shannon had the urge to snap, "it's just Play-Doh!" But she bit her tongue in spite of her exhaustion and irritation, reminding herself that Daniel was feeling confused and neglected by his parents and was the victim of an unfair life, much as she was.

"It's okay, sweetie." She bent and kissed his curly head. "We can rebuild it." She started to pick up the flexible material when she felt a hand on her back.

"I got this." Andy pushed her toward the door. "Go. Kurt's orders." He bent his head for her ears only. "He *really* cares about you."

She knew she should head straight to her stack of homework waiting on her desk, but first she stopped to play the piano, just let melodies flow from her soul and through her fingertips. Then she nestled down in a corner of the sitting room upstairs and sketched a few scenes from life. And a profile of Kurt. What on earth had he been doing in that frumpy old coat last night? He still looked good, though.

When she went back downstairs to get something going for dinner, she found Andy at the stove in an apron, dangling a spaghetti noodle above his mouth. He slurped it in noisily to the giggles of the onlooking Daniel. Gabby was setting the table.

"Dinner's ready!" Andy grinned at Shannon, noodle handing from his mouth. "Where's the strainy thing?" he sloshed, sucking the remaining noodle through his lips.

"You mean a colander?" Shannon retrieved the strainer from a cabinet. "You're gross, by the way. I don't know what Stephanie sees in you." The sarcastic tone turned her honest jab into a joke, and Andy started laughing, only to choke on the noodle.

After dinner he pulled Shannon into the family room and sat down next to her, examining the lines in his hand. "I'm sorry I wasn't honest with you about Stephanie. I didn't like hiding it. I knew you'd be hurt. But she didn't want you to know. I'm sorry I went along with it."

Shannon sighed. "Forget about it, Andy. We're cool."

"Good." He nodded. "Dad's mad at me about it. He's making me pay rent, you know."

Her mouth dropped open. "For real?" Finally Kevin did something she approved of.

But Andy scowled. "Such a double standard."

Shannon grew still. "What do you mean?"

"I probably shouldn't tell you this, but I'm sure you've noticed how scarce he's become."

Duh. Why else did she look like a 100-year-old insomniac granny?

"Anyway, I'm pretty sure he's hooking up with a lady friend after work."

Shannon's spaghetti immediately threatened an unwelcome return. "Are you serious?"

"I don't know for sure, but I know Dad, so yeah..."

"He is despicable."

Andy made a back and forth gesture with his hands. "He's not as bad as you think. He's just hurt and disappointed." He ran a hand through his messy auburn waves. "At life, at people, at everything. Carmen hurt him terribly, and he is trying to force himself to get over it and move on. He is disappointed at me, and—" he looked up apologetically—"at Laura. He doesn't know how to help us make better decisions, because he always made the worst ones. He's disappointed at..." Andy stopped and shook his head.

"At himself," Shannon said softly.

"Yeah." They sat quietly for a minute, each wrapped in their thoughts, when Andy spoke again.

"I'm really sorry, Shannon." He opened his arms, and Shannon dove for him. Man, she needed that hug.

"I forgive you," she mumbled against his chest. "I love you, Andy."

* * *

Kurt's big project for Friday was the renovation on Cabin #2. Late winter and early spring was the slowest time for his dad's vacation cabins, and the whole farm in general, so he'd been working on some updates. Andy was supposed to be meeting him there to see how much they could accomplish on their last day of spring break.

In fact, he had beaten him. Kurt parked beside Andy's car and found Andy sitting on the porch steps of the cabin, resting his chin in his hand complacently.

"Hey, man," Kurt greeted and handed his friend a hammer. "Let's finish that trim." They worked without speaking for about twenty minutes.

"So I heard a really interesting story last night." Andy shattered the silence. "At Mike's party. From which you were noticeably absent."

Kurt ignored the bate and continued working.

"What gives, man?"

He shrugged and brought the hammer down squarely on the nail. "Nothing. I just don't do parties anymore."

"Or Carolyn?"

Kurt jerked his head to look at his friend. "Okay, what story did you hear?"

"You turned her down twice? She's your kryptonite!"

Not anymore she wasn't. He still didn't respond.

"First flooring it across town loud enough that a whole room of partiers heard you. And then literally running away from your own house shirtless and not coming back?" Andy lowered his hammer. "She is livid. *Livid*. She was drunk last night and cussing you up and down to a friend. I simply overheard. Is it true?"

Kurt pursed his lips. "More or less. Except the shirtless part. I ran from my room shirtless, but I got one on before I left the house."

Andy waved his hand. "Technicalities." He set his hammer down. "Come on, take a break."

Obediently, Kurt followed Andy out the cabin's front door and sat down on the stoop. The view up here was magnificent since Dad had cleared some more trees. Mountains on every side for miles. Kurt loved his homeland.

Should he tell Andy? All signals said it was time.

"So... I don't do that anymore."

"Do what?"

"Girls. Sex. You know. Our routine."

Disbelief spread across Andy's face. "I knew you hadn't been as active lately, but—not at all?"

Kurt shook his head, feeling a sliver of pride.

"For how long?"

"I don't even know. " He spread his hands out in between his legs, examining them. "I messed up once, a while back, but other than that, I haven't been with a girl in three or four months. I don't remember when my year started."

"Your year?" He found Andy squinting at him. "What year?"

It was so freeing to finally share all the details of his dad's rules and his struggles. When he finished, Andy didn't say anything at first, simply sat studying the distant peaks with a furrowed brow.

"How come you didn't tell me sooner?"

Kurt considered this. "I thought I would fail. I wasn't sure you would encourage me. And I didn't want you to feel...pressured. We've played the same game together for a few years."

"I gotcha. 'Cause I'm still doing it." Andy turned to face him. "You have my respect, man. What you're doing takes a lot of self-control. I don't know how you're doing it."

"Hardest thing I've ever done."

* * *

"You know about Kurt's one-year abstinence challenge, right?"

"What?" Shannon squinted to stretch the skin across her forehead. She must have heard wrong. It was likely, after studying the past four hours for her huge Spanish test looming ahead. What a way to spend a Saturday.

"Obviously not. Pretend I never said anything." Andy scuttled out of the family room, and Shannon stared at the empty space he'd been filling, her mind grappling to process his words. Abstinence challenge? Kurt?

She breathed fast, suddenly desperate to know what Andy was talking about. Before she could convince herself otherwise, she jammed on her running shoes and took the driveway at a less than leisure jog. She hardly enjoyed the run while question after question propelled her forward. She reached the Blakes' front door panting like a dog and paused to steady her ragged breath. Hesitantly she rang the doorbell, disappointment settling deeper with each second. No answer. Turning away, she began a slow retreat, not ready to run back home.

The *whirr* of an electric tool screeched through the air, and she followed the sound to the shop at the side of the house. The noise ceased before she softly pushed the door open. Jefferson unleashed a round of joyful barks at Shannon's sight and bounded over to greet her. Mr. Blake lifted his head from where he was bent over a workbench, surprise registering on his face.

"Shannon! Nice to see you." He dusted sawdust off his trousers and stepped over to where she had squatted down to pet Jefferson.

She smiled and rose, feeling embarrassed. She suspected he knew a lot about her and Kurt. "Hi, thanks. Is Kurt here?"

"He's actually up at our rental cabins. Do you know where they are?"

"Maybe. He showed me once."

"Here." Mr. Blake motioned her outside and followed. "See that road there? Follow it until it branches, and keep to the right. Kurt should be in the second cabin." He glanced around. "Did you walk? I can drive you up to the cabins."

"Oh, no, you don't have to do that." Man, Kurt's parents were so nice. Shannon pointed at her shoes. "I'm getting my exercise. Thanks anyway, Mr. Blake."

"Anytime, Shannon. And please, call me Jason."

Shannon started out at a jog, but as the road steeply inclined, her pace slowed to a brisk walk, then ground to a trudge. Maybe she should have taken up Mr. Blake—Jason—on his offer.

She rounded a bend and saw Kurt in the distance beyond the first cabin, rummaging in the back of the Suburban. He didn't notice her approaching as he muttered to himself, obviously searching for something. She was almost to him when her foot snapped a twig, and he whirled around.

"Hey." A frown settled between his eyebrows as he shoved his hands into his jeans' pockets and lifted his shoulders in question. "What are you doing here?"

What *was* she doing here? It wasn't her business to ask the question burning in her brain. "You know what, never mind. I'll just—go." She spun around, her face on fire, but Kurt grabbed her arm before she could take another step.

"Please." He spoke behind her, his deep voice low. "You came for a reason. Tell me what's on your mind."

She turned back and found his face serious, but his dark blueberry eyes glimmered with hope. She took a deep breath and looked him in those amazing eyes. *Here goes.* "What's your one-year abstinence challenge?"

He sucked air in between his lips, held it, then puffed it out. "Did Andy tell you?"

"He assumed I knew. But I don't." She hesitated. "May I?"

Kurt took another noisy breath, then examined his dusty work boots. "Okay. Basically, my dad challenged me to one year without sex, or anything remotely to do with sex. He's keeping me accountable. Been three or four months since we started." He met her eyes. "There. I told you."

Shannon was silent for some time, too many thoughts careening crazily through her mind to respond. "Why didn't you tell me?" she finally asked. She couldn't believe he was doing this. Not Kurt.

He shrugged and looked away. "I was afraid I would fail."

"Did you?"

When he looked at her, she saw the truth in his bobbing Adam's apple. His eyes darted away to the trees. "Once." He cleared his throat. "I've almost messed up a few other times. Carolyn is determined to break me down."

Carolyn. Shannon *really* didn't like that girl.

"You want to sit?" Kurt pointed at the wooden steps leading up to the cabin door a few yards beyond them. She followed him and sat down, while he remained standing before her.

"What made you start this...challenge, as you call it?"

"You." The answer came too fast, like a reflex, and he smiled apologetically. "I mean, my dad. But it was directly related to you. I accepted my dad's challenge at first because I wanted to change *for* you. By the time he convinced me that might not work, I still wanted to change for myself. For the first time, I respect myself. And that's a good feeling. I have a lot of regrets. Not much I can do about that. I understand if it's too much for you to ever get past. But remember my letter? I told you I would change. I don't know if I even meant it then. But I do now."

Warm, weepy feelings were bubbling in Shannon like a soda fountain, but she tempered them down with a strong swallow.

"Has it been hard?"

Kurt flickered tortured eyes in her direction. "You have no idea."

And she didn't.

He sat down beside her, and they watched as the sun sank behind the mountains, a glorious sunset simmering beyond the trees.

"I need to get home."

"Can I take you?" he asked, his hair dancing golden in the light. "It'll be dark before you're home if you walk."

They rode in comfortable silence. Shannon didn't trust herself to speak until she processed things more, or she was going to blurt out something that was going to give Kurt too much hope. When they rolled to a stop beside the house, she opened the door, then turned to thank him, but he beat her to it.

"Thanks for coming over. I've wanted to tell you for a while. I'm glad you know now."

She took a deep breath and said the words silently first to make sure they were kosher. Yep.

"Well thank you for telling me. I'm really proud of you."

He merely smiled. "Good night, Shannon."

The side door opened before she even reached it, and Kevin stepped out, an angry scowl on his face.

"Where have you been? I've been calling your phone for an hour!"

She'd left the house in such a rush, she hadn't brought it with her, but she didn't owe Kevin any explanation. He was the one who'd been gone practically all week and hadn't cared then where any of his children were.

She tried to brush past him, but he grabbed her by the arm and yanked her into the kitchen.

"Ouch!" The surprised exclamation slipped out. "Let go of me!" She fought against him, but he only squeezed harder.

"Stop it!" Kevin barked, giving her a hefty shake. "I asked you a question."

Shannon froze at the tone of his voice, her heart racing at a terrifying gallop. Her hand was already going numb from the pressure on her arm, and he wasn't letting up.

"I was with Kurt."

"What were you doing with him? You listen to me. If you get pregnant, I will throw you out of this house!"

How could he say that? Why was he being so cruel when he knew she'd never do such a thing?

"Do you hear me?" He was yelling and shaking her, and tears stung her eyes as she stared at the monster before her.

"Yes, I hear you." She shook her head at him, ignoring the splash that landed on her cheek. "What is wrong with you?"

Kevin's hand fell away, and he took a step back. Shannon took the chance to escape and literally ran away from him.

He would never, never change…

The next morning, after she dropped Gabby and Daniel at their Sunday school classes, Jesse studied her face carefully.

"What's wrong?"

She shrugged, but tears sprang to the corners of her eyes anyway. "My dad." She closed her eyes to keep from crying in front of other parishioners milling about the hallway.

"Let's take a walk." Jesse placed his hand on the small of her back, guiding her out the door. They walked through the parking lot and onto the sidewalk, where he crossed his arms and tucked his hands under his arms. "Tell me what happened."

And she did, choking out Kevin's treatment last night and all the other times he'd berated her lately.

"Why doesn't he care about us? For a while I believed he did, but now I see that it was fake."

Jesse remained silent, looking down at her with solemn eyes. She knew what he would say. And she wasn't ready to go there.

"You've told me that I need to forgive him, but how can I when he keeps hurting me over and *over?*" Her voice rose in anguish as tears slipped down her face.

"God does." Jesse said the words as softly as the breeze. "Each one of us, you included, hurts God on a regular basis, and He forgives us every time."

"I'm not God, Jesse! I'm human—I have my limits."

They stopped walking and faced each other under a bare oak tree. Tiny buds were forming on the branches. Shannon shifted her weight from one foot to the other. These heels were not for comfort.

"What if Kevin never changes, Shannon?" Jesse asked her the question that had kept her awake half the night. What if he never changed?

"What if he never becomes the dad you want—the dad you need and deserve? Are you going to let that affect you the rest of your life? Are you going to stay hurt and angry forever?"

She shrugged and muttered, "maybe," avoiding his eyes.

His hand came down on her shoulder gently, holding her in place. "Shannon, if you want to be happy and free inside, you are going to have to forgive your dad, just the way he is."

He spoke of the impossible. "You have no idea what you're asking."

"I know a little bit. I had to choose to forgive my dad for ruining my life. Believe me, it wasn't easy or natural, and I couldn't do it on my own. God had to help me a lot. But how can I expect God to forgive *me* when I fall short, if I won't forgive fellow humans for their mistakes? Luke says to forgive, and you will be forgiven. That's the order it goes. Forgiveness isn't something you give because someone deserves it. No one deserves forgiveness, even when they're sorry. Forgiveness is a gift you give to others — and a gift you give yourself. Honestly, *others* can live without your forgiveness. But you can't."

But how could she forgive Kevin. *How?*

"I don't know how to forgive him, Jesse, I don't know how!" The words tore from her mouth before she covered her face with her hands and sobbed. Jesse's arms closed around her, and he rocked her back and forth, making gentle noises that slowly calmed her soul.

"God will help you. Keep asking Him to help you. Forgiveness isn't a feeling. Your feelings about your dad won't necessarily change right away. The hurt won't go away. But when you make that decision to forgive him, instead of holding all those feelings inside of you and turning them back on Kevin, you will give those feelings to God and let Him do whatever He does with our hurt."

Shannon listened intently as she sniffed against Jesse's chest. Slowly she pulled back. His shirt was soaked in the middle.

"I'm sor—"

Jesse cut her off with a finger against her lips. "Don't even think of apologizing."

They started walking again, Shannon wiping her face with her hands, hoping she hadn't completely destroyed her makeup.

"One thing to always remember, Shannon," Jesse was saying, and she focused on him again. "God is your true father. When our earthly fathers mess up, little or big, we are not fatherless. Your Father in heaven will do anything for you."

A calming wind traveled through Shannon straight down to her toes, and she smiled. She tilted her neck back and gazed up at the puffy white clouds. Her Father was up there. Now *that* was a thought to hold onto.

They walked on silently, her stilettos click-clacking on the cement.

"Anything else bothering you?" Jesse asked after Shannon had clearly gotten her emotions back inside where they belonged. She hesitated. Jesse's opinion of Kurt was as low as it could get, and she wanted to set the record straight. But she didn't want to hurt Jesse.

"Well, there is one thing, but I don't think it'll make you happy."

* * *

Jesse's heart shuddered. Instinctively he knew it had something to do with Kurt. Did he want to know? No. Would it hurt him? Maybe. Would he listen to Shannon anyway? Absolutely.

"Try me." He swallowed hard to steel himself against what was coming.

Shannon paused and started drawing circles with the toe of her sparkly black open-toed high heel. Her toenails were bright pink. She had no idea how hot she was in those shoes.

No. Jesse forced that thought away and focused on her face.

"I just thought you should know that Kurt really is changing. I know you think badly of him, and so did I many times, but I found out yesterday that for the past few months he has—well, he stopped sleeping with girls. His dad challenged him to one year of abstinence."

Jesse leaned back, stunned. Knowing what he knew about Kurt—which was far more than Shannon knew he knew—this news was astounding.

"Are you sure?"

Shannon nodded. "Yeah. His dad is keeping him accountable."

Jesse raised his eyebrows. Now that took some serious humility. A trait he'd never known Kurt to have in abundance. He couldn't help but feel some admiration for his former friend, but more than a little jealousy, too.

"Is he doing it for you?" He clenched his teeth against the accusing edge in his voice. As he gazed into Shannon's utterly beautiful face, he felt his heart cracking. He was going to lose her. He just knew it.

"At first. But now he's doing it because he really wants to change. He wants to respect himself."

Wow. That was amazing. Jesse really did admire him, albeit, begrudgingly. He forced himself to voice the question screaming in his head.

"Does this change your feelings about him?"

Her gaze shifted aside.

"About me?"

Her face jerked back to his. "What? No!" Without warning, she launched herself at him, and he caught her just in time, again hugging her snugly against his body. He tightened his arms. *Ahh.* This felt so right.

She pulled back slowly, and Jesse dropped his arms. This was too much for him. He had to be honest with her.

"Shannon, I am so … very … I hate to use this word … jealous … of Kurt."

Tender understanding sprang to her face, but Jesse forged on.

"He can see you much more often than I can. Your dad likes his family. They have money. Now he is trying to become a good guy, and soon he'll be everything any girl could want. As much as you like me, I know you have feelings for him, too."

A look of shame crossed Shannon's face. She didn't deny any of his words, only whispered a hoarse, "I'm sorry."

"No. Don't be. I'm just being honest with you about how I feel." He cleared his throat. "I like you so much, Shannon. Of course it's hard for me to not feel jealous of Kurt."

She smiled at him sweetly. "I understand. And all those things you said don't do *anything* to change how I feel about you, Jesse."

What Jesse wanted to hear was, *Kurt is nothing to me, and I love you, Jesse.* But he'd have to settle for her words without promise. That she liked him. But she hadn't denied that she liked Kurt too. He swallowed the hurt, the disappointment.

"Kurt and I were good friends once." The words blurted from his mouth before he could stop them.

"What?" Shannon gaped at him, open-mouthed. "What are you talking about?"

There was no going back now. "When I moved here, Kurt befriended me. Andy wouldn't have anything to do with me anymore. He told Kurt not to bother with me, but Kurt ignored him and got me onto the football team. He was starting to get more involved with girls, and I wasn't sure how I felt about it. Then I started going to church and became, as he put it, a goodie-two-shoes. When I told him I couldn't condone what he was doing, he got really offended and told me where to go. We've acted like strangers ever since." Sadness tinged his voice.

"How come you never told me? I had no idea! But it makes sense. You two knew too much about each other."

Kurt was his rival. They both liked the same girl. Why *would* he tell Shannon they used to be best buds? Obviously Kurt hadn't told her, either. Now the truth was out, and Shannon was free to make up her own mind.

"We better get back to the church," she said softly, touching his arm. "Thanks for telling me. I always appreciate your honesty."

"You're welcome." He smiled warmly at her as the breeze suddenly gusted, fanning her gorgeous red hair out around her face.

She was exquisite. But she wasn't his.

Chapter Thirty-Three

Shannon had been thinking on Jesse's words all week, but she'd come no closer to taking action on his whole "forgiveness" thing. Kevin was still either gone all the time, or she wished he was due to his constant nastiness. It was one thing to forgive someone for one wrong done—but for a continual string of wrong upon wrong? Never-ending wrong? She didn't know how to forgive someone who was going to keep on hurting her. It was just too hard.

Kevin's absence was taking a toll on Daniel and especially Gabby, and Shannon spent most of her "free" time trying to keep them too busy to fall apart. She tried to avoid any heart-to-hearts with Gabby. She had no counsel to offer. It had been a long week of homework and tests, too, and Shannon was just relieved to be cooking Friday dinner. Gabby and Daniel were both busy elsewhere, and all was quiet except for the steady *chop* of the knife on the glass cutting board as she sliced onions for spicy black bean burgers.

Bang!

She jumped as the side door slammed against the wall. A few seconds later Stephanie barged into the kitchen, tears streaming down an angry face.

"It's *your* fault!" she yelled, shaking her finger in Shannon's face.

"What is?" What *could* be? They hadn't talked in days.

"First you filled Kurt with your stupid purity junk, and then you pushed it on Andy. Now he says we're over. It's all your fault!"

* * *

"I feel like the biggest jerk in the world." Andy examined his hands after dinner. He'd come in quietly halfway through the meal. "I knew she liked me a lot, but, I don't know, I thought we were both just using each other to get what we wanted. Kurt tried to convince me that she was giving me what *I* wanted, in hopes of getting what she wanted, but I didn't listen..."

Apparently Kurt and Andy had a spent a lot of time talking during the last week. The result was tonight's break with Stephanie.

"I know I've hurt her a lot, but I can't keep using her." Deep guilt etched his features. He looked so much like Kevin, it almost hurt Shannon to look at him. "I hope she'll be okay."

Shannon hoped so too, but she didn't know how to help Stephanie if she didn't want to talk with her. The girl had run off before Shannon could even reply, and she had called her three times and texted twice, with no response. She was proud of her brother, but she was worried about Stephanie. Obviously she was hurt badly.

After another day of no answer, Shannon drew the courage to stop by on her way home from church. She parked the Explorer on the street and walked up to the grey door. It didn't take long for Stephanie to open the door. She stood in the doorway looking at Shannon from red eyes surrounded by dark puffy circles.

"What do you want?"

This wasn't going to be easy. "To talk with you. Can I come in?"

Stephanie sighed but opened the door wider. "I guess."

Shannon followed her and kicked off her purple heels. Stephanie threw herself belly-down on the couch, so Shannon settled onto the edge of a chair. "How are you doing?"

Stephanie jerked her head up and glared at her. "As if you care. You didn't 'approve' of our relationship. You're glad it's over."

Shannon waited a moment to reply. "I'm not glad he hurt you."

Stephanie lowered her face into the couch again, and seconds later Shannon saw her back shaking with silent sobs.

"Oh, Steph…" Shannon quickly crossed the room to her friend and put her hand on her shoulder. "I'm so sorry."

"It hurts so bad!" Stephanie wailed. "I never thought I would hurt this bad over a stupid guy!" At last the tears abated, and she pushed herself up beside Shannon. "I really thought he liked me. I mean, he never said he did, but I wouldn't have slept with him if I thought he didn't actually like me." Tears started sliding down her face again, and she swatted them away like flies. "I should have known, since he didn't ask me out. We never talked about dating. I assumed he wasn't ready yet. I never imagined he would dump me like this." Her face crumpled, and she wept into her hands. "I love him, Shannon. I gave my heart to him, and he didn't even know it..."

When she calmed down again, she looked at Shannon. "You're quiet."

"I don't know what to say. But believe me, I didn't have anything to do with Andy's decision. I never talked to him about it."

"Really?"

"Nope. Whatever Kurt and Andy have decided has nothing to do with me."

Stephanie studied her, then smiled sadly. "You really don't know your influence, do you? It has *everything* to do with you, Shannon."

Did it? "But I never tried to convince them of anything."

"You didn't have to say anything. Your life said it for you. They watched you, and they learned."

A shiver fluttered through Shannon. That was powerful. She hoped it was true.

* * *

"Where's Daddy?"

It was the question asked every day since spring break started. Now it was half over, and still no trace of Kevin during waking hours.

Daniel slid his fried egg around in a puddle of ketchup on his plate. Gabby hadn't even picked up her fork.

"I guess he's at work, Danny. But I heard him come home last night, and he checked on both of you. He didn't want to wake you up." That much was true. She'd heard the stairs creak, and she'd popped her head out her door to see Kevin peaking into Gabby's room, and then Daniel's. He didn't check on her and Laura, though. Probably didn't care.

"Oh." The little boy brightened. "I miss him. I hope he'll be home tonight."

"Maybe he will." Not likely.

While Shannon was cleaning up from breakfast, Gabby wandered into the kitchen.

"Hey, darling, what's up?" Shannon slid a jug of orange juice onto the top shelf of the refrigerator. "You sleep okay?"

"I was wondering..." Gabby hesitated. "I looked at the calendar in the family room. Next Sunday is Easter."

Shannon stopped mopping at a juice spill on the counter and focused on the little girl twirling her hair around her finger. "Do you guys do anything special for Easter?"

"Our mom always made an Easter egg hunt for us. It's not a big deal to me, but Daniel would be really disappointed if we didn't have it."

Shannon could tell by the look on Gabby's face that it mattered a whole lot to her, too. She started to reply with an "of course we can do an egg hunt," when an even better idea came to her. Gabby deserved it.

"How about..." she paused for effect..."we throw a big Easter party for all your friends? We'll have Easter snacks and Easter food and Easter crafts and Easter games, and end with the best Easter egg hunt ever!"

That was a whole lot of Easter, she could tell by the huge, excited eyes peering back at her. She was busy the rest of the week getting ready for the big event. First she had to track down contact information for Gabby and Daniel's friends, which was no small task. Some just didn't get an invitation. But by the end of the week, 17 small children had RSVPed, and Shannon was a whirlwind of planning and shopping. She managed to drag the kids off to church on Sunday morning, even though she still had a lot to do before their party started at 1:30. She didn't want to miss the Easter service. And it was beautiful.

A few hours later she found herself refilling the jelly bean dispenser while peering into the family room, which she had transformed into a tea-room for any mothers who chose to stick around, which was most of them. Every craft station she'd set up in the dining room was occupied. The Easter bunny canvas competition, sponge art, the pipe-cleaner egg basket, the foam cutout bunny with eggs, bead art, and finger panting were all busy, with more kids waiting. She'd set up the snack table in the living room, complete with homemade chocolate eggs and a bunny-shaped cake. Decorating that had been a challenge. She hoped to one day take a cake decorating class to improve her skills, but she was proud of the outcome.

The meal was served outside in the warm spring sunshine. Shannon had invited Stephanie over even though it was a kid-only party. They'd hung out a few times since Andy's breakup, trying to mend their friendship. Shannon had also gone running with Andy and Kurt twice, and Andy had shown face a lot more this week. At least someone had.

Stephanie stood with her watching the egg hunt, laughing at the over-the-top excitement of the pre-schoolers.

"Look, there's one in the glutter!" Daniel's shrill voice proclaimed, and Shannon smiled, especially when she heard Gabby's saucy response.

"You mean the *gutter*?"

When the last guest finally left, Shannon and Stephanie started cleaning up the leftovers. They were just about to carry the last load into the house when the crunch of gravel caught their attention.

"Oh no." Stephanie's face drained of color. "I'm not ready to see Andy yet." She looked around frantically, about to run. Shannon put a hand on her arm to calm her.

"It's okay. He probably won't come over here."

To her surprise, he did. Kurt was with him, but he only waved and headed into the house. Andy cleared his throat, his face a bright shade of red as he approached where the girls stood under a tree.

"Hey, Steph, you have a minute?" He plunged on before Shannon could excuse herself. "I am...so sorry for hurting you. And I'm sorry for using you the way I did."

Tears were sliding down Stephanie's face already, still-raw pain flexing across her forehead.

Andy took a deep breath, then sighed it out noisily. "Look, I like you a lot."

Stephanie's eyebrows rose, her tears falling harder.

Andy looked questioningly at Shannon, then forged ahead. "I have a lot of issues to work through before I can commit to a healthy relationship. It's not fair of me to keep using you — I like you too much for that. That's why I ended things with you."

Stephanie still hadn't said anything, but she nodded.

Andy looked instantly relieved. "I think we both need some time apart to...adjust. I can't promise anything else, but I hope eventually we can be friends again."

"I'd like that." Stephanie offered a wobbly smile.

"Okay." Andy stood, bobbing his head. "Well, I'm gonna—" he threw his thumb over his shoulder—"go find Kurt. See you two later." As soon as his back was turned, Stephanie sagged against Shannon. She left shortly after, with apologies for not helping clean up more. Shannon understood. Undoubtedly her run-in with Andy had been emotionally exhausting.

Laura was helping her fold up the two long, plastic tables she'd used for lunch when Kurt and Andy came onto the porch.

"Man, what happened in there, Shannon? It looks like an Easter bomb when off!"

Shannon grinned at Andy. "Shannon happened, that's what."

A wide smile filled Kurt's handsome face, and he chuckled. Gabby came running then, with Daniel trailing her from where they'd been picking up leftover eggs around the yard. Gabby flung herself at Shannon with arms wide open.

"Thank you for making the Easter party, Shanny! I love you so much!" Her small arms wrapped around Shannon's waist, and Shannon squeezed her tightly, a lump in her throat.

"I love you too, Gabby girl. I'm so glad you had fun." She staggered as Daniel crashed onto her back, dangling off her with his hands around her neck.

"Thank you, Shanny!" Daniel exclaimed. "I love Easter!"

She smiled in spite of the fact that she could hardly breathe. Behind her she heard Kurt's low, deep voice, "Man, they really love her."

Warmth spread in Shannon's chest. Gabby and Daniel loved her. And she loved them.

She wrangled Daniel off her back and carefully detached Gabby's clinging arms from her middle. "You're very welcome, both of you. It was a great success, don't you think?" She hesitated. She didn't want to preach at the kids, but this was important. "Do you know what Easter is?"

"It's the day Jesus came back to life," Gabby supplied confidently. "I learned that this morning."

Shannon's heart soared. It wasn't easy to wake up early every Sunday and get the kids dressed and out the door, but if it acquainted Gabby with Jesus, then it was worth every bit of stress.

"Yes, it is. Daniel, do you remember who Jesus is?" She wasn't sure how much he understood from his class at church.

"Yes. He was the baby who was born in the barn. At Christmas time."

"You're right. He was God's son, remember? And when He grew up, He helped lots of people, saving them from their sins and making them feel better if they were sick or hurt. But some people were jealous of His power or didn't like Him because He didn't do things the way they wanted Him to. So they decided to get rid of Him. They killed Him."

"That's sad." Daniel's little brow furrowed. "They nailed him up on a piece of wood, right?"

So he'd been paying attention in church, too. "That's right. They put Jesus on a cross, and they thought they had killed Him for good. But two days later, God made Jesus alive again. It was a Sunday morning, and an angel came to where Jesus was buried, and the angel moved the big rock that was covering the grave, and Jesus became alive again and walked right out!" Shannon's heart thrilled with the retelling of the amazing tale. There was no doubt in her mind that only God could do such a thing. Only God could do the impossible.

"Wow!" Daniel breathed, eyes wide and focused on Shannon. "God really did that? That's so cool!"

"It's way cool!" Shannon laughed, feeling free inside. "We all deserve to die because we do bad things, but Jesus died for us, so that we don't have to die. And then He rose again to life, so that He can keep on saving us every time we need Him. And that's why we celebrate Easter. Because Jesus is alive!"

The silence that greeted her announcement reminded her that Daniel and Gabby weren't her only audience. Laura, Andy, and Kurt all sat on the porch, staring at her. Feeling awkward, she shrugged.

"I just wanted to make sure you know what Easter is about. Easter parties are fun, but Jesus is better."

Gabby beamed at her. "Easter didn't make the party special— you did. And Jesus made you."

Her heart melting, Shannon pulled Gabby into another hug. "You are the sweetest."

* * *

As Kurt watched Shannon interact with Gabby and Daniel, her words refused to stop replaying in his head. Jesus is alive. Jesus is alive. Jesus is—alive? Could He be? Kurt had dismissed it long ago as a fable. But the way Shannon told the story was so simple and...convincing.

Could it be?

He shook his head soundly to clear the confusion.

What did it matter anyway?

* * *

"How are things with Kevin?"

Shannon set down her fork and looked at Jesse. "The same. Why?"

He shrugged, then suddenly leaned down with his forearms folded on the lunchroom table. "Because..." His dimples popped in, and he ducked his head. "I'm dying to ask you to prom. But I know I can't."

"Well, you can't pick me up at my house." Shannon threw the idea out with a flirty look, and he grinned.

"So, will you meet me at prom?"

No hesitation. Jesse was hands-down the nicest guy she'd ever met. "Of course. I'd love to."

That night she was surprised when the door opened at 6:30 and Kevin walked in. His pattern of absence and anger had continued for the past several weeks with no deviation. The only thing he'd discussed with her was college, and it hadn't been much of a discussion. He had decided for her—she was going to the University of Virginia in Charlottesville. All Shannon knew was it was four hours away. From Laura, that felt like oceans. From Kevin, nothing was far enough.

He stopped in the kitchen and nodded at Shannon. She almost gasped at the sight. His face was red and swollen, grey bags hanging under his eyes, and his eyes were bloodshot as if he'd been crying.

"Are you okay?" She couldn't help asking as she turned to slide enchiladas out of the oven.

"Yes, I'm fine, Shannon. How was your day?"

His words sounded hollow and forced, and he didn't even wait for her reply before continuing down the hall toward his bedroom. A moment later, she head the door slam, and he didn't come out for dinner. Five minutes into the meal she was genuinely worried and tip-toed down the hallway. She gave a timid knock on the door. No answer.

"Kevin? It's…it's me. Shannon."

There was silence, then, "come in."

Gently she turned the knob and cracked the door open. Kevin was lying on the bed with a cloth on his forehead, the room as dark as night.

"We're eating dinner, if you want to join us," she offered, wondering what was wrong, and not just with her for caring. He was a doctor, so surely he could medicate himself if needed.

His eyes were closed, but his hand flickered against the bed. "Thank you, Shannon, but I'm not hungry."

"Oh… Okay." She backed out of the room and closed the door. Maybe he just didn't want to be with them.

From then on, his pattern changed. He was home on time, but quiet and brooding. No more yelling, but still no fathering.

"I'm pretty sure his lady-friend dumped him," Andy told Shannon. "We're lucky he hasn't gone out drinking."

Shannon prayed it remained so. And she continually prayed to find forgiveness in her heart. Kevin never made it easier.

Chapter Thirty-Four

Shannon nervously approached Kevin in his office on a Tuesday night. Prom was at the end of the week, her dress was purchased and adjusted as needed. What she hadn't counted on was Laura getting asked to the dance by a junior. Her sister had surprised her a few weeks ago by joining the English Club. There was no end to the unexpected from Laura. She had started eating lunch with her fellow club-members, who seemed better characters than her former playmates. One of them had asked her to prom, even though he was dared to do it.

"I accepted so that I can be the sophomore who got into the junior-senior prom," she'd told Shannon with a twinkle in her eyes. Shannon was happy for her. But now she had to make sure Kevin would be home, or Jesse would be out of a date.

"Kevin?" She popped her head around the cracked open door.

He looked up and nodded her in. He looked worn and weary, the usual.

Shannon cracked her knuckles, wrung her hands, and stepped from one foot to the other.

"What do you need, Shannon?"

Finally she met his eyes. "Prom is this Saturday. I was wondering if you'll be home so I can go?"

He just looked at her. "Do you have a date?"

Shannon took a deep breath. She was done lying to her dad, God help her. "No one is picking me up, but..."

"But you're meeting Jesse there."

Why did he know her so well? Must be why he could hurt her so well, too.

He was quiet, then slowly nodded. "I'm not thrilled by the idea, but so be it. I'm on call, but I'll do my best to get back in time." He pressed his lips together and stared at the desk, a pained expression pinching his face. "I'm—I'm sorry for all I've put you through, Shannon. You don't deserve any of it."

Her heart nearly stopped. This was it. The time to forgive him. If she could just say it—

But she couldn't. He'd done too much.

* * *

"Are you sure?"

"Yes, just go. Your date's here." Shannon gave Laura a shove toward the door. "I'm sure Kevin will be here soon."

But he wasn't.

At half past 7:00, she called Laura and asked her to find Jesse.

"I'll come late if I can, but it doesn't look like I'll be coming at all." He assured her he understood, and Laura offered to come home and stay in her place, but Shannon refused. She held back the tears until they hung up, then sank to the floor in a heap of silky purple. She buried her head in her arms and sobbed. She was going to miss prom. Because of Kevin. He was so selfish. He didn't care about anyone but himself.

Why did she ever let her hopes rise?

Her hopes that Kevin would change, that is. She could live without prom. But sometimes she wasn't sure she could live without her dad.

She—she *hated* him!

No, don't say that.

The thought collided with her emotions, and she raised her head and puffed air from her mouth. Well she certainly didn't like him right now. With pinched lips, she reached for her Bible. It was the last thing she felt like doing.

Her page marker rested on Psalm 139. Progress had been slow.

She wasn't concentrating well until the words jumped straight off the page. "For you created my inmost being; you knit me together in my mother's womb. I praise you because I am fearfully and wonderfully made. . . All the days ordained for me were written in your book before one of them came to be." She read the words again as tears slowly filled her eyes. Jesse was right. She *had* been planned. By God Himself. He'd woven her together. He'd mixed her paint. She was *His* special creation.

Love wrapped around her as she read it again. All her days had been written down before they came to pass. That meant...that meant all along God had known this time would come. He knew she was going to miss prom because of her dad.

And he'd been preparing her for it. He'd been preparing her to forgive.

She flopped her head back against the side of the bed behind her and gazed upward.

"God, I'm so hurt. Kevin doesn't care how I feel. He doesn't care how hurt I am. He doesn't even care that he's my father." Tears fell rapidly from her eyes. "I don't think he will ever stop hurting me. I can't go on feeling like this. If he's not going to change, then I have to. *Help me.*" With shaking arms, she cupped her hands together over her heart, then held them out to God. She hoped He understood that she was giving Him all the pain, hurt, and anger in her heart, because she couldn't handle it anymore.

"Take it," she whispered.

A tiny prick began in her chest, and then it spread until she felt like she was floating on a cloud of peace, and joy, and…forgiveness. God had answered.

"I forgive him, God. I do. Please help me to keep forgiving and loving him every day, in the midst of the hurt."

* * *

"Shannon?" Kurt never knocked, but he definitely didn't have time for that tonight. "Shannon?" he called louder.

When she appeared at the top of the stairs, he forgot why he was here. Dressed for prom in a long, shimmering purple number that showcased her perfect shoulders and beautiful hips, she would have parted a crowd. Her hair looked freshly trimmed with layers and flowed freely down her back, a few strands framing her face.

Man.

He let out a low whistle as she came to a stop a few steps above him and pointed his finger up and rotated it. With a shy smile, she spun around slowly. The dress was form-fitting and giving him too many details. Forcing clean thoughts, he cleared his throat as she faced him again.

"You look amazing."

"Thanks." She smiled and plopped down on the stairs. "You're the only one who gets to see it, though. My dad didn't show up, so I'm missing prom."

Right. Back to why he was here. She didn't look nearly as upset as he thought she'd be. In fact, she was kind of glowing.

"You know, I'd volunteer to stay here with Gabby and Daniel so you can go, but I have another reason for being here." How could he tell her? "See, your dad actually has a good excuse this time. He was trying to make it home for you, but as he was leaving the hospital, walking to his truck, he was hit by a car."

"What?" Shannon's voice was suddenly thin. "Is he okay?"

Kurt took a deep breath, and before he could even answer, tears began to pour down Shannon's face.

"No, Kurt. Don't you dare tell me he's dead. I already lost one parent, I can't lose two!"

He sprang forward and put both hands on her shoulders. "No! No, he's alive. Andy and I were in Bristol at a car show when Andy got the call. I dropped him off at the hospital and came to get you all. Look at me." When she did, he didn't know how he could say what he had to. Her eyes were breathtaking, like her heart. He couldn't break it again.

"Your dad is hurt bad, Shannon. He's in surgery right now." He swallowed hard, and picked up her hand, squeezing it. "They don't know if he's going to pull through."

"Oh, God, *no*." She crumpled over on herself, sobbing. Kurt wanted to let her cry, but there wasn't time. He gently pushed her back up by her shoulders.

"Andy asked me to bring you all to the hospital."

She stared at him in horror.

"You go change, and I'll tell the kids." She nodded and stood, her teeth clacking together as she tried to stop crying. He longed to pull her into his arms and rub her silky back, but again, no time, even if she'd let him.

While she disappeared into her room, Kurt located Gabby and Daniel and told them the barest details. Their dad was hurt, and they all had to go to the hospital. Thankfully they hadn't changed into pajamas yet.

He had driven Andy's car from Bristol since he'd ridden with Andy earlier that day. He left it in Andy's parking spot and warmed up the Explorer. As they drove into town a few minutes later, Shannon called Laura and told her to meet them outside the high school. Apparently she didn't want to go inside, and he was relieved she hadn't asked him. There was bound to be any number of girls in there he'd rather not see. He was an idiot!

* * *

What if Kevin dies? The question was on repeat in Shannon's brain during the silent ride to Bristol. What would happen to them? And she hadn't told him that she forgave him! Panic welled up inside her, and she struggled to take in air. No, he had to be okay, he *had* to!

Kurt's phone rang, and she felt the blood drain from her face when she recognized Andy's voice on the other end. But he was calling with the good news that Kevin had made it out of surgery and was in ICU now. They passed a blue hospital sign as Kurt turned left and then right.

"Do you want me to drop you off at the door? I have to park in the parking garage."

Shannon was afraid to go in alone. "No, we can park first and go in together."

Kurt reached his hand to her trembling leg and gave a short squeeze. "Okay."

When they walked into the Intensive Care Unit, Laura still decked out in her prom gear, Shannon saw Andy pacing back and forth at the far end of the waiting room.

"Andy!" Her voice rang out louder than it was probably supposed to, but she didn't care. He bolted toward them and crushed Shannon into a hug. When she pulled back, she could see he'd been crying. He swept Laura and Gabby and Daniel into his arms simultaneously and squeezed them hard before turning to throw his arms around his friend, clinging to Kurt like a little boy.

"What's the update?" Kurt asked, gently prying him off his shoulder.

"Nothing new yet. He's going into surgery again in an hour, so you guys better see him now."

A nurse was approaching with an apologetic smile on her face. She pointed at the large-lettered sign above the registration window. "I'm sorry, but children under the age of 12 have to remain in the lobby. Who are you here to see?"

"Our dad. Kevin Conrad." Shannon barely recognized her own hoarse voice.

Worry flickered across her round face. "I see. Immediate family members over 12 can see him one at a time, for one minute only. The children cannot visit him at this time."

"I'll stay with them." Kurt put held out his hands to Gabby and Daniel. "Why don't you go first, Shannon?"

The smell of medicine stung Shannon's eyes as she followed the nurse through a door and down a white hallway, terrified of what she would find. Nurses and other scrubs-clad personnel scurried everywhere.

"He's in here." The nurse ushered Shannon through a door. "I'll come back for you in one minute."

The room was dark, machines beeping and whirring up a racket. Shannon crept toward the bed and thought certainly the nurse had been mistaken. This man wasn't her father.

She stepped closer, and her hand shot to her mouth to stifle her cry. She swallowed back her dinner and all the bile in her throat. It *was* her dad. The only exposed skin on his face was black from bruising, whereas most of his head, face included, were wrapped in white bandages. His hands were swollen and purple from the blood running wild underneath. There must be a million tubes and wires connected to him, and his arms and legs were strapped down and wrapped in more bandages.

"Oh, Dad." She wept into her hands, peaking through her fingers to look at him. Tubes were in his nose and mouth, breathing for him, *living* for him. How could he live? How? He was going to die, just like her mom had. He was going to die before she could tell him that she forgave him. He was going to die before she could tell him that she loved him.

Tears dripped from her face and hands, splashing around her, and Shannon couldn't take the sight anymore—her broken, crushed, dying father.

She ran from the room and down the hall, ignoring the staff who told her to slow down. She burst through the door and into the lobby. Surprised exclamations came from her family in the waiting room, and Kurt's fingers brushed her arm as he tried to grab her, but she kept running. Running. Running away from death. Again.

Chapter Thirty-Five

"Internal bleeding. Swelling of the brain. Punctured lung. Crushed femur. Broken wrist. Broken arm. Broken clavicle. Crushed foot. Ruptured spleen." The list continued, but Shannon didn't understand the rest. Kurt had found her in the hospital chapel and let her cry it out on his chest. When they came back, Andy passed on the doctor's warning: their dad had a 50% chance of making it through the second surgery now underway. They had stabilized him as much as possible for the surgery, but they couldn't wait any longer or they might lose him anyway. This surgery was to quell the internal bleeding. If he survived, there would be many more surgeries to come.

"I'm thirsty, Shanny." Daniel tugged at Shannon's arm.

Andy sat with his head in his hands, leaning his elbows on his knees. Laura, now changed into the jeans and hoodie Shannon had grabbed for her, hugged her knees to her chest, her feet tucked up on the edge of her cushioned seat. Kurt sat beside her, tapping the toe of his shoe repeatedly on the hard hospital floor. They had been moved to the operating waiting room. Kevin's surgery had been underway for three hours and still no word. Shannon felt like she was sitting on a cactus, praying unintelligible phrases in her head. Jesse had called her to find out what was going on and prayed over the phone with her. Stephanie had called, too.

"Shanny!" Daniel shook her.

"Okay, okay." She stood up, no idea where she was going. "Come on, let's go."

Kurt appeared out of nowhere and gently pushed her back down into her seat by her shoulders. Swooping Daniel into his arms, he took Gabby by the hand. "I got this, Shan. Do you want anything?"

She sent him a million thank yous with her eyes and shook her head. "No."

They disappeared from the lobby and Shannon pulled out her phone. Heading for one in the morning. Kevin had to be out of surgery soon…right? At least they knew he was still alive. No word was good in that sense.

Kurt returned with the kids and an armful of Gatorade bottles. He pushed one at Andy, then Laura. When he tried to hand one to Shannon, she waved it away.

"Please, Shannon. You need it."

She closed her eyes against the nausea rising in her throat. "I can't."

"Yes, you can." He squatted in front of her and pushed the bottle into her hands. "Just try."

She sat motionless with the Gatorade bottle limp in her hands.

Kurt patiently took it back, twisted the cap off, and handed her the open bottle. "One swallow to start. You can do it."

Slowly she raised the bottle to her lips and filled her mouth with the sweet liquid, letting it slide down her throat slowly. *Mmmm.* She took another sip, bigger this time.

"That's my girl."

I'm not your girl. The words drowned in Shannon's throat with the Gatorade. Did it matter right now whose girl she was? She just wanted to be her daddy's girl, and he might be dead for all she knew. Any second they could find out.

"Andrew?"

Shannon bolted up at the strange voice. How in the world had she slept?

A man in a white coat stood over Andy, his hand on Andy's slumped back.

Shannon staggered to her feet. "How's our dad?" Her voice was so thin, the doctor would probably think she needed oxygen.

"Dr. Richardson." Andy jumped to his feet, his face panicked. "Everything okay?"

"Good news. Your father made it through surgery, and we were able to stabilize him somewhat."

Somewhat. What did that mean? "So he'll be okay, right?" Shannon felt Laura creep to her side.

The weary looking doctor turned to her. "I don't think we've met. I'm Dr. Richardson." He held out his hand, and Shannon shook it. "You are…?"

"Shannon."

He smiled genuinely. "Your dad has told me a lot about you. It's a pleasure to meet you."

Shannon had forgotten her dad worked at this very hospital, and the people trying to save his life were his coworkers. They probably knew him better than she did.

"He is okay at the moment. I'm sorry I can't offer more assurance than that, Shannon." He looked back at Andy. "The next five or six hours will be crucial. We must do more operations as soon as possible, but your dad's system is in shock, and he has to be stable for more surgery." He paused. "We came very close to losing him on multiple occasions during this surgery. Right now he is being monitored in ICU. If you would like to relocate to the ICU waiting room, you will receive updates there."

"Is that all you can tell us?" Shannon asked, feeling helpless.

Dr. Richardson looked at her with compassion. "I don't want to give false hope. Please know that your father is not only a valued colleague of mine, he is also a treasured friend. I will do everything in my power to see him through. Beyond that..." He pointed his finger up. "If you're the religious sort, I'd be praying. I know I am." He nodded at them.

In the ICU waiting room they all curled up where available and attempted to sleep. Kurt settled beside Shannon, cradling a sleeping Daniel. Shannon helped Gabby stretch out beside her, using her lap as a pillow. The rest of the night passed in slow motion. A nurse checked in on them twice. Kevin was still stable, but showed no sign of consciousness.

Lord Jesus, save my daddy... The words played over and over in Shannon's mind and in her dreams. *Please, God...*

Morning came, and the nurse appeared to tell them Kevin would be going into surgery in 20 minutes if they wanted to take turns with him. Shannon passed. The children still sleeping on her lap were a good excuse.

The minutes ticked by after they once again moved to the surgery waiting room. Kurt took Gabby, Daniel, and Laura to the cafeteria for breakfast, but Shannon and Andy remained in tense silence. The rest of the group came back, and Kurt had just started a movie on his iPhone for the kids when the door to the waiting room opened. Shannon's breath caught in her throat. Kevin's surgery was done so soon? Did that mean—had he not—was he—

"Grammy!" Gabby catapulted from her chair, knocking Kurt's phone to the floor as she flew across the room toward the elderly woman who walked into the room past a receptionist, followed by another middle-aged woman. Andy hugged them both and led them over to Shannon and Laura.

"I don't know if either of you remember, but this is our grandma."

She was a small woman with a shock of obviously dyed red hair rising in the middle of her head like a tufted titmouse, and she surprised Shannon by leaning over to give her a tight hug.

"You used to come to my house every Thanksgiving when you were young. Both of you. I've missed you dearly."

Shannon patted her back awkwardly. She vaguely remembered.

"And this is your Aunt Kate," she introduced as she backed up. "You can call me Grandma Carol if you'd like."

Shannon didn't like anything except the idea of escape. This was Kevin's family, not hers. She slipped out of the waiting room and took a long walk around the hospital.

"Kevin's still in surgery." Andy greeted her at the door when she returned. "After he gets out, Aunt Kate is going to take Gabby and Daniel home. She'll stay with them."

Hours slipped by. Shannon skipped her opportunity to see Kevin again after surgery. Kurt left to drive Aunt Kate, Gabby, and Daniel to Claywood. Andy and Laura went with "Grandma Carol, " as she called herself, to the cafeteria for lunch. When they came back, Grandma Carol settled herself down comfortably beside Shannon.

"Well, dear." She patted Shannon's arm that was crossed across her chest. "How are you doing with your father? Emotionally, I mean."

Shannon gave the woman her best, "who are you and why are you talking to me" look, and Grandma Carol laughed.

"My, but you do look like your father. My precious black sheep may not talk to me much, but your brother Andy updates me on the family goings-on every week. I am well informed, trust me."

Shannon lifted her chin high. "We've had our differences, but he is my dad."

A smile spread slowly across Grandma Carol's face. "That he is. And my goodness, if you haven't grown up to be the spitting image. You learn from his mistakes and put your DNA to good work, and you will be one successful lady."

Shannon couldn't keep from smiling reluctantly. "Thanks. You think he's going to recover?"

"Oh yes. God knows you need your father. He'll take care of the details. Don't you worry."

It was the most comforting thing she'd heard all day, and boy did she need it.

Kurt strode into the room just then, and his face lit up when he saw Shannon. "Hey, Gabby sent a care package for you." He winked. "Change of clothes, phone charger, sketch book, and as she insisted, your Bible."

"Aww, that little sweetie." Shannon beamed at him. "Thanks for bringing it."

"Anything."

Grandma Carol chuckled beside her and shook her head as Kurt crossed the room to where Laura was sprawled, a second bag in hand. "Boy do you have a mess on your hands with that young man."

Shannon rolled her eyes. Discernment must run in the family.

A doctor came into the room with an update. Kevin's vitals had improved, although he was still unconscious. He would remain in ICU overnight and then early in the morning he would be having another operation. Grandma Carol and Andy debated getting a hotel room but in the end decided to spend the night in the hospital in case anything changed. Shannon settled in for another long night. At least this time she didn't have two children using her as a pillow. Instead she used Kurt's shoulder as a pillow, and she didn't even protest when he put his arm around her and pulled her against his chest.

* * *

Kurt shook Shannon awake gently at 7:00 a.m.

"I'm sorry, Shan, but I gotta head home. I have a final this afternoon and two tomorrow."

And he'd spent his whole weekend with her family. Sweet guy.

Andy insisted that she and Laura go with him. "I'll keep you posted, and as soon as Dad wakes up, you can come back."

If he wakes up.

Shannon shivered at the unwelcome thought. He was going to wake up. He *had* to.

"Please go." Andy looked at her with weary red eyes. "I don't know what I'm going to do about finals, but I'll worry about that later. Grammy is here with me, so I'll be okay."

Shannon nodded. "I'm going to ask if I can see Kevin before I go." Just in case. She'd never forgive herself if she kept avoiding him and lost her last chance.

He was as pale as the white hospital sheets, and looked much the same as he had Saturday night, although his arm was now in a cast. That's what the surgery this morning had been for. His legs were going to take a lot more work, Dr. Richardson said.

The monitor above the bed beeped to his heart rate. Slow, but steady.

"Oh, Dad." Shannon's voice trembled. "Please come back to us. Come back to *me*."

* * *

"He's awake."

"Oh, thank You, God." Shannon slumped against her locker in relief, nearly dropping her phone. It felt like she'd been holding her breath for three days, and she could finally breathe.

"My dad woke up!" she squealed to Jesse in English class.

Never had a week taken so long to reach Wednesday. Every night they had huddled together on the living room floor, Aunt

Kate, Shannon, Laura, Gabby, and Daniel holding hands while Shannon and Aunt Kate prayed. Laura had added her own prayer last night.

"Ready?" Kurt was waiting in Shannon's living room when she got home from school. The whole group piled into the minivan, and Kurt chauffeured them to Bristol again. Andy met them in the hallway outside ICU.

"He can't talk yet. He knows what happened, but they haven't told him yet how badly he was injured."

Shannon let Aunt Kate and Laura go first while she waited with Daniel and Gabby. They still weren't allowed beyond the lobby. When it was her turn, she anxiously followed the nurse down the hallway.

"Here he is, hun. Press the red button if you need me." The nurse waved her into the room and continued on her way.

Shannon tiptoed into the room. Kevin's eyes were shut. He looked better than on Sunday, but not as improved as she expected.

Maybe he was asleep. Reaching her hand out, she ran her finger over his puffy hand, brown and blue from the IV needle.

His hand jerked, and her attention flew to his face. His eyes were open, staring at her. His mouth moved to speak, but the tube in his throat was in the way.

Shannon forced a smile, nearly overwhelmed by conflicting emotions. She practically hated this man, but she'd forgiven him, and then he'd almost died, but now he was going to make it, and she was so glad. It was a lot to feel.

"Hi," she said softly. "I'm—I'm glad to see you awake." A slight nod indicated his understanding. "You had us pretty worried. We've been praying for you. I'm so glad—" The words choked in her throat as tears suddenly sprang to her eyes. "So glad we didn't lose you." He wiggled his fingers to where her hand rested on the bed and weakly squeezed her fingers. His mobility was limited, so the movement was awkward, but the sweetness of it, the miracle of it, broke Shannon, and tears poured down her face in a waterfall. He gave her hand another squeeze, and Shannon rubbed her tears on her shoulders.

"I'm sorry, I'm sorry. It's just, we weren't sure you were going to live." Her voice cracked and she took a deep breath, stared at the ceiling, and counted to ten. When she looked back at her father, he was watching her with tender blue eyes.

"Thank you for coming back to us, Dad." She hadn't said that word in a long time, and his face lifted up in a smile ever so slightly. Her time was almost up. "I'll be back to see you again soon. Keep getting better, and I'll keep praying for you."

He nodded, and Shannon moved in to drop a kiss on his cheek before she lost her nerve. She walked away briskly, then stopped at the door and looked back. He was watching her with tears trickling down his bruised face.

* * *

"I'm going for a walk. I'll be back soon."

Kurt cracked his eyes open. It was Sunday afternoon, and he had dozed off in the hospital lobby. Kevin had been transferred to an inpatient recovery wing where he would be recuperating for the next few weeks, and Kurt had brought Shannon and the rest down for the weekend. Everyone was more relaxed with Kevin improving daily.

"Can I go with you?" It was a bold request. She'd been increasingly quiet all weekend.

She flickered her eyes at him, then away, indecision obvious in her stance. "Um, yeah, I guess."

It wasn't the most encouraging invitation, but he took it. They headed for the main exit of the hospital and into the warm spring sunshine.

"*Ahhh.*" He breathed in deeply. "Clean air!"

Shannon chuckled half-heartedly. "What, you don't like that sterile hospital smell?"

He winked in response. "Are you kidding? I love it!"

"Whatever." She rolled her eyes at him as they paused to let a squirrel scamper across the walkway. "By the way, thank you for bringing us down here so many times. That was very generous of you."

He shrugged it off. "No problem." Anything involving Shannon was never a problem.

They walked off the hospital grounds and took a sidewalk into a nearby park. It was filled with children and parents chasing at a playground. A teenage couple were trying to get a kite flying and failing miserably. Kurt couldn't help smiling at the way they laughed at their lack of success. They were just happy to be together.

"I've noticed you've been pretty quiet. Everything okay?" The chance of her opening up to him was pretty slim, but he wouldn't be Kurt if he didn't try.

"Yeah." Shannon stopped and looked at him. Her blue green eyes held a hint of sadness. "I'm happy my dad is recovering, but I'm missing my mom. It's my first mother's day without her. Been thinking a lot about her this weekend."

Mother's day. The words sank through Kurt like a stone. It was mother's day? What kind of a loser son was he? He hadn't even known!

Shannon was walking again, and he forced himself to continue beside her. He'd buy flowers on the way home and surprise his mom at the end of the day. Oh, bless Shannon for reminding him!

"You know, my mom made a lot of mistakes, just like my dad. She had an affair with him. She wrecked his home. She lied to us about him my whole life. I found out the bad stuff about her *after* she died, and it changed how I look at my memories of her. I hate that, and I've been resenting her."

Kurt listened as Shannon unloaded her heart, clueless what to say, but thankfully Shannon wasn't looking for a solution from him.

"I forgave my dad on Saturday for every single hurt he has caused, but I didn't get a chance to tell him. If he had died, he wouldn't ever know about my forgiveness, but I would, and that makes all the difference. Forgiveness isn't so much for the offender, as much as it is a gift you give yourself. So it hit me today that I have to forgive my mom, too, although she'll never know it. I have to forgive her so that my heart can be free to love her and my memories with her."

She looked up at Kurt and smiled hesitantly. "If that makes any sense."

He smiled back, completely lost for words. She'd forgiven her dad? For everything? That was crazy.

"Besides," Shannon continued, "how can I expect God or anyone else to forgive me if I don't forgive my mom and dad?"

"As if you need forgiveness for anything!" Kurt exclaimed, incensed at the very idea. Shannon was so good, so pure!

She looked startled. "Of course I do. We all do. Maybe you don't believe in the Bible, but I do, and it says we are all sinners and deserve the death that Jesus died for us. Pastor read a verse that even says all the good in us is equivalent to dirty rags. It's only through God that we can do or be anything good. Any goodness in me comes from God, not from me. Don't you see? Without God we're worthless."

A constricting feeling was trying to close over Kurt's throat, and bitter, burning flames erupted in his stomach. Was he getting sick? He checked his phone, blocking out Shannon's words. For the love of birds, why did he suddenly feel like crying? He wasn't a child! What was his problem?

"We should head back," he muttered, his voice rough. "We'll need to leave soon."

They returned to the hospital in silence and had one last visit with Kevin. Kurt remained at the back of the room, brooding over Shannon's ridiculous words. She wasn't a bad person. Shoot, if she was bad, that practically made him the devil. It was all just religiously posed hogwash, rhetoricized for those not strong enough to stand on their own in this world. Some people needed belief in God as a crutch to get them through life, that's what.

"What's wrong?"

Kurt glanced at Shannon in the front seat beside him. They were halfway to Claywood now, and he hadn't said a word.

"Nothing." He turned his eyes back to the road.

"Liar."

He glared at her. "I don't want to talk about it, okay?"

Her eyes grew wide with hurt at his sharp tone. "Okay, fine," she huffed, turning deliberately to stare out the side window.

He grunted a sigh. Perfect. This day couldn't get any better.

After he dropped them off at their house, he drove into Claywood hoping some place in this miserable town would still have decent flowers for Mom. She deserved a lot more than flowers, but that would have to come later.

"Mom?" He found her in the kitchen making dinner.

"Hi, honey!" She smiled and came at him for a hug. "We missed you this weekend." Her arms were open wide, and suddenly he thrust a dozen red roses under her nose.

"Happy mother's day to the best mom under the sun and moon."

"Oh my goodness, Kurt!" She ignored the flowers and wrapped her arms around him. "I thought you'd forgotten, honest I did. Thank you so much!"

He pulled back with a smile. "I'd never forget about you, Mom. It was a busy weekend, though, so I'm thankful Shannon said something to remind me." There, that was a partial truth.

"Oh, I knew I liked that girl!" She winked at Kurt and grabbed the roses from his hand. "They're beautiful and oh, they smell lovely. Good choice, Kurt."

He grinned.

"Dinner's ready. Can you find your dad? I don't know where he disappeared to."

"Sure." Kurt went looking for his dad and came to a full stop when he found him on his knees, leaning into his favorite arm chair. "Dad, are you okay?"

Dad lifted his head and smiled. "Never better. Just praying for you."

Kurt's world rocked for the second time that day. "Praying for me? *Why?*"

Dad rolled back on his heels and stood up. "Because you need God desperately."

"No I don't. Why does everyone have to bring God into things?"

"Listen, Kurt. You've made some incredible decisions that have changed your life, and I am so proud of you. But what's been motivating you? First it was Shannon. You realized you didn't want to hurt her. Then it became deeper than that. You didn't want to keep hurting yourself. But what you have failed to see is who you've hurt the most, and that is God."

Kurt rolled his eyes. "What does God have to do with my mistakes?"

"Everything. God is the creator of all things, Kurt. We mess up a lot, and He works with us, but that doesn't mean that He doesn't want us to strive for His ideal. Even for sex. Sex was created to be between one woman and one man who have devoted their lives to God and each other through marriage. Sex is holy, Kurt, don't you see? It's a vow. Outside of marriage, it loses its holiness and becomes sin."

Kurt's head was spinning. When had his dad become a preacher? He hadn't even grown up Christian. His parents had just started going to church last year!

"That's fine, Dad, if you believe in God, but I don't, so what you're saying doesn't apply to me." Right? That's what he heard all the time from people around him.

"Just because you don't believe something is real doesn't make it so."

Kurt struggled to breathe, waiting for his dad to go on.

"Look at you. You're real. And you know it. But what if someone came along who absolutely refused to believe that you are real. In spite of your best efforts to show him that you really are real, he still chose not to believe it. Would that make you in any way less real? Same with God. He's real, whether you believe it or not."

Kurt stared at his dad. He felt like he was being split into two pieces. Like someone was on either side, pulling his arms in opposite directions. He rubbed his hands together and cracked his knuckles. He licked his lips.

"Kurt." His dad's voice was soft. Out of Kurt's peripheral vision, he saw his mom standing in the doorway, her hands folded against her lips. "I've been watching you struggle, I've been watching you fight, and as a dad, it breaks my heart, because I know there is an easier way. I want you to experience the freedom in Christ that your mom and I have found. We never told you this, but the reason we started going to church last year was because our marriage was all but over. We were so busy with our businesses, we had lost our love for each other. We tried God for the first time in our lives. I only wish we'd done so sooner. We fell in love with God together, and so fell in love with each other again."

Kurt looked back and forth between his parents. His mom's lips were moving silently, and he knew she was praying for him. What was going on in this room?

The tugging back and forth was stronger, the pain in his chest deeper.

He thought of Shannon. If she, a human being, was able to forgive her parents for all their offenses, then if God was real—and Kurt was beginning to feel for sure that He was—maybe He could forgive him for all the mistakes he had made. For all the times he had desecrated what God had meant to be holy.

He took a deep breath. "Okay, what do I do first?"

The tug-of-war stopped, and sweet calmness soothed his chest. Dad's face lit up with joy, and he gripped Kurt's hand. "You get on your knees and talk with God as a friend, Kurt."

"That's it?" *Whew*. Kurt blew air out between his lips. This was intense. This was crazy. He couldn't believe he was doing this. "Okay, here goes."

He lowered himself to his knees, and his dad knelt beside him. It took a while for him to find the words. He was so much better at writing. "Okay, God, I'm here… I'm not sure how to do this, but I need to tell you I am sorry for not believing in You. I'm sorry—for all the things I've done wrong. You know it all. Help me to be a better person. Please forgive—my sins." He tried to fight back the tears that pushed against his eyeballs, but they came anyway, and then he was sobbing. His dad put an arm around him and hugged him tightly.

"Thank you, God. Thank you for bringing Kurt Home."

Chapter Thirty-Six

"Careful, careful!" Shannon called out as Kurt and Andy carried her dad up the steps and into the house. He'd recovered in the hospital for three weeks, and today he had been released. She was glad the trips to Bristol were over. Maybe life could settle down and go back to normal, although Kevin was a long way from walking and would still undergo several reconstructive surgeries for his crushed leg, not to mention months of therapy.

Grandma Carol and Aunt Kate were long gone. The daily care of her dad was up to her now. Doctor Rasco had given her very specific instructions this morning for his medications and injections. In a few hours she would be giving her dad a shot.

Kurt grunted under the weight of her dad as he and Andy lowered him onto his bed.

"Thanks, boys," he muttered, quickly clenching his teeth. He'd been grumpier by the minute since they'd started for home, and Shannon had to keep reminding herself that he was in a lot of pain.

She followed Kurt and Andy out of the room and down the hall, heading for the kitchen. "You guys want a drink?" She poured three glasses of lemonade.

"Less than two weeks, huh?" Kurt guzzled half of his glass, then lowered it from his face.

"Don't remind me." Half a week of classes, then finals. Then graduation. She hadn't allowed herself to think about it yet.

Andy grimaced. "I'm still trying to make up my finals. Maybe I'll be done by the time you are, Shan." He flashed a grin at her, but Shannon caught the exhaustion behind his twinkleless eyes. The past month had taken a toll on her brother. On all of them.

"Ouch! What the heck, Shannon? Could you be a little gentle? I'm a human, not a horse."

Things were not going well. Shannon's hands shook as she set the needle down. Kevin was in a foul mood. No matter what she did, he found fault with it. She couldn't even take his pulse right. She was squeezing his wrist too hard, he said. He started gagging when she took his temperature. She spilled water when she handed him a glass for his pills.

Lord, help me.

"I'm sorry, Dad." She still had to force the name from her lips. "I'll try to do better next time."

In the morning she had to help him eat, since his right arm was in a cast. He got so irritated he threw a bowl of cereal across the room, and Shannon spent ten minutes picking soggy Special K off the carpet. When she stood up, Kevin sighed.

"I'm sorry, Shannon."

She swallowed all the irritation and smiled at him softly. "That's okay. I know you're frustrated with your recovery."

"I am," he huffed. "It's taking so long, and I'm bored out of my skull. There's not much I can do."

Sympathy flooded Shannon's heart. "Is there anything I can do to help? Anything I can get you?"

"I don't know. I'll tell you if I think of anything. Thanks for asking."

Well, that was the most civil way he'd addressed her in months. Maybe it was almost time to share her forgiveness with him.

That night the injection was easier to administer , and she detected his vitals with more precision. His temperature was running higher than it should, so she gave him Tylenol as the doctor had recommended. Kevin was grumpy again, though, so Shannon didn't say much.

Saturday morning she was waiting at her dad's bedside before he woke up. She was done with all her regular classes. Only finals remained next week. She couldn't wait a moment longer to talk with her dad about forgiveness. Why had she waited this long anyway? It wasn't like her words would do anything catastrophic. The change had already taken place in her heart.

"Shannon?" Kevin mumbled, cracking his eyes open. "What are you doing here?" He struggled to sit up, rubbing his eyes with one hand. "What time is it?"

"After 8:00. But Dad, there's something I need to tell you. Something I decided when I missed prom. Before I knew it was because of your accident."

"Sorry about that. I did try."

"I know. But I didn't then." Shannon took a deep breath, playing with her thumbs. Her heart was pounding. She didn't know how to say it. "I just want you to know that... well, I forgive you." The words blurted from her mouth. Kevin froze, his ice blue eyes locked with hers. "I forgive you, Dad." This time she whispered the words. She reached for his hand and held it. "For everything. For all the times you hurt me, when you knew and when you didn't, I forgive you."

Shannon's heartbeat slowed as she waited for a response from her dad, who stared at her.

"Okay. Uh, thanks." He cleared his throat. "You making breakfast? I'm hungry."

That was it? As hurt blasted through Shannon, she forced herself to her feet and out the door, saying something about eggs and hashbrowns.

It wasn't about Kevin. The change had been in her. She had just told herself that. Nothing catastrophic was going to happen.

But she was still hurt.

Lord, please. She sighed and wiped the tears falling from her eyes. *Help me to forgive him. Again.*

* * *

Two hours, 38 minutes, and 15 seconds.

Shannon was graduating.

She set her phone down on her desk and flopped back against the pillow with a smile at the ceiling. She pushed away the sad thought that her mom wouldn't be here to see her graduate. At least her dad would.

Jesus, please, touch my dad's heart. Please...

She pushed herself up and out of bed with a sigh. Standing in front of her closet, she tilted her head in perplexity. What was she going to wear?

Nearly two hours later, hair styled, nails painted, and dressed in a sky blue pencil skirt, loose black sheer blouse over a yellow shell, and yellow stilettos, Shannon teetered down the stairs.

She had gotten Gabby and Daniel ready first, so they were already waiting in the living room beside Laura.

"Oh my, Shan, you look gorgeous." Laura nodded her approval from her seat.

"Aww, thanks, sis." Shannon flashed her a smile and headed down the hall to check on Kevin.

To her surprise, she found him still in bed under the covers, his back to the door.

"Dad?" She knelt with one knee on the bed and peered over him. "You okay? We need to leave in a few minutes. I thought Andy was helping you get ready."

He groaned and rolled onto his back to look at her. "I'm not going."

"What?" His words slashed Shannon's heart, and she blinked at him, willing away what he'd said. He closed his eyes and turned his face from her.

"It's my graduation, Dad." Her voice cracked. No, this couldn't be happening. She had to have a parent at her graduation. "Please. I want you to be there."

He ignored her and rolled onto his side, again giving her his back. "Just go, Shannon."

Tears ran down her face as she backed from the room. Would he ever stop hurting her?

Probably not.

God, help me.

She batted at her tears as she returned to the living room.

"Okay, let's go."

"Where's Daddy?" Gabby asked.

"He's—he's not coming." She could barely choke out the words.

"What! Why not? The jerk!" Laura fumed, but Shannon shook her head.

"Don't say that, Laura. Come on. I'm going to be late." She had to be 30 minutes early.

Andy was waiting in the Explorer. He gave Shannon one glance and looked away.

"I'm sorry. I tried."

"It's not your fault." She swiped at the tears that refused to stop falling. How could her dad do this to her? It was the ultimate rejection, the deepest hurt he could thrust at her.

"We're graduating!" Jesse greeted Shannon in the cafeteria, where the seniors were lining up. "Hey, what's wrong?"

"My dad's not coming."

"Oh, Shan..." Jesse quickly gave her a hug and murmured against her hair, "I'm so sorry." He pulled back and held her at arm's length. "Just remember no matter how much he hurts you, you have a Father in heaven, and He is perfect."

She knew that. But was it asking too much that her earthly father not wound her heart on a daily basis? She reminded herself that she had forgiven him even if he never changed.

God, help me to keep forgiving.

Stephanie bounded over, and Shannon hugged her, giving in to the excitement in the room. They really were finished with high school! She wasn't going to let her hurting heart spoil this day. If her dad was never going to change, well neither was she. She would keep on forgiving him. And loving him.

Finding a quiet spot, she fished her phone out of her pocket under the depths of her white graduation gown. She started typing slowly, speaking out loud. "Hey Dad, I hope you feel better soon. Laura is going to take pictures for you." Her finger hovering over the send button. "I love you." Send.

It was the first time she had said she loved him since she was a little girl. She stared at her phone screen, needing him to appear and say, "I love you too, my daughter."

Swallowing a lump in her throat, she glanced upward. God would tell her.

* * *

Kurt was almost to the high school when his phone rang. He grabbed it out of the console.

Dr. Conrad. What in the world?

"Hello?" he answered, quickly pulling over.

"Yeah, Kurt, are you going to graduation?"

"Sure am." What a strange question. Wasn't *he* going?

"Great. Do you think you could come give me a hand?"

Now Kurt was really confused. "You're still at home?"

"Yeah. Think you could help me out? I'd really appreciate it."

"Sure thing." Kurt turned his truck around and floored it in the opposite direction. They didn't have much time if they wanted to catch Shannon marching in.

He found Kevin on the edge of his bed, trying to button a shirt over his chest.

"Thanks so much for coming." He nodded distractedly. "I might need some help here."

Kurt did everything he could to help Shannon's dad get ready. He couldn't help tapping his foot and checking the watch his mom had given him for his birthday. He couldn't bear to miss Shannon's graduation.

Finally Kevin was ready, and Kurt helped him out of the house and into his truck. He was supposed to use a wheelchair if he went out, but Kurt would carry him if he had to.

Kurt cleared his throat as he started back into town. "I'm not sure what's going on, but I'm glad you'll be there for Shannon. She needs you."

"I know. I wasn't planning on going, which really hurt her. Then she sends me this text."

He handed Kurt his phone, and Kurt took his eyes off the road in spurts to read it. He could hardly process it before Kevin spoke again, his voice unsteady.

"I've known Shannon loves me, but I wasn't expecting her to say it—especially after all the deliberate pain I've put her through. Kurt, I've spent most of my life running away from God because I didn't think He could forgive me for all the mistakes I've made. But if my human daughter can forgive me for all that, I'm thinking God really can forgive me."

Kurt knew the love and forgiveness Shannon had displayed could only come from God living in her heart. What an amazing testament to God's reality.

"I agree, Dr. Conrad. Don't sell God short."

Shannon's dad looked at him in surprise. "The religion bug's bit you, too? Never thought I'd see the day. If Kurt Blake is believing in God, then for sure I believe, too."

He winked, but Kurt sensed the sincerity in his words.

"You're a good man, Kurt. I'm deeply grateful for your help today and many other times."

"Any time." If only Shannon felt the same as her dad. He tightened his hands on the steering wheel. What was he worrying about? His challenge wasn't even half over, and look how much his life had changed. No telling what the future held. One thing he knew: he wasn't giving up on Shannon any time soon.

* * *

Laura sat demurely with her legs tucked under the chair, waiting for her sister to march. What a year it had been. She remembered last's year's graduation in Chicago for a niece of Alan's. They had gone to see Mom in the hospital afterward. They had been a family. Now life was so confusing. She was sitting in between Andy and Gabby, her half-siblings. Her anchor was graduating and going off to college. Sometimes she still curled up in a ball and cried. For her mom. For the stupid boys she'd thrown herself away with. For her baby. Maybe she should try counseling. Or God. That had worked for Shannon.

This was supposed to be a happy day. Why did she feel so blue?

Stupid Kevin! The thought erupted inside her. He had ruined this day for Shannon! Would he always ruin anything good in their lives? Why couldn't he just be the dad they needed?

Why couldn't he just be the dad *she* needed?

She blinked away the sudden liquid in her eyes.

He'd never asked how she was doing after her miscarriage. Never.

There was a commotion in the aisle. Laura raised her head, and her jaw slackened. Kevin. He was here? Kurt was his crutch, helping him shuffle down the row. He was coming nearer, and then his eyes locked with hers. She felt her heart squeeze like a fist. He motioned Andy over, and Kurt lowered him down beside her. Laura froze. Why had he sat beside her? What did he want with her?

An arm snaked around her, the touch shocking her system with a jolt. *Kevin's* arm.

"Laura." His voice was close to her ear. "I'm sorry for leaving you when you were a little girl. I'm sorry for not showing my care as you grew up. And most of all, I'm sorry for not being there for you this year when you needed me most. Do you think you can forgive me some day?"

Laura buried her face against her dad's chest and sobbed.

She had the dad she needed.

* * *

Shannon breathed deeply, waiting for the signal. She began walking down the long aisle. This was surreal. Screams surrounded her, and she focused on the blond hair of the girl in front of her. Not too fast. Not too slow. At last she reached the front of the gym and climbed onto the risers that had been erected for the graduates.

She scanned the audience. Where was her family? Someone was waving from the back of the room.

Kurt.

He was pointing. There they were. Daniel, and Gabby, then Laura and—

Shannon straightened, not believing her eyes.

Dad was here!

She gripped the chair with her hands to keep her in place. She wanted to run straight to him.

Laura pointed right at Shannon, and Dad's hand shot into the air with a frantic wave at Shannon. She waved back, blinking desperately against tears.

He had come! Her *earthly* dad had come.

Thank you, God!

She didn't hear a word of graduation. The speaker spoke, and the valedictorian spoke, and all Shannon could think about was how much she loved her dad. She couldn't wait to tell him.

"Shannon Rose Conrad." Her name boomed through the mic, and people were screaming her name. She heard Kurt's whistle as she crossed the stage. Someone moved her tassel, and the diploma case was in her hand.

Pandemonium erupted when the whole class stood and began their recessional through the gym. Shannon searched the sidelines. There was Andy, taking a picture with his phone. Where was her dad?

The graduates poured outside into the grassy courtyard. Shannon fought to get back inside, but she felt like a salmon swimming upstream. She made it inside the door and pushed herself through hoards of parents and friends and cap-and-gown clad teenagers. Where had her family been sitting?

"Shannon." Kurt swept her into his arms. "Congratulations."

"Where's my dad?" she blurted.

He grabbed her by the hand and tugged her behind him, plowing through the crowd. Then there he was. Her dad. Sitting where he'd been, because of course he couldn't get up. His arms opened up, and Shannon was running. Running. Running to her dad.

She threw herself into his arms and clung to him. Tears ran down her face, and when she pulled away, she saw that his face, too, was wet.

"Shannon." He looked at her with wonder and amazement. "I love you so much."

Finally. Finally she could voice the words she felt she had waited a lifetime to say.

"I love you, too."

He crushed her with another hug, and Shannon let her eyes gaze upward to where she knew her Father was watching with Heaven's biggest smile.

Thank you, God. You sure do know how to paint.

Acknowledgments

There are many people who have influenced the shaping of this book. To mention them all would be another book. A few simply cannot be skipped, however. My college professor Dr. Rachel Byrd truly demonstrated how to be a Christian in the literary world. She also taught me how to write, and rewrite, and rewrite. Four drafts were required for each essay in her expository writing class. There are four drafts of this book.

I am thankful for all the girls I worked with in North Dakota for the school year of 2011-2012. Jenna, Lexi, Sara, Gina, Sierra, Kathryn, Brienne, Trisha, Christine, Abby, Nicole, Katy, Jessica, Hope, Taylor, Mary Alice, Hannah, Mint, Pam, Jill, Brooklyn, Britney, Leilah, and Shania—this story is for you. You ladies were my inspiration. And a big thank you to Ruthanne, who let me craft more than half of this masterpiece in her office.

I'm grateful to my parents for encouraging my love of writing from a young age. My mom is the one who taught me to write in the first place, and my dad is always eager to read anything I wrote.

My husband Zahger has been my biggest supporter, and he encouraged me to keep going every time I wanted to quit. His belief in me led me to actually finish the first draft. I don't know that I would be publishing this book if not for him.

Most importantly, I am thankful for my savior, Jesus Christ. He was with me on every step of the journey, and I wrote this book with the hope of bringing glory to Him and bringing my readers to His glory.

Coming Summer 2019...

"The Art of Messing Up"
Family Fruits of Faith- Book 2

Chapter One

"Nineteen, twenty, ready or not, here I come!" Shannon straightened from where she'd been stooped to sweep under the massive oak dining room table and leaned the broom against a chair as she rubbed her back. Did she really have to go hunt down more children? She'd entertained hordes enough of them already today.

"Playing hide and seek with a broom? Only you."

She swung around at the unexpected voice behind her. "Are you ever going to stop showing up in my house unannounced?"

Kurt cast his ever-ready grin at her. "Where's the fun in that? Sorry I missed the party."

"Well, I assume you're over the age of five. If so, you didn't miss much." She ignored his chuckle as she headed into the living room and began looking behind the larger furniture, Kurt trailing close behind. "You gonna follow me everywhere?"

"I just wanted to talk with you for a few minutes."

She gave him an apprehensive glance. Kurt's talks could be life-altering. And she didn't have time for that right now. "Okay, talk. I gotta find these kids and put an end to this hide and seek business."

"They didn't have enough games at Daniel's party?"

Shannon snorted and started up the stairs. "You would think. But I asked for help cleaning up, and they bargained. So hide and seek it is. Oh, Danny, I know you're up here!" she raised her voice as she stepped into his room.

"You want a summer job?"

Shannon stopped, then slowly turned around. Kurt wasn't even looking at her, instead prowling around the room checking all the corners. She hadn't even thought of getting a "real" job with how busy her siblings kept her. Especially with Dad still in recovery.

"Working for your dad?" It wasn't a bad idea. Close by. "Could I be part time?" That might actually work.

"Aaaaand… Gotcha!" He pulled a laughing Daniel out of the closet and playfully shoved him onto his bed. "Yeah, part time. And actually—" He faced Shannon, suddenly looking nervous. "You'd be working for me. My dad made me summer program manager." He offered a casual shrug, but she could tell it was a big deal to him. As it should be.

"That's awesome, Kurt. When do you start?"

"Monday. It'd be really good experience for you, if your dad can spare you. And of course I'd love to have you there." He didn't try to mask the feelings in his word, and Shannon wondered if it was a good idea to work for him, given the rather messy history between them.

"I'll see what my dad says," she replied, pretty sure her dad wouldn't be keen on it either. "Let's find Gabby." After they found her nine-year-old sister in the shower, she and Kurt walked side-by-side down the wide, curved banister. "Want some leftover dessert? I made it."

"Naturally. And yes, I thought you'd never ask. But can I take it to go? I'm supposed to meet with my dad in ten minutes to work on summer planning."

When they walked into the kitchen, Shannon's eyes honed in on the bushel of strawberries sitting on the counter beside the sink. She slipped a hand to her hip and turned to Kurt.

"What? You'll make an edible masterpiece out of them."

"Aren't you supposed to sell those? You know, make money for your dad's business? That's a lot of strawberries. Does he know you keep giving me produce?"

The guilt on Kurt's face answered her question, and Shannon knew she should discourage him. Again. But past experience told her she'd just be wasting her breath.

"I suppose I should say thank you." She *would* turn them into something scrumptious. Several things, in fact. Her mind was already conjuring up a few mouth-watering ideas.

She shoveled a huge piece of cake onto a foam plate and carefully tucked cling-wrap around the edges. "Here you go."

Kurt flashed her the grin that always made her heart trip. "You're the best. Call me tonight if you want the job, 'kay?" He vanished from the kitchen, the side door slamming behind him.

Shannon put the rest of the cake away and slid the strawberries into the fridge along with it. She sat down on a bar stool at the counter and rested her chin in her palm.

A summer job. Working for Kurt, of all people. It smelled of trouble. The thought of seeing him every day set her heart to racing, and that was a recipe for disaster. Good thing Kevin— Dad—would save her from herself.

In spite of all that had happened, she still slipped up sometimes and called him by his name. He always understood, though.

She looked at the time on the stove clock behind her. He should be getting back from physical therapy any minute. He'd left as soon as Daniel's birthday party ended with Andy as chauffer. He should be able to drive again soon, but the accident that nearly took his life in the spring had left one leg almost useless, and he was regaining mobility slower than he'd like. Funny how doctors were the most abominable patients. Shannon had never known her dad to be a patient, easy-going man, but in recovery mode, he was a downright beast.

Speaking of the devil, Shannon thought with a smile as the side door opened.

"We're home!" her brother's cheerful voice called out, and she heard her dad's shuffle-thump gate as he came through the door. His face was lined with pain as he eased into the kitchen, but he smiled at Shannon.

"Made it. That was intense, though. Worst session yet."

"I'm sorry." She stood up to give her dad a hug, just grateful he was alive. And more thankful than words could say that they were finally having a healthy father-daughter relationship after the roller-coaster that had been the past year's ride. And the previous nine years. "Anything I can get for you?"

"No, I already took painkillers." He grimaced and sat down on a bar stool. "At this rate, I'll be addicted before I recover. Good job cleaning up, by the way. It was a total wreck when I left. What did you do, work magic?"

"Let's just say I used my powers of persuasion to enlist the help of the birthday boy himself and his sister."

Dad assessed her with mock admiration. "Impressive. Well, I'm gonna head to bed. I know it's early, but that PT wore me out."

"Before you go." Shannon's mouth suddenly went dry. Why was she nervous to ask? He was going to say no, anyway. Even though she wanted the job. Wait, did she? She gave a tiny shake to her head, trying to clear her confusion.

"What is it?" He frowned, clearly sensing her distress. He'd always been a little too intuitive with her.

She licked her lips. "Kurt offered me a job for the summer."

Andy poked his head out of the refrigerator where he was searching for something. "He did?"

Shannon gave him a little nod, more interested in her dad's reaction than Andy's.

"*Hmmm*." Dad studied Shannon until she started to squirm. "And how do you feel about it?"

"I mean, it would be good to have a real job before I go to college. Babysitting my little brother and sister has made me pretty good at tiny tot crisis intervention, but I'm not sure how far that'll take me in life."

Her dad laughed and shook his head before quickly sobering up again. "I will admit I was just thinking the same thing earlier today, although somewhat less descriptively. But working with Kurt wasn't exactly what I had in mind." He gave her an apprising look, and Shannon felt her cheeks growing warm. If only her dad didn't know every little detail that had happened between her and Kurt.

"He would actually be my boss. If that changes anything."

Dad's eyebrows rose slowly. "It might. Andy? Care to weigh in on this?"

Andy looked surprised to be included, but he joined them with a glass of chocolate milk in hand. "Jason made Kurt manager for all the summer workers."

"And what do you think of Shannon working for him?"

Andy looked deep in thought before he spoke. "It should be all right. Kurt has done a lot of changing, for one thing. He'll respect Shannon's boundaries if she sets them."

Shannon lowered her head at the dig. That had definitely been a problem in the past.

"Second, Kurt will be her boss, and that should make him very careful. Also, his dad is still in charge overall, and he watches Kurt like a hawk."

Shannon knew that firsthand.

"Aaaand…" Andy drew the word out, along with an expanding chest, "Jason made me Kurt's assistant manager."

"No way!" Shannon exclaimed at the same time their dad said, "That's great, Andy."

"Yeah, so I'll keep my eyes on things, too."

"Well." Dad drew air in through his nose thoughtfully. "I hope I don't regret this. But I'm going to give you the green light, Shannon—pending your sister agrees to pick up your slack at home. I'll probably have to pay her to do it."

Shannon pouted her lips with feigned indignation. "You never paid me!"

"I know. I took shameful advantage of you. But you let me. I know Laura won't."

"Okay. Truth. I guess I better go talk with her."

"Sounds good." Dad stood to his feet with a wince and groan. "Now I really am hitting the sack. Oh, when do you start, Shan?"

Man, this was for real. "Monday."

I hope I don't regret this. Her dad's words played over in her mind as she trotted up the stairs to find Laura. She hoped she didn't, either.

* * *

"You *what*? Kurt, we already have everyone we need. I told you that yesterday."

Kurt stubbornly avoided his dad's eyes, focused on the receipts on Dad's desk that he kept rearranging.

"Look at me." Dad's voice had softened, so Kurt raised his eyes. "I know you want to keep her around you. I get that. But do you think it's a good idea? You're doing so well. I don't want anything to mess that up."

Doing so well leaving his stupid past behind, his dad meant. Shannon wouldn't mess that up. She was too good to do that.

"Too late. I already offered her the job. I'm not going to take it back."

Dad growled in his throat. "Let's hope Kevin is smart enough to stop her from accepting."

Let's hope not.

Dad speared him with a look. "I don't want to see any more behavior like this from you as my summer manager, do you understand?"

Kurt straightened, remembering the responsibility his dad had given him. He couldn't let his feelings for Shannon interfere with that. "Yes, sir."

"Good. Here's your employee list. The only full-timer is Andy, obviously, since we're making him assistant manager."

Kurt let his eyes roam over the list of names on the paper his dad had handed him. He stopped at a name, and his heart followed suit. Then his eyes landed on another.

He slowly set the paper down and met his dad's eyes.

"What's wrong?"

Kurt swallowed hard. Why had he been so stupid?

He pointed at three names in total. "Her, her, and her. They can't work here."

"Well why ever not?" Dad sputtered. "I've already promised them the job, and they filled out all the paperwork." He stopped and looked closely at Kurt, before blowing air out of his mouth. "I see. You've...been with them, I take it."

Not one prone to blushing, Kurt felt heat in his face nonetheless. He lowered his head.

"Yeah." The word was hardly audible, barely able to work its way out around the shame.

"Well, son, if you hadn't slept with half the girls in town, you wouldn't be facing this problem," Dad said briskly. "You're just going to have to find a way to handle it professionally."

"It wasn't half," Kurt defended wearily.

Dad sighed loudly. "I'm sorry, Kurt. You know I am really proud of the changes you've made, and I don't want to underplay that. But your past actions certainly do make your present ones more challenging, don't they?"

Kurt nodded and kept studying the list.

Jesse Kowalewski.

He met Dad's eyes again. "Jesse applied?"

"He will be afternoons only. He works nights doing security, oh I don't remember where."

Kurt knew. The lumber yard.

"I know it's a lot for him, but it sounded like he really needs the hours, and he looks like a hard worker. Which you should know." Dad eyed him. "He was your friend once."

Yep. He would be an exemplary worker. Kurt smiled humorlessly and threw his head back. He'd asked Shannon to work for him in order to keep her close. Meanwhile Dad had hired the guy *she* liked. So basically Kurt had just handed her off to Jesse. He was an idiot.

His phone started ringing the special ringtone he'd set for Shannon. Not like she called him often. Had she ever?

He looked at his dad. "That's her."

"Well get it, son." Dad was frowning at him, and Kurt was afraid he was already wondering if Kurt could handle his management position. He was wondering the same thing.

"Hey, Shan." Wait, should he have answered more professionally? "How are you?" he threw in to make up for his casual greeting.

"Just calling to let you know I'll take the job." He sensed her suppressed excitement.

"That's great." His tone lacked matching enthusiasm, but he couldn't help it after his conversation with Dad. He was half-way surprised Kevin had agreed to let her take the job. He knew too much. But maybe Kurt had proven himself enough to the man. He'd have to be very careful this summer to fully convince Kevin that he had changed. It might take longer than that to convince Shannon. Unless she was already convinced. She confused him to no end. Sometimes he could swear she still liked him, and other times he was certain she didn't. It drove him crazy.

"You okay?" her question brought him back to the moment, where it didn't actually matter what she might feel, because he was going to be her boss for the next few months.

"Yep. I'm glad to have you on board, Shannon. We'll need you here at 9:00 a.m. sharp on Monday for new employee orientation. Report behind the orchard stand. Oh, and bring your license and social for paperwork. We'll do that real quick before you start."

"Okay. Thanks, Kurt. Good luck getting ready. Relax. You'll be a great manager."

Her words gave his heart a mini massage. There were so many reasons he liked this girl, her thoughtfulness being one of them.

"I appreciate that. Good night, Shan."

When he hung up, his dad was simply staring at him, his chin cupped by his hand as he leaned his elbow against his desk. He shook his head ever-so slowly.

"This spells trouble, Kurt. Trouble. With a capital T."

"It'll be fine, Dad. Trust me."

To be continued...

Subscribe to my blog

www.yourstrulyemily.com to be in the know,
so you can be the first to order Book 2 when it is complete.

Follow me on Facebook @Yours Truly, Emily or
Instagram @your_true_emily

Thanks for reading!

Made in the USA
Las Vegas, NV
15 March 2024

87227361R00236